# "LOVE, POLITICS. SEX, VIOLENCE . . .

It has everything—but these Texas Starrs shine, and the company they keep is very grand."
—*Houston Chronicle*

"Realistic and well told. Lovers of family sagas will find the book hard to put down. . . . A good story with believable characters."
—*Boston Herald American*

**"SUPERB . . . INFORMED . . . SPICY . . . SHOCKING** . . . The fine quality of Leslie's story-telling goes far beyond his tales of fashion intrigue and into the realm of human relations."
—*Los Angeles Herald Examiner*

"Hard-to-put-down reading . . . engrossing and entertaining . . . a natural!"
—*Indianapolis News*

# Warren Leslie

# the Starrs of Texas

P A KANGAROO BOOK
PUBLISHED BY POCKET BOOKS NEW YORK

Distributed in Canada by PaperJacks Ltd., a Licensee
of the trademarks of Simon & Schuster, a division of
Gulf + Western Corporation.

*All the characters in this book are fictitious, and any resemblance
to actual persons, living or dead, is purely coincidental.*

 POCKET BOOKS, a Simon & Schuster division of
GULF & WESTERN CORPORATION
1230 Avenue of the Americas, New York, N.Y. 10020
In Canada distributed by PaperJacks Ltd.,
330 Steelcase Road, Markham, Ontario.

Copyright © 1978 by Warren Leslie

Published by arrangement with Simon and Schuster,
A Division of Gulf & Western Corporation
Library of Congress Catalog Card Number: 78-7902

ISBN: 0-671-81773-6

First Pocket Books printing August, 1979

10 9 8 7 6 5 4 3 2 1

Trademarks registered in the United States and other countries.

Printed in Canada

To The Memory of
Kay Daly Leslie

# PROLOGUE

RAMSEY, TEXAS, well into the second half of the twentieth century, had a symphony orchestra, a baseball team, a football team, a civic opera, an art museum, a university and other attractions, but if you mentioned its name almost anywhere in America, many people who knew nothing of its other assets would say, "Ramsey . . . oh, Starr's." People who had never been to Ramsey, never been to Starr's, knew its legend. It must be, they thought, the most fashionable, expensive, opulent store on earth, and entering it would be like entering the world of the Arabian Nights. Such a legend had been built deliberately by the founder, his wife and their three sons, Adam, Louis and Bernie, all of whom worked at the store. It had come about through genuine quality of goods and genuinely high prices, but also through guile, imagination, a sense for the spectacular and location; for it was in Texas, land of tall tales where dreams could come true. Starr's in Nebraska or in New Jersey would have been another store; in New York, one of many on Fifth Avenue. Starr's belonged to Texas.

On a blistering August day, not so long ago, several things happened which affected the store in unusual ways. After that day, nothing was ever the same again.

AT ABOUT six-thirty in the morning, a handsome black girl in her twenties was lying on a couch on the second floor of Starr's. The couch was covered in beige suede, an impractical fabric for the use it was getting. It stood directly under a superb seven-foot statue of Kwan Yin, the Chinese Goddess of Mercy. Since the second floor was where Starr's sold its most expensive apparel, visitors sometimes congratulated the Starrs for placing a goddess of mercy there; a gracious touch, they thought.

1

The handsome black girl lay on her back with one leg on the floor and the other draped awkwardly over the buttocks of a white man named Bart Struther who was plunging all he had into her. He was the superintendent of Starr's, a position he had held for eighteen years, having served an earlier seven as assistant superintendent. Within his direct responsibility lay many of the mechanics of running a great store, such as warehousing, packing, trucking, ticketing and scores of other glamorless functions, including housekeeping. This girl was a housekeeper. What he was doing with her was nothing new. He had been doing it for a number of years with various of the girls who came and went. In his stable of housekeepers, there was always one, like this one, who, for a modest contribution toward her rent, could be persuaded to meet him early some mornings under the Kwan Yin. There was not the smallest possibility that he would be caught. He knew where everyone in the store was at this hour, a tiny group, all of whom worked for him and were located by him. That morning he was caught.

Eli Goldstein, senior vice-president of Starr's, arrived at the store at this hour for the first time in his life because he could not sleep and went to the second floor to look at some draperies which would have to be replaced. Struther, finished, lifted himself to a sitting position from which over perhaps sixty feet of space he saw Goldstein watching him. Each stared silently at the other for a matter of seconds. Then the courtly, white-haired, elegant vice-president of Starr's turned slowly back to the up escalator and continued up to his office while Struther watched, his mouth open as though someone had driven a fist deep into his belly. In that one moment, Struther saw the eighteen years of twelve- and fourteen-hour days he had spent running the minuscule details of operating Starr's extinguished like the last of a cigarette. He stayed where he was, his fly still open. The young black girl now rose to her feet and straightened her uniform, smoothing out the creases in her skirt with her hands. She was a pretty girl with a pretty figure.

"You better zip your fly, baby. Gonna look funny you roamin' around with your fly open all day."

He zipped up his fly. "It won't matter much," he said. "You and I, we ain't likely to be here all day."

The black girl's face suddenly changed. The simplicity left it, her eyes narrowed and even her lips seemed to thin.

"What's that you say, Bart?" When there was no answer, she grabbed his lapel and pulled at it. "What's the matter with you, Bart Struther? Now get your mouth to movin'."

The fierceness in her tone reached him. He turned to her, a hardworking, middle-aged man with a beer belly; a man who knew one thing, Starr's, inside out, and nothing much else.

"The matter with me is, sweetheart, that what we just did, there was a man watchin' us. His name is Eli Goldstein and he is senior vice-president of this store. And you and me're gonna be out on our ass, right out there on Maple Street, in just about three hours, just as soon as Eli gets a chance to talk to Adam Starr and tell him what he's seen. . . ."

"You're tellin' me Mr. Adam is gonna fire us?"

"Mr. Adam," he said, leaning heavily on the Adam, "is gonna fire us so fast you better get to the little girls' room right now if you wanna go because you ain't gonna have the time later."

She spoke softly enough, but her face was dangerous. "For what? We didn't steal nothin'. We didn't do nobody no harm."

The rage in him boiled out.

"You dumb bitch, okay, I'll explain so you get it through that cotton in your head. I'm what they call a middle executive of this here store. And they got a policy which they ain't exactly put in writin' but they got it—that executives like me don't spend their mornin's gettin' a piece of nigger poontang on the second floor of Starr's. Not on the Second Floor, get that through—"

She hit him so hard he lost his senses for an instant. Before they returned, she had run her nails from his forehead to his collar and the blood was already leaking on his shirt and jacket. He hit her once in the stomach, she sank back on the sofa, and the fight was over. Vaguely he became aware that she was speaking.

"All my life," she was saying slowly, "I been wantin' to work at Starr's. I been wantin' to see all them pretty clothes up close, to feel 'em, to put 'em up against me. And someday, I been wantin' to sell 'em to all them white cats so I could learn how to be like them. Learn how to say yes and how to say no. And which is which. 'Cause I'm gonna be a customer here onea these days." She paused and looked at Struther with hatred. "If Adam Starr fires me on accounta you . . . I'm gonna cut his balls out, you hear me?"

Struther laughed without mirth. "Why not me too?"

Her eyes were fierce.

"What balls?" she said.

Her name was Tennessee Bower, and she was not without friends.

By EIGHT o'clock, the machinery which ran the store was humming. The beige-and-brown Starr's trucks were on their way from the central warehouse to the two stores, the downtown flagship and the northern suburban branch. They carried merchandise from all over the world to the store's receiving rooms, big, ugly cellars where the goods were marked, sized, inspected and then delivered to the various departments. The minibus was making its first trip downtown from the warehouse, carrying buyers or their assistants, some glad, some sad, depending on whether their purchases had arrived. Few people are sadder than a buyer whose merchandise has not arrived.

But the saddest buyer in the world is she who has an ad running in that morning's newspaper and no merchandise to cover it. "The manufacturer promised . . . the plane must have crashed . . . there was a strike . . ." None of these excuses will work. Late deliveries mean you have promised customers something and have gone back on your word. That, if it should happen enough times in a single department, is a firing offense.

All of which was well known to Emma Goldman, the second-floor dress buyer, a stout, shapeless woman in her late fifties, with dirty gray hair and the plodding force of a medium-sized tank. Like this tank, Emma rolled through life, flattening all obstacles in her straight ahead path, keeping her side turrets open, guns at the ready to protect her flanks. Arnold Starr had once remarked to his wife, Jenny, "If I were a young girl in retailing, I would marry the first young man with reasonable expectations I could, and never see a store again except to buy something. Otherwise, I would turn into Emma Goldman. On a big jet airplane with two hundred people aboard, I can pick out the Emma Goldmans in five minutes. Of course, it's good for us that there are so many lonely women with no one to take care of them. Where would we be without our Emmas? Our Emmas who travel on planes, but listen to no music, see no movies and read no magazines because they are too busy refiguring their open-to-buys."

"Buyers have personal lives," Jenny had said. Emma was her closest friend; she came to dinner often, though not to the important ones. She was not appropriate for them. But she and Jenny covered the market together and talked confidentially. "Emma has a beau she sees in New York."

Arnold had chuckled. "And he is married, and she sees him two or three times a trip, and since his arthritis is very bad, it's not a matter of great passion. No. Buyers of a certain age have personal lives between fashion seasons and not during sales. That leaves about two weeks a year."

On this particular morning Emma arrived at the store unusually early, since there was a difficult phone call to make before she met with the salespeople at eight forty-five to show them the new merchandise. She was calling Mr. Ben Zucker, one of her prime manufacturers, whose expensive clothes had been carried exclusively at Starr's for more than thirty years. She was calling him at nine o'clock in the morning New York time because she knew that Zucker would be in his office that early as he had been for all his years on Seventh Avenue, and that his secretary would not, and that he, therefore, would answer the phone and not be able to evade her, which he would undoubtedly otherwise do.

She dialed directly and, as she had expected, Zucker himself answered.

"Hello, darling, it's Emma. How are you, lover?"

She could almost hear his sigh over the wires.

"What is it, Emma, what's the matter, dear?" It had to be something the matter. It was much too early in the season to be calling about reorders. He was an old man, over seventy, and knew better, he was thinking, than to answer his phone at nine in the morning.

"Well, dear heart, it's those Chanel copies . . ."

"Every button is changed, all the linings are different, you wanted the good wools in Italian silk, which has been done, though the tailoring, of course, is not the same tailoring because you cannot tailor that silk like you can that wool . . ."

"I'm sure . . ."

"So the goods are exclusively Starr's, at least you can bend the point and say so, and there are the ten models I have not sold to anyone else in Texas, not even Houston, the whole of *Texas,* and . . ."

"Ben, my own true love, I'm sure the goods are beautiful, just as all Zucker goods are always beautiful because no one cuts clothes like Ben Zucker, and I'm sure they will sell to women who appreciate quality, but you see, Ben, the goods are not here, do you see my point?"

There was silence. "No," he said. "So what, they are not there yet. They were shipped three days ago, they will be there, your ad is not for nearly a week, you have samples to sketch . . ."

"But, Ben, how do you know they were shipped three days ago? What if they were not? Then, you see, my darling Ben, my ass would be in a crack."

"Excuse me, Emma my love, but that is horseshit. The goods will be there tomorrow, maybe the next day . . ."

"Tomorrow, love, no later," she said flatly. "Three days in advance of the ad or I have no ad. That is the rule here, darling, as you know."

"The next day would still be in time."

"Not for me, darling Ben. It is a matter of sleeping at night, which you know I have trouble doing in the best of times, and if the goods are not here with twenty-four hours to spare . . ."

"What are you telling me, all this sleep talk? Emma, I have heard you before like this and it is always bad news for me, a chill is going through me right this minute."

She smiled. "Then we will both feel better when you have put a duplicate shipment on an airplane today."

A kind of anguished yelp came across the wires.

"And then they will without doubt be in the store by tomorrow, no later. I am so sure of that I will meet the plane myself."

"Emma, if you *were* my sister and you were on your deathbed, I could not do that for you even if it were your last request, because the goods are not in the house, they are going all over America . . ."

"And you can change the labels on a Magnin's shipment or a Field's shipment . . ."

"They have . . ."

"Or a New York store like Bonwit's . . ."

"Emma, your mind has gone, darling, it has cracked into smithereens just as we are talking here."

"Because if you do not do this, I am looking at a piece of paper here . . ."

"And it is sad that this should happen to you . . ."

"Which is your confirmation on my order, and if I should meet the six-o'clock plane tomorrow evening and that plane does not contain my precious, lovely Chanel copies . . ."

"Em-ma!" But he was beaten and he knew it.

"Then I will have to reconsider this confirmation and perhaps cut the order by forty, fifty percent because I have been thinking that out of my love for you, I might have overbought the line anyhow. It is not your greatest line, Ben."

"God damn it."

"And I will be sparing myself the pain, the physical pain I get from markdowns, it is around my heart, Ben, you wouldn't believe . . ."

"I would believe, Emma, I would believe." He sucked in air and exhaled audibly. "So you will ship me back the duplicates when your goods arrive . . ."

"Air collect, dearest, and I love you with all my heart."

"You have the heart of a witch, cold as seaweed . . ."

"Goodbye, darling Ben." And she hung up. It was now Emma Goldman who sighed. She had had no doubt that Ben Zucker would do as he was told because in the rest of Texas put together he could not sell the dollars he could in Starr's. Not yet. Oh well, she thought, we'll both be dead before that changes. She did some paperwork until it was morning meeting time. She was sure she could sell her old friend Ben Zucker's Chanel copies. Almost sure.

IN NEW YORK, a tall, lanky, grizzled man in his fifties came out of the Plaza Hotel and stepped into the back of a large Continental limousine, and sat down next to possibly the richest furrier in America, one Samuel Rosengarden. Rosengarden was rich because his merchandise was meat and potatoes to practically any retail fur operation of any consequence in the country. He did not try to be fashionable, or to make news in the fur business. So he did not go up and down like a yo yo as many furriers do. He was steady. He was stout, perhaps sixty years old, and his hair was dyed black with a little gray at the temples for appropriate distinction. He needed the thin man badly, for this was Joe Fox, senior merchandise manager, furs, for Starr's, generally thought to be one of the great fur retailers in America. He needed him not for profit on the Starr's account, but because the name Starr's, the name Joe Fox, sold his goods to the hundreds of buyers who would buy anything Joe Fox had bought. Sell the star and he sells the rest of the world.

At this moment, Joe Fox was red-eyed and his face was still flushed from the night before's Dewars, but he was grinning. Hungover or not, Joe Fox was nearly always cheerful; loose.

"I will have to admit I'm surprised," said Samuel Rosengarden.

"At what?"

"Your smile. I didn't think you'd be feeling well."

"I feel terrible." Joe paused, thoughtfully. "In fact, we could skip the airport and go directly to Riverside Chapel. I smile because I assume you have a restorative handy as you always do."

Samuel Rosengarden reached forward and pulled open the bar behind the front seat. "Harvey here prepared a thermos full of Bloody Marys. Would you like one?"

"Harvey here has a grand future. And since I know you do not drink, Sam, I will not only have a Bloody Mary, I will have the whole thermos full."

"Well," Joe Fox said, after awhile, "I have left Lupe."

"Your Mexican mambo dancer or whatever?"

"Singer. Not too much in demand."

"I thought you were devoted."

"For many weeks that was true. She could, after all, break your back in fourteen places. Conversation was always limited. At the beginning, it was all right, but lately she has been discussing the matter of apartments and rent. Those are words I do not understand. So, sadly, we parted."

Samuel Rosengarden was thoughtful. "You gave her a basket from Cartier, I assume?"

Joe Fox drank a bit of his third Bloody Mary as they began to near Kennedy. "Oh, sure. But after she threw a soft-boiled egg at me, I had to add five more big ones. I thought she might move up to Plaza lamps . . . One grand. Well, four months . . . it was worth it." He sighed. "The restorative is working. I feel much better."

Samuel Rosengarden reached into his inside pocket and took out a plain white envelope. He handed it to Joe Fox.

"Four percent off the top," he said.

Joe Fox, quite serious now, said: "And that leaves the three percent for advertising?"

"Of course. It amounts, altogether, to twelve thousand dollars. Six is in there, and the rest is set aside for your promotional fund."

"Okay."

Samuel Rosengarden cleared his throat. "I have read and you have told me that Bernard Starr has assumed general merchandising responsibilities for furs as well as other departments. Is that going to affect our little arrangement?"

Joe Fox laughed. "Christ, no. Bernie doesn't know shit about furs. Or anything else. Forget it, Sam. I might have lunch with him once a month. That's what it'll amount to."

Samuel Rosengarden nodded. "I thought I should ask."

"Same as always," Joe Fox said. "No problems."

On the drive back to the city, Samuel Rosengarden was silent. Eventually, Harvey said, "What's botherin' you? That was funny about Lupe and a five-hundred-dollar soft-boiled egg."

Samuel Rosengarden said, "Funny? Yes, but he left her, you know. Someone leaves you, it is sad, Harvey."

Harvey shrugged, "She has a basket of green stuff, Sam."

Samuel Rosengarden leaned forward.

"Would you leave me for a basket of green, Harvey?"

"Of course not," the young man said, readily.

Samuel Rosengarden sighed. "Well, that is lying, of course, but then I am the one giving out the baskets. For business or for . . . a warm body on the cold nights . . . They tell me there are people who are given those things. I always paid . . . So be it."

INSOFAR AS customers and most of the employees were concerned, the business of Starr's went on as usual that day. For major executives like Bill King, the senior financial officer, it was a day unique in their experience; a day with no Starrs on the scene; of waiting for the second shoe to drop. Adam Starr, the eldest son, had called King at home at seven that morning.

"I don't think he can last another night," he said, hoarse from too little sleep.

"That weak?"

"There's nothing functioning . . . except his mulishness of course."

"Jenny all right?"

Adam did not speak for a moment. "It's as though somebody carved her in stone," he said, slowly. "In the rocking chair with a shawl around her. She looks at him as though he were being—irritating. Or . . . something." He stopped.

Bill King cleared his throat. "Okay. I'll keep you posted."

The chief financial officer of Starr's was exactly fifty years and nine days old, exactly six feet tall and weighed exactly one hundred and sixty pounds. He had gray, medium-clipped hair, a prominent aquiline nose set in a small-boned face with rather too large ears and a pale complexion that dramatized the unexpected, stabbing blue of his eyes. Within the year, he had affected a small, neat moustache. He dressed conservatively: his jackets had no padding, his narrow ties were in regimental stripes, mild foulards or solid colors and all his shirts took a collar pin. He drove a four-year-old Ford to work each morning, leaving the big white Cadillac for his wife, Kathleen, and he arrived without fail between nine-thirty and nine forty-five. He was by far the most influential officer in the corporation with Adam Starr. No other officer knew more about his field than Adam himself did. But King knew more about finance than Adam did. And Adam trusted and relied on him.

Now, as he walked into Starr's on a day when there was no Starr present, authority came easily to him. He greeted people pleasantly as always and told those who asked that Arnold Starr was growing weaker. No one had made a pretense about the seriousness of Arnold's illness, so it was assumed within the store that he would die. This seemed proper to King since, in fact, Arnold *would* die, barring a miracle, and there seemed no reason why the people of the store should not be prepared for this fact. He took the elevator to the executive floor and walked to his office, two doors away from Adam's, separated by Louis's. "Good morning, princess," he said to Julie, his secretary, "how did we do?"

"About even," she said. She was a plain girl with stringy

blonde hair and thick spectacles and a slim figure. She knew her business, and his. She adored him, she was a superb secretary, and a fine colleague. He was well pleased with her. "But it wasn't a good day, really," she continued. "Jewelry wrote up the twenty-three thousand dollar earrings, or we would have been ten percent behind."

By this time King was in his chair, studying the flash, the sheet that came out daily giving the quick totals by department for the day before.

"Accessories a standoff, Junior and Younger Set ahead, Better Apparel behind, Sports ahead . . ." He looked up from the figures at Julie. "How are you doing on your five-year job on Emma's department?"

She turned her spectacles on the floor. "Finished," she said, quietly.

"And?"

"Thirty-two percent dollar increase." She seemed about to continue, but did not. Emma Goldman had many friends.

"That's mostly inflation," King said, gently.

"I know."

"Well?"

"Number of transactions . . . There is a two percent decrease."

King blew out his breath. "That," he said, "is appalling. Saks would have a fifteen percent increase. Well—that's for another time."

"Junior Shop show," Julie reminded.

He snapped his fingers. "Oh, yes. All right, I'm going up and have a look. I want to hear Peter Shaw announce it."

In the restaurant, on the top floor, the show was already in progress when King arrived. The place was packed with some three hundred people. Salesladies, college girls, some high school seniors; young women who fitted junior sizes. King only glanced at the makeup of the audience. He watched and listened to the commentary of Peter Shaw, the young sales promotion director. He was relaxed, easy, often humorous and good looking. He held his audience like a practiced actor. He should, Bill King was thinking, be doing the commentary on all the shows. Louis Starr, the second son, who liked to give the commentaries, bored an audience. But the announcer of a big fashion show is highly visible; before he had given it up, it had been one of the devices Adam himself had used for maximum public exposure. It would be difficult for Adam to fire Louis from commentating. But not impossible. Bill King sighed. Change was unpleasant, and much change at Starr's had been averted by the old man's presence on the scene; Arnold Starr had his bind spots. But Adam, of course, had not.

King looked at his watch. Cullum Roberts, president of the Chamber of Commerce, and Riley Clark, president of the First National Bank, were coming in to see him at ten-thirty, and it was nearly that. He took the elevator and returned to his office. When he was seated, Eli Goldstein poked his head in.

"Are you free?" he said, gently.

"Not for long. I have some visitors coming in. Why?"

"I've talked to Matilda. We need to have a chat with you."

"Serious?"

"Yes."

King again sighed. "Okay. When they've gone." Matilda Johnson was the personnel director. A meeting between the three of them meant something was awry. Matilda normally handled her fiefdom by herself.

Roberts, a long, thin man whose family ran a chain of supermarkets, came in with Clark. Obviously, they had walked over together. King knew Clark well, since the store did its major business with his bank, but Roberts was only an acquaintance. As head of the Chamber of Commerce, he was a figurehead presence in the community, whose duties were limited to meeting visitors of note, trying to attract conventions and signing his name to much of the Chamber's voluminous promotional mail. But he was also president of the Ramsey Citizens Council, an organization of roughly one hundred of the most powerful businessmen in the city. The Citizens Council, with the active backing of both newspapers, controlled Ramsey. Practically everything that happened in the city had been worked out by the Citizens Council, which stood, politically, to the far right and thus gave the reactionary flavor to the community which was known nationally as Ramseyism. Moderate liberals such as Adam Starr could be members, could be heard and would be outvoted. The Council was a kind of right-wing Politburo, a term which would have amused its members.

Cullum Roberts came straight to the point. "Bill," he said, in a soft drawl, "what we came here for is a little advice." He crossed his long legs and smiled. "I wouldn't be surprised if that wasn't about the only thing here at Starr's that's plumb free."

Riley Clark, a stocky, florid man, also smiled. "Well, they don't charge for the drinking water. Anyway, Bill, Cullum here asked me to bring this up with you since you and I are buddies and we do a whole lot of business together. See, Bill, as you know the Citizens Charter Association will be runnin' a slate of candidates for the City Council same as it always does, come the next elections."

"Which will win. As it always does," King said.

"Which *might* win. And which might *not* win," Roberts said. "And which might win most of the seats, but not all of the seats. Or, even worse, might win some of the seats but not most of the seats."

"One problem, Bill, is in Adam's district," Clark said. "Where he lives. East Ramsey. I don't know whether you ever noticed it because the papers don't give it exactly page one, but there's a black boy in Adam's district who's announced he's gonna run."

King shrugged. "So what? You've already got a black on the Council."

Roberts sighed. "Bill, that's Tom Estes, and Tom Estes is a personal friend of mine. He owes me. I own him. Now this other black boy—Stacy Kirk, his name is—none of us even knows him. Not at all. But we hear he's already beginnin' to talk about the power structure and all that other shit we ain't heard around here since Catfish Sanchez got in in 1938."

"Why has he got a chance? Seems to me you boys would just step on him."

Riley Clark squinted. "Can't. He doesn't owe us. He's a disk jockey for one of the radio stations, and they tell me he's got a hell of a followin'."

"Kids," King said. "They don't vote."

"Not just kids," Clark said. "Kids, Chicanos, young white people. Not so young white people. And all—*all*—blacks who listen to the radio at night. He's got the biggest following of any DJ in the state. Now just for the black part . . . Adam and his father own great property over there, but a few miles away there are three separate areas which are almost all straight black. Maybe thirty-five percent is the black vote in East Ramsey. This young fella catches on, I'll tell you, Bill, he just might take it. If he did . . . I doubt we'd all get along too good. That could cause all kinds of trouble, and right now, Ramsey don't need no spikes in the wheel."

"So what are you suggesting?" King said, wary.

Roberts cleared his throat. "Soundin' you out, Bill. Just soundin' you out. How would it seem to you, you bein' Adam's closest associate, if Adam was to run for the Council?"

Bill King blinked. "You must be kidding."

"Naw, Bill, not at all," Clark said. "Adam can win. Truth is, Adam could run from any district in the city and win hands down. Everybody knows Adam Starr. He can kill this black boy."

Bill King spoke slowly. "I don't think Adam would be interested in running for a place on the City Council," he said. "Just another Councilman. I don't think so."

Roberts nodded. "Exactly so, Bill. We didn't either. What about for Mayor?"

King's eyes were bright. Mayors were not elected but appointed by the elected Council in Ramsey. "You'd be in a position to guarantee that?"

Clark shook his head. " 'Course not, Bill. The elected Council, they're the only ones who can do that. But should we get our men in, I think they'd be mighty amenable to seein' things our way."

"Oh, I'm convinced they would, Bill," Roberts said. "Just convinced of it. 'Mayor Adam Starr' has a fine ring to it, just like an old church bell."

"What do you want me to do?"

Roberts shook his head. "Nothin'. We'll talk to Adam after this sad business with his Daddy is done. Nothin' till after that. But if you were in favor, why I'm sure that would carry a lot of weight with Adam."

Bill King rose. "Thank you, gentlemen," he said.

Riley Clark shook hands with him. "For or against, Bill?"

"I'll have to think. There'll be a lot to do here."

Roberts nodded. "A good man always takes on more'n he can handle, Bill, you know that. And then handles it."

"There are . . . good things about it," Bill King said.

Riley Clark paused a minute at the door, then turned to Roberts. "Cullum, you wait out there in the hall one minute, will you? I got one thing on business to say to old Bill here."

Roberts waved and left the other two men.

"What's up, Riley? We miss a payment or something?"

Clark shook his head. "Bernie," he said.

"What about Bernie?"

"He's into us for one hundred and thirty-seven thousand, Bill."

"What?!" King's shock was total.

"One-three-seven grand. Of course, it's all collateralized. But the collateral is all Lone Star Electronics and your own stock. And your own stock has the value you put on it, Bill."

"The public has some of it."

"Damn little. It's not a normally traded stock. Oh, it's okay. But I hear things that're not too good about Lone Star Electronics. Now if something happened to that stock . . . well, we'd have to take steps. So there's nothin' to be done right now, but Bill, a lot, maybe all that borrowed money . . . well, mighty big checks get written out to some names we know in Vegas, Bill. I have looked into that. I would not personally have loaned Bernie any of this money, in spite of the collateral, if I'd known how he was usin' it. Or at least I wouldn't unless you told me to. And signed."

"No more. Not a penny more. Until you talk to me first. You should have talked to me before."

Clark shrugged. "He's a big boy. And he had the collateral. Anyway, now you know, and personally, I feel much fuckin' better. So long, Bill."

Bill King sat silently. He knew something about Lone Star Electronics. What he knew was that the company had overextended itself, and he had sold his own stock six months before at a good profit. The stock, he felt, had to go down; even out. It would have to slide. He was also sharply aware of the value of Starr's stock; it had no absolute market value while seventy-five percent remained in the hands of insiders.

"Well," he muttered to himself. "I can hold off Riley if things get bad. We could even co-sign . . ."

"What?" Julie said. "If you don't see Mr. Goldstein, he's going to have a fit. And Miss Johnson."

"Okay. Send them in. And put on my calendar to have a talk with Bernie. And Adam."

Eli Goldstein's way of explaining what happened that morning was hesitant. Matilda Johnson, an Irishwoman in her mid-fifties who had been personnel director for fifteen years, had to help him.

"What Eli is trying to say, Bill, is that Bart was screwing one of the housekeepers under the Kwan Yin at six o'clock this morning."

"Under the Kwan Yin?" Bill said, in a somewhat strangled voice.

"Under the Kwan Yin," Matilda said firmly.

Bill King burst out laughing. It had been an unusual day. In a moment, Matilda joined him and finally, even old Eli Goldstein was laughing.

"If I could tell Arnold this, he'd recover," King said, at last.

"Yes, all right, but what do we do?" Matilda said.

Suddenly, the laughter was gone. It was basically Matilda's decision, but she was looking at him, and King knew it was his.

"Do you have much choice, Matilda?" he said.

"Not much," she said.

"The years he has . . ." Goldstein began.

"Should we call Adam?" Matilda asked.

King was silent. Through his mind went all the conjectures: What Arnold would do. What Adam would do.

"We won't call Adam," he said. "He's at his father's deathbed. If we did call Adam, Adam would say to fire him. And her. He would say that what they were doing was . . . insulting . . ."

Matilda spoke quietly. "Are you sure, Bill?"

Bill King, like Arnold Starr, and like Adam Starr, made decisions and did not then agonize over them.

"Adam would fire him," he said. "The least we can do at this point is do it for him."

And so Adam's name was called into a decision he knew nothing about. Both Struther and Tennessee Bower were out of the store before the end of the day. Matilda Johnson took care of the details. Struther said nothing. Tennessee said, "It ain't fair."

"Yes, it is," Matilda said. "You're a grown woman."

"Some day . . ." Tennessee began.

"Some day what?" said Matilda.

"I'll get even," Tennessee said. "Big-ass honky dike, you wait and see."

At a quarter before six that evening, Arnold Starr died.

# PART ONE

# 1

ARNOLD STARR, son of Morris and Janina Schatzki, was born in Brooklyn shortly before the turn of the century. He grew up with his parents in their rooms above the delicatessen they owned. Working after school, he learned in the store something about buying, marking up and selling. He was a reader from his early years. He read everything, and his parents encouraged: history, poetry, good and bad novels, old and new; at one time he thought he might become a professor of English. His father discouraged him.

"Retail," he said. "Retailing is easy for Jews. People expect Jews to be good peddlers. It is not so easy when Jews try to be good something elses. We are not welcome everywhere, which you do not know yet because most of the people around us are also Jews, but you will discover I am right. Many changes will come in this country, but we have been good peddlers for thousands of years and our place will always be reserved for us. Be a little safe. Why not? Life is hard enough."

So Arnold grew up, full of book knowledge, drawn toward ideas and elegant phrases, but speaking in the accents of the street people around him. He studied merchandising at night at New York University while selling shoes during the day at Abraham and Straus and working on Sundays at the delicatessen. His parents died within six months of each other and he went south with seven hundred and fifty-six dollars, their savings after forty years of sixteen-hour days. He chose the South because it was warm, New Orleans because it was a big city purportedly cultured. He got a job in an old New Orleans store which still had a good deal of carriage trade and he learned a great deal about quality in goods and how to sell expensive things; and that the name Starr was preferable to Schatzki

20

in the South. He then learned about buying, and finally merchandising, at which point he decided he was marriageable.

He married Jenny Goldsmith, a customer of the store and a young lady of breeding and comfortable means, who seemed to him to know everything about the proper way to live that he could not learn from his books and that no one had known on the streets of Brooklyn. One night he said to her, "I am hearing many good things about Texas." He was twenty-seven and she was twenty-two.

"What things?" she said.

"I hear they are eager there and full of energy and talk all the time of the future instead of like New Orleans where yesterday was always better. And I hear the money is young and can be educated, and here the money is old and knows it all."

"You think we should start our store in Texas, then?"

"I think we should look at Ramsey. It is centrally located, and whatever happens to Texas, everything will have to go through Ramsey. And if the people there are smart, they will end up financing everything in the state. Would you hate leaving your home?"

"I would open our store in Alaska if you asked me to."

On Goldsmith family capital, Starr's opened in 1926. Adam was born. At equal intervals of two years, Louis and Bernard followed. And, in time, Jenny and Arnold had all the world's good things and lived in a mansion, on which, Arnold always considered, the down payment had been $756.

At the store, Jenny Starr provided the fashion flair and authority, and Arnold Starr provided everything else. When the prosperous old store had become a new one, six stories high and nearly three hundred thousand square feet, located way uptown at the center of Ramsey's new commercial development, it was almost as if there had never been an old store. And when a year later, the Starrs moved into the big house on sixty acres of East Ramsey, it was as if they had never lived anywhere else. The fifteen bedrooms and twenty-foot-high ceilings became their natural ambience.

It had never been considered by Arnold and Jenny that their three sons would not go into the store. So ingrained was this thinking in the boys themselves that it is doubtful, except for fleeting moments, that any one of them ever seriously considered an alternative career. The contrasts between them were, however, striking. At six feet four inches, Adam was two inches taller than Louis, six more than Bernie, but he carried himself with a careless slouch and rolled like a swimmer when he walked. Louis was stick-straight and moved with the quick, short steps of an elderly governess. Each had the bold Starr nose, but Adam's forehead sloped high to his brow, while Louis slicked down his black hair which grew lower above his eyes. The eyes were similar: brown, rather small, deeply set. Lines had wrinkled the corners of Adam's, giving him a somewhat quizzical expression, but Louis's skin was unmarked by the years; darker, oilier than Adam's, it would age less quickly. Louis's chin and jaw were tentative; Adam's long and assertive. Each had heavy shoulders and a slim waist, but Louis kept his shape because he was always on a diet and did calisthenics daily. Adam ate and drank what he wanted, never exercised (except for occasional weekend tennis) and still remained hard. It was one of the major indications to Louis that the world was going to be unfair to him. There had been earlier ones, though not at home. There, the three brothers were treated scrupulously as equals, Arnold Starr having convinced himself, for his own reasons, that they *were* equals. Yet, at Exeter and Harvard, Adam had managed to struggle out only Bs and Cs, while Louis earned a long string of straight As. But Louis had graduated only Summa Cum Laude, while Adam had been president of his class at both schools. Adam had also been president of both the *Exonian* and the *Crimson*, and had been an oarsman. Louis had been president of the debating society and a champion chess player. These two brothers dressed conservatively and without particular flair. But Louis's jackets were always buttoned; Adam's forever flying open as he walked the streets.

The third brother was Bernie. After struggling through day school in Texas, he was accepted by Exeter on the reluctant basis that his brothers had done well and that his father had contributed generously to the scholarship fund. Exeter had but three unbreakable rules; no women in bedrooms except at prescribed times, no smoking in these bedrooms and no drinking at all. When Bernie was found in bed with a town girl, dead drunk and the bed on fire, he was launched on his pilgrimage through four prep schools and a year at the University of Colorado before his father finally gave up and put him to work as a stock boy at Starr's. After stumbling through a year of this, he was put into training and learned how to write a sales check. Eventually, not knowing what to do with him, Adam suggested that they put him in the Men's Store.

And so Bernie joined the Men's Store, where he was a qualified success. He did bring in the young Turks of the area who bought their shirts and ties and socks from him, swapped stories with him, had drinks in his tiny office, and were introduced to the new talent among the Starr models and salesgirls. And so, when it came time to make him a vice-president, his father assigned him to a short spell of associate merchandise manager for the Sports Shop, and then gave him the title of merchandise manager of the Men's Departments.

"That he will fuck up," Adam said to his father, dubiously.

"No he won't. He can't. The three best buyers in the store are Jefferson, Cohn and Philbrick. He'll get in their hair a little, but they can comb him out and go on doing their jobs. All he has to do is initial their orders."

"Bernie is very high on lavender shirts this fall, Father. I think he also sees a return to spats."

Arnold Starr burst out laughing. Adam did too.

"That's all very well," Adam said, finally, "but what is Cohn supposed to do? Turn him down?"

"Tell him to buy a few lavender shirts, six pair of spats and run a thirty-inch ad on the shirts when he's running color . . . I think we won't advertise the spats."

The structure of the brotherhood was complete: Adam executive vice-president, chief operating officer; Louis executive vice-president, merchandising; Bernie, vice-president, merchandising, Men's Store. A year or two later, they also gave Bernie furs to increase his income. There, too, it was thought he could do no damage, since Joe Fox was the best fur buyer in the country, and was also genial and understood that Arnold Starr was only trying to justify a little more money for his youngest boy.

Within the store, Arnold was Mr. Arnold, Jenny, Miss Jenny, Adam, Mr. Adam, Louis, Mr. Louis, but Bernie, just plain Bernie.

"Why," he asked his father once, "don't they call me Mr. Bernard, like the others?"

Arnold Starr had looked at him long and fondly. "It just isn't possible, my boy," he had said.

The store prospered. Pushed ahead by the expanding economy of the Southwest, its volume grew between fifteen and twenty percent annually, and volume will cover a multitude of operational sins. It was not, of course, without competition, but it did an annual volume larger than that of any department store in the city despite the fact that it sold no refrigerators or furniture or other high-ticket items. It was a phenomenon of retailing. Part of this success had to do with outstanding buying, editing of stocks and selling. But another and vital part stemmed from the constant flow of national publicity about Starr's, which had turned it into something of a legend and made it synonymous with Ramsey, Texas. Nearly all this publicity was engendered by Adam, who had understood long ago that Ramsey by itself could not support a high-fashion, high-priced store. It would need business from all of Texas and from the five states surrounding it, and the store would need to become a mecca for visitors of all kinds, including conventioneers. Accordingly, Adam had set out to make Starr's a national institution. He did it by national advertising and by such tricks as his Fall Fashion Gala, at which Starr's presented awards for distinguished contributions to fashion to designers and consumer-celebrities from all over the world. He gift-wrapped packages so opulently that he lost nearly one hundred thousand dollars a year on the operation, and charged it off to promotion. His October Foreign Fortnights drew thousands of visitors and increased late Fall volume by nearly three-quarters of a million dollars when other merchants were using stale off-price promotions. The store's Christmas catalogue regularly featured a few improbable gifts, at astronomical prices, which were not expected to sell and almost never did, but which would creep into magazines, newspapers and television shows as the ultimate in luxury or foolishness. In either case, the annual media roundups of what was being offered for Christmas that year were never released before the appearance of the Starr's catalogue. And Adam made speeches and gave interviews. He was the face, the voice, the flesh and blood of the corporation. Few people understood that Adam, in all his glory, did not run his store. For his father had given him plenty of rope. Arnold Starr was proud that his son had become a celebrity before he was thirty-five. It seemed quite proper to him. The fact that his other sons were lost in Adam's shadow seemed appropriate because they were younger. The eldest, in his opinion, should always be the spokesman. As for himself, he was too old for prolonged exposure to the sun. He reserved only the simple prerogative of making personally every major decision regarding the store, whether Adam, his other sons or anyone else for that matter, agreed with him or not. In advance of a decision, he was hospitable to argument until it wearied him; having decided, he became concrete, would hear no further controversy and did not carry doubt to bed with him. He had never taken a sleeping pill in his life.

This was not to say that he could not change his mind. He could: "In one to three years," Adam had once said, wry, if not bitter.

But he had run things. Now he was dead. It was up to the rest of them.

# 2

THE MALEVOLENT Texas sun seemed to wither the necks of the small group standing around the gravesite, for their backs were to the west and it was four o'clock in the afternoon. The heat was a physical thing, hazily visible. It steamed off the grass, off the trees, off the monuments themselves and hung like a vapor over the endless acres of cemetery. Several of the men used sopping handkerchiefs, but the women did not, though sweat glinted on their upper lips and trickled down from behind their ears into their hair. The rabbi spoke in Hebrew. Not a soul in the gathering understood a word he said; it occurred to them all that he might never finish. They responded in the Kaddish from printed cards which they pronounced phonetically and hoped for the best; each hoped someone else would say the word first and, as a result, their responses were ragged. Adam Starr did not respond. The metal casket containing the body of his father shone brilliantly in the sun. All the women and all the men were dressed in black. The widow, veiled and tearless, stood to Adam's left with Louis on her other side. She was a tall woman, and her eyes were even more deep set this afternoon than usual. Louis also was tall, but Adam towered over both of them and everyone else at the grave. Plump Bernie, standing next to Louis, scarcely reached Adam's shoulder and was already balding. From Bernie's eyes, tears ran, mixing with the sweat; and he was gulping, because Bernie did not do things gracefully. Adam noticed the tears and was saddened, at least partly because no tears had come from the others, not from Jenny, not even from his own children. Some tears should fall for the death of such a man, he thought, and he glanced at Nancy, nineteen, and Bobby, seventeen, but they stood solemnly with their mother and their faces were inscrutable, an inscrutable age, one might say, and yet the adults were as inscrutable as the teenagers. Claude, Adam's wife, on whom so much of Arnold's tenderness had been bestowed, was expressionless. Perhaps, in this family, the tears would have to come later when each was alone. Except, of course, for Bernie; for a moment, Adam envied his youngest brother.

While the rabbi prayed, Adam thought, "The Old Man is dead, he is really dead." The sentences had been going through his head for two days; from the moment his father, lying in the same big bed in which he had slept forty years with his wife, opened his eyes, saw nothing, grunted and died. The doctor had closed his eyes, and the words came to Adam, "The Old Man is dead. He is really dead." Yet thousands of words later had not yet convinced him.

To his surprise, the ceremony was over. Someone in the group must have known it, for there was a quick rustling and murmuring even before the rabbi walked over to Adam's mother.

"Well, Jenny, that's it," he said.

"Thank you, Levi," Jenny Starr said, and shook hands with him. The rabbi, short and stocky, wearing thick, rimless glasses, stood six inches shorter than she, was her own age of sixty-six and had been a friend for twenty-five years, though in all that time the Starrs had been in his synagogue no more than once or twice, except for funerals.

"Arnold," said the rabbi, "would have liked the words in English. I've marked them for you and give this translation to you with my love. Some evening, read them, and they will sadden you pleasantly."

He handed her the battered old prayer book and she thanked him again and held it with both hands against her chest.

"Hello, Adam." The rabbi extended his hand.

"You always did have a beautiful voice," Adam heard himself saying, as he shook hands.

"Unfortunately, you've mostly heard it in a living room. You must come to the synagogue sometime, perhaps on the High Holy Days. Just for the music. I was once a cantor, you know."

"I didn't know."

"Good. After twenty-five years, we are still discovering things about each other."

By this time the small group was around them, and Rabbi Levi Moskowitz shook hands with all the men and kissed all the women and children lightly on the cheek. Louis Starr said to Adam, "See any reason not to pile into the cars?"

"None at all."

"You still plan to sit shiva through today only?"

"I'll come over part of tomorrow."

"Well, Bernie and I'll do the whole time so Mother doesn't have to go through it alone."

"That would be helpful. I can't face it at all."

"It's all right, Adam. You really ought to be at the store. Things get mixed up when none of us is there."

"Well, thanks, Louis, anyway."

"Don't forget, at shiva, none of the family can mix a drink." He smiled, "Including Becky . . . who knows how to mix a drink."

Adam smiled at his brother. "So she does," he said.

As he spoke, a sudden roaring sound came from above them. Both brothers looked up and saw a covey of six Air Force fighters flying in perfect formation. Symbol of war, Adam thought, and wondered fleetingly if the planes were a message or warning to him. "Well, let's get the cars loaded," he said.

Three black limousines were parked near the gravesite.

Adam took his mother's arm and began the walk to the first one.

"I wonder . . . always at funerals . . . whether we have missed something along the way," said Jenny Starr. "About this religion, I mean."

"You're letting Levi shame you."

"Oh, that. He's shamed me for twenty-five years. I'm past it by now. No, simply an element we've not had. An element which seems to comfort many people."

"Father never missed it."

"Arnold and I were not identical, you know."

"Personally, I resent it. Not Judaism. All of it. Judaism, Catholicism, Methodism, if there is such a word."

"Do you remember your Bar Mitzvah?"

"Without pleasure."

"The only one who enjoyed it was Bernie. He had a very good time and drank a good deal of wine."

"That was what he enjoyed."

"I suppose it was."

They had reached the cars. Adam, his mother, Claude and the rabbi would ride in the first car; Louis, Aunt Bessie Goldsmith, Jenny Starr's sister, and Adam's two children would ride in the second; and Bernie and his wife Becky would be in the third. They would be twenty-five minutes getting to the house of Arnold and Jenny Starr. In the first car, Adam sat between his mother and his wife in the back seat and the rabbi on the jump seat facing them. The motor was running and the air-conditioning was a shock. Jenny Starr shivered.

"Do you want it off, Mother?" Adam said.

"No, I'll be used to it in a minute."

"There's a shawl back here," Claude said, reaching in back of the seat. "I thought of it at the last minute. Put it around you, Mother, you'll catch cold."

"What about you?"

Claude smiled. "I brought two. I'm always cold in these cars."

Rabbi Moskowitz also smiled. "It's like my apricot brandy. On the rocks with a little soda. I've gone to many houses for many years, but yours is the only one where I can be sure there will be some apricot brandy. I think you are the genius for kind, little things, Claude."

They rode silently most of the way. Adam looked out at the browned grass. Even for Ramsey, Texas, it had been a hot, dry summer. Water supplies were low and home-owners had been restricted to watering their lawns on alternate days. The battle with the sun had thus been an uneven one and the green things of Ramsey were not very green. The leaves on the trees and the grass broke off easily, like split human hair. The limousines were traveling from the north of Ramsey to the east of it, from the new to the old. The east, once the fashionable section of the city, still had its sections of grandeur, like the sixty acres Arnold Starr had bought in 1920, but most of it was middle-income housing now. These areas were interrupted by blocks of barracks-like shotgun housing, some of it public, where the blacks and the Mexicans lived uneasily side by side. The poor white sections, while not adjacent, were close by. It was not a pretty ride.

"At these times," the rabbi said, "one always thinks of change and cities are always changing. But I think Ramsey may have had more of it faster than any place else in the country."

"Well, it's young," Adam said. "It never got locked in."

"Space," Jenny Starr said. "We have enough of that in Texas. You can go as far as you want. Even downtown. To the south, to the east, even west across the river. Apartment buildings, office space . . ."

Adam was silent. About downtown, he did not agree with a word his mother said, and she knew it. He had fought his father for better than five years on his conviction that downtown Ramsey would never be residential; that Texans of means liked land around them, disliked apartment living, and that Starr's, to maintain its local trade, must build in a major way in the north suburbs. He had won and lost. Starr's had built in the north suburbs, but in a minor way; almost a service store. So now the long battle would continue with his mother; that battle, many battles.

The black butler, Maitland (William S. Maitland, precisely), stood at the open door as the limousines pulled in. There were no white butlers in Ramsey. A few suddenly rich families had tried the importation of English butlers to go with their Venetian bathtubs, but these experiments had ended in failure. Butlers have a tendency to hang out with other butlers. When the Englishmen found that their Thursdays off would be spent with black men, they returned to New York and other civilized places. Like

Arnold Starr's Tudor mansion and much of what was in it, Maitland was aging and massive. He had been with the Starrs twenty-three years and would have been at the graveside, except for his job of preparing for the visitors.

"Is that candle lit?" Jenny said to him.

"Yes, ma'am."

Jenny smiled at the rabbi. "That's for you, Levi. A single candle for sitting shiva."

The rabbi laughed.

"We'll go to the living room," Jenny said.

In the enormous room, they took seats, the adults surrounding Jenny, the children off to one side. It was an awkward time. Maitland offered them drinks, but no one accepted. There is a lull before any party, complicated in this case by the fact that about the death, and for that matter the life of Arnold Starr, they had all for the present used up all their words. Fortunately, they did not have long to wait for the first arrivals, and by six o'clock the mansion was filling up. Jenny Starr sat at one end of the living room with a tea service in front of her, but she neither poured nor drank from it. The service, Georgian, eighteenth century, had cost thirty-seven thousand dollars in London seven years before. Today it was a prop, indicating where she was, making it easier for people to file toward her, shake her hand or kiss her on the cheek and move on. The place for food and drink was the dining room, where both tables overflowed with roasted turkeys and chickens and endless kosher delicatessen. Bottles of red and white wine, as well as champagne, were open, glasses on the table, for the guests to help themselves. Hard liquor was served by Maitland and five assistants, who circulated through the rooms with silver trays.

Adam, as head of the family, stood at the front door greeting people and bidding them goodbye. Louis stood near his mother, in case she should have trouble remembering a name; or to pry loose someone who was taking too much time and slowing the line. Bernie and the wives wandered. Bobby and Nancy sat together in a far corner of the living room talking to each other and responding properly to those who knew the family well enough to greet them.

Promptly at seven, as he had promised, the Mayor entered with the Governor, the Senator and the Congressman, and Adam personally walked them around the line

to his mother. She greeted them by their titles except for
the Congressman, whom she called Mr. Twill, but they all
called her Jenny, and the Governor and the Senator kissed
her on the cheek. Adam then introduced them to Louis,
who had met all of them and winced when he was called
Louie by the Governor. Adam then went back to the door,
and the politicians dispersed through the rooms to shake
hands with their supporters and enemies.

Eventually, the Senator joined Adam at the door, and
the two men walked over to a corner of the hallway to
avoid the interruption of saying goodbye to people. The
Senator was as tall as Adam, much heavier and had some
whisky red in his face.

"Sorry about Babydoll. It's a silly female operation, but
the doctors wouldn't let her out."

"That's okay. Give her our love."

"Well, you know you got hers." The Senator paused.
"So you're finally gonna have the whole kit and caboodle
to yourself, Adam? Funny thing, most people think you
already had it for years."

Adam laughed. "Not anyone who worked there."

"Oh, I guess the old man was on your ass inside. But he
let you run pretty good outside. Hell, half this state don't
know your Pa's first name, Adam, but they know yours."
The Senator paused. "Arnold was smart about that," he
continued. "He knew how to run a good store, but he
didn't know how to make a goddamn tourist attraction out
of it. You got hotels, trade centers, roads, plane schedules,
a soft goods industry . . . you got a lot of things here in
Ramsey might not be here except for Starr's, Adam."

Adam looked at Hayden Calhoun, senior Senator from
Texas, twenty years older than Adam, deep-lined leathery
face, gray hair long and piled on the back of his neck, and
said to the second or third most important man in Washington, "All right, you old bastard, what do you want?"

The Senator's pale blue, heavy-lidded eyes sparkled.

"New stores, Adam. I want to see Starr's in Houston,
San Antonio and Fort Worth. And I don't want no measly
little sixty thousand footers. I want the big babies, with
plenty of Eyetalian marble and all that other crap."

"The grave's barely covered yet, and Father's already
spinning in it," Adam said, smiling.

"I know the old man was fightin' expansion, which is

why we're talkin' right now. If you start tomorrow, it'll be years before you open any doors. I know that."

"So you're saying, 'start tomorrow.'"

"I'll help."

"You'll have to."

"We got some things goin' for all those towns, Adam. New business. Lots of jobs. Some government offices. Important ones."

"Well, we'll expand," Adam said. "We have to."

"Where to first?"

"Houston."

"Ain't that the toughest nut?"

"Yup. But it's got the best potential. We're already late. We should've been there years ago before the New York chains. But we have a Texas name, and in Texas that still counts."

"Well, you got more'n that. The New York stores, they're just stores. Starr's is a dream. People'll always buy a dream. Something like Saks, they already live with. You'll put in a two-ton Henry Moore sculpture, twenty good paintings and ten thousand dollar robes—now they don't live with *that*. And the art'll probably appreciate and the robes'll sell to some idiot, and people'll think you're Oz, just like they always have. Everybody wants to go to Oz."

Adam was wry. "As long as they can find a good dress for a hundred bucks there."

"The Henry Moore'll sell that dress for you."

"You would have made a pretty fair merchant."

"Pro'bly," the Senator agreed. "Family gonna fight all this expansion?"

"Sure. Father casts a long shadow."

"But you'll win?"

"All the first battles anyway. Which gets you your Texas stores. If they work, I'll be all right. If they don't, I won't."

"They'll work, Adam," the Senator said. "This ain't a one-crop state anymore." He looked at Adam sharply. "How long do we know each other, Adam? Twenty years?"

"I guess so."

"And you were outa Harvard for the summer, and I was runnin' for Congress from south Texas. And you come down to south Texas with money and a Harvard accent and went to work for us."

"Everybody else in the state made Coolidge look like a Communist."

"I know why. But you did, anyway. And there ain't many things we ain't said to each other since, includin' quite a few four-letter words . . ."

Adam grinned. "I only use foul language when you get in bed with the oil lobbies and the National Rifle Association. I use sweet words for all the civil rights legislation you got through and when you prove to me you've learned who Henry Moore is."

Senator Calhoun shook his head. "You know about guns and oil. Adam, you live in Texas. That's survival. So forgive me that and we'll stay friends. I'm a better friend to have than you are." The Senator laughed. "I get to go to the Senate dining room where the food is terrible. You eat in your Garden Room where the food is good. So who's ahead?"

Adam laughed. "You are," he said.

"Right now." He smiled. "You learn enough about survival, you might be a senator some day, Adam. First Jew senator from Texas."

"That's *Alice in Wonderland*."

"Maybe not," the Senator said. "You ain't *too much* of a Jew . . . Look at Goldwater. Arizona's not so different from Texas. Hell, he ran for President. I don't know, maybe down here, one day . . . Well, if I ever think that day has come, I'll tell you."

The Senator looked at his watch. "You know, we gotta get out of here. We got a plane to catch, Congressman Twill and I."

Adam looked toward the door.

"Nobody outside yet. We can go in and round them up."

"I think we oughta. I hate to face it. Just on the way to the airport, that peckerhead Governor of yours is gonna hit me up for four new highways and three lakes, I can feel it comin'."

The two men walked slowly back toward the house. For the moment, there were no moving cars and the only sound was the buzzing of the crickets. Not the smallest breeze rustled a leaf. Adam, caught by the silence, stopped suddenly and turned his back to the house and its lights. He looked out on the old live oak trees and the long meadow, partly lawn, partly grown up crabgrass and eventually woods. The Senator stopped, too.

"What are you thinkin', Adam?"

"The stars," Adam said.

The Senator nodded. "The stars of Texas. Grow up here and they go with you everywhere the rest of your life."

Inside, Senator Calhoun stopped suddenly. "Adam," he said, slowly, "you know there's nobody in Washington I can't bullshit with. That's my act. And drink scotch with. Now on nine days outa ten I bullshit and drink scotch, though the papers say it's bourbon because Texans are supposed to drink bourbon. And on the tenth day I break their arms. Crack 'em right in two, so they're screamin'. And there ain't a son of a bitch up there who don't pee in his pants when he sees me comin', because he doesn't know whether I'm gonna shoot shit with him or crack his arm. Nothin' happens if you don't scare people, see? Now, you, you're gonna build an empire and I'm gonna help. Everything you do is gonna be for that empire. So . . . you're gonna have to be plumb sure that the people you deal with piss white when you're around. And in your case, I'm talkin' about your own blood. Can you do that?"

"Yes," Adam said.

The Senator nodded. "I think you can, too," he said. "Le'ss go. Time to go home."

When the politicians had left, Adam looked around the grand room. The temporary help had left and so had most of the guests, and these too now disappeared, couple by couple and finally in a clump. Only the family remained, and they sat together in the living room, sipping final drinks. The departure of the last guest seemed to have severed some wire within Jenny. She sat on a corner of the sofa now, slumped back, her face gray with fatigue.

"You should go to bed, Mother," Claude said, tentatively.

Jenny nodded silently. She seemed to wish to close her eyes but did not.

"What's the matter?" Adam said to Bernie.

"Nothing. Momma's a little tired, that's all. I wish the bastards had gone home an hour ago." Only Bernie called Jenny Momma; to the others she was Mother.

Adam looked around the room. "They're gone now. Maybe I'll take that drink."

"What do you want? A scotch?"

"Yeah. I'll go over and see Mother."

Adam bent over and kissed his mother on the forehead. The lines were deep from her nostrils to her mouth, as they became when she was tired. And she was pale.

"Okay, dear?" he said.

"For a little while longer."

"You can go now, you know. I'll take you upstairs. Everyone's gone."

"I'd like a pony of brandy."

Adam spotted a waiter and ordered the drink. As he did, Bernie arrived with his scotch.

"Thanks, Bernie. We've got Mother drinking now. Just ordered a brandy."

"You old lush," Bernie said. His mother smiled. She took perhaps a half-dozen drinks in a year.

"How many people do you think we've had?" she said.

Bernie shrugged. "Off and on, over a thousand. Wouldn't you say, Adam?"

"Arnold would be interested," Jenny said. "He was a good merchant. He was always interested in traffic." Her sons smiled.

"He was that," Adam said.

"Well," Louis said quietly, "it's all over now."

Jenny did not reply; there was silence in the huge room. Suddenly, a paralyzing fear seemed to come over all the Starrs at once. Jenny's eyes opened wide. It seemed for a moment that her mouth would fall open, but instead, she set her jaw consciously. What had happened was simply that the silence brought home to all of them that Arnold Starr was dead. During his lifetime, there had been no such thing as silence. Arguing, laughing, discussing, the Starrs had made noise when they were together. In character, some of them were private people; Louis was; Claude; Jenny; Adam less so; Bernie and Becky, not at all. But even the private ones, during Arnold's lifetime, uttered many words. With the Irish it was always the word, Sean O'Casey had written; so it is with some Jews. Perhaps the words had not always contained the full truth; among Starrs, too much was withheld for that. But always, family gatherings had produced sound, and now there was none. And it occurred to Adam and the others that perhaps Arnold had willed them silence. By questions or answers, statements or rambling discourse, he had been their sound switch. And that very sound seemed always to prove to them that they were indeed a family and that they knew each other.

Did they not then? Adam asked himself.

On the evening of his father's funeral, was there nothing they had to say to each other? Had Bernie no stories, Louis no laconic comments, Claude no kindnesses, Becky no small idiocies? And what of himself? Had the plucking away of his father's flesh and blood drained him of his own?

Adam felt a chill. He looked at the others. Each pair of eyes was on him. Even his two dark-haired grown-up children regarded him. And all of them were asking that he break the spell. Adam, they were saying silently, it is up to you. Give us back life and character. Restore us to what we were, for something has happened. At this moment, we are not sure we exist. We never really existed as individuals, only as threads in a family web. Now the major thread, the strong and vital one which has supported the web, has been broken. It must be replaced or the web will fall. Starrs, whether by blood or marriage, are a family or they are nothing. We may fight and even hate, but we are locked together, and our strength is only that of the strongest member. Now, Adam, the eyes of his kin told him, all your press clippings will not help. They represent only what people have said about you. They have created a posture for you, but a posture is not a person. Where is the flesh and blood, Adam? Produce it. Break this ghostly silence in this ghostly room, where nothing seems real, where all is a dream and unfamiliar.

All of this Adam felt. His mouth was dry and he felt sweat stinging under his armpits. He looked at the drink standing on the table beside him. After a moment's thought, he picked it up and drained it. He then rose to his feet. When he spoke, he half expected his voice to crack, but it was steady and strong, just as it had always been. As the words came, the chill left him. The sweat dried. He was all right. So then would they all be.

"The Fashion Gala," he said, "comes about a month after Father's death. It's occurred to me, as I guess it has to all of you, that maybe we ought to cancel it—the parties, the show, the whole bit. Anybody want to comment?"

"Of course we should cancel it," Louis said.

"Why?"

"It's a matter of simple decency."

"I doubt it," Adam said. "We don't put the damn thing on for fun, after all. It's business, just as much as opening the doors in the morning is business."

"It *looks* different," Louis said. "There's something about square dancing at a Western party . . . Father just barely in his grave . . . It's obscene."

"Father will not be 'just barely in his grave,'" Adam said, quietly. "He will have been dead a month."

"Which is not what you'd call extended mourning . . ."

"How extended do you want it to be?" Adam said. "There's a specific reason for the Fashion Gala. The temperature down here is about a hundred degrees in early September, and our stocks are full of fall goods, including several million dollars worth of woolens. We have to hit our customers with a hammer to persuade them to get out of cottons and into wool, or we won't start selling until the November markdowns."

"I know the reason for the Gala," Louis said sourly, "at least as well as you do, since I control those goods."

"And you also know that the Gala sells your goods for you and sells them early."

"Of course it does," Louis snapped. "I'm simply saying that it's inappropriate this year, this soon."

"What's inappropriate?" Adam said. "Selling goods? Dad would never agree with that, Louis."

"We'll have to use other means, that's all."

"What other means? If I knew of other means, I wouldn't spend the money for two huge parties and two huge fashion shows. I'd use the 'other means.' But I don't. We know this works and we don't know what else will work."

Bernie broke in.

"Anyway, we've already notified the fashion award winners," he said. "What do you want us to do, Louis, write and tell them they haven't won after all?"

"We can send them the plaques," Louis said.

"Come off it, Louis," Adam said. "Those plaques are given so the winners will be in the store for a few days and customers will come in to meet them and buy their goods."

"I know that," Louis said, angrily. "Stop holding my hand and explaining things. I'm not six years old. Why don't you just cut that goddamn patronizing of yours! It makes me a little sick. Going ahead with the Gala is just plain bad taste and you know it."

Louis was now angry, Adam not. He had expected this reaction from his younger brother, just as he could predict most of Louis's reactions. And Louis had a point. There would be criticism of them for going ahead with the Gala. On the other hand, the occasion brought more than a thousand out-of-town customers to Starr's, who used the Gala as an excuse to come to Ramsey and do their fall shopping. Would they still come if the Gala were cancelled? Certainly not more than half of them, Adam thought. You had to have a compelling event to attract them. Otherwise they would do as so many of them easily could: go to New York for shopping and the theater; or London, or Paris for that matter. He was convinced, as he had been twenty years before when he had invented the Gala, that Starr's early season, high-ticket fashion business depended greatly on staging the most elaborate fashion show in the nation, bringing well-known designers to the store with their complete collections and throwing a couple of parties to which customers would be embarrassed not to wear fall clothes. His father was dead, but the business was alive and must proceed as usual. So he had made Louis angry enough to say more than he wanted to and in an ugly way. Adam was confident enough now to look at his mother.

"You've always been our taste barometer, Mother. How do you feel about it?"

Her black eyes fixed on Adam for some moments. It seemed to him, improbably, that there was amusement in the gaze. Then she shrugged. "It's a business matter. It's your decision, Adam."

Adam drew a deep breath.

"We'll proceed as usual then."

Louis rose to his feet. He looked tired. Defeat always made him look tired

"I think it's time to go to bed," he said. "It's been a long day for everyone."

"You're in your old room," Jenny said.

"I know. Shall I take you upstairs, Mother?"

"Yes. Please. Bernie, you and Becky are in the green room."

"Thanks, Mother."

Ritually, each one kissed Jenny good night. As she left them, Adam looked at Claude. She rose and called to Bobby and Nancy, sitting near each other silently in another part of the room. In a few moments Adam and his family were gone, leaving the downstairs to Bernie and Becky and the servants cleaning up in the kitchen.

"Hello, baby," Bernie said. "Want a nightcap?" She had been a cocktail waitress in Houston, supplementing her income in other ways. She had been an unpopular choice with Bernie's parents. But Adam, convinced that his youngest brother was helplessly in love with her, had said simply, "I know her. I like her. Bernie's over twenty-one. If he wants to marry her, he should marry her." Adam had never met her. He had carried that furious day's battle. Bernie, who had always loved him, now thought he was God.

"Sure, why not? . . . Gee, Louis was sure mad at Adam, Bern."

"He nearly always is. Cuts himself up." He went over to the bar and mixed their drinks. By now the bar was pristine. The debris left by a thousand people had disappeared. He poured a tumblerful of scotch for each of them, threw in some ice and splashed the results with water. "Like, you know, he should take up yoga. When they make Adam president, he'll hear it in a straitjacket."

"Does Louis think he's gonna be president?"

"Oh, no. He'll just keep wishing Poppa'd come back to life. Poppa kept things balanced. Without Poppa, Adam is Mr. It, which is fine with me, of course. But not good for Louis."

"What about your Momma?"

Bernie was silent. He stared ahead of him with wrinkled forehead, which for Bernie meant thought.

"And I'll be in the middle," he said, quietly.

"I said Momma, not you."

"Momma'll be like me. In the middle. Oh, she'll be chairman or something. And she'll go on selling expensive clothes, just like always. Difference is, Momma owns exactly as much stock in this company as the three of us combined." Bernie paused. "She could cut the heart out of any of us if she wanted to."

"Well . . . I mean, she's certainly not gonna do a thing like that. To her own sons?"

"If Louis says it's green and Adam says it's red, she's gonna cut somebody's heart out. So I guess she'll go the easy way. Adam's president, you let him win. But if she gets to thinking he's running too fast, she can always pull out the rug. Either way . . ." He grinned. "Old Bernie's safe."

They fell silent. The house was still at last. The servants had finished up. The kitchen was dark. Only Maitland would still be up. He would be in his small sitting room, waiting to turn off the lights and lock the doors.

After a while, Becky asked, "What time is it?"

Bernie looked at his watch.

"I'll be damned. After midnight."

Becky ran her fingers through her hair. "Funny," she said. "They covered that hole up long since now. Your Poppa's really gone, Bern."

"Yeah. Well, let's go to bed." He pushed out his cigarette and they started upstairs. When they came to the door of Jenny's room, they stopped short. From behind the wall, they heard the sound of a woman half-gasping, half-grunting; refusing, by some effort of consciousness, to sob. Bernie and Becky looked at each other. They were both pale.

"Go on," he said. "I'd better go in."

She left him and he knocked softly. When there was no response, he opened the door as softly as he could. His mother sat on the end of a chaise lounge. She was in her nightdress and a silk peignoir. Her mouth was contorted in the effort to prevent sound from coming from it. Her black eyes, darker and bigger than ever, were fixed on the double bed and her thin shoulders shook.

"Momma, Momma, what is it?" Bernie said, frightened.

She turned and saw him but only shook her head and returned her gaze to the ancient, carved oak four-poster, possibly even antique at the time of its purchase. Too expensive for Arnold alone at the time, it had been partly paid for by Jenny. Forty years she had slept in it with the man now dead, and in her present gaze was horror.

Bernie knelt by the edge of the chaise and put his arm around his mother's shoulders. With relief, he noted that she did not pull away; perhaps the gesture was even welcome; the shaking began to calm and soon stopped.

"You got to tell me what's wrong, Momma," he said. "No way I can help you unless you tell me that."

"The bed," she managed.

"What about the bed?"

"I can . . . not . . . sleep in that bed," she said.

Bernie thought he understood; all the years of closeness

together ended; the shock of this first night after the finality of burial.

"You don't have to, Momma," he said. "There's a dozen bedrooms you can have tonight. Any one of a dozen. Why not the yellow room? Next to us. That way, if you want anything, we're right there."

She shook her head. Only the brass reading light by the chaise was burning, and the room was full of shadows. They were dark under her eyes and under her open lips down her long, thin neck and its network of age lines.

He tried again. He kissed her cheek and found it cold. He repressed a shudder. He was not an appropriate character for a Gothic tale.

"Why not, Momma?" he said. "That's what those rooms are for. Don't sleep here tonight if it's too sad for you . . ."

The enormous eyes looked squarely into his. A flicker of amusement passed over the harsh features.

"Sad?" she said.

"It's natural enough."

But she had turned away. The corners of her mouth drew down. She placed her hands, gripped into fists, on the chaise and forced herself to her feet. She took a step toward the bed.

"I can't figure why you're doing this," he said. "I don't see why you don't come down the hall."

Her voice under control, she said, "If I don't sleep in this bed tonight, I'll never sleep in it again."

She walked forward to it. Her face was now composed. Lightly she dried the wetness under her eyes with the back of her wrist. She pulled the covers over herself and lay back on two pillows. And closed her eyes.

"I'll turn off this light," Bernie said, tentatively.

"No," she said. "Leave it on, please."

He went to his mother and kissed her on the forehead. It was still cold. Her eyes opened. She smiled and said, "Dear Bernie . . . don't try to understand, child."

Puzzled, for it seemed easy enough, he said, "All right, Momma."

"And now go to Becky."

"You sure you're all right?"

"I'm glad it was you who came in. Somehow, you're the only one who could make it less—mysterious. The only one. You don't try to see too far."

"I don't understand."

She was still smiling faintly. "That's what I mean," she said. "Good night, Bernie dear."

"Good night, Momma."

He left her side. At the door, he glanced back. Her eyes were still open but no longer on him; they stared blankly ahead. The smile was gone. He started back, thought better of it and closed the door noiselessly. For some reason he found himself tiptoeing down the hall toward his room.

SOMETIME IN the forties, Jenny discovered that her husband was unfaithful to her. She did not mention it for some time. The discovery itself was not difficult. While looking for a checkbook in his desk, into which she had never been, she came across a St. Louis hotel statement for Mr. and Mrs. Arnold Starr. She had never been to St. Louis, but he had ("to see some shoe people"), and the bill reminded her of when and for how long. She looked for others and found a few: Philadelphia, Atlanta, Houston, Los Angeles and some from New York, all marked paid. The New York bills were from the Stanhope, where they had never stayed together. Though they were often in New York simultaneously, they were sometimes not, and he occasionally stayed longer than she did. They also traveled separately on store business, from time to time.

She became violently sick to her stomach and remained so for several days. She was adjudged to have some form of intestinal flu and was sent to bed. Arnold, to allow her to rest more easily, moved down the hall. When she arose from her sick bed, she took a bus down deep in Elm Street, the shoddiest section of downtown, full of used-clothing stores, vile-smelling beer holes and pawn shops. At one of these, she bought a .22 caliber revolver and some bullets. No questions were asked (they never are in Texas), and the man who sold her the pistol was bleary-eyed and dirty and did not appear to recognize her. He did, however, show her how to work the gun, even as she was recoiling from his sour breath. She took it home with her and placed it in a hat box, along with her carton of bullets. She put the hat box under many others and stored her murder materials with an old lavender picture hat she had not worn for years.

She was now prepared to shoot her husband.

She bided her time. She did not bring the matter up for some weeks. She wished to examine their life together. She wished to look at its physical routine, at its minutiae: the risings in the morning, the breakfasts (for each, a soft-boiled egg served in a procelain egg cup), the discussion of the Starr ads (even before the front page, normally), the comparison with competitive advertising (always cheering), the drive to the store (chauffeured by Maitland, in a Lincoln automobile; Arnold, smallish, liked room around him), his meetings for the day; whether they would lunch together (once or twice a week, normally, always in the store restaurant, no cocktails), which customers she had appointments with and how much they could be expected to spend; then he to his office, she to her second-floor desk (all she needed) by no later than eight forty-five. In the evenings, she picked him up in his office at six-thirty (no later; the boys could stay on, they had the youth and were still earning their keep); home, a drink or two for him, a cup of tea for her, dinner by eight with a half bottle of wine (sometimes champagne), some jokes from him which perhaps a visiting furrier had told him, an anecdote or reports from her on how things had gone in the fitting rooms; one or two hours of reading, often portions of things aloud; then bed. Or there were the parties, some small, a few forty or more at dinner. At these, the two of them moved easily as always; he discoursing, occasionally too long, she briefer; smiling often, listening well or seeming to, since Jenny could turn off anyone for a good while before he knew it, if indeed he ever did. The guest of honor might be a visiting actor on tour, a soloist with the orchestra, a painter, writer, politician; everyone of note came to the Starrs', and many notables came to the bursting city of Ramsey.

The business of life.

With curiosity, she allowed him to make love to her when he wished. He was, as he had always been, gentle and kind. She did not think he sensed the distaste within her. At least, when the sex was done, he held her head on his shoulder as he liked to (as she had as well) and did not seem to feel the tenseness of the muscles in her neck and shoulders. This was in the mid-forties, after the war. Jenny had heard of female orgasm. She never expected to experience it.

So life, after the finding of the hotel bills, was as usual. They were a great and famous couple. With the exception now that she hated him; had not known what hate was; now she did.

She chose a Sunday night after she had made their chili to bring it up. It had been a dull autumn day with a light frost. They had taken a long walk, lunched with Adam and Claude, read the *Times* (flown in daily) and he had napped briefly. At night they sat in bathrobes at the small round table in a corner of the kitchen. All the lights were on. Sometimes she turned them off and they ate by candlelight, but not this night. She did not wish to miss the smallest flicker on his face.

"Who was the woman in St. Louis?" she said, calmly.

She had been right to leave the lights on. His mouth tightened almost imperceptibly. His eyes barely narrowed, and only for an instant. But they did.

"The woman in St. Louis," he repeated, slowly. "Oh, well . . . you don't know her."

"I didn't expect to know her. I don't know whores."

He shook his head. "As it happens, she's not a whore." He smiled. "I wonder if I ever heard you use that word before."

"Who is she?"

"What does it matter?"

She was sure she had the advantage. "Because I say it matters."

He sighed. "Her name is Edith Stevenson."

"How old is she?"

"About thirty-five, or less. She works in an antique shop. I met her through some shoe people in St. Louis. I spent a day or two . . ."

"Three days."

He smiled faintly. "You found the hotel bills. I knew I should have . . ."

"Thrown them out? They were paid. You wanted me to see them. Philadelphia, Houston, Atlanta . . ."

"Maybe."

"With Miss Stevenson?"

"Good Lord, no." He chuckled.

"And all the other bills. The ones I haven't seen."

He pursed his lips. "Not really so many."

Her body was suddenly so tired it ached. She started to pick up a cup of coffee and found that her hands were trembling. She put it down and it clattered loudly.

He said, kindly, noticing: "Very few in twenty-five years, Jenny. Fewer than average, I think."

She wanted to throw the cup at him, but she hadn't the strength.

"Just one," she managed. "Only one. It's the same as fifty, a hundred, five hundred."

He became sharp with her. "Nonsense. If it were one, it'd still be going on, which would be serious. And if it were fifty . . ."

"Shut up!" she heard herself say, loudly.

But he saw his chance now, saw that it was he who had the strength.

"Oh no," he said. "We'll finish. There have been other places, other times and there will be others again. What does it matter to you? Who cares, the names? You say names, I don't even remember some, more than a few. Names are nothing. Don't exist . . ."

"Disgusting." Again, the word was almost more than she could manage.

"But I remember their faces and what they did." He leaned forward, looking at her intently. He did not seem to mean to be unkind. "At a certain age, a man realizes he does not know it all. At least that he has not done it all. For somebody, somewhere, that's all right, you see, maybe so. But not for me. Now, Jenny, that's very important you realize. Not for me. When you and I got married, I didn't know so much, but more than you. But I heard, men told me, I should experience . . . things should be taught to me. About it all. Now, I have been finding out about these things. They are, from time to time, necessary. Now is it that you want me to teach you these things I have learned, Jenny? Do you want that?"

"No, God Almighty, no!"

"Well, it isn't all turning to the same woman once or twice a week after twenty years. After ten, even five, whatever. There are mysteries. They must not go . . . uninvestigated. Things must be recognized, understood. Things must be done that have *never been done*." He paused, then continued gently. "And, of course . . . most vital . . . there must be new bodies. Stretching fantasies. Living them. Dreaming others." Again, he stopped. "It does no harm, Jenny. It separates a man from the wallpaper."

"And the woman . . . his wife?"

He shrugged. "I supposed it would be up to the woman. Some women are what they seem. Happier that way."

"But then there is what you do to her. Crucify her. Destroy her in your filth. You are supposed to love your wife. You do not do these things to your wife."

He lightly rubbed his forehead. "Do what things? Sex? Variety in sex? Sex is overrated in matrimony. Love? I don't know. I've read of love. A few people have even told me that love is terrible and fierce. And full of fear. I've heard about lovers. That each must tear the flesh of the other. To bring the blood. To possess souls. Things like that. Do you want your flesh torn, Jenny?"

She whispered: "No."

"No. Not me, either. Our gain. Our loss. Who is to say?"

"The sacredness . . ."

He was again curt. "Do not use that word. Something is sacred. I don't know what is sacred, but I'll take some people's word that it's so. But sex is not. Sex is the least sacred of anything. By definition, sex is profane. Do I mean 'profane'? Well, it will do. Whether it's a thought, or a dream, or a hotel room in St. Louis. I am not Aristotle. I am Arnold Starr, formerly Arnie Schatzki, shoe buyer. I know only me. I do not go to Africa to shoot animals. I fuck a strange woman now and again."

At the expression on her face, he smiled. "You die. At the word, only the word, you die a little."

But he was wrong. The word had given her a flash of strength.

"I know the word. I taught you to read, you Arnie Schatzki, shoe salesman. To speak. To sit in a good house. I almost held your hand when you picked up a fork."

He nodded, cheerfully enough. "And I gave you a good life for it."

"You betrayed me for it."

He laughed. "If I betrayed you, it was only because I didn't tell you these things. Instead of leaving hotel bills around."

"Why didn't you?"

He sat silently. "No good way of putting it, I think. Bringing it up. A man has to be caught. On the defensive. So he can be clear, I mean. So that lying is . . . impossible."

"You've lied to me."

"Never. Not once. What for? You never forced me to. You never asked."

Now they were both silent for a long time.

"What you have," she said, slowly. "You owe it all to me."

"Such as what?"

"The store. Which is what you are. It was my money."

"And my vision. *I* found Texas. If it hadn't been your money, it would have been somebody else's."

"I had the taste."

He nodded. "You had. And taught it to me. For your own sake. You would not be married to a man without it. You saw it could be there. You developed it."

"The fashion sense . . ."

He was cruel. "I can hire that."

She closed her eyes. It seemed to her that hard fists were pummeling her. There would be black bruises. Blood. Without thinking, she put her hand to her mouth, to her nose, even to an ear. There was no blood. She threw a card out without examining it.

"Suppose it had been me?"

He looked away from her and was thoughtful. "With the brain, I say, okay, why not?"

"What would happen to you?"

"I don't know. But remember I said with the brain."

"What do you mean?"

He smiled. "Lavender and needlepoint."

Angrily, she said, "I haven't worn lavender in years. And I don't do needlepoint."

"A figure of speech. You were never Jenny Goldsmith, shoe salesman. For you, it would be . . . artistically wrong."

From the years of habit, she corrected him wearily. "Aesthetically."

He was again cheerful. "You see? Still teaching. Tell me the difference."

She shook her head. "No."

He rolled his eyes, helplessly. "I'll never learn."

"Our children . . ."

"Have nothing to do with it. Know nothing about it. Never will."

She said, slowly, "I wanted you once very much. I wonder why?"

He said slowly and seriously, "I was the best of a bad lot, Jenny. All those young propers with their New Orleans accents and dances and white gloves. I was little and smart and ambitious and said some wrong words. There was adventure in you, too, Jenny. Still is. Not my kind. Not *all* my kind. And you were younger. You spit in the eye of New Orleans and gave me money and came with me to this scrub country."

"Was that love?"

He was silent. Then he said, "As you and I know it. As we will ever want to know it. For us, love is what fits well. Well, it all fits well. Now we will throw away the hotel bills and it will still fit."

"The new ones . . ."

He shook his head. "There won't be any more left around. The old ones must have been there . . . for a purpose. Whatever it was, it's gone."

Jenny took a long deep breath. "I'm empty," she said. "And very afraid."

"It's Sunday night. The whole world is empty and afraid on Sunday night."

"I bought a gun the other day. I was going to kill you with it."

He looked at her in astonishment.

"Where?" he said, finally.

"On Elm Street. In the colored section."

Arnold Starr twinkled. It was not his style to laugh uproariously. Now he suddenly did. "Jenny Starr. Probably in a thousand-dollar dress by Norell. In a hock shop on Elm. Did Maitland drive you?"

She shook her head. Even this was an effort. The weariness was now overwhelming. She had lost this battle and she knew it.

"I took a bus."

"It must be thirty years since you took a bus anywhere. Well, are you going to kill me tonight?"

Dully, she said, "No."

"Good," he said.

She tried once more. "But maybe I will someday. It's not impossible."

"Do it like Alcoholics Anonymous. Don't say you never will. Just say every morning, 'I won't do it today.'"

She put her head in her hands.

"It's late," he said. "An early day tomorrow."

She half rose. "I'll clean up."

He put his hand on her arm. "We pay the servants sufficient."

So far as she could tell, he slept soundly enough that night.

As THE things happened again over the years, she always thought she knew when, though she never again saw a hotel bill. It was as though he were lifted by them; grew an inch or two. They never discussed the matter. She only felt sick for a little while, and sometimes did not let him touch her; though, if her hunches were right, he usually wanted her more rather than less after an "episode." But on the night of his burial, it was all she could think about; absolutely all. Not a good moment in their years came to her mind. And the rage in her grew to nothing she could recognize in her sixty-six years. She shook with it, huddled her arms around her shoulders, stopped shaking by this physical effort, took her arms away and shook again. Eventually she rose and went to the smallest of her three closets. In this were clothes she seldom wore, perhaps would never wear again. They were by Dior, Balenciaga, Trigere, Norell, Galanos, Givenchy, a few odd things by Bonnie Cashin, some Claire McCardells, many others. They were classics, simple clothes, for Jenny wore no others. But they had been worn often. Soon they would go to the Jenny Starr Fashion Collection at the Ramsey Museum of Fine Arts.

She found all the old hat boxes, dozens of them, piled all on one side. Women were beginning not to wear hats, but Jenny continued. She knew exactly where the box was. She simply threw the others into the room. Tops fell off and the room looked like the remnants of a child's Christmas, all the presents having come in round boxes. The last box contained her old picture hat. And under it was her revolver. She took it up and fingered it with wonder and, perhaps, love. How phallic it was after all, she thought. How slim and elegant, not blocky and thick like Arnold. She walked with it, carrying it with both hands to the French windows, now closed because of the air-conditioning. She opened the windows and stepped out on the balcony. Overhead, the sky was a mass of tiny lights. In more than twenty years, she had never unloaded the pistol. It took her a little while to remember how it worked. But it was simple enough. She pulled back the hammer, and

slowly fired six shots into the Little Dipper. Even holding
the gun with two hands, the recoil startled her. Then she
threw the pistol over the balcony railing to the lawn below.

Bernie arrived in his undershorts. Louis, almost simultaneously, in his Liberty silk robe. She faced them, smiling
and at ease.

"What in God's name . . ." Louis began. Bernie stood
pale and silent. And now Becky crept to the doorway in a
kimono. Downstairs, there were noises of servants.

"You must mean the shots," Jenny said, still smiling.
"Oh well. I just found an old pistol and I thought I'd
empty it."

"An old pistol?" Louis said.

"I had no cannon. We had no cannons at Arnold's
funeral."

"Where is it?" Louis asked.

"On the lawn. I did not have twenty-one bullets. Only
the six. But the salute is over."

A long silence. No one moved.

"Dirt he was. Dirt he has become," Jenny said, slowly.

"Ashes," Louis said, almost inaudibly.

She looked thoughtful.

"Perhaps you should call Adam," she said. "To say that
I won in the end. Tell him Arnold is dead, but I am alive.
Tell him Jenny Starr is still alive. And may not die. Not
ever."

She paused, then frowned.

"No," she said. "Better not. You'd wake the children."
Again, she paused. "Go to bed, all of you. I had a dream,
is all. It's over. I am perfectly fine. Please, now go to
bed . . . I will sleep very well. Now that the dream is
over."

After a moment, Louis nodded at Bernie. They said
good night. In the hall, Louis said to Bernie and Becky,
"Go on back. I'll take care of the servants."

Downstairs, he told Maitland that all was well. Nothing
more. Maitland nodded. Two of the black maids shivered
behind him.

Louis walked through the great hall and out to the lawn.
After a search, he found the revolver. He looked at it
curiously. Then, not knowing what else to do with it, he
slipped it in the pocket of his bathrobe. (Eventually, with
some thought of keeping it away from his mother, he
would take it home and place it in a bureau drawer.) Then

he walked a couple of hundred yards to the pond between Arnold's property and Adam's. He walked halfway across the bridge that straddled the nearly dried-up bottom. The night was steaming. He looked toward Adam's house, hidden by the cedars and live oaks.

"Well," he thought, "I guess she can tell you whatever she wants herself."

He went back to his mother's house and to bed.

# 3

IN ADAM'S house, they didn't hear the shots. But, sometime after they were fired, Adam emerged from the house and drove off aimlessly in his black Rolls-Royce. The night was still hot, yet he left the air-conditioning off and allowed the wind to blow in his face through the open windows. He did not wish to be closed in, not even for comfort. The jacket to his black suit had been flung carelessly to one side and he had pulled down his tie and loosened his collar. Still he sweated, and this pleased him. He would have liked to be sweating more. He would have liked an axe and a cord of wood to split.

He drove downtown, through the maze of tall, broad buildings of steel and cement and lately aluminum. He passed the hotels, the banks and the insurance companies, and found he was going the same route he always did, directly by the store. He hadn't had that in mind, but the sign Abe Weinstein's Prairie Club caught his eye, and before he quite realized it, he had parked in the garage next to it. He had known Abe Weinstein since he had been a teenager. Abe ran many of the strip-joints, all the gambling and who knew what else in Ramsey. Kind face, kind eyes, soft voice. But you do not run all the gambling anywhere by simple kindness.

Abe Weinstein had been in the store hundreds of times. He had once said to Adam, "I owe you."

"What for, Abe?"

"My girls, they ain't the Queen of England. You treat 'em like they are. They didn't come from nowhere and they ain't goin' nowhere so for them Starr's is their heaven. I owe you."

Remembering, Adam smiled. Better to be owed than owe, he thought.

Standing under the neon Prairie Club sign, Adam stared across the street at the famous store he had helped to build. The odd feeling came to him that he had never seen it before. The six stories of white marble were strange to him. What was inside? Who lived there?

He shook his head impatiently and ran his fingers through his dark, short-cropped, gray-flecked hair. He stepped into the street. A cruising car screamed to a stop to avoid hitting him. A storm of profanity came from the driver's seat. Startled, Adam looked back and realized it was directed at him. He half-waved an apology and went to the employees' entrance. No one was there. He rang the night bell. After a while, a plump, elderly man wearing the broken leather face and the belt and braces that introduce old Texans came into view. He put his face almost flush against the glass of the door. When he recognized Adam, his mouth fell half open. He reached for the keys, remembered something, threw on his jacket and only then opened the door.

"Mr. Adam . . ." he began.

"Evening, Fred."

"I was . . ."

Adam nodded. "You've got to make your rounds. I know. Will I set off any alarms if I walk the store?"

Fred shook his head. "I can fix the signals."

"Will you do that?" Adam paused. "And turn on the escalators, please."

He walked on past the punch-in register and the rows of employee tags in their slots against the wall and past the big, padlocked room which was known as store call. From this room, all Starr's employees picked up their own purchases to take out of the store. Each package was coded and matched carefully against the employee's sales check. Often there were long lines outside the store call at the end of the day; and there was still grumbling among the old-timers that such a thing existed. Once they had walked out with their packages like ordinary customers. As he looked at the locked window, old dialogue came into Adam's mind. His father. Arnold Starr, was speaking angrily:

"Do you really think I'm gonna tell people who've been with me twenty, twenty-five years that all of a sudden I don't trust 'em? You've got another think coming, sonny boy."

"It's not personal, Dad. You're making it too personal."

The older man was white with anger.

"Personal? Of course it's personal. There's nothing about this store that's not personal. That's what built it, don't you know that? It's what sent you to Harvard . . ."

Adam's voice could be as loud as his father's and just as angry. "One, one and a half percent pilferage we can afford," he shouted. "That's how it's always been. We can live with it, other stores can live with it. Now we're at three plus and heading for four. That, Father, is the profit."

"Then fire that goddamn ex-G-man you brought in and hire somebody who knows a shoplifter when he sees one!"

"That's not the problem . . ."

Arnold banged his fist down on his desk. "And prosecute," he said. "I gave you permission. Use it. Prosecute."

A LONG FIGHT, that one, Adam mused, walking slowly through the first floor. One of hundreds in the twenty years since he had come down to join his father in the small, respected little retail business Arnold Starr and his wife, Jenny, had founded. Secretaries in the executive area grew so accustomed to the shouting between father and son, they scarcely bothered to listen. When the tumult grew too distracting, Rosemary King, Mr. Arnold's secretary for thirty years, got up and closed the door. That helped a little, but it did not improve the scorched nerves Adam took home with him every night; and the battle fatigue. Arnold Starr hated change. The old man was frightened of it and fought with Adam because it was always Adam who proposed it. It took five years to get the escalators on which Adam now rode.

*Arnold* (looking up from the figures he had been studying): The cost of these escalators is just under ten times what your mother and I spent to build the original store in this location. Before the additions. It is more than one hundred times more than the original store downtown—including all the merchandise in it which we paid for in cash.

*Adam:* We don't have to pay this in cash.

*Arnold:* In the end, it has to be paid. You borrow, you just pay more.

*Adam:* You buy the time. The escalators pay their own bill.

*Arnold* (looking down at the figures): Where is such a guarantee? The escalator company is making it? I don't see it. Or maybe you personally are making it? You are such a big man now, you are personally guaranteeing these millions whatever-it-is dollars, which is five times that in sales to make up for it? You are getting a very big head, Adam. Maybe you are believing some things they write in the papers about you, is that it?

*Adam* (wearily): Every new store has escalators. In an elevator, a customer goes where she meant to go and that's all. Escalators take the blinders off. Every floor is its own show window. Escalators sell.

*Arnold* (spit on his lips): Stop! You can sit in that chair, Mr. Harvard Business School Man, and tell me what is a sales tool? Forget that I am your father. Just remember that I am Arnold Starr who knows how to buy and sell since before you were born.

*Adam:* I didn't mean . . .

*Arnold* (leaning forward, eyes glittering): Without that you are my son, you should be selling shoes. Since you are my son, you are vice-president. *Only because of me,* you hear that? You are nothing, zero, except for me. Zero.

ADAM NOW reached the top of these escalators. He walked slowly back through the Gift Shops, past the Credit Department and the Advertising Department and through the door marked Executive Offices. In this area there were no night lights; only a faint glow from the Gift Department allowed him to see where he was going. He walked directly into his father's office and stared at the huge mahogany desk and the high-backed leather chair behind it. The office was simple and ordinary.

Three round-backed wooden chairs with seats and the backs of leather faced the desk. A couch, again in black leather, was against one wall, with Chinese red lamps at either end. The only wall decorations were a large framed photograph of the first Starr's store and a collection of early advertisements. On the desk, however, were pictures of every member of the family. The largest, and the only one done in color, was of Jenny Starr, Arnold's wife and partner, Adam's mother.

Adam stood just inside the doorway remembering the battles. He said quietly to the empty chair behind the desk:

"In the end, I won them all, you old son of a bitch. Every one. But it was so goddamn tough," he whispered.

With these words out of him, Adam suddenly felt weak. He slumped down into the sofa and leaned back and closed his eyes. The picture of his father, so much smaller than he, white-haired and bright-eyed, came to him. He remembered how his father had loved his merchandise, loved his people who worked for him, loved his spotless, elegant store; probably had loved him, Adam—probably, hell, certainly. And Louis. And Bernie. And Adam's wife and Adam's children, and maybe even at last Bernie's wife. And he remembered the endless talk from this man, the philosophizing, the meandering sentences that twisted and turned and came out with gold in them, though you had to wait for it and recognize it when it came. And he remembered that everything his father knew he had taught himself, with the help of Jenny. And he remembered, amidst all the battles, laughter and agreements and understandings and the pride his father had had in him which he had never expressed openly but which sometimes shone on his face. And he remembered the great joy on the days the store broke records, and more than once a cork popping from a bottle of Dom Perignon for a sip to celebrate.

Adam leaned forward on the couch and put his head in his hands. The tears now ran down his face to his lips, and licking them, he tasted the saltiness. The lump in his throat was nearly choking him. To the empty chair, he said, quietly and with difficulty, "See, I never understood why you couldn't make me president, Dad. You'd still have been the boss . . ." The actual saying of the words brought on the sobs; even as he was saying them, Adam knew he had not called his father "Dad" since his childhood. Always "Father." Arm's length. Ritual kiss on the cheek after absences. He wanted now to hold his father in his arms, that gallant little man with the elusive gold in his heart and mind. He wished to tell his father that he, Adam, had always loved him; through every battle, had always respected him. He cried that he could not do these things.

He stayed a while in his father's office and his eyes felt swollen when he left. He passed by the watchman quickly; the eyes were a private matter.

But he still did not wish to go home. He got the Rolls and drove north from downtown, having no idea where he wanted to go. Within minutes, when he had passed all the automobile showrooms and battery and muffler sellers, he was at the Expressway; he drove up the ramp and turned north. Now he knew where he was going. He was heading for the ranch he and his father had owned jointly. It had once been a Hereford ranch, but now there were strong, healthy Black Angus on it. And Adam and his father, the joint owners, made some money on the cattle, so that although the tax advantages were not what they had once been, the working aspect of the ranch was practical. But the fun of it was in the horses which both Starrs liked to buy and trade and even ride. Both of Adam's children had learned to ride out on these thousand acres. They had learned Western style, but four years before, Adam had bought a five-gaited English mare and taught Nancy, then fifteen, to ride English style so she'd be at home in the East where someday she would go to college. Nancy was a natural; now she sometimes showed horses. Bobby, at seventeen, rode tentatively, as he did everything else having to do with sports. He had never got the hang of posting, and even in the Western saddle he still bounced when he trotted. Essentially, as Adam knew in his heart, Bobby hated the horses and was afraid of them. But it was not possible for Adam to admit the existence of fear in his son. And so for years, on Sundays, he had taken the boy from his books and his Mozart and forced him up on the beasts, keeping him there until dark, until father and son were both worn out; and then told the boy he was improving all the time, acting proud, lying. Bobby would smile faintly.

The buildings were nearly a century old, ancient by the standards of Ramsey, which had been a general store and a post office until the turn of the century when some adventurers decided to make a city out of it. In those early days, most of the county was cotton and cattle land, like the rest of Texas. It was hard, tough country for the animals and the men. Northers, dust storms and periodic droughts plagued them, and there was never quite enough for the cattle to eat or to drink. People and animals existed, no more. The men were glad enough to sell their acres as the city began to develop. There were few ranches around Ramsey anymore, and those that were left were more for pleasure than profit.

The Starrs had done little with the buildings. The two old barns, the bunkhouse and the main house were as they had always been. Fixing up was done as it was needed. Ben Sanders, a descendant of the original owner, lived in the main house with his family, and he kept a couple of hands in the bunkhouse. The three of them kept the place going.

Adam pulled up in front of the stables. In all, there were a dozen horses, fewer than the barn would hold and more than were needed. One of the jobs of Ben and his hands was to keep them all exercised. They were good animals. A man could take pride in them. The cattle were all right, but the horses were better and Adam looked at them with pleasure. One of them, a new Appaloosa, took his eye. A superb animal, it had scarcely been ridden yet. This would be the horse for tonight, Adam thought. No saddle, just a blanket and a hackamore. He needed, he realized suddenly, combat. He threw his jacket on the ground. He had no trouble getting the hackamore on. He set the mounting block and made the mount, talking softly to the big stallion. "Let's go!" he yelled suddenly and dug his right heel into the horse's side. "Jack! Your name is Jack. Your name is Jack for tonight. You against me, Jack." And Jack took off into the blackness.

"Just don't step into a gopher hole, you bastard," Adam said. He was grinning. All the sweat seemed to be gone. What was left was the swell of power in the man and the beast, one feeding the other, until they were a single being with fear and exultation blended in it: power, Adam's bad need, strong as an alcoholic's for his drink on this strange night.

On they sped, long after the light from the ranch house was out of view, faster than the wind which whistled at them as though in warning. Twice the horse shied, spying something on the ground. The first time, Adam held, but the second was too sudden and he shot from the animal and landed on his shoulder but rolling so that, after a moment, he knew nothing was broken. Blood ran from his scraped cheek and forehead and some minor cuts. The horse grazed quietly, perhaps twenty yards away.

"You son of a bitch," Adam whispered. "You fucking bastard, you are going to El Paso tonight."

He crept up on Jack. At the last second, the horse moved, but too late. Adam had the rope and brought the head down hard and talked lovingly into the animal's ear. "You are a bastard," he was saying, "and you'll drop tonight, or I will, but it's going to be you." His voice was very gentle. Since he had no idea where they were, he could not lead the animal to a sunken road and he had no mounting block, could not even know where a log or a rock might be. So he put his arms around the horse's neck, leaped, pulled himself over, and on his third try, made it. And now he dug his heel into the flesh and bones and again they were off.

There was no way of telling how long it was before the horse began to slow. Lather was all over his face, but spit was on Adam's too, and his lungs felt as though they would burst. He kicked the animal fiercely and Jack gave what he had left. He gave longer than Adam expected, like a boxer who would not stay down. And there was a huge feeling of pride in the animal for Adam, but it was only a part of what he felt for himself.

At last, Jack was through and Adam knew it. They stopped and Adam talked to him for a while. There seemed to be no noise on the prairie except for the breathing of the two of them. Perhaps it was too desolate even for crickets out there, or perhaps the horse and Adam were simply too much together to hear them.

Adam turned him finally, and they began the long walk back. Sooner or later, Adam thought, they would see a landmark for they'd gone straight, he thought, all the way. After a while, Adam leaned forward and put his head on the horse's neck and rested it there. Eventually, they reached the stalls and Adam washed down the horse and put him up. "I love you," he said.

At home, at nearly four o'clock in the morning, Nancy was still up reading. She was in the living room, curled up in one of the big Dunbar easy chairs, sitting on her legs. At nineteen she was long and lean, like Adam and his mother. Her forehead was high and sloping and her short black hair was rough and wiry and would always look tousled. It framed well the brown eyes that often looked black and her nose that was long and just slightly curved. Someday she would perhaps have it operated on, and this might be a mistake because the nose went well with the wide mouth, the lips a touch too thin and the jaw that told people who she was. With her grandmother, she was the most Semitic looking of the Starrs; not pretty, but striking enough to live up to her name. When Adam walked in, she looked startled for a moment, and then laughed.

"As they say, look what the cat dragged in," she said. "Or rather, you look like the cat after a bad night. Have you been on the town, Adam?"

Both children called their parents by first names, not unusual in the East and in California, but rare still in Texas.

He slumped into the twin chair next to her.

"I had a go-round with Jack out at the farm," he said. "Took him with a blanket and a hackamore, and we went fifteen rounds."

"And you won."

"I won. What are you reading?"

"Evelyn Waugh. *Officers and Gentlemen.* I've been going through all of Waugh, one after another."

"I did that when I was your age. There wasn't so much to go through then, of course."

"You don't read as much as you used to, do you?"

"No time. Too many memos. The trouble with the world is too many memos. Including mine. And too many magazines and reports that seem to have something to do with my work. Businessmen eventually become illiterate, you know. Like doctors."

There was a pause. Other things should have been said. Questions should have been asked. Something major had happened and they had not discussed it. They had now the time for it and the aloneness. But the time passed and there was no discussion. Neither of them knew quite how to start it. Each was perhaps afraid to try. Neither wished to push the other. Safer to stay on the surface. Each was saddened by this.

"Couldn't you sleep?" Adam said finally.

Nancy shrugged. "I don't know. I didn't try. I will after a while. I've nearly finished this."

Adam pulled himself to his feet. "Well, I've had it. Upstairs for me."

He leaned over and kissed his daughter on the forehead. "Good night, dear."

Impulsively, she brought his head down a second time and kissed him on the cheek. He looked down at her, startled. Nancy absolutely never did that; did not care for shows of affection.

"Do you care that you're filthy?" she said, embarrassed.

"No." And that moment, too, passed, leaving important matters untouched. But Adam did not, for the life of him, know what more to say; and so he left her.

Upstairs, he sat in his dressing room and removed his shredded trousers and the shirt. He looked in the full-length mirror at himself naked and grimaced. What he saw was caked blood and dirt, a good deal of both on his face. He considered brushing his teeth, which he had probably not failed to do each night for nearly forty years, and decided against it. In the big, king-sized bed, his wife, Claude, lay breathing evenly. She too would be naked. They wore nothing to bed, ever.

He crept under the covers like a thief, so that he would not wake her, rose up on an elbow, looked at her, and felt the power of the horseback ride rise up in him and woke her anyway by putting his arm around her, cupping her small breast in his hand, black with the soil of the farm.

Her eyes opened slowly but without surprise and she turned to him. Neither of them said a word. They spent a good deal of time silently touching. And then they began a major reason for their existence. For this as much as for anything, Claude Duvalier, a famous mannequin in Paris, half-English, half-French, kept by good men and bad, loved by experts and amateurs, loving back or not, had left her Paris for this wilderness called Texas with a tall man called Adam Starr twenty-one years before. And after that twenty-one years, she knew him less than she had known him then, was confused by him, overwhelmed by her role as his wife, solaced but often puzzled by her role as mother; and nipped a little vodka in the kitchen now and then to help her get through the dinners for twelve, or, more important, the dinners for two.

But there was always this; and sometimes, not invariably, it answered questions and solved problems. Every ounce of strength and power that Adam distributed in bits and pieces throughout his life, he concentrated in this act and it transfigured her. He knew, or so she imagined, for they had never discussed it, what she had been; others certainly did, though none perhaps in Texas, and it was long ago now and few would care. But he would care, good God how he must care, and it was as though each time they came together he attempted to wipe out this past of hers. The force of the effort always astonished her, touched her, made her wonder fleetingly whether he had succeeded. When it was over, of course, he had not. But she responded to the effort with all her senses.

"Adam, Adam," she whispered. Only silence from him.

When it was over, he dropped his head between her neck and shoulder, as he always did. And it was almost the position he had taken with the horse on the way home. He had won it all. Conquered. And also wept. He could sleep now.

# 4

BUT CLAUDE did not sleep immediately. Instead, she slipped from their bed and threw on a light silk robe. She walked to the window. Outside it was still dark, but it would not be long before the first light of dawn would be creeping in. She went to the bathroom, tidied herself up and left the light on, closing the door all but a fraction so that she had some vision in the bedroom. She sat down in one of the twin, round-backed chairs and examined the prone body of her husband intently. He slept on his back; never snored. He had, she reflected, a fine body for a young man, never mind a man of forty-two; broad, sloping shoulders leading to a flat waist and hips and strong, straight legs. His head was large, his dark eyes set deep into craggy features like his mother's, his hair was only lately touched with gray and his nose would have been too bold, but his long jaw balanced it. Claude was sick of people saying he looked like Lincoln, but so he did.

Well, she said to him silently, whatever you had to prove, I seem to have proved it for you. Repository for your seed, symbol of your triumph. Whatever you needed

I gave, and what did you give me in return? Emptying yourself, what did you fill in me? No loving phrases, not even a word. There are no words for repositories. You bring me to climax, I moan for you, and that is enough for you. Checked off on list: Satisfying wife. Other check-offs in the supreme order of your life: Consult wife on plans by informing her as to what they are. Be logical, reasonable, kind in all matters involving wife and children. Do not lose temper, even if wife or children do. Do not scatter emotion; that is senseless. Therefore, do not look probingly at wife or children but invent roles for them and be satisfied that they are indeed the roles: strong, healthy, loving of each other and you, and in charge of life, like you.

Continuing to stare at him, Claude said aloud, but very softly: "Adam, we aren't those characters. Cut us and we bleed, and the world does cut us and none of us is able to show you our wounds. Poor Adam. Poor all of us."

He stirred and his eyes opened briefly.

"Nothing, dear," Claude said. "Close your eyes."

Without a word, he did.

Claude rose and went back into the bathroom. She let her robe fall to the floor and examined her body in the full-length mirror. Here and there now, the suggestion of softness. Well, at forty . . . in the hips, the lower belly, first hints in the breasts. She ran her fingers through her hair; still soft brown with golden streaks, not the first thread of gray. Adam, she thought, what will you do when I grow old and round; for that can never fit into your play at all. She put her robe back on and went downstairs. Nancy, still reading, looked up in surprise.

"Did Adam wake you?" she asked.

"Yes, he did."

"Wasn't he a sight?"

"Was he? I didn't notice. Oh yes, I did see some blood on his face."

"Bloody but very much unbowed. He won a fight with a horse."

"Adam always wins his fights." Claude went to the enormous window which looked out on the lawn and finally to the woods. "At last, morning," she said, for now the light was rising over the trees. "Shall we have a drink?"

Nancy hesitated, then said, "Why not?" She rose and

went to the pantry, returning shortly with two glasses of straight vodka over ice. She handed one to her mother and the two women sat together on the huge Dunbar sofa.

"Your father," Claude said, "is perfect."

Nancy frowned. "Thinks he is?"

Claude shook her head. It was important that she be clear; no whining. "Really is. He's never knowingly unkind. Thoughtless. He does all he knows how to do."

Nancy did not approve. "You make him sound stupid. He's not."

"I wish he had once cried today."

"He rode a horse. Same thing. Partly. Also of course, he was dominating. And in control." Nancy paused, leaned forward and lit a cigarette. Light was quickly filling the room. The paintings were coming to life. The smoke curling up from the cigarette looked fragile and pretty. "He's not perfect, but I see what you mean," she said. "In control."

"I cried for a while tonight. But it was somehow all wrong. It wasn't for Dad, it was for me. He was the last person who loved me foolishly. Like your father loves you. And Bobby."

Nancy shrugged. "Foolishly? I doubt it."

"Yes. He can't help it."

"Or anything. He is what he is. And that is a lot. I agree with you. There is . . . splendor in him. He loves you, Claude, you're not doubting that?"

Her mother shook her head. "All he can," she said. "And I love him all I can. I just feel . . . used. Sometimes." She hesitated and sipped her vodka. "But then, what else am I for?"

"No one is here to be used," Nancy said, angrily.

Claude said calmly, "Adam is a superb man. In the end, he may turn out to be a great one. Who knows where it may end for him? We are *not* equals. I supply what I can . . ."

Nancy stubbed out her cigarette bitterly. "That makes me sick," she said. "And I promise you that if you mention the word inadequate, I'll throw up. Any single person who comes to this house and feels a smidgin of warmth has felt you, not Adam. You can get a stranger through an evening with your gentle talk, your smiles, and Adam waits and expects and offers nothing because he doesn't know how. And the stranger withers . . . Are you going to cry?"

Claude shook her head with determination. But her eyes were full. The vodka was warm in her stomach.

"Put your head on my shoulder," Nancy said. And she leaned back against the arm of the sofa and took her mother's head in her arms, so that the two lay side by side and eventually fell asleep like that. When the butler found them later, they looked like spent lovers.

# PART TWO

# 1

"I THOUGHT," Karen Woodward said, "you weren't going to have a Gala this year. I thought it was too soon after your father's death."

"It has been decreed that we will," Louis said into the phone.

Karen laughed. She had a low, gentle laugh with much cheer in it. People enjoyed hearing Karen laugh.

"Who did the decreeing? Adam?"

"Of course. Who else?"

"From what you tell me, Adam seems to do a lot of decreeing. Didn't they listen to you at all?"

"Oh, yes. It was felt that my father would rather do the business than have us mourn his death."

"And Adam decided this?"

"Mother decided this. Mother has the final say. Mother's final say happened to be Adam's final say. Anyway, the point of the matter is, are you coming down?"

Karen was silent.

"Well?" Louis said.

"I don't know, Louis. It seems like . . . a commitment. You've been moving rather fast. I've known you three months and I'm not sure at all that I want to come to Texas to see you."

"No commitment is involved," he said, impatiently. "As a matter of fact, I don't even know what you mean. It's a four-day weekend over Labor Day, it's quite a lot of fun, and I'd like to see you on my home ground—or you to see me, maybe."

Again Karen was silent, but this time she broke it herself. "All right," she said finally. "I'll come down."

"I'll send you a ticket," he said, more relieved and pleased than he would like to have confessed.

"Of course you won't," she said, sharply. "I'll get my own ticket. You can get me a small suite at the best hotel and that you can pay for since I am your guest. Didn't you ever invite a girl to a dance? She transports herself. What will I need to bring besides daytime and evening?"

"There's a Western party . . ."

"I'll get that in your store down there. I'll let you know my flight number. We'd better hang up now before I change my mind."

Karen Woodward was close to a classic beauty. She was tall, slim and moved like a dancer. Her hair was black and she wore it short and loose so that it looked as though she never had to comb it. She was thirty-one years old and had sculptured features, pale skin, blue eyes, a quick smile and a lilting voice. She was the kind of girl who had never met an artist who had not wanted to paint her; and many had. Not one of their portraits was in her apartment. They were all with her father and mother in Locust Valley. Instead, the paintings in her apartment on Central Park South were by Chagall, Matisse, Picasso and Modigliani, among others; Karen Woodward was rich. Her father, now retired, had been a copper tycoon, and it had been his policy from the day his only child was born to buy her whatever she wanted and a good deal she discovered she didn't want, including, when she was twenty-two, a poor Italian prince. She looked like a princess, she should be one, he decided, and she thought he might be right. She struggled through five years of marriage, living in Italy, France and New York before the thrill of watching the prince play polo and picking out his suits died, as did all other thrills, and she realized that he bored her. To her parents' mild regret, she divorced him, dropped his name, kept the New York apartment, a maid and a cook, and began to live the free life of the very rich. She had several affairs, none lasting longer than a few months, chaired a few charity balls, bought paintings, traveled with friends, skied a lot, weekended wherever she wished and was happy that she was childless. Was, in fact, happy, she supposed. She had what she wanted, did what she liked. She had been seated next to Louis at a party, found him a good dancer and pleasant. She was fascinated by the legend of the store, fascinated by the stories he told of Texas and the Southwest, and let him sleep with her on their fourth date. She also enjoyed that; and the fact that he was wryly deprecatory about himself and his role at the store. Adam, Adam, Adam this, Adam that; much of the wryness from these references. She was tired of Adam before she had even met him. The Gala: well, why not? she reasoned. It was no more a commitment than sleeping with him, which had been no commitment at all. It would be amusing. A square dance! The nation's most elaborate fashion show, so he had promised her, and she loved good clothes.

And Louis. Not bad at all. He knew music, art, literature and fashion as well as she did, and he was a tender lover. One difficulty: he was also in love with her. Well, that was not so awful. Many men had been in love with her, some were now, and they were not problems. She had wondered once or twice whether she were falling in love herself, but the months had said no. Perhaps it would be Louis Starr. Since the most attractive men were almost inevitably homosexual, straight men of the second rank were welcome enough, and Louis was probably better than that. He was, she thought, certainly the most attractive man in her life at the moment and led the most interesting life.

Karen rang a bell and a middle-aged, white-haired lady appeared in the living room.

"Anna," Karen said, "I'm going to Texas, what do you think about that?"

The old woman looked disbelieving. "Texas," she said. "Don't they still have Indians?"

"I hope so. And villains and heroes and six-guns. Wouldn't it be fun to see a showdown at the old corral?"

Anna smiled, "I like Mr. Louis. He knows who he is. He worships you but he's not foolish about it the way the run of them are. His flowers are nice and not too much."

"The Starrs of Texas," Karen said, musingly. "Well, they've built something out of nothing. Like Daddy did. And they seem to know how to take care of it. That's something. That's quite a lot."

## 2

AFTER HIS father's death, Adam took a number of immediate steps. He moved his office to his father's and moved Louis to his. He did this the day after his unanimous election by the board to be president of the store, and Louis's to be executive vice-president.

"Otherwise," he said to Louis, "the office stays vacant and becomes a shrine. Do you agree?"

Louis nodded. "Absolutely. And I would get your own things in as quickly as possible. As I will. He's gone and we're here, so let's say so."

For the moment, however, his father's office, where they now sat, was still his father's. They were relaxed. It was three weeks after Arnold's death.

"You heard about Struther?" Adam asked.

"Just yesterday. What an idiotic thing."

Adam was silent, shifting uncomfortably in his father's chair. He would have his own things in as quickly as possible. He was accustomed to creating his own surroundings, slightly uncomfortable when out of them.

"Would you have fired him?" he said to his brother.

Louis did not hesitate. "No," he said. "I would have lacerated him, scared the shit out of him, but no, I wouldn't have fired him. Eighteen years, for God's sake. But I don't blame you. It was correct, if that's the word."

Adam laughed. "Blame me! Blame me for what? I didn't fire him."

Louis looked at him in astonishment. "I thought you did."

"I didn't even know about it until a week after I got back. Matilda, Eli and Bill did the work. They thought they were doing me a favor. It never occurred to them that, like you, I would never have fired him. Or the girl."

69

"I'll be damned." Louis whistled through his teeth. "Well, hire him back."

Adam shook his head. "I can't make fools out of our three top executives. Which I would be doing since the story's around. He's all right anyway. I got him a job down in San Antonio. Not quite as much money, but he'll come out all right. But I can't do anything about the girl."

Louis shrugged. "The girl . . ." he said, without interest.

"When you come right down to it we had less right to fire her than Struther. She did what the boss asked. There's nothing to be done about it, but—it was certainly unfair."

Adam stood up and stretched. He walked to the window and looked down at the street below. A line of cars was waiting to get into the parking garage. A good sign. They were good cars. The occupants would be shopping this afternoon. Adam wrestled silently with all that he had to say. He wrestled with the order of items and with his tone of voice. He tried to avoid hating himself in advance. There would be time enough for that later.

He returned to his chair and looked at his brother's expectant face. The conversation was not over and they both knew it. ". . . this too, too solid flesh," suddenly ran through Adam's mind. Solidity, stolidity. You can teach a man anything except flair, exuberance, daring.

"I think," Adam said, slowly, "we should go ahead on a new store in North Ramsey."

Louis sat back, comfortably. He had a surprise for Adam. "Expanding what we have?"

Adam shook his head. "You know the difficulties where we are. Not enough parking, too much congestion now, never mind after expansion . . . and we're not far enough north. We're a little behind the way the city's moving. I'd rather be a little ahead than a little behind."

Louis was silent.

"Wouldn't you?"

Louis nodded. "Yes. Well, that leaves Hammond's proposition. You like it?"

Adam looked off. "He's got his location right. His accesses are good. There's plenty of room. The key for him is us. If we go, he'll sell it out in no time. Major department store, specialty shops . . ."

"Will he build the store?"

Adam nodded. "We'd fixture it, of course. Ninety-nine-year lease, we choose the architect and the center would follow our lead. Architecturally, I mean."

"What happened to the old store?"

"I'd say Hammond would have to take it over." Adam smiled. "On our terms. He could lease only a discount store. Or outsizes. Or furniture. Or something. Nothing competitive with us."

"Would he do it? That's putting handcuffs on him."

"He'll have fifty million in the new center, Louis. Every cent of that rides on us. Otherwise, he's got to go to Saks or Stix or somebody, and they're all afraid of us. They want no part of Ramsey. At least not yet."

"Does he know about this plan?"

"Not the last part of it. And he'll kick—for about ten minutes—until his fifty million hits him."

Louis laughed. His laugh was gentle. Adam loved to hear his brother laugh, for it came not so often and it meant he had not been hurt. A deep sadness went through him for he would have to hurt Louis this very day. "What do you think?" Adam said.

Louis continued to smile. It pleased him to surprise his brother. It pleased him to please his brother.

"You're talking about a hundred thousand square feet or so?"

Adam shrugged. "One twenty-five, about. We'll lose some business downtown, but we're losing it anyway, or will be, the more small, high-quality shops go in out there. And Ramsey's getting more than its share of convention business so the visitors'll take care of part of the sucking out of downtown."

Louis said, "Well, this may surprise you, but I think you're one hundred percent right. And I think if we can make a deal with Hammond we should make it tomorrow."

Adam sat silent, stunned. Finally, he said, "I thought you were dead set against expansion. Like Dad."

"A while ago. But since you were so strong for it, I did a serious analysis of our business out of city. Sixty percent of the downtown business in some of the top-price lines is already being done out of town. Amarillo, Abilene, even Memphis and Chicago. And conventions. Doctors' wives. Lawyers' wives. Meanwhile, in the suburbs, we're obviously losing business to the shops you're talking about. I think we can do fourteen million out north and maybe not cost ourselves two, three million the first year, less after that."

There is a peculiarly empty feeling when one has gained a victory after long struggle. Adam could say nothing.

"Have you discussed this with Mother?" Louis said, helping him.

Adam shook his head. "Only Bill and you."

"Well, we'll have to discuss it with Mother."

"She'll hate it."

"Not if you and I are *both* for it. She couldn't be against anything that unusual. Incidentally, Adam, I am for *this* expansion. Not *any* expansion. My doubts about Houston and Fort Worth remain."

"That's another subject. Another time."

"So . . ." Louis got up to leave. "Let's go."

"Louis," Adam called him back, and then nearly changed his mind. Why not another time? Because it had to be done. When unpleasant things have to be done, let them be done quickly. For all Adam's life he had believed that, and so he said: "How important . . . how important is announcing the Gala fashion shows to you?"

Louis sank back in the chair as though Adam had struck him. Commentating the Gala fashion shows before one thousand people in black tie one night, one thousand women the next afternoon, was the only time during the year when he, Louis Starr, was the focal point of Starr's. He worked on his commentary for nights, well into the mornings. He felt he did them well, that his vast fund of fashion knowledge was transmitted to the audience, that he educated them. No one knew all this better than Adam.

"Not . . . important at all," he said, his face pale.

Adam looked at him hard and unblinking. He did not know whether in business or personal life he had ever done anything which hurt him so much to do. But the comments had been coming for years. From the staff, from the audience, even from the models. Louis's commentating simply bored people. Nothing could have been done with Arnold Starr alive. Nothing could now be ordered with Jenny Starr alive. Louis would have to be forced to decide himself. "It isn't the best thing you do," Adam said flatly. "I think you know too much. And try to tell it all."

"Why don't you just come out and say it, Adam?" Louis said, angrily. "You want to give them to Peter Shaw because he's an actor. He doesn't know his ass from his elbow about fashion, but he looks good and makes an audience laugh."

Adam said, quietly, "I think Shaw should handle them, yes. Actually, by right he should. Fashion shows are part of his division. They are sales promotion. As you say, audiences do like him."

Louis once again got up from his chair. His eyes were smarting, and he was not entirely sure what he might say. He had told Karen he would be announcing the shows. He had, after all, announced them for five years, ever since Adam had given them up as beneath his dignity. They were his moments in the sun, and the world was not filled with these.

"Tell him. And while you're at it, tell him that if he wants to know the difference between a mink and skunk to write me a note."

"I'd rather you told him," Adam said, plowing straight ahead. "It won't look right if I do."

And Louis exploded. "You're goddamn right it won't look right. Because Peter Shaw will know that what you've done is cut my throat. And that he won't like. He'll do it because you tell him to and because he has ambition and ego. But he's also a decent man. He won't like the fact that one brother cut the heart out of another and he's in the middle."

Adam shook his head. "Skip it, Louis. We'll go on just the way we always have. I just thought from the store's standpoint . . ."

"I know what you thought. You have no monopoly on thinking about the store's standpoint, Adam. We all do a little of that. But all of life is not this fucking store."

"Of course, it isn't. That's why I said, skip it."

Louis shook his head. "Do you really think I'm that dumb?" he said wanly. "Don't you understand that I know what you're doing? All right, you've done it. It worked. I won't announce the shows and Peter will. Now, tell me . . . why should I make things easy for you by telling Peter this myself? Why shouldn't I make this hard and nasty for you by making you tell him? Can you think of one good reason?"

And Adam was now angry. "Why shouldn't you? When it's the proper way of handling the matter. Why shouldn't you do what is correct? What is best for this store? Because without this store, you are nothing, Louis, and neither am I. So why aren't you doing some of the tough things instead of hiding in a corner and letting me do them? Well, I'll do them, all right. Somebody has to. But if you think I admire you . . ."

"I'll tell Shaw."

"You should."

"I realize that. You're quite right. It was simply a shock. I'll attend to it."

"Louis, there's another part of it. I think I should welcome the guests as usual. But I think you should give out the awards. After all, they are awards for distinguished design in the field of fashion, and you supervise our fashion image."

Louis might have turned him down. But then Karen was arriving.

"Thank you for them there crumbs," he said. He turned to leave. At the door, he turned again to face his brother. "You're going to have one awful time running this joint without Dad," he said. "There are tougher things to be done than this, you know. Deadwood. Dad was the excuse not to do them. I honestly don't think you want to hurt people, Adam, but now you're going to have to hurt and even kill. Good luck. I don't envy you."

When he had gone, Adam sat for many minutes staring straight ahead. He felt exhausted, used up. Louis's last words beat against his brain. He had made a change that should have been made five years before. A compassionless move. Against his brother. And it was, as Louis had said, only the beginning.

Wearily, he pulled himself to his feet and walked across the hall to Bill King's office. "Louis is in favor of North Hills," he said. "We'll tell Mother and sign the lease with all the covenants on the old building."

"Good for you," King said, in surprise.

"I don't feel 'good for me.' Are you working on Houston?"

"In a dark room with the blinds drawn."

Adam smiled. "For God's sake, keep them drawn. Anyway, we've got plenty to do with North Hills. I guess we can spring the architect's sketches on Mother now. As though I had had them done on spec. In a way, that's what I did do . . . Incidentally, Shaw will commentate the Gala."

Bill King nodded. He said nothing, figuring enough had probably been said.

FROM WHERE she parked her car, near the university's Arts Building, Nancy had a three-block walk to her dance class. They were quiet streets. A few frame houses were set well back from the roads, but much of the area was wooded and overgrown. Old people lived in these houses, had lived in them since before the Arts Building, a few of them since before the university. In the early evenings, as Nancy was going to class, they often sat on their porches, looking silently out into the hot nights, but by the time class was over and Nancy, in shorts and a shirt, was walking back to her car, the old people were nearly always inside, the lights were off and the streets were dark. Nancy went to dance class every Tuesday and Thursday night. She did not expect to be a professional dancer (though who could tell?) but she danced well. Her long, supple, small-breasted body could do things most of the other students couldn't do, and occasionally she danced exhibitions with Ronnie, who was a professional and who taught dancing during the summer only. For Nancy, the classes were exercises she did not do at home.

One of the good things in the mixed view she had of her father was admiration for his self-discipline. She liked the way he sat down for his breakfast at seven, read his paper until eight and was at his desk at eight twenty-five. She liked to see him leave the pool at four o'clock on a Sunday afternoon and sit in his study dictating until he had finished; and then return to his study after dinner if he had to. Her own mind, she was convinced, was too scattered, flailing out at ideas without ever grasping and hanging on to them. And yet she did not wish to reach the point she considered Adam had reached when convictions have hardened into clichés—the cliché storekeeper, the cliché merchant prince, the cliché charmer when charm was of use, the cliché liberal, the cliché husband choosing to ignore the nips of vodka Claude took, the cliché father full of reason and good advice and proper love; love without outbursts, without resentments, without hopelessness. She wanted bits and pieces of her father but not without a part of her mother's vulnerability; her understanding of the vulnerability of others. In her dance class she practiced exhibiting emotion under the strictest kind of control; but she did not wish such control to govern her life, rendering her mechanical and predictable. She could see the flesh and blood of her mother, not so easily that of her father. She wanted to be parts of each.

One night a little more than two weeks after her father had become president of the store, she left the Arts Building and began her three-block walk. Later, she remembered only that as she passed the wooded area she heard a whisper, "All right, now." Then she heard a rushing in the branches, felt a soft cloth smashed against her face; the cloth smelled sweet. She knew nothing else until much later.

When she awoke, she was lying on a double bed and her head was splitting. At first, she was conscious only that she was looking blearily straight up and that she was staring at a dirty white ceiling. It seemed to her that there was murmuring in the room, but she had hardly time to know before she tried to move her arms and then her legs and could not. With a rush, consciousness came back to her and she knew that she was tied, spread-eagled to the bed. She thought she was going to scream, but, strangely, all that came out was a long, low wail and her head began twisting back and forth, back and forth, on the bed. She saw the shadow on the ceiling before she saw the man. A great shadow, arising from somewhere and moving toward her. When she turned her head to look up at whatever the shadow represented, she thought she had lost her mind. She was looking at Donald Duck—pink skin, big yellow bill, sailor's cap. Her wailing did then become a scream, several screams, until a big flat hand whipped across her face hurting her. She now only whimpered.

"We's a long ways out in the country, sister, but that's just too noisy, heah?" This came from Donald Duck, and the voice was deep and husky. Nancy could not see all of him because of the way she was tied, but she saw that the top half of his body was massive; huge shoulders and chest and even the mask could not cover all his face. She saw that he was black and that he was dressed in black; black sweatshirt, the tops of black pants. She looked around the room, hearing giggling, muttering, unable to distinguish words. She saw Dopey and Doc, Mickey Mouse, Snow White, and bodies moving about. Five, six, eight people; she could not count. It came to her that she was looking at masks and that all the figures were in black.

"Sister's done woke up now," a voice murmured. "Pretty sister's just 'bout ready."

Another voice: "She ain't even seen the color yet. My what a pretty color, now they ain't no way you could miss our sister, even on a dark night."

Nancy looked down at her body. Now she began to cry, softly. She was totally naked; she had expected this. Also her body had been painted an orange-red, the color of fire; every inch of her body, with the brush strokes carefully circling the black pubic hair.

"Color of sin," Donald Duck said. It seemed to Nancy that she had never heard so deep a voice. Yet it was calm and somehow she became calmer herself. "See, you might never say what happened here. Probably wouldn't. The paint will say it. We got to be sure some people know what happened or it ain't no good. Color of sin."

"Who . . . who are you?" she said, trying to force her teeth not to chatter, realizing that sweat was pouring off her. The temperature of the room seemed well over one hundred degrees. Yet her teeth kept wanting to chatter, even as her own perspiration was stinging her eyes.

"Just . . . an arm," Donald Duck said, still standing over her. Now he sat down on the edge of the bed, to one side of her hips, and he folded his arms. "One time one of the brothers saw a Scotch plaid and he found out it was called Black Watch, an' there's some of us who like that name. We're all black, see, and, workin', we wears black. Me, I think that sounds like a TV series. I don't set much store by names. You gets to namin' things and sooner or later the name gets to be more important than the thing."

"Why . . . what will you do with me?"

A high-pitched giggle came from one of the masks.

"Shut up, Chigger," said another, "or I'll slap you good."

"No names," said Donald Duck, sternly. "Well, sister . . . you notice I call you sister? That's because you gonna suffer like us. Now, it may be that you *deserve* to suffer. That sure is possible. But we don' know that. We brought you here and we done painted you the color of sin and each one of us is gonna fuck you for somethin' you didn't do." Donald Duck laughed softly. And as quickly, became serious. "You ever hear of Tennessee Bower?"

Nancy shook her head.

" 'Course not. Kind of thing your pa wouldn't bring

home with him. Wouldn't be in his briefcase, the story of Tennessee wouldn't. Well, Tennessee was a housekeeper in your father's store, and she got caught fuckin' a white man, her boss, early one mornin'. An' your pa, he fired 'em both, but you see, what happened, that was mainly the white man's fault. Now Tennessee was to blame, too— nigger woman fuckin' a white boss man—and takin' money she didn't share with the rest of us. But that ain't for your pa to judge. That's for us . . . Chigger," he said, forgetting his own advice about names. "Bring in sister Tennessee." And Chigger went out the door. The door and the walls were peeling paint as though no one had been in this room for years. In a moment, the creaking door reopened and Chigger, masked as Dopey, a little man, not half the size of Donald Duck, smaller even than the girl he led in, presented Tennessee Bower.

"Take off your shirt, sister Tennessee," Donald said.

Tennessee, hollow-eyed, silent, unbuttoned her shirt and let it fall to the floor. Her handsome breasts pointed out toward Nancy.

"Now turn around, sister," Donald ordered.

Tennessee turned around and for the second time that night, Nancy screamed; and then quickly thrust a second one back into her mouth before she could be slapped again. The black girl's back was in ribbons. She had been whipped mercilessly, but some time ago. The welts were beginning to heal; but she would be scarred for life.

"Thank you, brother. You can take her back now," Donald Duck said. He regarded Nancy for some time without speaking. "Sometimes, Tennessee, she been my old lady. An' when she turned her tricks, why we shared and shared alike. Like we always do for a heist, a rolled honky with some bread . . ." His tone was derisive of his own phrase. "Tennessee forgot that part of it. Tennessee wanted to be white. Well, we pulls out the whip for that. She don' wanna be white no more." Donald Duck paused. When he spoke again, his voice was measured. "Jus' in case you be thinkin' somethin' anything at all, we'll all be gone tonight. On our way—New Orleans, New York, Memphis, who knows? Gone . . . like ghosts."

Once again he paused, and when he spoke again, the hard edge was gone from his voice and it was almost gentle. "So, why you, sister? We coulda killed your poppa, but he'd never've knowed what for. So what's the good in that? White people've killed niggers, God knows, but mostly they've . . . humiliated 'em. Humiliate . . . I was twenty-two, maybe twenty-three when I knowed what that word even meant. But I know now. An' when somethin' comes up, like what happened to Tennessee, see, that's humiliatin'. So we humiliate back. We rob and steal to live and maybe they's been a dead white man left along the way when it couldn't be helped. We don't like to kill nobody. Death, that gives dignity. To the trashiest bastard that ever lived, all he has to do is die and he gets dignity. So we aim to take that away. Now the worst thing we could do to your poppa was to do it to you. So, sister Nancy, you gets to be called 'sister.' 'Cause you is a victim of bad, bad injustice. Jus' like niggers . . . niggers."

Abruptly, Donald Duck got up. "You can scream all you want now," he said. "Before it just burst my ears. Chigger, you want to start, go ahead."

Nancy did not scream. She choked back any utterance whatever while, one after another, they thrust themselves into her. She found herself thinking of sizes, the big, the medium and the small, and at one point she had a mad wish to giggle. She was mad anyway, she thought; or perhaps she would wake up, or perhaps the dream would take some unexpected turn, or, if it were not a dream, the Canadian Mounted Police would come to the rescue. She waited for the door to open and Nelson Eddy to appear, sing an aria and disperse the villains as he did in the old movies she had seen on television.

At last they were all done, except Donald Duck. So he would after all maim her, she thought. Instead, he cut the bonds holding the upper half of her body.

"Get on your side, sister, 'cause you gonna take it in the mouth," he said, harsh now.

"No," she whispered.

"On your side, sister." And he dropped his pants and there was the erection. "You just take it in and you move the opposite of the way I move, and you use your tongue and you keep it sucked, but you try anythin' else and I cut your throat, sister. Like I say, they's been *some* dead men along the way. An' if you never done this before, why you're learnin' somethin'."

Into her mouth, it came and began to move. Instinctively, she drew back because it was big and choking her, but he had the back of her head with his hand now, and was controlling the motion. After what seemed forever, the thing in her grew larger and she knew he was coming. "In your mouth, sister, you takes it in your mouth and you swallow it." And the slime went down her throat; and the thing, depleted, was at last out of her. She sank back on the bed staring, unseeing, at the ceiling.

"Now you see, sister, that wasn't so bad, was it?"

No longer caring whether she lived or died, loathing beyond anything she had ever thought possible and nearly wretching from the slime, she said: "It was smaller than I'm used to."

His fist crashed into the side of her face and perhaps, she thought, broke something. She did not care.

"Cunt," he said. She had beaten him. They both knew it.

They blindfolded her and let her off somewhere. The blindfold was put on with yards of adhesive tape. The car had plenty of time to drive away before she could take it off. When she could see, she found that she was at her own driveway, naked and all orange-red with a sticky place of blood on one thigh. The side of her face ached. She walked slowly down the long drive to the door of Adam's house. It must be very late, she thought. She rang the bell.

When her mother answered the door, she tried to put a hand to her mouth, but her mother's high, terrible scream woke the household, and Nancy began to sob, out of control, something she continued to do, softly or loudly, depending on the sedation, for five days.

During those days, much of her thinking was disorganized and irrational, just as the images of the people coming in and out were jagged and distorted. The crazy dime-store masks would not leave her mind and at one point she was sure the doctor was wearing a Donald Duck mask and screamed at him to let her alone. But almost instantly the mask disappeared and it was only Elias Fry's familiar old face. She screamed erratically for several days, but finally she quieted. There was no night and day for her, or at least she did not seem to know which was which, but whichever it was, a figure, either her father or her mother, sat in the highbacked wooden chair by her bed. Her mother did not try to talk to her, but took her hand now and then or kissed her forehead. Her father's face was stained with tears once; she remembered that; and he smoothed her hair. After a day or so she remembered something, and she pulled up the covers to look at her body. It was white and clean. She looked at the chair and her father was in it.

"How?" she said.

"It washed off," he said.

"Who . . . who knows?" she said, terrified.

"You, mother and I and Bobby, who saw you. And the doctor. We had you upstairs before the servants could see. They think you have mild pneumonia."

"But you . . ."

Adam said, "I've gone to work every day. I had no choice, of course. I've come home at noon and a little early in the evenings. Nobody knows."

"Have I mentioned . . . Tennessee Bower?"

His lips became very tight. "Yes. Many times. She had been whipped."

Nancy turned away from him. "That was horrible. Mutilated."

"In case you care," Adam said, "I didn't fire that girl. She was gone before I even got back to the store."

Nancy shook her head. "Have I blamed you, Adam?" she said.

"Off and on," he answered.

"I'm sorry. Did I tell you about the blacks?"

"Yes."

"And what they wanted."

"Humiliate, you said."

"Yes. Humiliate."

Adam looked her straight in the face and she saw that the tears were streaming from his eyes though there were no sobs. "They're madmen, of course, lunatics, but they didn't succeed. They didn't . . . humiliate me. They couldn't *humiliate* me through you. Oh, they could break my heart, but that's not what they want. They failed. Utterly failed. They're mad and, what is worse, stupid. Do you feel humiliated?"

The memory of the response she had made at the end to Donald Duck came back to her.

"I humiliated one of them," she said.

"How do you mean?"

But the Donald Duck mask was passing before her eyes, and she always had to squeeze them shut to make it disappear. When it had gone, she was lucid again.

"Adam, you know I'm going to live through this all right," Nancy said.

He was silent.

"You're thinking it may come back to me in the middle of the night. I can handle that. At least, I think so. Anyway, what happened was *not your fault*, Adam. That is the clear thing. Whatever I've said."

For a long time he continued to be silent. When he did speak, it was very softly. "I honestly don't believe in the punishment of sins. I don't believe in hell. I don't believe in punishment here on earth. I've seen sinners live happily ever after and saints die on the cross. But there must be some reason for this. I can also not believe in blind, crazy chance. Not on a thing like this. There must be something . . ."

"Nothing. There are crazy groups now. They're everywhere, even here where we expect they're not."

"This is not California, this is Ramsey, Texas. We are in control here."

"No one is in control anywhere. Craziness is in control. Even in Ramsey. It's a warning, if it's anything. There is no such thing as control."

He nodded. "I understand that," he said. He looked at her seriously. "I feel it myself," he said. "If we were to report this to the police . . ."

"No," she said, sharply.

"Of course not. We haven't. Not going to. It's gone. But if we had, and the police had caught them, I would not have wanted them arrested. I would have wanted them machine gunned. I would have wanted to hold the gun myself. I would have machine gunned them from the legs up so they could feel the pain. So you see, I accept what you say, that the irrational is in charge. I'm no better than they are. It's five days now, Nancy, and this is still what I would do."

"No police, Adam. *I will not tell the police what happened.* Or anyone."

He said, quietly, "Not the police, honey. I promise. Remember what I've said, though."

She smiled and said nothing.

On the fifth day she got up. Her father was already at the store, but her mother was sitting by the bed as usual, and helped her into her clothes.

"I'd like to see Bobby," Nancy said. "But before I do, I want to say that you and Adam have been fine."

Claude said nothing.

Nancy laughed. "Cat got your tongue?" she asked.

Claude shook her head. "I've been wondering whether to tell you something, and I still don't know."

Nancy stopped pulling on her stockings and looked at her mother intently.

"I think you can say it. I don't think there's anything I can't hear."

"It goes away," Claude said, briskly. "Not ever for good, but it becomes just another bad memory and life is full of those . . ."

"It happened . . ." Nancy began, almost in disbelief.

"Not as any form of punishment. Just some drunken Englishmen in Paris. I was seventeen and in the wrong place at the wrong time. Now," she looked at Nancy, rather defiantly, "should I have told you or is it a bad mark against me? That it happened, I mean."

Nancy hesitated. "And you're . . . so good . . . after it," she said. "I think it helped. A lot. Thanks, Claude. I do love you."

Not a word Claude had said was true. She had simply thought it might be helpful to a girl unsure of her sanity. She also loved her daughter.

To Bobby in his room, Nancy said: "You now know something that happened to me that only my mother and father and a doctor know. It was as awful as anything that can happen except that I'm still alive. Ghastly. Terrifying. All the bad words. Now, there are things in you that you think are horrible. I'm sure of that. And that you can tell nobody. I would have told nobody about this, but I had no choice. So you know it all. My point is that whatever you ever wish to tell me, it cannot be shocking to me. It cannot be too horrible, too ghastly, too strange or too terrifying. You cannot top me. You need to talk to someone and it may not be Claude and God knows, not Adam. It can be me. You should say nothing now. Only when you are ready. All right?"

She turned and left him sitting on his bed, silently looking after her.

ADAM STARR had attended Exeter and Harvard, traveled the world and had no trace of that drawl that is the mark of so many Texans. He was nevertheless, in many essential ways, a Texan. He took chances, was decisive, energetic, even flamboyant. He believed strongly as Texans have from frontier days in the protection of his property and his kin; and in taking vengeance on anyone who would damage either. Like other Texans, he believed, without ever having quite said it to himself, that when the law would not or could not help him, then he would be the law. He had cried for Nancy during the first horrible days, but these were not only tears for her, but tears of rage. The rage lasted. He was consumed by it; and had no idea what to do about it. Until, one morning, driving to work, something occurred to him. He made a phone call. Half an hour later he was sitting in the Eatwell Cafe, a shabby diner down the street from the Prairie Club. At that hour of morning it was quiet. The booth in which Adam sat across from Abe Weinstein was isolated on both sides. Nevertheless, he spoke softly to Weinstein. When he had told the story, Weinstein's face was dead serious and did not seem so kind.

"What d'ya want to happen, Adam?" Abe asked, quietly. "You talkin' about the whole bunch?"

Adam shook his head. "Mainly the big one."

Abe nodded. "Makes it easier. Not real easy, not if they've plumb disappeared. But this Bower broad was his old lady, which is somethin' to start with." Abe's face wrinkled up in disgust. " 'Black Watch'! Chickenshit jigs. But we might need to find him through our own chickenshit jigs. Or maybe not, 'cause a'course I got the numbers business around this territory." He looked hard at Adam. "So we find him, Adam. What do we do?"

Adam said quietly and carefully: "Not kill him. That's the only 'not.' "

Abe Weinstein's eyes were ice cold as he looked at Adam. "Whatever you say. Me, I'd leave the pieces of him scattered in the street. But that's your business. Five grand all right?"

Adam nodded.

"Might take a month, a year, more . . ."

"I understand. The only thing—you've got to be sure you've got the right man."

Abe Weinstein shrugged his shoulders. "If he answers

to the name Donald Duck, why I reckon we got the right man."

They had little more to say to each other. Adam went back to the store. He felt better.

# 3

FALL CAME to Ramsey as it always did: imperceptibly. The steaming August days turned into steaming September days. The temperature continued to hover around one hundred degrees and there was little relief at night. Yet, from the middle of August, retail business began to pick up. The salespeople rubbed their eyes after the somnolence of summer and began to work again. A certain pace came into daily operation. The credit phones were busy, the cars began to line up at the garage across the street, the restaurant filled up at lunch time and there began to come about at Starr's and at all retail stores that most desirable of all conditions, traffic.

The Fashion Gala and the parties surrounding it, which attracted so many good out-of-town customers to Ramsey, were planned as carefully as the Normandy invasion, and then reviewed by Adam in detail. The award winners had been selected to provide as much interest on as many floors as possible. For the couture floor, the second, there was Charles Teal, an ageing perfectionist, whose clothes sold for up to five thousand dollars. For the Younger Set Department, Irene Von Hoffmanstahl, who called herself a princess and perhaps was, would be on hand. Her dresses did not get up to five hundred, but she was a member in good standing of the jet set and had a scandalous enough love life to be the most highly publicized designer of the day. For shoes, there was René Tanguy, and for children,

Hattie Bell. No one argued with these choices. They were the best in the world.

All proceeds would go to the Ramsey Museum of Fine Arts. Close to two hundred of the store's own suppliers would be present. They had not been invited purely out of friendship.

"How much will they spend?" Adam asked Louis.

Louis shrugged. "For courtesy buying, forty to fifty thousand. Gift wrapped, Christmas buying, maybe another twenty-five."

Adam nodded. "Well, then, I guess we're set."

The show itself was all that actually interested Claude about the four-day weekend. As a onetime model, she had never forgotten the excitement of a major opening, and she always watched the presentation eagerly. The rest of the long weekend was frightening. The job of hostess was not one she relished at any time and, as Adam Starr's wife, she was stuck with it constantly. Anyone who was prominent and visited Ramsey normally took a meal with the Starrs, or at least a drink. Celebrities are most comfortable with other celebrities, and in Ramsey the Starrs were the local celebrities. But in other years Arnold and Jenny had shared the responsibility. The enormous Sunday night lawn party at Gala time, for example, had always been at Arnold's. This year that house was in mourning. Jenny was making token appearances at the various events. Claude was the official hostess; Sunday night would be on her own lawn. She told herself that giving a party for a thousand people is far easier than giving one for eight, and while she was right, it did not comfort her.

On the surface, the long weekend went smoothly and easily. The Western party was gay and a good ice-breaker for all the visitors. The Seventh Avenue manufacturers, in their dark business suits and wearing their Jewish accents, struggled gamely with the square dancing until the people from Abilene and Amarillo, flushed with whisky, dressed in bright embroidered Western shirts and pants, took them in hand and blundered them through. Adam, dressed in an all-white costume and Stetson, and Claude, as bejeweled as any of the visitors, danced all night, pointing the way. She only needed a little vodka to get through the Western party. When it was over, the award winners, Louis, Bernie and Becky, and Peter Shaw and his wife, Amanda, were invited back to the house for a nightcap, and it was there Adam began to know Karen Woodward.

THEY HAD all known Louis was bringing a guest, and nothing more about her. He was normally closed-mouthed about his lady friends, and Karen Woodward was a name unknown to the other Starrs. He had met her at the plane by himself and brought her to the hotel, picked her up for the party and only then introduced her to his family. That afternoon she had purchased a Western outfit at the store. It was black, relieved only by simple embroidery on the shirt and by her wide white hat, which she sat back far on her head. Among the jewels and the conscious overdressing of most of the guests, she looked starkly chic. Now, at the house of Adam and Claude, she looked even more understated and elegant, as Charles Teal told her.

"My dear," he said, "when we get out of this wilderness, you must let me dress you completely. Come to the showroom, pick out what you like, we'll fit it there . . ."

"And of course you'll charge it through her account at Starr's," Louis said, smiling.

"Don't be ridiculous, my boy, designers should pay to have their clothes worn by bodies like this."

"I have some of your clothes," Karen said. "I'll start sending you bills. Who are you?" she said to the tall young man standing next to her.

"Bobby Starr," he said, solemnly.

"Adam's son. Were you at the party?"

He grinned. "Insignificantly."

"You play the piano and read a lot. Louis has talked about you. You play very well, I hear."

"He's the only one of us without a tin ear," Adam said, putting his arm around his son's shoulders. "One year I was president of the symphony and I never could understand why, if they hadn't any money, they didn't just fire some oboe players."

Karen looked at him a moment silently. "Of course you understood that," she said. "What an odd thing to say to me." She paused, then: "I hear you have a good tribal mask collection. Would you show it to me? My father owns some first-class ones."

While Adam took Karen off to the small room next to his study, Claude watched and Irene Von Hoffmanstahl spoke to Bobby. "Do you play serious music?"

"Mostly." His slender face was slightly flushed. He was not accustomed to being the object of so much attention. "I play Bach, Mozart, Scriabin . . . and Cole Porter and Rodgers and Hart."

She smiled. Claude's living room had more than its share of beautiful women on that night. "You are a show-tune buff?"

"I suppose so."

"He's as good as a professional," Bernie Starr said. "He'll go into the store, of course, but he could make a living anytime playing piano."

"*Will* you go into the store?" Irene Von Hoffmanstahl asked. "Is it written?"

Bobby smiled. "It is written. But I may or may not. I don't believe in what is written."

A blond, quite handsome man, perhaps thirty, perhaps older and cared for, appeared at her shoulder.

"Oh, this is Guy Racquette," Irene said. "He's an old friend. Does all my makeup. Happily, his cosmetics company has sent him here for the Gala. Otherwise, I would have had to bring him myself. Paid his way, for God's sake!"

Racquette, slim and tanned as a ski instructor, shook hands. "As you can see," he said, "making up Irene is a very difficult problem."

"Will you make me up while you're here?" Becky Starr said. "Now that *will* be a problem." Her voice had a slight edge to it. In this group, she felt just slightly coarse.

Guy Racquette reached out and gently touched her face. "Of course," he said in a soft, velvet voice with just the suggestion of a French accent. "What's the problem?" He looked over toward the corner of the living room, where Jenny sat talking with Tanguy, the shoe designer, and Hattie Bell, who made the exquisite children's clothes. "The Starr women do not need makeup men," he said. "To touch that face" (he indicated Jenny) "would be something like sacrilege. And Claude" (turning back) "you do everything yourself, no?"

"I was once a mannequin," she said. She was drinking, and her voice was slightly blurred from the alcohol. "Makeup people have done me. I remember once . . ." For a second she forgot what she remembered. Then it came back. "For Norell, in this country, my eyes were all smudged. Like a clown's. And my lips were scarlet red, like blood."

"Van Dongen," Racquette murmured.

"I dislike fashion which tries to bring back other eras," Irene said. "Such a bore, the twenties look, the thirties look. Fashion is now or it is nothing."

"It may be now, but it's never new," said Charles Teal, stiffly. "What you are doing with your sexy fabrics and bias cuts, my dear Irene, they did in the twenties—rather better, I'm afraid. Your girls could go off to a party at Gatsby's and look right at home." His own collection was based rather firmly on the elegance of the thirties.

"Do you feel like playing something?" Claude said to her son.

"Oh, no," he said at once, horrified.

"But you *must*," Irene said. "This gorgeous room . . . I love the extraordinary black-brown of the walls against the cold white of the gallery, Claude . . . But we must have live music. We have the paintings and the people, now we need the player."

Bobby felt someone catch his arm. Looking down, he saw his sister, smiling up at him. "Go on," Nancy said. "Be a hero."

"If you'll come and stand next to me." This almost a whisper.

"I will."

He played Chopin first, a waltz and two nocturnes, and this is what he was playing when Karen and Adam returned to the room. Karen looked at the tableau seriously: quiet, intent, people listening. The boy, with usually too pretty a face, now quite subdued in the soft light as he played; his striking sister next to him, so clearly proud. Karen caught Louis's eye and smiled. Gratefully, he smiled back. She stole a look at Adam and noticed that his eyes glistened. Good Lord, how this boy could hurt him, she thought. And probably not mean to, even know it. But after the Western group it was an enchanted moment, she was willing to admit that. And she was willing to admit that Adam's mask collection was outstanding and that his collection of paintings was his own and not something bought with the help of an adviser; and that he talked simply and originally of what he owned. So she listened when he spoke.

"Whenever he plays, everything the rest of us do seems rather unimportant," he said.

"Well, it is."

He smiled down at her. "I know. I made that point, Karen, not you. You'll make your points, but that one's mine."

She laughed. "The problem is I've thought of you as a sultan," she said. "Surrounded by untold riches, improbable gifts, the opulence of the world. I have this impulse to prick you, thinking you'll burst like a bubble."

He burst out laughing, enjoying her. "I might," he said.

Bobby switched into show tunes. He was playing "Bewitched, Bothered and Bewildered," encouraging people to talk again, not wanting too heavy a weight on him. Irene sat next to him at the piano.

"You are absolutely lovely," she said.

He nodded and smiled. Nancy drifted away. Once he had begun to play, her brother needed no support.

"Your wife is stunning," Karen said to Adam.

"Yes, she is. She was once a mannequin and I think she could wear the same clothes now as she did then. She's tender and kind and altogether too good for me."

Karen looked curiously at him. "Yes, well, I shouldn't think you'd need anyone too terribly tender and kind," she said.

"Claude needs no help," he said, sharply. "She's quite enough her own woman."

She switched direction, and laughed. "I was thinking of you and your thirty-thousand-dollar sables and ten-thousand-dollar antique boxes. So much of the world thinks all that is dead. In fact, that *you're* dead."

He thought of Donald Duck. "I try . . . we try . . . to provide some relief from the world as it is. Some light-heartedness."

But she saw she had hurt him some way and placed her hand lightly on his arm. "Are you fond of Louis?" she said.

"Yes. Is he fond of me?"

She frowned. "Oh, yes. There's no doubt of that. He thinks of you, though, as a giant. Larger than life. I should change that in him, don't you think?"

He smiled. "I gather you intend to be around for a while?"

"Would you like that?"

"Of course."

She shrugged. "Louis hasn't asked me to be around at all, yet," she said. "Though I imagine he will."

He smiled. "He may be too kind and tender for you."

She laughed, delighted. "If I should stay . . . we'll watch each other like hawks, you and I. All right?"

"All right."

"What," said Charles Teal, "are the plans for tomorrow? I'm already reeling. New York is a rest home compared to Texas."

"Lunch at the Petroleum Club at one o'clock," Louis said. "After that, we'll take you sightseeing or let you rest, whichever you like."

"Sightseeing?" Charles Teal said, in mock horror. "In *Texas!* My God, we saw cows tonight. What else is there?"

"Would you take me to the party tomorrow night?" Irene Von Hoffmanstahl said to Bobby.

He looked startled. "Hasn't somebody been assigned . . . I mean, aren't you going with somebody?"

She laughed charmingly. " 'Assigned' was correct. Yes, Guy. I requested him. But he'd much rather be free. He's a very free soul. Would you take me?"

"Of course," Bobby said, awkwardly, aware that there was no rule against taking a woman seven or eight years older to your parents' party; he rather wished there was.

"Guy? Guy?" Racquette appeared at her side. "I've asked Bobby to take me to the party tomorrow night. You don't mind, do you? Just as long as you dance with me occasionally. I've told Bobby you'd rather flirt anyway and be free, isn't that right?"

Guy looked at Bobby and patted his shoulder. "You're doing all right, my friend. And this is the lady you're doing all right with."

"We have to say good night to Mrs. Starr," Irene said.

Jenny was still going strong with Tanguy and Hattie, both of them old friends. The excitement of the evening had lifted her, and there was color in her cheeks. Now she was gracious to each of the guests who came to bid her good night and be driven back to the hotel in the limousines assigned to them. Karen stayed. Louis would drive her, dropping his mother across the way.

Only one thing untoward took place. When Claude tried to get up, after everyone had gone, she wobbled and nearly fell. Bobby caught her, then Adam. She shook her head, smiling. "My foot went to sleep," she said.

Saying nothing, they led her to the bedroom. The long night of trial for her was over.

"Do you want to go to my house?" Louis said to Karen in the car.

"Of course not. What would I wear tomorrow?" Gently, she put her hand on his arm. "You can come to the hotel. But you must leave early. I don't want you running into your award winners tomorrow morning in the lobby, looking like Tom Mix. You would be so horrified, my darling."

READING THE morning paper on that Sunday morning, Karen began to develop a strange feeling of displacement. She could not identify it for a long time, and smoked cigarettes and drank coffee trying to think of what might have brought on her mood. She got up and threw on a robe over her naked body, and looked out of her window. From here she could see part of the skyline of Ramsey, many tall, gleaming buildings with spires, some of which, Louis had told her, had been added or planned in a height competition between banks. Outside it was sunny, and she knew the heat would be murderous. Here in her room, she was almost cold. Perhaps, she thought, it is the artificiality of the air-conditioning; perhaps the fact that one so seldom feels a chill or heat from nature but only from machines.

"Business is God in this town," Louis explained to her, driving to the Petroleum Club. "There's no organized labor to speak of, the newspapers both say the same thing, and the city is so right wing, a movement to boycott the symphony for playing Shostakovitch was seriously considered a few years ago."

"If you're telling me that's conservative, I tell you it's lunatic."

He looked at her quizzically. "It almost comes to that . . ."

Finally, she said quietly, "It reminds me of some German city back in the thirties."

"You're thirty-one years old. How the hell do you know anything about German cities in the thirties?"

"Because I can read," she snapped.

"Oops, sorry. Anyway, whatever you want to say—or bitch—this city's a comfortable place to live."

She examined his profile as he drove. He was a good-looking man. His dark-eyed swarthy face took the eye, as the faces of all the Starrs did, except Bernie's. Also, he was not bleeding from her lances. She knew what he was doing. She was aware that his liberal senses would be offended by all the things he was saying, but she also knew that he must *explain* to her his home ground; that he would not accept obvious judgments from her.

"I greatly dislike too much comfort," she said, further testing. "It's corrosive. Look what it's done to you. You're as smug as a Rotary Club chairman."

He smiled. "That is idiotic," he said. "Of which you are quite aware. And you've been at least as comfortable as I have all your life."

Pleased, she said nothing more until they arrived at the Petroleum Club.

## 4

THE DAYS were better for Jenny than the nights. In the mornings, when she awakened, a short period of confusion and dislocation ensued. Not a great deal had changed in her routine. Clarissa, her personal maid, a black woman in her fifties, still appeared at seven-thirty carrying a small silver tray containing her orange juice and coffee, and she continued to smoke her cigarette with the coffee. What was missing, of course, was the sound of Arnold showering and dressing in the next room. The hissing of the water, the clearing of his throat, the flushing of the toilet. There were never sounds involving the actual use of the toilet.

"Mother," she had said to him as tactfully as she could, forty years before, "told me it was more attractive to run the tap water when I was using the bathroom. Where people could hear."

Arnold had roared with laughter. "With a few exceptions, taking a pee and a crap are the most satisfactory things we do," he had said roughly and looked as though he would say more. But he saw that she was pink with embarrassment and he only smiled. "Well, I never thought of that," he had said. And had used the tap water the rest of his life.

Jenny missed these sounds early in the morning, but only for a short while. By the time she had finished her coffee and cigarette the small feeling of loss and queerness had passed. But the evenings were a problem. During the first month after Arnold's death, she dined once with each of her children and refused their other invitations. She disliked the thought of being a burden. Bessie Goldsmith, her sister, came out twice, but Jenny had always found Bessie a bore and her widowhood could not alter that. Her old friend, Emma Goldman, buyer of better dresses, suited her better. They talked of customers and salespeople and manufacturers and designers and the whole small world which they knew in common. Such evenings were relaxing for Jenny. A few of the friends she and Arnold had, had called on her; the wives of lawyers, real estate men, bankers, insurance men and others with whom Arnold had done business over the years. But she soon realized that these relationships had depended on the men; the wives were appendages, extra baggage. For such, she had no words.

At night she read as usual; magazines, current books, but she missed being interrupted by Arnold. She missed the sound of his breathing and the smell of his cigar. She found that she put down her book at ten o'clock because she was expecting Maitland to enter the library with the light whisky and soda he had brought to Arnold at this hour. Reading had ceased when the whisky and soda arrived. During the half hour or so it had taken Arnold to sip his drink, they had talked. There had always been something to talk about. When she had accepted his infidelities as successfully as her nature allowed her, and had taken stock of what was beneficial in their marriage, high on the list (after joint ownership of the store and other worldly goods and joint parenthood) was the fact that there had never been awkward silences between them.

After Arnold's death, the silences disturbed her greatly. Sometimes, climbing the stairs to her room, they brought her close to tears. And she felt tired and weak then, as opposed to the daytime, when she was always strong and sure. She was at her best when, for the first time during the Gala weekend, she came face to face for any length of time with Karen during the luncheon at the Petroleum Club.

Like everyone else, she had known from the beginning that Karen was not a casual date. Louis did not import casual dates from New York, and Karen herself, in the way she spoke, in the set of her mouth, in the aliveness of her eyes, in the way she dressed and the way she carried herself, proclaimed herself as important; not just important to Louis; a significant person. Looking at her seated between Charlie Teal and Louis, Jenny guessed that she would eventually be forced into a relationship with this young woman; for the moment at least, she was drawn to it. As she smiled at what Teal was saying, agreed with some comment from Louis, introduced remarks of her own, she watched the woman across the table from her and admired what she saw: the soft hairstyle, balanced by the quiet smile which crinkled her eyes and the musicality of her voice as she varied the pitch of her words. Jenny liked the fact that she could speak conversational French with her two luncheon partners, Tanguy and Racquette, and better than that, she shortly forced them back into English so that the others at the table were not excluded from their talk. She liked Karen's camel-colored jersey dress, cut by Trigere on the bias so that her slim and elegant figure was recognized but not displayed. Eventually, feeling that sooner or later she would have to and curious enough to wish to move closer to this girl, she turned to Louis and said, "Why don't you bring Karen back to the house after lunch? Perhaps she's brought a bathing suit and would like a swim."

In astonishment, Louis said, "Good Lord, Mother, don't you want to rest?"

His mother smiled. "If you mean do I wish to take an afternoon nap, I do not. I loathe afternoon naps. They make me feel guilty and put a funny taste in my mouth."

"Well, maybe Karen would like to lie down."

"Of course she wouldn't. She's young and full of energy and has the kind of skin that takes the sun well." Jenny reached in her purse and extracted a Parliament. Louis fumbled for a match, but Charlie Teal was first.

"You look too biblical to smoke," he said; an elderly

homosexual with a skin stretched tight from all the face-lifts.

"I smoke five cigarettes a day. With my morning coffee, after each meal and before going to bed. I enjoy them all immensely."

Charlie Teal laughed. "And I—I smoke five cigarettes before I even tinkle in the morning. I enjoy none of them. I tried giving them up and went into such a screaming fit my whole staff threatened to resign, my business partner wanted out, which was fine except that he wanted his money back—and my lover moved to a hotel."

Jenny smiled. "How long did you last?"

"Eight lunatic days. Stopped on a Saturday, resumed on a Monday. When I walked in that Monday with a ciggy hanging from my lips, there was cheering from the multitudes. Not my fault, of course. God's. He gave me no will power."

"But think how *irresistible* he made you," Louis said, smiling.

"Well, that's true, of course."

The waiters finished serving the coffee, and a restlessness came over the luncheon group. For the time being, they had said all they had to say to one another. They had two more nights and days to be together. They needed a respite. They needed to stop smiling. Which was why Karen was surprised and a bit dismayed at Jenny's invitation.

"Did you bring a swimsuit?" Louis asked.

"Well, yes, but . . . does she really want us?"

He shrugged. "Apparently. And just us, it seems."

She considered this. "Oh, dear, it must be 'look her over' time. Well, I suppose that can't be avoided. Anyway, I don't suppose this is exactly an invitation?"

"We can't invent a previous engagement," he admitted.

"No." And then she was cheerful. "Why not? A swim would feel good."

Louis drove her downtown to pick up her suit. By four o'clock they were sitting by the cabanas next to the big pool and Maitland was pouring iced tea for them. The sun was still broiling hot, so they sat around a table under the roofing of the indoor-outdoor bar. The pool area was a kind of mini-housing complex. The bar, fully stocked and operational, was part of a lounging area which contained eight or ten white, round wrought-iron tables and accompanying chairs. A small but adequate galley faced the bar, offering the promise of hot meals served from it, and the dressing rooms and bathrooms extended to both sides.

"Do you like a sauna?" she asked now. She was wearing a short terry-cloth robe which concealed her body but not her legs. Her legs were exceptional for a woman of her age and she knew it.

"Not much," Karen said. "It's like doing a hard penance."

"Penance. Are you Catholic, then?"

"Oh, no. Nothing, really. I was christened in the Presbyterian church, but I don't go."

"We're not religious, either. Though Louis sometimes goes to temple."

"For the sound of the language," he said. "Not for my soul. The sauna's better for my soul."

"It's on," Jenny said. "I had Maitland turn it on as soon as I got back. In case."

"Really? Okay. I'll have a go. Tell Karen how worthy I am, Mother."

She smiled. "You are worthy," she said. When he had gone, there was a short silence which Karen broke.

"This must be hard for you. This festivity so soon after your husband's death."

Jenny thought for a moment. She had decided before this girl arrived that she would be surprising to her. So she said, truthfully, "I feel a certain amount of guilt that it isn't harder. When people die, guilt is often more severe than grief."

Karen was not jolted; mildly surprised. "And longer lasting," she said. "Is it progressive?"

The old woman nodded. "Yes, it's harder now than in the days after his death. No one has ever loved anyone properly. Death is God's doing. Loving is ours. And so, after a loss, we feel guilt. After a time, after it builds up enough, I suppose one is able to block it out. Arnold, of course, should feel it as much as I do. He died before he could love me enough. But then, death is the end so it was Arnold who got off easy."

"You are very certain that death is the end?"

Jenny was silent a moment. "Within my intellectual capacities it is. That's the best I can do."

"It's an odd conversation. For a Sunday afternoon in Texas. However . . . do you . . . do you not love your sons enough either?"

Jenny smiled. "What is enough?"

Karen also smiled. "That would be for you to say."

"Well, then . . . I say enough. But they might possibly say 'Not enough.' Since I don't have—don't *admit* to having a favorite . . . one could even say I don't love them at all."

Karen, deciding to be no more careful than Jenny, said, "Perhaps you don't. I can't imagine doling out love in equal cupfuls."

Jenny looked straight ahead to the green lawn and the woods behind it. She thought, had been forced to think, about what she meant. "If one of them were downtrodden," she said finally and slowly, "then he would be my favorite." She looked at Karen and smiled. "That hasn't been tested yet."

It was now Karen's turn to look away. Jenny examined her once again. I wonder, she was thinking, if Louis is secure enough for this girl. For it seemed to her that what she had been saving of love might be as true of Karen as it was of herself. And that might be the reason for Karen's silence.

"A woman," she said, "is by the laws of men weak. If loving someone becomes a madness, as I am told it can, then a woman is only weaker . . ." Jenny stopped, startled. She noticed that Karen was watching her. It was important that she correct the half-truth. "I said . . ." Her voice was much weaker, "As I am *told* it can . . . No . . . That is not quite true."

"You *know* it can." Karen said.

Jenny spoke slowly. "When I married Arnold Starr, I was weak from love. It never occurred to me that perhaps I should have been president of Starr's. And hired *him*. He had no less to learn than I did. And I understood fashion and I had—or could get—the money. But of course, I was a woman. It could not have been a serious business if I had headed it. Not in those days. I would have been the first to agree. Since also I loved him."

"You seem to have made a good team . . . as you were."

Jenny reflected. The sun, still scorching, had dropped lower in the sky and now peered under the roofing and warmed their bare feet. The door to the sauna slammed, and Louis emerged, breathless and dripping.

"God!" he said to them and plunged quickly into the

pool. The women watched him as he flipped over in the water and commenced a slow, smooth backstroke.

"Louis is an excellent swimmer," his mother said.

"So am I," said Karen. Startled, she looked at Jenny and they both laughed.

"There was a time," Jenny said, "when we had reached just the level of sales to give us solidity. In other words, Starr's was a good, small business in an excellent business community. A strong competitor could have come in then. In the middle forties or even the early fifties. And challenged us. No one did. It would have made no difference whether Arnold or I had been president. We needed a certain type of executive. With different skills from ours. Someone who would make us legend. Make us look stronger than we were. To discourage competition."

"And this, of course, was Adam."

"If I hadn't given birth to him, I should have had to hire him."

"Would you also have hired your other sons?"

The old woman was silent. "I doubt that I should answer that question, but we seem to have decided to be honest with each other. Or rather, I decided and you agreed. I would have hired a Louis, yes. Adam is very intuitive and maybe impetuous. Louis is exceedingly careful. He creates barriers for Adam and I think this is beneficial. If Bernie had not been my son, I would not have hired him, no. But I might . . . I might have adopted him."

"The store, the store," Karen said with impatience. "You're all indivisible from the store. What kind of *people* are you?"

Jenny thought for a moment. "All of us are corporation people, of course. Much of our thinking revolves around the corporation."

"Do you run it? Or does it run you?"

Jenny smiled. "We can make a place for Bernie, which shows that we run it." She paused. "What do you do with your days, Karen?"

Karen sat silently, watching Louis stroking. He must have set a goal, she thought. Ten laps? Twenty? She rather wished he would stop and splash some water at them.

"I don't know," she said finally. "The days come and suddenly they're gone. I can never make out what became of them." She looked at Jenny, challenging her. "Why do you want to know? We've barely met. Why are we having this conversation?"

Jenny was gratified. She had won.

"I have the feeling you are going to affect this family strongly," she said evenly. "Of course, it is only an idea. What do you think?"

"I have no idea," Karen said. Her tone sounded defiant to her. She corrected this; turned back to Jenny and smiled. "Maybe it will be the other way around. Or, of course, neither way . . ." She paused. "Shall we go in the water? And keep Louis company?"

"You go in, my dear. I'll watch you."

Karen nearly said something, but did not. Instead, she rose and walked to the edge of the pool. Jenny, looking at her in a sleek white swimsuit, thought she had one of the most perfect bodies she had ever seen. She watched in amusement as Karen picked up a big beach ball and bounced it off the moving Louis, causing him to disappear momentarily. When he emerged, Karen called to him. "Stop being Johnny Weissmuller and play with me." And she jumped in the air curling her legs under her, and landed as a human cannonball, in Louis's arms.

No set to her hair, therefore no "unset." She would only blow it dry, run a brush through it and go to tonight's party. With a slight glow from the afternoon sun. The blessed of the world are so often blessed in everything, Jenny thought.

The sun was beginning to creep up her own legs. She allowed it to do so. The sun mixed well with her olive skin. After all, she too was one of the blessed.

FOR THE party at Adam's, one hundred and twelve tables for ten were decorated with light-blue tablecloths, candles and Texas bluebonnets in superb Viennese decanters which served as vases. The elms and live oaks, lit softly in blues and greens, dotted the huge lawn in back of Adam's house. Two long buffet tables set off the party area on each side and eight bars were scattered around the perimeter of the dining area. In earlier years, Arnold Starr had liked enormous ice sculptures on the buffet tables, but Adam and Claude, Claude really, had decided against this touch.

"I only think," she said, "it's too much what people expect us to do. In Texas, I mean."

He nodded. No ice sculptures. Ritually, huge tents were ordered in case of rain, but traditionally it had never rained at Arnold's party and it did not rain for his son's. At seven o'clock, as they were dressing, the sunset was just finishing. The night was hot but there was a slight breeze. In an hour or so, the evening air would be comfortable. Outside, the orchestra was setting up behind the raised dance platform. It was big, twenty pieces, and would be spelled by a black Dixieland band Peter Shaw had brought up from New Orleans for the occasion.

Claude stood in front of her mirror, naked to the waist, and applied the small amount of makeup she used. Adam, unlike himself, was sipping an early scotch and soda. He sat on the closed toilet of her bathroom, watching her.

"Are you nervous?" he asked.

She shrugged, penciling her lips carefully. She finished and looked at him. Smiled. "All right?" she asked.

"Lovely. You are spectacular tonight. What are you wearing?"

"The white Galanos. I suppose Charlie Teal will be angry."

"It's your party."

"Nervous? I suppose. More . . . floaty. The long weekend. Like a continuing dream. One thing leads into the next. No periods. Hazy. You always think something will happen . . ."

"Good or bad?"

Claude looked at him seriously. "Not awful. I don't think anything really awful could happen to us, could it, Adam?"

He put down his drink on the basin and took her in his arms. Surprised, she stiffened momentarily, then put her hands against his back.

"Of course not," he said, quietly. "Nothing awful is ever going to happen to us. Ever."

After a moment she said, "Shall we have our drinks outdoors? I should be checking."

"Fine."

At these times, when she was arranging things or rearranging, giving instructions, turning an acute eye to the flowers, the china, crystal, silver and so on, Claude was confident. She was by nature skillful at the physical arrangements for a party; the machinery of hostessing was familiar to her. Her sureness ebbed only when not a single flower could be changed. Adam watched her with admiration.

"You're still putting Mother in the receiving line?" he asked.

"At the head of it. She can put more names with more faces than any of us."

He nodded. In a moment he sat down at one of the tables and indicated the chair next to him, which she did not take.

"I'm going to walk the party." She left him at the table, and he took a short sip of the scotch he had brought with him. Somehow, as he watched her floating through the crepuscular setting in her long white chiffon dress, he felt sad. She seemed very gallant to him. She was doing what she did best and yet he was aware that she did not look forward to the evening but hated the thought of it. And he knew also that there was much else in life that she dreaded: nothing more than the long days when he was at the store and she was coping with nothing more arresting than the evening menu or an afternoon swim. This kind of sadness came to him often; in a glance at Bobby, after a word with Nancy, or watching his wife, as he did now. He felt a failure with his family. He felt that he had not managed to bring ease, spontaneity, cheer to them; at least not in relationship to himself. He noted the affection between the three of them and longed to share in it. But he could not because he was not an equal citizen of this household, he was the chief executive of it. Not for him were the quick touches, the surprising laughs, the gentle tones. Everything, with him, was correct; intelligence was at work; no one was silly, foolishly gay; and love was proper. He lacked the gift of foolishness. He would be poor at it, and Adam did not do things he did poorly. He supposed Claude and the children were not unhappy. He worried about Bobby's shyness, his lack of assertiveness and felt sometimes that Nancy was not simply responding to him, but judging him. He worried often that Claude needed a touch too much vodka to get through evenings, but the condition was not disastrous and it was incomprehensible to him that it might become so. He felt that he was admired by his household; he would have given much if he could have brought them joy. In his heart, if he was naming it correctly, was all the love his wife and children could wish. He would have to assume they knew this since, by nature of their relationship, it could not be discussed.

"My God," he thought, "sentimental on half a scotch."

He got up and drew a long breath. Still warm, but cooling. He looked at his watch. Quarter before eight. When he looked up again, Louis and Karen were approaching, and he saw them and before thinking, he burst out laughing.

"What have we done?" Karen said, smiling.

"Is my fly unbuttoned?"

Adam indicated Karen. "You're wearing Claude's dress," he said.

"Oh, my God!"

Louis snapped his fingers. "Damn it! I forgot she had that dress. She never wears it."

"She did tonight," Adam said.

"Oh, well," Louis said. "All she has to do is run upstairs and change."

But this is not what Claude did at first. Instead, she took it rather badly. Her eyes filled for a moment, she looked as though she might cry.

"I have no intention of changing," she said.

"Why not?" Louis said. "Karen would have to go all the way back to the hotel."

"We'll both wear the dress. I didn't choose it casually and I'm sure Karen didn't. We'll simply be sisters for tonight."

Louis looked at Adam. "That isn't a good idea," he said uneasily. "Customers complain when they see themselves at parties in expensive dresses. Two Starr ladies in the same dress would give them a lot of ammunition. I'm afraid it's bad business."

Karen looked at Claude oddly for a moment, and it was Claude who looked down. "Drive me back to the hotel," Karen said to Louis. "I'll wear my ball dress here and this one to the ball."

There was a silence. Claude took a deep breath. "That is stupid," she said, finally. "If people should arrive . . . Here's Mother now. Please receive with Adam, Karen. I'll be down in a few minutes."

But when she did come down, in a slim, black Dior, she did not look quite so spectacular. For the soft blue light, the white had been the clear choice. And once again, Adam, though irritated by her quick bad temper, saw gallantry in her. Clothes are, after all, the way we present ourselves to the world. And now Claude, on the biggest night of her official life, was at her second best and knew it.

Not fair. Unlucky accident. Not good on Louis's part. He was supposed to know who owned the important dresses and where they might be likely to be worn. Starr's tried hard not to sell two women the same expensive dress for the same occasion. Difficult to believe that Louis would not remember his sister-in-law owned and might be likely to wear the dress his date was wearing when he picked her up at the hotel. A phone call would have turned the incident into something amusing, easily rectified. Adam mentioned this to his brother later in the evening.

"Did you really forget that Claude owned that Galanos? And very likely would wear it?"

Louis looked surprised. "Of course I forgot it. Why else . . . ?"

"You shouldn't have," Adam said, shortly. "That's a three-thousand-dollar dress. And as such memorable."

"I said I was sorry . . ."

"Well, you didn't, but I assume you are." He turned away.

At Adam's table, Irene Von Hoffmanstahl put her hand on Bobby's arm.

"Your son," she said to Claude, "is the most divine dancer."

Claude smiled. "I know," she said, "I taught him. Did he do his Fred Astaire routine?"

"Claude," Bobby protested, redfaced.

"No," Irene said. "What's that?"

"A combination of the Castle Walk which nobody but Bobby has danced since 1925 and a whole group of steps I think he invented. At least, I didn't teach him those. I can hardly follow them."

Irene, her eyes bright, her breasts nearly exposed under the light, gauzy top she wore over them, kissed Bobby on the cheek. "Dance for me, my love," she said. "Take your mother and show me."

"God, no," Bobby said, in sudden fright.

"Please," Irene said. A young, shy boy made her slightly giddy. The makeup man, Guy Racquette, in a flowing tie, a ruffled shirt and a velvet dinner suit, pursed his lips disapprovingly at Irene, but she tossed her head and persisted until finally, laughing, Claude got up to dance with her son.

At first, they had too little room. But then, as the other dancers perceived what they were doing, they moved to one side, stopped and watched. Eventually, Claude and Bobby were the only ones dancing. And what a dance it was. All kinds of footwork, double and triple time, lifts and twirls, jazz and burlesque, classic, full of humor and grace, and with extraordinary anticipation, one for the other.

"This is fantastic," Karen said to Louis.

"He's a superb dancer. And anything else that has to do with music."

"Well, so is Claude." Karen paused. "It's practically indecent how good they are together. Mother and son."

"They're very close."

Karen watched with pleasure. When it was over—they did no finale, just stopped, perspiring and breathless—she applauded with everyone else and called out, Bravo. Irene rose and hugged them both. Adam, who had seen it before of course, laughed and was proud. His mother, sitting next to him with a half smile on her face, said, "If there were money in sweetness, Bobby would be very high-salaried." Claude and Bobby had a triumph.

LATER, LOUIS said, walking toward the table after a dance, "Would you like to marry me?"

"Would I *like* to?" Karen said, musing. "There was a day when the question would have been put another way. You would be on your knees begging, imploring . . ." She was only half joking.

"Would you like that?" he asked. He was very serious, not smiling.

"Well . . . better than 'may I borrow a banana?' which is how you sounded."

"I'm sorry."

"And Adam never seems to touch Claude in public," she said, musing. "And your mother didn't weep when her husband died."

He smiled ruefully. "You make us sound like such cold fish. We're really not, you know."

She laughed. "Scratch and blood will come, I suppose. You're all rather touching, really. Such effort it must take. Always to be in control."

They had stopped walking now and were standing underneath one of the elms. "I would like a cigarette now," Karen said. He fished in his pocket and gave her a Marlboro, then lit it and one for himself with a gold lighter. Laughter and music filled the air. The black Dixieland band was holding forth playing "At the Jazz Band Ball," and many couples were doing the Charleston. White-jacketed black waiters hustled from the tables to the bars and back. Dinner was over and now the party settled into drinking, dancing and flirting.

"The question, the way you phrased it, leaves in doubt whether you want to marry *me*," Karen said.

"I do. Very much."

"You oughtn't to be too sure of that. I'm not an easy person. Not on myself, but particularly not on others. My father adores me, but he finds me very difficult. Tells me so all the time. Because he tries to handle me, to put me in a category titled 'Only Daughter.' I think you would also put me in a category. 'Starr Wife.' Number two ranking. After Claude. Before Becky."

She was not smiling, not even looking at him. She looked at the sky, examining the Little Dipper without noticing it. With her black hair and in the white dress whose flowing skirt sometimes moved with the soft breeze, she looked like an old-fashioned cosmetics advertisement. "I don't think," she said, looking at him now, "you've thought how difficult it would be for me to be Number Two anything."

"Not much I can do about that," he said, coldly.

"You shouldn't try," she agreed. "That would be my problem, not yours." She paused and laughed. "This is your way of telling me you're in love with me? That's never been mentioned, you know."

"It's my way. Yes . . ." He stopped and stamped out his cigarette on the lawn. "I did think you knew that, though. I've thought you've known that since we met."

"Well, I did," she said, kindly. "And you have tried to say so a few times in bed . . ."

"You wouldn't let me," he jumped, looking up.

"I know." Again, kindly. There was a long silence.

"Those accents," she said.

"What?"

"I might hate Texas, you know. I've no idea . . . I tell

you . . . It's a long weekend. Tuesday is a luncheon show, right?"

"Yes."

"And I was going back that afternoon. Why don't I stay over? We can have dinner alone Tuesday night. And see what we think."

"I know what I think."

"Do you? Well, I don't."

NANCY KNEW she'd lost Ronnie when he met Guy Racquette. The elegant dancer and the elegant makeup man did not attempt to disguise the attraction between them. They flirted lightly but with a serious edge, and Nancy, theoretically not minding it—she had no romantic interest in Ronnie—nevertheless felt shut out and minded that a bit. She sat alone for a while, looking out at the Texas women and thinking of the emptiness of their lives and how much she would hate to grow into one of them; yet very well might: the drawling, giggling women with too little in their lives of value or even of interest.

"Fools," she said aloud, "You all need to be raped."

"What's that?" Bobby said, suddenly at her side.

"The women. The sheep."

"Never mind them. Remember who you are. Nancy . . . Marvelous Nancy . . . Come and dance with me."

"All right. The exercise might exorcise me."

"My, my," he said, laughing. In spite of himself. She also laughed. "What a silly line," she said. "Whirl me away, dear, darling Bobby." So he did. But he could not whirl away the bitterness within her. And glancing down at her now and then, he understood that he couldn't and wondered who on earth could and when.

ON THE dance floor, Adam asked Karen, lightly, "Have you come to any conclusions?"

"About what?"

"About us. You've been in Texas two days now. Many journalists have written learned articles about Texas on the basis of a two-day visit. Learned and inaccurate."

"With all the clichés."

"All of them. Mainly focused on money. Every Texan is an oil man and drives a Cadillac. Nonsense, of course."

"Certainly," she said. "You drive a Rolls-Royce." She laughed. "Forgive me. I do see what you mean." She was silent for a time. They were not really dancing. There was not room for it. They simply rocked back and forth and swayed from side to side, trying not to bounce off too many people. At last, she said, "How close are you and Louis?"

Surprised, he was honest. "As close as two brothers in the same business can be. At least I think so. We have disagreements, but if you mean do we love each other, sure."

She made up her mind. "Louis has asked me to marry him."

"I'm not surprised. If I were Louis, I would have, too. You're rather exceptional, as I'm sure I don't have to tell you."

"Do you think I should?"

He looked puzzled. "Isn't that up to you?" he said. "How do you feel about him?"

"I'd like to know what you think." She smiled. "I must be getting into the Starr syndrome. 'What does Adam think?' "

"Well, how *do* you feel about him?"

"Enormously fond. And drawn to him."

He smiled. He wondered if the feeling he had was relief. How would he have reacted if she had told him she was madly in love with Louis? Having Karen in his arms, watching her move, listening to her talk made him feel very strange. He was not a man whose eye wandered. In all the years of being married to Claude he had not had a single extramarital adventure. He had looked with interest upon hundreds of women and pursued none of them; nor had he any regrets. The prospect of one-night stands or illicit weekends did not appeal to him. He was not a drinker so he did not get himself into positions he had not meant to. To be faithful had cost him very little.

Karen made him uneasy. Nor was it just her looks. He felt challenged by her. Her smile was not casual but teasing; at least to him. In her eyes, sometimes even in the tone of voice, she seemed to say, "Be careful, Adam. I'm your match." And for him, this was something new in a woman.

"That doesn't sound too promising," was all he said.

She shrugged. "Why not? I'm not a schoolgirl, you know. I'm not likely to pine away and wither for love like a Southern magnolia flower. Fondness and physical attraction make a very good basis for marriage. I should also respect him, however. Should I respect Louis?"

Adam hesitated. The words physical attraction had bothered him, and this annoyed him. "Of course you should," he said, shortly. "Louis is kind, thoughtful, gifted in his fields and intelligent. Now if that's enough then you will respect him. But it may not be enough for you."

"Exactly what do you mean?"

"That he is not President of the United States, nor likely to be. That he is not sole owner of Starr's, not even chief executive, by accident of being born two years after I was born."

"That he is not God—as you are God."

"That's not what I said or meant."

"It's what you meant. Or at least what people think about you. I don't blame you, however. One does begin to believe what other people believe. However . . ."

"However, what?"

"I have no intention of marrying an attendant at the Sacred Temple of Starr's," she said sharply. "An acolyte. Any more than I would be an acolyte to Louis."

Just as sharply and with some anger, he said, "Louis can do as he likes with his life. Nothing outside the store itself is beyond him. He can be president of every civic organization in the city . . ."

"After you've turned it down."

"Not necessarily." He twirled her rather angrily.

"How would you like it if Louis were to become a bigger man in the city, forgetting the store, than you are?"

"Fine. I'd be proud of him. Delighted. You're confusing the fact that I have to make final decisions at the store—some of which are against Louis's thinking—with what you seem to think is a monumental ego trip for me."

"I think your ego is burstingly healthy, yes."

"Isn't this all a little unfair? You've known me two days."

"Through Louis, I've known you for months. Through *Women's Wear Daily* for years. I have yet to see Louis quoted in that newspaper, though it is Louis who actually runs the fashion business and buys the collections, not you."

"They always like to go to the head man."

"Then until a month ago, they should have gone to your father, not you. No, I think your public relations girl has done a remarkable job for the store, but I think she may confuse the store with Adam Starr. Is she in love with you?"

"Don't be silly."

He felt stung and angry, and this too bothered him, for he was seldom stung. Anger usually came to Adam because of other people's slowness or their mistakes; not from criticism of himself.

"You started this," he said, coolly, "by asking whether or not I thought you should marry my brother. We have now degenerated to a discussion of my ego and our public relations operation. What the hell has that got to do with whether you should marry Louis? If it would please you better if Louis ran the store, forget it. He doesn't and won't."

"It would please me better, yes." She smiled enchantingly. "If he did, I wouldn't hesitate to marry Louis. If I do anyway, I will certainly push him to become absolutely everything he has in him to become—including recognized. That's why your ego has a lot to do with all this."

He laughed. "I'll do everything I can to help you. Except resign."

She also laughed. "We'll see." She paused. "Do you actually dance?" she said. "Or just sway?"

Now he laughed merrily. "Fair enough. All right, let's see how we do."

He did then actually dance with her, their bodies pressed close together, and he was a good dancer, though not in a class with his son, and they were very much aware of each other. Toward the end of this dance she had decided that she would indeed marry this man's brother, and she knew that she would be marrying not just Louis Starr, but also a brother to Adam. And she understood too that she would be close to Adam, but whether as friend or enemy, she did not know.

AT ONE o'clock the band packed up, and the last third of the guests began to take their leave. Jenny, who had decided to stay to the end, joined Adam and Claude in saying good night. She seemed buoyant; not tired at all. His mother was quite remarkable, Adam thought. She might well live to be one hundred.

From the bandstand came the sound of the solo piano. Once again Irene Von Hoffmanstahl had Bobby at work, and they were all singing. The song was "Always," and Bernie and Charlie Teal, arms around each other's shoulders, were singing harmony, audibly if not musically. Both of them were a little tight, and Claude, with the nervousness behind her, took a large vodka from the bar.

"Shall we all sing?" she said gaily.

And so they did, the award winners, their guests and the Starr family, gathered around the piano. They sang old songs well into the night, and the sound wafted over the blue lawn seemingly carried by the smoke from their cigarettes on up toward the sky until at last the melody and the smoke disappeared into the stars.

AT FOUR-THIRTY that morning, Irene Von Hoffmanstahl held Bobby in her arms and tried to comfort him. "It doesn't matter," she said, "it happens to every man once in a while. Ssh . . . my baby. Go home and sleep, and tomorrow it will be all gone. I just surprised you, that's all. What is an older woman doing fooling around with a young boy anyway? I have no shame. In the end, it is my fault. Go home, Bobby, it's late."

He dressed silently, leaving her naked on the bed in the hotel suite. He could not bear to look at her naked body, a slightly older body than he had expected. He managed to say good night, and he meant to say that he was sorry, but these words would not come out without the threat of tears. He walked quickly to the elevator, and then to his small Triumph parked in front of the hotel and drove home very fast.

In the suite, Irene dialed Guy who was just down the hallway. It was several rings before his voice answered.

"Hello, darling, it's Irene," she said.

"Of course it's Irene," he said, groaning. "Nobody else would have the ghastly manners to call at this hour. How was 'graduation day'?"

"Well, that's what I called you about. I have a feeling Bobby may be more your cup of tea than mine."

"I could have told you that."

"Did you really know?"

"Guessed. If you're thinking of sending him down the hall, forget it. I have company."

"I was sure of that," she said, rather acidly. "I'm just mentioning it for your future files."

"Thanks, Mommy. And for God's sake go to sleep. You'll look sixty-eight tomorrow. You know how the silicone slides when you get overtired. Like bubble gum . . ."

But she had hung up.

# 5

BOBBY HAD lived alone for his first two years at Exeter, but in his third year Max Larousse was placed with him and his life changed. Max was short and stocky and good at sports. He even played guard for the junior varsity football team. But he also read a great deal and wrote well. He became a contributor to the *Exeter Review*, the school literary magazine. His short stories were rather vague and surrealist and his readers did not know whether they understood them or not, but the language was effective. On the other hand, he was very bad at the mathematics at which Bobby was good, so Bobby tutored him; and he loved to listen to music but knew little about it, so Bobby explained it to him. And he read Bobby's music reviews for the *Exonian* with admiration. Midway through the fall term, when Bobby, assuming that Max was asleep, was beginning to masturbate, Max rose quietly from his bed, slipped in beside Bobby, and said, "Don't do it alone. There's much more to it than that."

And they became lovers. It was Bobby's first sexual experience with another human being and at first he was consumed with guilt. But Max said, "It's nothing to worry about. It's a stage. A time of life. One of these days we'll both meet a girl, we'll go to bed with her and the stage will be over. It's in Kinsey."

Little by little, the guilt disappeared. They were suspected by no one. They were immensely happy.

"What would your father do if he knew about us?" Max asked once.

Bobby was thoughtful. "I think he'd kill me," he said, soberly. "Or maybe just you."

Max laughed. "Let's not tell him."

Obviously Bobby, through invitational dances, through family friendships and the normal course of growing up, had dates with girls. He and his date were nearly always in groups, but, when he got his Triumph, he did take the girls home, and learned that they expected that he would make a pass at them. So he did. He learned how to kiss them and fondle their breasts, even feeling excitement in his loins as he did so. This encouraged him. Max was right. It was only a stage. Eventually he would go all the way with one of these girls and the experimental days would be over. Only one nagging worry persisted: once in a while, he was certain, a girl wanted him to go all the way, and at these times, he pulled back. The excitement in his loins died, and he acceded to the girl's half-hearted protests that they had gone far enough. But that, too, he was sure would pass.

In fact, it was Max who changed. They had planned to go to Harvard together and had applied to room together. But at the beginning of this very summer, six weeks or so before his grandfather died, Bobby received the following letter from Max:

"Dear Bobby,

"This is to tell you that I have transferred from Harvard to Amherst for the coming year. After the largeness of Exeter, I think I would like to go on to a smaller school and have that new experience. I visited Amherst and it is a beautiful place with a superb faculty and a silly football team that I may even be able to make. It seems to me a good idea.

"There is another reason. I have met a girl, and as I said would happen someday, those other days are over now. She is not the only girl in the world, not the final girl, but she has ended the time of life you and I passed through together. When I remember the good things we have had, a good deal of sadness is in me, but I must confess there is much more joy. We are really not meant to be in life as you and I have been. What is happening now is the right way and it is what I want. And so, in time, will you if you don't already. I have the feeling it may have happened to you, too, this summer. I hope so.

"Good luck, my dear friend, and if you are sad, it will be only for a little while.

"Max."

But Bobby had been addled the whole summer. Furious at first, he relapsed into a melancholy that his family remarked on from time to time. He had never answered the letter. Oh, he had written all right; letters of fury, beseeching letters, sadly philosophical letters, falsely cheerful letters and lying letters. He wrote one that was all about a girl with whom he was spending the summer and went into the most minute detail about their erotic times together. He tore everything up. He had no dates, he read, played his piano, conversed properly with his family and hid as best he could the hurt in his heart. And then Irene Von Hoffmanstahl had come along and forced his hand.

He had had no doubts as to what might be coming when they had left the party together to go back to her hotel. He had known quite well that she would ask him up, and that in some way, she would make it clear she wished to go to bed with him. In the exhilaration of his success at the party, he had felt a certain confidence, and even looked forward to success. So this would be it, he had felt. This would be the end of "that time of life," and with a famous princess at that. It would be the ultimate destruction of Max and of the Maxes to come.

It had been a disaster. She had excused herself and returned in a negligee, nearly completely sheer. She had opened a bottle of champagne and they had sipped from it until at last she had drawn his head down and he had kissed her long and deeply. There had been no escape. Soon they were in bed without clothes and he was doing all the things he knew he should be doing, and she was crooning to him, and he was touching her and using his fingers and then she was moaning. And he grew large, but the fears were flooding him, paralyzing him, and he tried to enter her quickly before it was too late. But it was already too late. The excitement ebbed and he had no chance. She had done everything; stroked him, kissed his ears, finally taken him in her mouth as Max had done so many times. And in desperation he had thought of Max, tried to imagine it was Max, even thought he was feeling stirrings; but just as he did, she raised her head and smiled at him.

"My lovely boy, it just isn't your night," she had said. "Here, put your head in my arms and rest a while and maybe later . . ."

But he had not been able to stand that. He had stammered apologies, said he had drunk too much, babbled. The only important thing to him in the world had been to get away, and finally he had.

Now, driving fast through the night, he was consumed with horror. It seemed to him that his life must be over. Surely there was no disgrace, no humiliation so great as this. Through clenched teeth, he actually grunted in the car as the fierceness of his failure came, abated, came again in terrible waves. Of course he could not face the woman again; he did not think he could face anyone. And the specter of his father was before him; that strong, strapping man who could never in his life have had such an experience. And he hated his father, whom he tried to please, to whom he tried so hard to be the son he wanted; hated his father for wanting this kind of son, hated him for being who and what he was. And he hated Max for deserting him and leaving him to a silly nymphomaniac designer who called herself a princess. But more than anyone, he hated himself. For in his heart he was convinced that a man could not be a man until he was having straightforward, normal sexual relationships with women. In fact, he believed that men should probably be having as many of these as possible. Monogamy was suspect in his mind. Men were supposed to have many affairs, during which they learned to be expert lovers, sought after by the most desirable women in the world. His father, he was certain, was such a man.

But when he was in his bed, in the small, dark-brown room which was his refuge, the anger left him. Humiliation remained. There was no question of sleep. In his life he had not known the total inability to make his body do what he wished it to do; which is to say that he could not run a hundred yards in record-breaking time, but he could run a hundred yards. He had not known a moment of total despair which is the moment of impotence in a man's life. This kind of helplessness had not visited him. He did not see that a quixotic impotence can be and often is a matter for some humor; in the life of a man unexpectedly too drunk or just as unexpectedly overcome by nerves or guilt. But this would not have helped him anyway, for such humor can come only after the fact; and then only after successful efforts have succeeded it. It was for him the cruelest blow he had known. It was too early in his life to know whether the impotence and his schoolboy homosexuality were related, but he could not perceive this at all. That he might prove quite adequate at some later date, under different circumstances, seemed to him out of the question. He would never be adequate. He was homosexual or he was nothing. He could see no difference. Either was death. He was not quite eighteen.

He put on pajamas, left his bedside light on and turned on his small portable radio. Sometimes, late at night, good music could be heard in Ramsey when station officials assumed their audiences were asleep. And he did find a station playing "Tales from the Vienna Woods." He had always enjoyed the waltzes of Strauss and he left the music on. Lying back on his pillow, he imagined himself at the ball, dressed in full cavalry uniform, dancing with a bewigged girl of twenty in a hoop-skirted dress cut low across the bosom. As the dance went on, the floor was cleared for them, as it had been earlier for his mother and himself. But at last, the dance was over and they were in a glorious hotel suite with lush Louis XIV furnishings, and the beautiful young girl, smiling at him, was removing her dress. But it was Irene after all, and the fears exploded in him once again, and his legs and arms became unbearably tense as the tide within him receded. And, certain that his life was over, he began to cry.

CLAUDE COULD not sleep. She tossed restlessly and looked at her husband with irritation as he lay on his back, head turned to one side, breathing deeply and silently. She often envied Adam's sleep. No matter how difficult his day, he was usually able to fall off within minutes of turning off the light. Often, after one of the endless arguments with his father, he would sit in the big armchair at the end of the room and tell her bitterly of what had occurred. At these times the anger and frustration within him poured forth and he might sit for an hour letting it loose for only her to hear. But then, purged, he would climb into bed and, sometimes after making love to her (for rage often made him want her), he would close his eyes and soon was gone. Nor did he seem to dream as she did. A day was a day for Adam; not part of some continuing process that led drearily into nights full of chilling dreams. For him, that continuing process was divided into segments; and he awoke fresh each morning to deal with the next segment. For her, the nights were often difficult and even frightening. When she had been drinking, she slept restlessly until the liquor wore off and then woke with a jolt and no hope of going back to sleep. On these occasions she rose, turned on the bathroom light and sat in the armchair, smoking cigarettes. Most of the time she took a sleeping pill and smoked and thought until the pill promised to take effect. Her thoughts were sad at these strange hours; lonely thoughts. Sometimes they grew sad enough so that she went downstairs and made herself still another drink, and drank this in the silence of the vast living room, with only her cigarettes, the vodka and one lamp to keep her company. But she did this seldom, for the next morning her face would be drawn and gray and she knew, above all things, that she must keep her looks. Her face and figure, she was sure, were all that kept what she had together. She discounted kindness; the world was full of kind people, barren of beauties. That the beauty appealed to Adam was shown by the fact that he made love to her often enough, perhaps more than was usual after so many years of marriage. More than that, she was convinced it was all she had of which he could be genuinely proud. At times, in the eeriness of the night, it did occur to her to wonder where she would be if Adam left her. Wealthy enough; the settlement would be generous and no great strain on him; more than enough so that she and the children could live comfortably somewhere, anywhere, perhaps even back in Paris. For the children certainly would be with her; not only because of law and custom but because of their own preference. Her children, she knew, did not consider her the intellectual equal of her husband, who was perhaps not really an intellectual, but was brilliant. But they did love her. How much this love was tempered with sympathy, even pity, she was not prepared to guess. It did not matter. They loved her. That was certain. In any case the proposition was absurd. Adam was not going to leave her. She thought it likely that someday he might have an affair with someone, if indeed, he had not already (although this she somehow doubted). He was lusty enough and sooner or later there would be a younger woman he would set up somewhere and visit occasionally. But he would be discreet, if this should happen, and if she should guess it, it would not destroy her; only a casual affair. Strict fidelity did not seem to her as God's command, yet she felt it less likely that she might be unfaithful to him. She did not travel as he did and Ramsey was a very close community. An affair of Claude Starr's in Ramsey, Texas, would be no secret for long. Adam might find someone young and delicious in New York or Paris or California or Florence, where he often went without her, but she went almost nowhere by herself and probably never would. But insofar as his marriage and family were concerned, he was, she felt, as committed as he was to the store. They were all a part of his flesh and spirit; they were inseparable from him. And so they would go on, and the only complaint she had, really, was that he was Adam Starr, which he could not help, and that by this fact she had been placed on a stage where she was uncomfortable and not herself.

On this night she was not sure what was keeping her awake. Her party had been a success, she had drunk very little, and all that bothered her was the matter of the dress. She had acted badly; all right in the end, but badly at first. She knew this was because it had been Karen wearing the same dress. If Susie Snow or Ellie May Harwood had shown up wearing her Galanos, she would have laughed and gone up to change. She was not at all sure what it was that bothered her about Karen. Perhaps it was a simple feeling of competition. If Karen married Louis, there would be a second Starr wife at least as beautiful as she and considerably cleverer. She had no doubt but that Karen was clever. Watching her in conversation with Adam, dancing with him, left no doubt of that. She handled him easily. Adam Starr meant nothing to her. He was a man, that was all, and Karen obviously knew how to handle men. Adam was easy for Karen; and after all these years, difficult for herself.

She sighed and decided to get up. Perhaps she would make a small drink tonight. She threw on her robe, turned on the bathroom light, quietly opened their bedroom door and went out into the house. All was in darkness. She switched on the lamp at the top of the stairs and quietly descended them. In the half-light the furniture seemed ghostly and menacing, but the paintings stood out like the wild kind of dreaming one does with one's eyes shut and not quite asleep. There were places and faces and strange designs and myriad colors and they all seemed to be grinning at her. They frightened her. She was used to the paintings lit; not so, they seemed alive. She went to the pantry, and made herself a drink. Then she went back to the living room and switched on a lamp by the sofa. She sat down and sipped the vodka. It went down her throat hot and then was warm in her stomach. She felt better. The paintings were just paintings after all. How stupid about the dress. Even more stupid to worry about it. It was all over and no harm done. Tonight at the ball, she would say something to Karen. Or perhaps not. It wasn't important enough. The hell with it.

She sat for some time before she realized she heard the faintest sound of music coming from somewhere in the house. She wondered whether any of the servants were still up. But the music was not coming from the servants' quarters. She realized it was coming either from Bobby's room or Nancy's. These were at the opposite end of the house from her own and Adam's room and were separated by a guest room and two baths. Since there was no overnight guest, one of her children was still up. Curious, she rose and walked toward the wing where they slept. The hall was dark, but light came from under Bobby's door and the music was clearer now. Strauss waltzes; she did not know which one. Well then, he was still up. She wondered about his ride home with the Princess and smiled.

"Barracuda," she said to herself.

Well, it was no business of hers, and she turned to go back to the living room. Some sound against the music caught her ear and she stopped. She crept close to the door and listened carefully. She could not really tell, but she thought she was hearing sobs. She strained to hear better, but could not. No one in this Starr house ever walked into a bedroom unannounced. She knocked gently at the door. There was a rustling and the sound of sobs seemed to stop; but then suddenly started again.

"It's Claude, darling," she said. "Are you all right?"

She heard his voice struggle to say yes, but the sound

was muffled and the crying continued. This, too, was his business. Whatever was going on with him was his affair. And yet she could not leave. She stood still for a minute or so and the crying continued; so she made a decision and opened the door and walked into her son's room.

She found Bobby's long body stretched out on his bed. He was lying on his back and one arm was across his mouth and nose as though he were trying to smother himself to quiet his sobbing. His eyes were wide open and had been staring at the ceiling. Now they shifted to meet hers. This was the first time she had seen Bobby cry since he had been perhaps seven years old. The sight of it brought a quick fear to her which quickly passed. She spoke calmly: "My poor Bobby," she said. "What did she do to you?"

He shook his head, still unable to get words out. His shoulders were trembling. He had taken his coat and tie off, but was still in his shirt and evening trousers. Next to him, the tiny little portable radio played on and only his bedside lamp was lit. She walked over to his bed and sat on the edge of it. She removed his arm from his face and took his head in her arms and lap and stroked the wet side of his face with one hand.

"Cry then, my love, cry," she said. "Tell me what you want. Or nothing."

He did cry for some time. There was no control in him and he could not have spoken if he had wished to. She did not move and said nothing more, but continued to stroke his face.

At last, he began to quiet. She kissed his forehead and his cheek, and allowed him to roll over so that he was on his stomach, his face away from her. And she simply sat and waited.

Soon enough, he told her what had happened; told her jerkingly, his voice breaking often, sometimes caught up in yet another sob. When he had finished, she was silent for a moment, then said, "There is probably no man in the world that hasn't happened to. Most often, I should think, it happens on the first time. Through a lifetime, it happens often."

"Does it," he said with great bitterness, "happen to Adam?"

She knew instinctively that she could not lie in answer to his question.

"Adam doesn't start things he is not going to finish," she said. "So quite often, he doesn't start things. Sometimes . . ." She paused. "Sometimes when he's aware that I would like him to. It is the same thing."

"No," he said.

"It's a minor, silly thing. You'll laugh about it some day. How you failed with a visiting princess who sells dresses and chases teenage boys."

"It's not . . ." He faltered. "The point . . ."

"Someday, at the most unexpected moment, probably with some girl who has not made it so clear what she wants . . . it will happen. Perfectly natural.

"You don't understand," he said.

"Of course I do. You think it has never happened to me? When I was younger. You surely don't think your father was the first man I ever knew. God knows *he* doesn't. I loved a young man very much once," she lied, "and that was how it started." It startled her to think that she had lied to both her children on matters involving sex, about which she was supposed to tell children the absolute truth, or so she had been told.

He said nothing for a while. When he did, it was this: "What is the most terrible thing I could tell you?"

She said without hesitation, "That you were dying."

"The next most."

"There is no next most. That is the only thing."

"What if I told you . . ." But then he could not go on, and was crying again. This time she simply stroked the back of his head, his black hair and waited. But when he did not speak, she finally said, meaning it, "If you told me you had murdered a child, I would still love you."

"I am," he said suddenly, "a homosexual."

Through the last few minutes, she had been expecting this, but yet a chill went through her and she had to force herself not to shiver. This was because she had the certain, absurd feeling that her husband was outside the door listening. She could think of nothing in all the world which would destroy Adam so quickly and completely as what she had just heard.

"There is nothing wrong with that," she said, quite calmly. "It's just one kind of life," she said, "like another."

He turned his face up toward her and it was still wet with tears.

"You're just incredible," he said.

She was suddenly angry. "You underestimate me," she said. "You think this house and this life are all I've ever seen. You think I've never lived because you see me making motions here, playing a part. Well, I've seen a great deal and I know a great deal. Now if that's all you have to tell me, then it is very little. If you want to talk to me some more, I'm here."

So he told her about Max. He left out nothing. He concluded with the letter at the beginning of the summer. He never looked at her as he was telling her all this, but his voice came evenly enough. And all the words that he said thudded against her like heavy stones, for she had known many homosexuals, male and female, and knew from them how lonely a life it is. One is always leaving or being left; they had told her this and she had seen it. And in Bobby's position one would be in perpetual hiding. It was Claude who now wanted to cry but she could not. Instead, she lay down beside him, and pulled his head across her shoulder to her breast.

"When you were very much younger, you often lay with me this way," she said.

"Did I?"

"Often."

"I never . . . never thought I'd ever tell anyone."

"Who is 'anyone'? Your mother? I am not wise, I make many mistakes, my education is lacking, but I am your mother, not anyone."

"That's true," he said.

They lay in silence for a while, and then he put his arm over her body. They were quite still. Something occurred to her, and she reached over with one arm and turned out the bedside lamp. Then she unbuttoned her robe swiftly and put his head between her breasts. After a while, as she had expected, she felt him grow very hard against her thigh. She knew that he would not dare to move. Slowly and effortlessly, she moved for him. She stroked him gently. She should have been terrified, she felt; terrified that he would recoil. But she felt no fear, had great confidence and security. And it gave her more pleasure than she had felt in years to be so gentle with him, to be helpful to him. She had, she was thinking, done this for gifts, for money, for a place to live and for no reason at all. She could see no reason why she could not do it for love. And with all the sweetness and this great love, she did not let him hurry, but brought him into her slowly, and even then did not let him rush until she was sure he was ready. And then she let him come.

Neither of them said a word. He only lay panting in her arms. For herself, she felt only joy and knew that she must say this to him. But it was a long time before she said anything. So it was he who spoke first.

"Thank you," he said, his voice breaking.

She continued to be silent for a while. Then she said, hesitantly, "Were you . . . were you pleased?"

He hesitated. "Yes," he whispered.

Again, she chose her words carefully. "We have always been . . . tender with each other. Now we have been as tender as God lets two people be."

"I understand."

"Go to sleep, my dearest."

After a while, he did. And much later, not long before dawn, she slipped away from him. She buttoned her robe and switched off the little portable. She kissed him on the forehead and tiptoed out of his room.

At least he has the choice, she thought. She returned to her bed, not waking Adam, and lay awake until the dawn did come, feeling the greatest happiness she had ever felt in her life.

# 6

THE NIGHT of the Fashion Gala was in two parts: the fashion show itself and the following ball, so, with typical Starr exuberance, it took place in two hotels. The show was given in the Ramsey Hilton, only three years old, and the ball was in the Sheraton Busch, which was fifty years old. The reasons were simply that the newer hotel, whose ballroom was low-ceilinged and ugly, nevertheless had staging devices devised primarily for conventions which allowed the store to pull all the tricks it wanted to. Lighting was sophisticated, and the level could be varied by rheostats and flickered all over the stage and runway by means of a switchboard. Slides could be shown, flicked off and replaced by live models brilliantly lit in any color. Flats were easy, and there was room and capability for the revolving stages by which the store introduced many of its groups. The older hotel had none of this sophistication. It had instead a lovely, high-ceilinged ballroom which hotels built in the twenties and thirties and in which one could give a gracious party. So, following the fashion show, the guests simply walked across the street to their tables. Everybody was invited for seven-thirty, were in their seats by eight and, with luck and a good many prayers, would be out of one hotel and inside the other by nine-thirty.

Backstage at the fashion show was as always—grim. Nearly eighty people were there for this night, counting the thirty-odd models (who would wear one hundred and twelve changes after heavy editing), twelve dressers (and undressers), shoe people, bag people, jewelry people, starters, hairdressers, six children, four dogs, a cheetah and two kittens. The children were not shielded from the chaos; if one of them began to cry, he was allowed to cry and jerked out on the runway by a hard-eyed model because nothing will bring an ovation faster than a child, except a weeping child. Animals are a child's only competition. The animals, however, were carefully walked just before the show: peeing on the runway or on one of the front-row guests is not considered attractive. Models, colleagues and friends all year, were filled with bitterness toward each other, for some girls always have better changes than others and are not forgiven for that.

Peter Shaw, a lusty, masculine man in his early thirties, wandered in among the chaos, thinking, among other things, that he had never seen so many bare boobs in his life. Shaw had announced scores of fashion shows but never one of this magnitude; so the sheer number of boobs bemused him. Before a show, models have no time to notice who is looking at them and most of them do not care anyway. Models' faces and bodies are to be admired or they would not be models. But Shaw himself had work to do. In his hand he carried his lineup, a listing of every piece that would be shown and a short description of it. He was backstage to make sure he noted any last-minute changes. It is embarrassing to be talking about one dress when quite a different one is traveling down the runway. One should not be discussing mink when the model is showing sable. And because the lights would be in his eyes, he would not always be able to distinguish between the two. He would be depending on his lineup and luck.

There were enough last-minute changes to keep him busy. Rachel Ritter, the fashion director in direct command, was everywhere, switching bags, gloves, shoes, jewelry, supervising hair styling, and even, within the limits of timing possibility, changing what girl would wear what outfit. Dressed as she was in pants and a silk shirt, she looked not unlike a ranch foreman whose cattle were the models. One of them began to weep when she was informed that she had been switched out of a sequined Norell, a great showpiece, into an ordinary black ruffled dress. Ritter looked at her through slitted eyes and said to the starter, "If that girl hasn't stopped sniveling in thirty seconds, cut all her changes and send her home." But when another girl came back from the bathroom having thrown up for twenty minutes and looking pale and wan, Ritter was approving: "She looks better. More ethereal. Whiten her makeup and be sure to blue the lights for her."

Ritter said to Shaw, "The thing is pace. Just move it. You don't move it and I'll kill you right on your podium."

Shaw did. Which was why so many people thought it was the best show in years, including Karen.

"That was," she said, crossing the street to go to the ball, "absolutely spectacular."

Louis nodded. "We're known for that," he said.

"I thought you announced these shows."

"I used to. This was Peter's first year."

"Why didn't you do it this year?"

He looked down at her and smiled. "Because he does it better than I do," he said.

"I see," she said, after a moment. "Was that your decision?"

"Yes," he lied, without hesitation.

The ball guests were substantially the same people who had been to Claude's party, but on this night they were much more elegantly and expensively dressed. On the lawn, the greatest number of dresses had been short, but now they were all floor length, and the family jewels were out in abundance, including a number of tiaras. There was, in the dress of these Texas women, essentially no more or less vulgarity than there is in the dress of women in New York, Chicago or Los Angeles, Karen thought. If anything, the Texas ladies, trained and reared by Starr's advertising and a sales force trained by Jenny Starr, tended to be somewhat more conservative than their peers in other American cities. "Texas has one thing," Karen said to Louis, sitting at their table in the huge ballroom with the immense chandeliers and the graceful arched doorways. "It grows handsome women."

He smiled. "Yes, it does. Most of the models who did the show tonight started with us as college girls, sometimes even in back-to-school shows, as teenagers. They're so good, a lot of them go to New York for the collection showings and work for the designers who've seen them here."

"I didn't mean the models, though I'll agree they'd hold their own in New York. I'm talking about the ladies at this ball."

Louis looked around at the swirling mass of a thousand people. "They have the problem Californians do," he said. "They get too much sun. The skin shows it. Women should avoid the sun like disease."

"I don't know," she said, thoughtfully. "It makes them look active—alive. As though they do something. Every time I have lunch at a good restaurant in New York, I look at the women and I'm positive all they're going to do after lunch is spend the afternoon at Bergdorf's." She smiled ruefully. "Including me. These women look like at least they play golf, or run the League of Women Voters."

He was amused. "On behalf of all of them, thank you."

"I'm impressed."

THAT MORNING, Claude had waked to the same happiness she had felt the night before. Adam had been already up and out, down at the store, and she had stretched and taken her time getting dressed. It was not until she was prepared to go downstairs for breakfast that she began to feel fear. For herself, she had no sorrows from the night before. She felt exactly as she had then. But what of Bobby? What was he feeling? Horror? Disgust? Humiliation? It had not been until they were getting ready to dress for the evening that she had seen him at all. He, too, had spent the day at the store and had returned about six o'clock. He had kissed her as usual; no more nor less affection than usual; and had gone to his room. In the bustle of getting downtown, meeting the award winners, getting seated and proceeding to the ball, she had scarcely seen him since. And the fear grew in her. She had no thought that anything would be discussed between them; was resigned to the probability that no mention would ever be made of their experience. There would only be silence about that. What frightenend her was that there might only be silence between them on all matters; that she had done irreversible damage to him. The accident of fate, as she thought of it, which had brought them together was no sin at all to her. But then she, Claude, did not equate in any way the sexual with the sinful. It had been a major reason why the Roman Catholic Church had dropped out of her life. She could still remember the priest's oniony breath coming through the confessional to her when, as a young girl, she had confessed to touching herself; still remember the penance he had given her, which had taken nearly an hour to say; still remember that she had continued to practice this sin and simply omitted it from confession until, in her late teens, she stopped going to confession and Mass as well. Now, walking toward her table at the Gala ball, she expected that she had committed what must be considered the greatest sin in the lexicon of the Church; and did not care. Unless Bobby cared. Unless he hated her and himself. Unless some latent Jewish conscience had brought him to his knees.

But when they were at the table and she looked at him almost furtively, she found the opposite of what she had expected. He was gayer than she could remember seeing him. Seated next to Irene Von Hoffmanstahl, he was laughing and joking with her and soon after their arrival took her to dance. While they were gone, she was herself withdrawn, perfunctory in her answers, distracted in conversation. Dancing with Adam, she could not keep her mind on what he was saying. He seemed to be talking about the business day, seemed to be cheerful about it, was commenting on the show, was saying that she seemed tired; she caught that and jumped at it.

"Tired?" she said. "That's not the word. Exhausted. Sick of every face in the room. Sick of faces . . ."

Adam looked at her, concerned. "Has something happened?" he said.

She looked at him sharply. "What could have happened?" she said. "You've seen it all. Aren't you ready to vomit?"

"What's wrong, Claude?"

"Nothing," she said, too loudly. She was behaving unlike herself and knew it. There seemed to be nothing to do about it.

"Well, if it's just this weekend," he said, stiffly, shut out, "then you have one more day and it's over."

"You actually seem to enjoy all this—shit," she said, using a word she had probably never used in his presence in her life. He was genuinely shocked.

"Are you feeling ill?"

She shook her head almost violently. "That's not the point," she said. "I painted a smile on my face three days ago and the paint is cracking. Does that satisfy you? Do you understand?"

He was silent. Then, "I suppose this is a great strain on you," he said, quietly. "I'm sorry. But I don't know what there is I could have done about it. You've been beautiful, sweet . . . quite marvelous, in fact . . . through it all. We haven't even had a complaint from Charlie Teal except about the size of our order, which you can do nothing about. You're a remarkable, wonderful woman and there is not one soul in this room who wouldn't agree."

And of course she felt a rush of compassion for him, and her eyes filled and she kissed his cheek. She had never, she was convinced, been good enough for him and now she had betrayed him in the most unspeakable way. She only said, "You're right. I'm just very tired and bad tempered. Take me back to the table and I'll excuse myself and patch up the cracks in the paint."

Returning from the ladies' room, she paused a moment and looked at the party. The dance floor was packed, and the orchestra was having a go at rock-and-roll and the mainly middle-aged dancers were having a go at dancing to it. She smiled: They looked so silly. Yet it was a pretty party. The display department had done loose flowers on the tables instead of elaborate arrangements and the effect was careless and appealing. The old hotel, seedy in spots now, still had its original silver and crystal and the tables had elegance. The ballroom, scene of every debutante party since Ramsey had discovered what a debutante was, had the grandeur none of the modern ballrooms have; and people, she reflected, looked marvelous in it. For no reason she could understand, she felt in her fear and sadness a sudden affection for these Texans. They were hard-bitten, tough, reactionary and inclined to think they were a race unto themselves. But they were also warm and generous and hospitable and they knew how to enjoy themselves. She remembered that when she had first married Adam, they had never put her down. One could say that was because of Adam, but she knew better. It was rather in spite of Adam. Adam was the catch of Ramsey and he had gone to Paris to pick out a wife. She had been fair game. Yet, they had all been kind to her, quickly forgiving her for being French. Her own French people, in like circumstances, would never have forgiven her for being a Texan. She was sure of that.

These were the things she was thinking as she returned to the table, the smile quite firmly back in place. She danced with Charlie Teal, with Guy Racquette and with all the others who owed her duty dances, and her responses might have been mechanical but they were adequate. Through it all, she could not keep her eyes from wandering in search of her son. To her amazement, he was table hopping, dancing with the mothers of girls he had been to school with and the girls themselves if they were present, and he was laughing a lot. Louis remarked on it.

"Bobby is suddenly the life of the party," he said.

"Isn't he?"

"It's good for him. He doesn't have enough fun."

"How is Karen enjoying herself?"

He made a face. "I'll know that better tomorrow night. Or Wednesday."

"She seems to be having a good time."

"With Karen what seems to be and what is are not necessarily the same. Mainly she's asked a lot of questions. She's been short on answers."

"You make her sound rather mysterious."

He shrugged. "More . . . unexpected. She's hard to predict."

She looked up at him, as they danced. "You'd like it better if she were predictable? Like me?"

"Are you really?" he said, seriously. "I often wonder."

Too hastily, she said, "Oh, yes, completely."

"I think you have many thoughts we none of us know anything about."

She looked at the chandeliers. "Oh, well . . . thoughts.

I was talking about actions. Everyone knows what I will do before I do it."

His voice continued serious. "I think that is a matter of discipline. You're a very disciplined lady. Which I suppose is a virtue."

She danced with him for a while, saying nothing. Then finally, "Would you prefer that I throw shoes? Or candlesticks? Or scream? I often want to scream . . ."

"Then you probably should. That's not to say I'd like it or Adam would. It would be disturbing." He suddenly seemed almost angry. "The point is, Claude, nobody ever told you what you had to be. Nobody. Nobody *said* that, as Adam's wife, you have to be X or Y. You assumed it. That's been your decision. What you've been, what you say, what you do, especially what you do—all these things are your own little decisions. You make them. By the minute, maybe. You want to say something and decide against it. You want to challenge and don't. You're fifty times as intelligent as you'll admit. That's a defense. An excuse. You play a role, but *nobody ever told you to*. You invented it yourself."

They were looking at each other edgily. She had not had such a talk with Louis before.

"Why are you angry?" she said.

He turned away and laughed. "Oh . . . because Shaw did the show very well. Because I'm frustrated and envious. Because I'm a bad polo player. Because I'm second-rate at everything. Not quite first-rate in anything. Because you're too goddamn perfect. Because you've made that role you play and what you are the same thing. Because the only thing you do to fight back is to take an extra drink, instead of throwing it in somebody's face."

"Whose?" she said, stung.

"Mine right now," he said. "I'm very sorry. Amazed. At myself."

"There's a reason for all this. What is it?"

"I think it rubs off," he said, after a moment.

She flushed. Looked down at the floor. "Oh, I see," she said. "You think Karen is looking at me and saying, 'Claude's what it is to be a Starr wife.' And that she wants no part of it. You're telling me that Karen might not marry you because of me."

"I didn't mean . . ."

"Of course you did. But it's absurd. If she does marry

you, she can do exactly as she wishes. And will. My God, Louis, you actually underestimate her. Now listen . . . I will give her no advice, even if she should ask for it, which she won't. I will do nothing—nothing—for or against her. Consider me . . . indifferent."

"Which means," he said curiously, "that you don't like her."

The question resolved the matter for her. "Not yet. Perhaps later on."

"I . . . very much hope you will."

"What does it matter?"

"Whatever we are, we are it together. We Starrs, that is. It would be more comfortable if you and Karen liked each other."

Claude laughed. "You seem to think she'll marry you?" she said.

He shrugged. "I don't know. She hasn't said so, God knows."

"Why shouldn't she? You're very marriageable, you know. Even if your polo isn't very good. You dance well. And you have steady work."

"Well," he said, quietly, not looking at her, "if she does decide to marry me, there'll be one small problem: I won't have any idea why."

As he twirled her around, she caught sight of Bobby. He was dancing with Irene and putting her through some of his steps. She was doing well with him. She was a woman who would do everything well, Claude thought. And her mind left the conversation with Louis, though he was still talking, and fastened again upon her fears. They became so strong within her that she lost track of what was going on around her; sat down with Louis; danced with other people; heard things and responded without interest or more than the scantiest knowledge of what was being said, until, late in the evening, Bobby finally came to get her and took her out on the floor. She looked at his silent face and noticed that his eyes were bright, and that there was a slight flush to his normally pale face. He held her close and guided her expertly through the other dancers, but it was a long time before either of them said anything. She would have given anything in the world to have opened the conversation, but the terror was too great. Whatever came to her mind to say seemed inappropriate, potentially dangerous or absurd. In her frustration, tears came and filled her eyes and dribbled down her cheeks. Furious, she had to dab at them with her hand, and this he saw. He said nothing, but he put his hand up on the back of her head and drew it down to his shoulder, and then danced with her this way; the way in which young lovers had once danced in the days of the big bands. She was thus able to wipe the tears against his dinner jacket and no one could see that she was crying. When he finally spoke it was very slowly. She could tell that he had worked on his words; that his silence had been while he tried to phrase them.

"I don't think," he said, "that anything that will ever happen to me in my life . . . can be as important . . . as last night. I feel . . ." He hesitated, "I feel that the world is full of things that I can do. Instead of things I can't. Do you understand?"

She moved her head against his shoulder, nodding.

"You are . . . my own mother . . . the most extraordinary person I've ever known. You must . . . you absolutely *must* . . . know that. And remember it. And . . . that I love you. Everybody loves you, but I . . . I love you most."

In a little while the tears stopped and the fears went away. She said nothing to him for a long time. Only kissed him softly on the cheek. Finally, she said, "I was so afraid."

"Not any more?"

"Not any more."

In TRUTH, the world was filled with things Bobby could do. He began that very night. He drove Irene home in his little Triumph, and, in his exuberance and with the help of some champagne and a good deal of enthusiasm from her, fucked her grandly, to her surprise and just slightly his own. Then left her to drive home whistling. In the days and weeks to come, he was to reflect that nothing that had happened to him was quite comparable to the experiences with Max; either physically or, certainly, emotionally. But he left that, quite cheerfully, as a situation to be examined later; or even left alone. He simply felt free, unlocked, alive. And with these new feelings, there came to him a new way of looking at things; a rather measured approach to living, which happened to coincide with his becoming eighteen years old. As he embarked upon his first year of Harvard, he found that his attitude toward people, his schoolmates, the faculty, girls, had become careless. Status no longer concerned him particularly, and as a result it rose. Though his music continued to be his best subject and he wrote occasional reviews for the *Crimson*, his grades in other subjects improved and his relationship with his peers also improved. By midterm, his confidence was such that he sought out a position which, during the previous year, would have been most unlikely for him. He went into debating, became a member of his class's debating team and, as he practiced in joint debates with other colleges and schools, became one of the best public speakers on the campus. He also found that he had an extraordinary talent for mathematics and that his English essays, while perhaps not gifted, were logical, organized, well thought out and lucid. Sexually he supposed himself to be ambivalent and did not worry about it. He had no homosexual affairs during his first months at Harvard and did indeed go to bed with one or two of the Radcliffe girls with whom he found himself at the end of theater or concert evenings; he did this without difficulty and without emotional involvement. By spring, two important things had happened. The first was that he was elected secretary of the freshman class, which he took in stride but was immensely pleased for his father; and the second was that he stopped for a few days of vacation in New York to see some theater, and there he ran into Guy Racquette on the street and had dinner with him at a lively restaurant in the Village. He spent that night and most of a week at Racquette's apartment and left for home thinking how pleasant it had been. From home and then school, he and Racquette began to correspond, and as sometimes happens, in that correspondence a kind of love began to grow.

ON THE night the Gala weekend ended, Louis did not go to Karen's suite for dinner as she had expected.

"I thought you'd want us to be alone," she said in surprise.

"No, I really don't. I think I'd feel I was in the dean's office waiting to find out if I'm being expelled. And you might as well see our best French restaurant here. It's part of the scenery you'll learn to love. Or won't."

So, he picked her up at seven-thirty. She wore a light camel tunic and skirt with a white wool top and he wore a dark business suit. She liked the restaurant at once. It was one smallish room with ordinary stucco walls which, in New York, would have been decorated by one of the more fashionable French muralists. Instead, quite good abstract paintings were hung on them; a fact on which she remarked.

"The place is run by two Poles," he explained. "Man and wife. These are their paintings, and they have taste. They buy them sometimes in New York, but Ramsey has about five good galleries and you can hang a decent collection just from them. The waiters and captains are almost all Poles, and one of them was a judge before the Communists took over. Practically any Pole on the loose in Texas can get a free meal and sometimes a job. Alex is a soft touch. And here he is."

Alexander Brailowski was a tall, solid man with silver hair and a ruddy complexion. Louis introduced him to Karen and he kissed her hand.

"You are coming up in the world," he said to Louis. "She lights up the whole restaurant."

"It's a charming place," Karen said.

"Are you from New York?" Brailowski asked.

She nodded. "I came for the Gala."

"Then you'll find us in the second rank of New York restaurants. Last month, we were in the first rank, but the chef left. Chefs stay six months. Chefs go out with other chefs after work. Unfortunately, in Ramsey, there are no other chefs. French ones. They are black barbecue cookers. So my chefs go back home or take to drink. Speaking of which, what would you like?"

They both ordered martinis and Brailowski told a waiter.

"The chef is feeling homesick and has made a cassoulet," the owner said. "You might want to try it. Everything else is as usual. If you're hungry, you could have the Chateaubriand and a bottle of Chateauneuf du Pape. You are so beautiful, mademoiselle, that if I stay here much longer I will sit down and not give you a check. So I will leave you alone."

In the back of the room, centered, was a grand piano and at it was a slim, elegant lady with white hair and wearing a long black dress to the floor. She had a strong, biblical face and she was playing Chopin. She played with enormous grace as well as precision.

"She seems too good to be playing in a restaurant," Karen said.

"Not quite. She tried it and it didn't work. She teaches during the day."

"Well . . ." Karen slipped back against the banquette, letting her head rest at the top of it. She looked at Louis with an amused expression.

"Well what?" he said.

"So the famous Gala is over at last. And everybody's exhausted. Or at least I am. Was it a success? From the store's point of view?"

Louis offered her a cigarette which she took and lit one for both of them. "I imagine it will be," he said. "We count Gala spending over a five-day period: Friday, Saturday, Monday, Tuesday and Wednesday. The first three days were ahead of last year, especially Monday which was a big gain. And we did well in Better Apparel today, though I haven't seen the flash sheet for the whole store. A lot depends on tomorrow. If those ladies who went to the luncheon today come in tomorrow and buy what they saw, we'll be all right. If they don't . . . we won't."

"Well, the publicity . . ."

"Oh, we'll get that. And happy to have it. I thought you meant pure dollars and cents."

"Actually, I did. I'm curious about how you spend so much money and still profit by it."

Louis smiled and sipped his martini. "Good shot," he said. "I can't really tell you how profitable that Gala is. Certainly a lot of out-of-towners come in for it, and they spend a hell of a lot of money. But we've painted ourselves into a corner with all those parties. It didn't used to be so expensive to give a party, but now it's a fortune. Personally, I think the Fashion Gala is marginal—Bill King and Adam say it's not."

"What if you cut out the parties and just put on two shows?"

"That's what I mean by painting ourselves into a corner. Women get their husbands to come because of the parties. Without their husbands, they might not come. If we cut the Western party, and Adam's, we'd look like we were cheapskating. Which Starr's can't afford. Very un-Starr's. Very un-Texan."

"But surely this has been rather an opulent weekend? Even for Texas."

He nodded. "Oh sure. But Texans do entertain a lot and they do it up brown. During the football season there are three or four parties on Saturday you could go to, the same on Sunday. Some people don't even see the game. It's just a blur."

"Do Texans drink harder than other people?"

He shook his head. "I doubt it. We have our share of two-fisted drinkers, but they seem to be able to sober up pretty quick if the talk turns to business. Some of the second generation crowd who don't have enough to do, at least yet, and do have a lot of money . . . they can pour it down. And chase starlets. And fly everybody to Hawaii or Mexico at the end of a party. But I've seen a lot of kids recover from that. Dad gives them a few years and then cracks down. They go to work or else. So they go to work and some of them are pretty good. More sophisticated than their fathers."

"Did you chase starlets and fly people to Acapulco?"

He laughed. "When I got out of college, Father gave me a year to play. I wasn't really very good at it. From the end of that one year, I've been working my ass off. Bernie's more that type than either Adam or I. He still gets his fun in and he won't die of overwork."

She said, musing, "I like Bernie."

"So does everyone else. How did you like Becky?"

"Fine. I like them all really. Claude, the kids, your mother . . ."

"And Adam?"

"Oh yes. Maybe especially Adam. We developed a mildly adversary relationship, you might say. But he has strength and power. And good will, I think . . ." Her voice trailed off and she became thoughtful. For a while, they sat silently, listening to the piano, smoking, sipping their drinks.

"Would you like to order?" he said at last.

"Not for a few minutes." She laughed. "I'm trying to think how to put something."

"Oh. All right."

"Look," Karen said, after a while. "I don't want this dinner to turn into a suspense thriller, so let's get flat out with it. Do you really want to marry me, Louis?"

"Yes, I do."

"You're absolutely sure of that?"

"Yes."

"All right, then. Louis . . . my dear Louis . . . I'll be very happy . . . and proud . . . to marry you. And I'll do my best to make you a good wife."

For the first time in his adult life, Louis's eyes filled with tears and he was unable to speak. He simply put his hand on hers under the table and kissed her briefly on the cheek.

"I think you must have expected that," she said. "You would guess I wouldn't have stayed over to say no. I'm not such a bitch as that. And I want you to know that I accept very happily. And that I think we can *be* very happy. But I must ask you one thing before we start calling up preachers. You understand that I'm not wildly, school-girly, head-over-heels in love with you?"

Louis nodded. He had recovered his composure. "I understand that."

"And does it bother you terribly?"

"It bothers me. I can live with it. I asked you to marry me knowing you didn't feel that way. It's all right."

"Well, it's not your fault. I've *never* felt that way. I don't know what it's like. I don't seem to know how to lose my head over a man. I wish I did. And if I did, my dearest Louis, I'm sure it would be over you."

"I accept that. It's good enough."

Karen said, "And even that may happen . . ." She smiled. "So the suspense is over and we can order now. Accepting a marriage proposal makes a girl hungry."

They ordered the Chateaubriand and the Chateauneuf du Pape and Louis talked quietly and affectionately through their dinner. She responded appropriately, but her mind was wandering. Amid the bustling of the waiters and while the little restaurant grew crowded and noisy, the pianist switched to Rodgers and Hart and then to Lerner and Lowe. She seemed at home in almost any music. Karen half listened to the piano, half to Louis, all the time wondering why she had said she would marry him. Was she really bored with, had she reached an end to, the skiing in Gstaad and the weekends in Southampton and the life and pace of New York? Did she really believe this Texas provincial city to be the appropriate substitute, the life she wanted? She was well aware that she had done through the course of her years exactly as she liked. She had never known what it is to want what one cannot have. Money had always been there, leaving her the kind of freedom only family riches can provide; money without responsibility. At various times in her life, she had worked for a museum, a bookstore, an art gallery and a good many charities. None of these jobs had involved heavy responsibility, though she retained a financial interest in the gallery and did go to it a few times a week. She had many friends and they occupied many hours. But they had not seemed to involve her in any very deep emotional commitment. She worried sometimes that one day emotions would suddenly explode within her and unprepared and defenseless, she would be shattered. That frightened her. So she was relieved about her feelings for Louis. She liked him, perhaps loved him lightly, respected him, liked to go to bed with him and was not bored by him; sound enough reasons to marry him, it seemed to her, especially since most of the men she knew within ten years of her age were sexually dubious and some of the most attractive not even dubious. I cannot be dubious, she thought. She turned to Louis and said, "I'm glad I'm going to marry you."

Throughout the weekend and even now she had been fascinated by the idea of marrying into a kind of feudal hierarchy, nearly a monarchy, complete with courtiers and serfs. She liked the legend of the store and she loved the power of the Starrs. Like their home state, they offered something larger than life and bursting with energy. Well, she had those qualities. So she was marrying Louis and not Adam; all right. That was the challenge to her. To build Louis by definition, meant to diminish Adam. Or at least to do battle with him. Such a prospect greatly excited her. She could feel it in her loins, for she sensed the flaw in Adam, the king, had sensed it all through the weekend, during which she had watched the store spend a small fortune.

Profit. Adam spent too much money. In his heart, she was convinced, he saw Starr's as a romantic adventure; always accomplishing the unexpected and heroic. Bound for glory. Anyone whose life pursuit is in any way romantic is vulnerable. She did not underestimate him. She supposed he would make all the necessary hard moves to insure pace and productivity in the business. But this wildly expensive Fashion Gala convinced her that he was, essentially, a man of the theater. Therefore, an exposed man. Chinks in the armor of highly visible people are easily perceived. Such people can be gunned down before they know what is happening. Adam, she thought, set himself up for a shootout. She knew she was greatly attracted to him, sensed that he was to her. He was as strong as she; not many men were. What a grand battle it could be, with Jenny in the background holding all the cards; Jenny Starr, who she was certain could be made her ally.

It was his use of Adam's name that brought her attention back fully to Louis.

"What did you say?"

He looked surprised. "Just then?"

"Just then."

"I said, of course, I'll ask Adam to be best man."

She laughed, and part of the reason was her secret.

"What's funny?"

"Nothing, really. It occurred to me you couldn't possibly have asked anyone else."

"Why not?"

"It's just obvious. Banal, really."

"He is my brother."

"So is Bernie."

"My senior brother."

"In the end, you're all like your father. Everything is proscribed. It doesn't matter. Rather silly. I would love to have Adam as your best man. Maybe I'll ask Claude to stand up with us. For me."

He looked at her oddly. "Isn't there somebody up north?"

. She shrugged. "Fifty people. Or no one. We might as well keep it in the family."

"She'll be surprised, I think."

"Surprises are good for Claude. She could use more of them. Why? Do you think she'll refuse?" Karen smiled, mischievously.

"Of course not," he said stiffly. "She'll be delighted."

She decided to get into specifics. "The first time I was married, five hundred people were on the lawn of my father's estate to witness the event. I thought it was no fun and slightly vulgar, though people say it was beautiful. I was, of course, in a white bridal gown though I had been sleeping with Paolo for nearly a year, and I threw a bouquet and we went to Europe to honeymoon. A good part of the trip was really on a yacht belonging to a friend of Daddy's. Because of my husband's family, I had to join the Catholic Church for the occasion. I left the church one minute after the priest had married us. The whole thing cost Daddy about twenty thousand dollars, and it got a good deal of space in the newspapers. I don't suppose you want to go through all that?"

"Not in the least," he said. "I'd suggest city hall, except that you have to stand in line."

So they decided that the wedding would be small and that they would be married by a civil justice.

"Won't your mother mind?" she asked. "I don't mind a rabbi. I just don't want to go through a month of instruction in the Jewish faith."

"Well, with a rabbi around, you might have to. And she will mind, but not much. I've been meaning to ask you. How are your parents going to feel? Your marrying a Jew?"

"They won't like it. But they won't say anything. Even to me."

"Why not?"

"I've trained them."

They decided to be married in the Library Suite of the St. Regis Hotel in New York. "I suppose it ought to be in my territory, at least," she said.

"But you really will have to come down this month for a while. To look at places to live."

"All right," she said and fell silent.

After a time, he asked, "Where would you like to go? For a honeymoon?"

She hesitated. "Do you really want a honeymoon?"

"I don't know. Fairly traditional."

"I always think a honeymoon is for people who have to learn how to sleep together. We know how to do that. I think I'd rather take a trip later on. When we actually want to go somewhere. I think I'd like to get on with life . . . Will people give parties for us?"

He was wry. "Oversufficiently."

"Well, that's fine. If I'm going to be a Texan, I want to be a Texan right away. I'm very impatient, you know."

He said nothing, smiled at her, watched her, pleased, while she grew genuinely excited. "I think," she said, "we could spend a week in the city after we're married. I'll finish up the moving business and we could look at some pictures and go to the theater. By then, we'll know what sort of flat we have and can start buying for it. We'll need two cars, won't we?"

"Absolutely."

"Then that's what Daddy can give us as a wedding present. The second car. That'll please him. Something he understands. He'll expect me to want a picture and he hates what I like. How will you tell the family?"

"Why don't we tell them together? Stay over and I'll give a luncheon and we'll announce it."

She was silent. Her eyes had brightened now that she was thinking in terms of specifics and she looked to him ravishingly beautiful in the soft lights of the restaurant. He noticed again how little makeup she used, even in the evening.

"I think," she said slowly, "I'd rather they wrote me. When they've had time to think. I'm curious about what they'll say. If we tell them together, they'll just react, but I won't learn anything."

"What do you need to learn? Everyone is going to be delighted. They'll be astonished I've done anything so obviously right, and gotten away with it."

"Oh, well," she said cryptically, "one can always learn."

Dinner was finished. Neither of them could have said whether it was good or not, but it seemed they had eaten it. They suddenly ran out of things to talk about. Louis had in his mind that something quite essential was missing, and he knew what it was. He wished to tell her of the greatness of his love for her. He wished to discuss the newness of such a feeling in him and the deep happiness he now felt. But he said none of these things because he felt it would be awkward for her. About love, the romantic notion of love, she had already said all she could. She would not be able, as she had already confessed, to respond in kind to what he had to say. So he said nothing of these things. It came as a great and happy surprise to him then when she turned to look at him, almost fiercely, and then threw her arms around him and kissed him hard in front of the other diners who looked at them in astonishment.

"I'm so tremendously excited," she said, pulling away at last.

She was not lying. She simply did not know exactly why she was excited; or at least all of the why. Since she didn't, she said something else that was also quite true.

"And I want you to know I've never cared about anyone else so truly. What I want to do now is go back to the hotel and go to bed."

Which was more than enough for Louis.

## 7

As THE letters arrived from the Starr family, Karen read them with great care. Becky and Bernie wrote together; two pages of her rather childish scrawl, defaced by exclamation points and dashes, full of good cheer and warmheartedness. Bernie's contribution was "All Becky wrote goes for me, too. It's just great, great, great. Best thing that ever happened to us. Come back soon. Love." Bobby and Nancy wrote short, proper notes and she threw them both away, along with Becky's. Karen did not keep old letters, photographs or locks of hair. Claude's letter surprised her. "Louis," she wrote, "so far as I have seen is a completely honest man. He never says what he doesn't mean. If he says he loves you, then you can be certain he does. Isn't that good? I hope you will love him, too. And the rest of us. It is an interesting family. Since my own parents have been dead for many years and since I have no brothers or sisters, the Starrs have been my only family since I married them. And I used that word with care. Whatever you have been, you are a Starr the day you take the name. As I looked at you over the weekend, it seemed to me you were born to be a Starr, which I wasn't, though I've managed. So I'm not surprised that you have decided to join us. I hope that you will make Louis happier than he is. And feel more important than he does. And I hope that we will be friends. Sincerely."

Karen reread Claude's note a number of times. With reference to her becoming a Starr, she felt nettled. Her own father had begun with nothing better than a high

school education and had fiddled unsuccessfully with gold
and oil before establishing the copper and aluminum company which had made his fortune. She would be willing
to bet that his personal assets would exceed those of any
one Starr and possibly all the Starrs together. But his
company was publicly held, did not bear his name, had
no progeny in office since there was only herself, and had
retired him when he came of age. So Louis could not lose
his identity and become a Woodward, since the name con-
notated only past history and now only an old man and
his wife, her parents. Whereas Louis Starr or Mrs. Louis
Starr were living representations of a living institution.
No escaping it. In name, she was marrying above herself.
Well, she consoled herself, cross a Woodward with a Starr
and the result would be a different sort of Starr from
Claude.

She looked forward eagerly to what Adam would say,
and was sharply disappointed. "I think," he wrote, "Louis
is very lucky and has shown his usual good taste. As a
matter of fact, I think we are all lucky that you are going
to be one of us. I look forward to that. Sincerely."

Nothing, no hint. He might have been writing that he
was happy she and Louis had won the mixed doubles.
She was certain that she had disturbed him over the long
weekend and the blandness of his note did not alter her
thinking. She did not like his note simply because it was
careful. Such propriety did not suit him. But, she told
herself, in consolation, he would not be able to sustain it.
She would see to that. Still, she threw his letter away
with the others that did not matter.

JENNY WROTE:

"I am very happy to hear about you and my son, Louis.
I had suspected it might happen, which is why we had the
kind of talk we did at my pool that Sunday. I was pleased
by that talk and I hope you were.

"Louis has for years gone out with young girls who
present little challenge to him. Therefore, I have always
thought it likely that he would eventually choose someone of great strength to marry. You have such strength and
I hope you will lend some of it to him, and not crush
him with it. Louis is not fragile as Bernie, for example,
is fragile. But he is vulnerable. I do not think my husband
was vulnerable to another human being and I do not think

Adam is. But Louis is. I ask you to keep what I have written in mind, since your response to it will determine the relationship between us. If that should sound threatening, let me balance it by saying how much I liked your mind, the sound of your voice and the way you move and look. We are used to beautiful things, we Starrs, and you are one of those.

"Claude and Becky call me Mother since they have no mothers of their own. I expect you should call me Jenny. I hope I will sign my future letters to you with great affection. Meanwhile, I think I shall sign this one,

"With great expectations,

"Jenny Starr."

JENNY'S LETTER was received on a crisp sunny day in late autumn, the kind of day when the air seems fresh and clean whether it is or not, and when New Yorkers can feel that they live in the most generous of all cities. Karen read it while breakfasting in the small dining room of her apartment on Central Park South. She could have had her breakfast in bed, but she made it a point each morning to bathe and dress and then sit down to breakfast with the *Times,* the *News* and the mail. That had always seemed important to her. The apartment itself was good-sized, had a superb view of the park and was filled with pictures, constantly being changed, by the artists who showed in her gallery. Like Adam's, it was a personal collection. Karen trusted her taste in all things. Some of the art was already valuable, some not yet and perhaps never would be; projections which had nothing to do with what she hung; she hung what she liked.

Jenny Starr's letter bothered her. She did not answer it until two days after she received it. It took her that long, after a number of tries in her head, to decide what she wanted to say.

She finally wrote:

"DEAR JENNY,

"I have turned over in my mind many times how I should reply to your letter. I think my best course is to be brief—and as honest as you were with me. As to my feelings about your son, they are the deepest I have known. You should think of me as an ally he has never had before. You seem to think of me as hard. That is a mistake. Louis doesn't think of me that way and none of you will when we know each other better. I am simply, I hope, not silly.

"Your most urgent consideration is obviously what kind of wife I will be to Louis. Well, in short, I intend to love him well, to fill his needs, to help him accomplish his goals, and to have him very proud of me. That is all I can say. I hope it pleases you just as I hope I will please you. And that you will give me a chance. And understand that I can't be perfect any more than you can—or anyone else. Sincerely."

AT THE moment of posting the letter, Karen knew at last that she was really going to marry Louis Starr.

HER PARENTS were in their sixties. Edward Woodward was six feet tall and had snow-white hair, a lined pink face and cold blue eyes. His wife, Katherine, was tall and elegant and her skin was young. At "21" they had a table front-center in the first room of the bar. It was a better table than Louis could have gotten and he said so.

"This place," Mr. Woodward said reflectively, "remembers old friends. When I first did well, I used to come here often. I tied up a lot of deals in this place. Now I don't come much, but they remember."

"Daddy, are you playing your rough diamond part tonight?" Karen asked lightly.

"Dear, it's the best part he knows," Mrs. Woodward said. She spoke with the suggestion of a sexy lisp. "In fact, it's the only part." Louis looked at her in surprise. Somehow, he had expected a mouse in company with a lion, but her voice and the way she used her eyes and smiled informed him immediately that she had been a highly sensual woman, still was. When she examined him, as she did from time to time, it was as her own woman. He even thought she might be flirting with him from old habit. "Do you have parts you play, Louis?"

"I suppose so," he said, easily. "I couldn't name them for you."

"Does he look like a polo player?" Karen asked.

After a moment, Mr. Woodward said, cheerfully, "Well, yes, to tell the truth."

"Is that bad?" Karen asked.

"Depends on how well he plays it. If he plays it well, it's a good way to get killed. If he's a three-goal man man, he might as well be ridin' a merry-go-round." As he spoke, he was looking quizzically at Louis.

"I've broken two arms, or rather the same one twice, and one leg, and I have a seven-goal rate," Louis said.

Ed Woodward nodded. "So you play to win. Good enough."

"Well, that's one of Louis's parts that he plays."

"Why do we not go into all the others, Karen, dear?" her mother interrupted. She smiled at Louis. "Never strip a man before dinner, is my thought."

Louis burst out laughing. Mr. Woodward shook his head. "You have to get used to the fact, Mr. Starr—Louis, rather, I keep forgetting you're about to marry my daughter—my wife has a lively mind. And expresses it often. For my benefit and any company we may have. But especially for me, since lively minds grow more appealing as you grow older. So I like it. Would you like another drink?"

They ordered another round and dinner at the same time.

"Most people, including Katherine and the various people Katherine hires can't cook a pheasant, but they can here. So if you like it, have it."

They all had it except Karen, who ordered duck. "Even here, pheasant is stringy," she said.

"So is all game," her father commented. "That's why people order game." He turned to Louis. "I'm acquainted with your store, you know."

"No, I didn't," Louis said, genuinely surprised. He looked at Karen, who shook her head and shrugged her shoulders.

"Well, no, Karen wouldn't know about it, though I may have told Katherine about it. In my youth, I used to work on a pipeline in West Texas. Out of Odessa. And we worked such long hours, when the day was done, the only place a man could eat was in the local whorehouse. You could sleep there, too, they had plenty of rooms and no favors given or asked. You bought their merchandise or paid two bucks for a cot. Nice lady ran that place. So when I had my wad, I went to Ramsey and bought nearly twenty presents for those girls. That was the old store, of course. When your Daddy and Momma was just startin'. I bought all those girls handkerchief roses from Starr's. One of your parents must've thought them up."

"Mother. And we still sell them."

Mr. Woodward nodded. "And I made a bouquet of them for the Madame. Clarissa was her name. Always struck me as a strange name for a Madame. Should have been Belle—or Texas Flo."

"Pun," said Mrs. Woodward graciously.

"I didn't know you were in oil," Louis said.

"I wasn't. Took some flyers and always landed on my ass. That was a pipeline, not a rig. I headed up the paint gang. Odessa was basically a roughneck town in those days. No, copper was my way, and then zinc and aluminum. And I moved the company to New York so we'd be closer to Wall Street and supported '21.' My company built by expandin' into other fields. You expandin', Louis?"

"Modestly," Louis said. "We're building a suburban branch to the north of Ramsey. We've had a small store there, but this one is about a hundred and twenty-five thousand feet. Which is major."

"What's the cost?"

"Developer pays the cost, except for fixtures. We'll have to pay four or five percent of sales."

Mr. Woodward looked blank. "Four or five percent? There's a hell of a lot of difference between four and five percent. What volume are you talking about?"

Louis shrugged. "It's our first try. Twelve million, maybe, to start."

"So that one percent is one hundred and twenty thousand dollars of straight expense. You shouldn't be guessin' there."

Louis, deflated, said, "Adam's working on that now."

Mr. Woodward said, "Who's Adam?"

Karen laughed heartily, "God," she said.

"My older brother," Louis said stiffly.

Aware that he had touched someone's nerve, Mr. Woodward said, "Too bad you can't keep those Mom-and-Pop businesses these days. Got to expand. Got to be big."

"You sound like Adam," Louis said, goodnatured again.

"Well, it's true."

"No, it isn't," Mrs. Woodward said to Louis's surprise. "Not if their city grows like it has been."

Mr. Woodward shook his head. "Even then. Growth attracts the suckers. I don't mean suckers in the usual sense. I mean suckers that grow up around trees. Those damn little good-for-nothings that grow straight up from the trunk or the roots of the big tree. In your case, suckers have names like Saks and Lord & Taylor."

"So what do we do?" Louis said, defensively.

"Beat 'em to it, of course. Do some suckin', on your own. You got a great name, national name. Sell it. In other cities. And then, when you need to . . . why you boys get yourselves some good workin' contracts and sell out."

"That," Louis said heavily, "will never happen."

The old, tough man looked at him a moment. "Maybe not," he said quietly. "You know your business, I don't."

The subject was immediately dropped, and for a few minutes they sat silently listening to and watching the bustle of the restaurant.

Mrs. Woodward turned to Louis. "Tell me why you want such a small wedding, Louis? Are you ashamed of marrying our daughter?" But this was said lightly.

Louis was startled. "I? I couldn't care less, Mrs. Woodward."

"Katherine, please. And he is Ed."

"Katherine. This is all Karen's thinking."

Karen sighed. "We're doing all this rather soon after about two dozen parties in Texas, for one thing. I never want to go to another party again. And, anyway, last time . . ."

Mr. Woodward nodded. "Last time we beat the drums a little loud for what finally happened. The only thing missing was the Goodyear blimp. And that's only because we didn't think of it. But . . ."

And now his ice eyes softened and he turned to his daughter. "That don't mean I won't throw you a bigger barbecue than they ever saw in Texas, if that's what you want. I'll even make it an *asado* and fly up fifty Argentine folksingers. *And* hire the blimp."

"At least, I think you should have a small reception somewhere," Katherine Woodward said. "Among us all, there must be two hundred people or more who would be genuinely hurt if they weren't asked to *something*."

So it was decided that there would be a reception on the St. Regis roof. And that Karen and her mother would attend to the arrangements but that Louis, in collaboration with his family, would provide them with the Starr list. At the end of the evening, Ed Woodward put his arm

THE STARRS OF TEXAS 149

around Louis's shoulder and stopped him by the cigar stand just outside the bar.

"You know, I guess that her mother and I've done very well with Karen. She's a good girl. I suppose you think so, too, since you're marryin' her."

Louis laughed. "True."

"Well, I thought I'd tell you how we did that. From the time she was three feet high we gave her every goddamn thing she wanted, and when she didn't tell us what she wanted we made some guesses. She ought to be the most spoiled little bitch God ever brought forth. Now I don't see that, do you?"

"She knows what she wants. But no, I don't really see that."

"What I'm sayin' is, you might. It's probably there somewhere. Her mother and I shouldn't have been that lucky. See, we're simple people. We never knew what to do with a beautiful child except make a princess out of her. Princesses notice peas in their mattresses, so I've heard."

"What are you trying to say, Ed?"

The old man thought for some moments. People went past them, to and from the bar and upstairs, and occasionally a voice rang out, "Table for four in the bar for Mr. Ringling." The husky man at the door examined cold-eyed the people coming into the restaurant for signs of drunkenness or other undesirable characteristics.

"What I'm tryin' to say, Louis, is that Karen never once has reached out for somethin' she couldn't have. If she should do that—well, you might have another of your famous tornadoes down there."

"I can give her most of what she wants. I think."

"Most," the old man said, heavily, his face now sad. "Some things no man controls. Some things a person wants, only God can give him. Or her. And He ain't always in a givin' mood. For instance, I wanted a boy worse'n just about anything in the world and Katherine did her best. But after Karen, there were two stillbirths, both boys, and you see, there wasn't anything Katherine could do about that. And for God's part, He may not've been so keen on why I wanted a boy. I wanted to leave my name on that company I founded. Thirty years ago, I could've set up things so when the sellout came . . . as it had to sooner or later . . . my son and I would've done the sellin'. And he would've had the management contract, just like I was talking about you boys a while ago . . ." His voice trailed off and he was silent for a moment. Then he smiled and his blue eyes lit up. "Well, if you can't figure a way to give her what she wants, I reckon the best way is to figure a way so she don't want it. And what's more, I don't know what in hell I'm talkin' about anyway. Let's join the ladies and have a nightcap somewhere."

THE ST. REGIS LIBRARY is really two rooms, the larger of which is lined with real leatherbound books and has a certain warmth most banquet rooms do not have. It leads into a smaller room for dining. Since there would be no dining, the bride and her father came out of the small room into the large room where they met Louis and Adam, his best man, and Rosalind, Karen's matron of honor. "I suppose," Karen had said, "that if I ask Claude your family will think I have no friends at all. And anyway, Ros is an old pal of all the Starrs as well as me."

The music for the occasion was supplied by Joseph Krutcher, a ranking concert pianist and a friend of both Louis and Adam. He played Bach.

A circuit court judge, Mr. Woodward's contribution, conducted the ceremony. White calla lilies in one lovely old urn borrowed from one of the store's Gift Shops were the only flowers. Karen was dressed in a pale-blue silk jersey dress with a softly full skirt, but with a top that curved with her figure gracefully. The dress set off dramatically her black hair, graced for this occasion by a single gardenia. Her eyes were clear and bright and her face had more color than usual; from excitement and from the glass of champagne she had had with her father before entering the main room. Ed Woodward gave her away, and the entire ceremony took less than twenty minutes. The men were in dark suits, no cutaways, and the women wore suits or dresses like Karen's. There were fewer than twenty people at the ceremony, most of them Starrs (Nancy and Bobby had come down from college) but with a few friends of the Woodwards as well. Adam supplied the ring, ordered the opening of the champagne and gave the bride her first kiss, a very light peck on the cheek, before everybody in the room kissed her.

She felt gay and a little giddy. She took another glass of

champagne, Taittinger Blanc de Blanc, took both of her husband's hands, leaned back smiling at him, burst out laughing for joy and fell forward into his arms. She had been, she thought, a lovely bride.

And then there was the reception on the roof.

"I think we should have something old-fashioned about the whole thing," Karen had said to Louis. "I think we should be married at two and have the reception a tea dance from three to five."

"Tea!" he said. "My brother Bernie will faint."

But she didn't, of course, mean to serve just tea, though it was available along with everything else it is possible to drink. The St. Regis waiters passed all the food, flaky hot hors d'oeuvres, potato balls filled with caviar and a variety of things which could be nibbled at all afternoon. Plenty of tables filled the room, but there was also ample space for dancing, and for this Peter Duchin's orchestra played. The guest list had grown to nearly three hundred and fifty, but the room held them well, and since it was a brisk, clear day, people wandered about the windows of the old roof, scene of a hundred debut dances since shortly after the turn of the century, looking out at what view was left from this spot, once the tallest hotel in the city of New York.

Adam danced with Karen just after his brother had whirled her around gaily.

"You dance better than I remember," she said.

"We have more room here. You should see my open work."

"Not like your son's."

"Nobody dances like my son."

Bernie cut in. "Will you dance with me again?" she said to Adam.

"Of course."

"I have something I want to talk to you about," which she didn't really.

"All right," he said cheerfully, and walked off, his jacket flying. Even for his brother's wedding, Adam could not remember to keep his middle button closed. He always looked as if he were going to take off his jacket and sling it over his arm. She noticed that he found his daughter and began to dance with her.

"You know something?" Bernie said. She was nearly as

tall as he was and his face was flushed. He had been after the scotch early.

"What?"

"I'll bet there aren't three brothers in the country who have wives as pretty as ours."

It was the best he could do and she loved him for it. She drew his head close to hers and began to hum with the music: "Just One of Those Things." Music her father could dance to. Dancing school music. The music she remembered as a small girl and that she had wished to be played on her wedding day.

"Dear Bernie," she said.

He laughed. "Just like a teddy bear, I know."

"Why don't we get some champagne or whatever you want?"

"Sensational idea."

And so she began doing her rounds with Bernie, while Louis danced with Claude. Photographers snapped her with many people. They already had dozens of pictures of herself and Louis. But the crowd was varied and interesting. There were businessmen with whom her father or the store dealt, many designers (nearly all of whom had brought their models since their boy friends had not been asked), theater people somebody knew, painters and sculptors (some her friends, some Adam's, a few Louis's), a number of gallery people, some old school friends of somebody; and the columnists and their photographers had plenty to do. It was probably, Karen reflected with a good deal of amusement, the poshest second marriage of the year; month anyway. She drank more champagne. And then she came to Jenny, who sat at a table with her father and had before her a glass of champagne and a plate of delicate little finger sandwiches.

"You got my letter, Jenny?"

The old woman's dark eyes gave nothing away. "Of course, my dear."

"Was it all right?"

There was something so anxious in Karen's voice that Jenny took her hand and gently pulled her down so that she could put her head next to Karen's. "It was a lovely letter," she said softly. "You are just fine. We are going to love . . . we are going to be very close, you and I."

And Karen put her arms around her thin shoulders and

hugged her. "I always wanted us to. Even by the pool. When you were testing me."

Jenny, nodding, moved the skin of her face against Karen's.

"We were testing each other," she said. "You and I will know what has to be done."

When Karen's face came away, her eyes had tears in them. She smiled gaily and plucked the white handkerchief from her father's breastpocket. "That's what fathers are for," she said.

By late afternoon, Karen was, for one of the few times in her life, a little tight. And reckless. And it occurred to her that Adam had not after all come back to dance with her. She searched the room with her eyes, could not find him, and so began to wander. She found Claude and hugged her for no reason and was hugged back, but did not find Adam. On a hunch, she went to the house phone and rang his room. The line was busy.

"Making money," she thought, wryly. "On my wedding day." And this irritated her. He ought, she was sure, to be present—with her—on this occasion.

She said to Louis that she was going to her room for a moment and he offered to go with her and she said not to bother. She took the elevator down to the eleventh floor and walked straight to Adam's suite. She knocked at the door.

"Just a minute," he called out. When he came to the door he was in his shirtsleeves. His eyes were suddenly astonished. She thought he looked like God in a white shirt.

"You didn't come back to dance with me," she said.

"I would have." He indicated the telephone. "I had it in mind to come back. Just a few calls . . ."

Karen felt herself grow moist between her legs. At another time, she would have turned and left. Done something. But he stood there, waiting for her to speak, long and lean and surprised, probably her enemy, and she said, "Oh, Adam . . ."

It was only a step between them. He took it and his hard arms were around her and he sank his lips against hers and his tongue deep into her and his penis was hard against her wetness. She pressed with all her might against him and gave him back all she knew how with her mouth. She felt that if he went on long enough, she would have her orgasm standing up, in a pale blue dress, and that he too would spill all over himself and her. But he pushed her away sharply. Apart, touching nowhere, they stared at each other. His mouth was still slightly parted. To her surprise, so was hers. She ran her tongue along her lips. Both of them were breathing hard.

"Almighty God," Adam said.

"I must," she managed to say, "get back upstairs."

The words seemed to shake him. "Of course," he said. Then, briskly, "I'll be back up in a few minutes. For that last dance."

She turned and nearly ran to the elevator. Upstairs, Louis was dancing with someone she did not know, and she went up to them rudely. "Do you mind if I cut in?" she said, lightly. "I haven't seen my husband almost since I married him."

And began to dance with Louis. "I love you very much," she said.

He held her close. The wetness came no more, but was sticky against her thighs. Adam returned but did not ask her to dance. She understood. She had no more wish than he to mention what had occurred between them. It was gone, banished. That night in bed, she did things to Louis she did not know she could; amazed him; gave him the greatest night of sex he had ever known. And when it was over, she said to herself, as her husband slept, "Forgive me, God."

On the following morning, Karen Woodward, a free woman, began life as Mrs. Louis Starr.

# PART THREE

# 1

WINTER CAME early to Ramsey that year. The blue northers roared down from the Panhandle one after another,
starting in early December, dropping temperatures thirty
degrees or more in an hour. Finally in January, snow and
ice hit, throwing the city into chaos. Texans have no idea
how to drive in snow, few own snow tires, buses are
hours late or don't arrive at all, and cities seem in one
long, endless skid.

Karen found it funny. "They won't give up," she said,
laughing. "They get on a hill and start to skid and ac-
celerate and everybody else is doing the same thing and
they all look like children's tops spinning."

"It also absolutely kills business," Louis answered,
ruefully. "We might do eighty thousand on an average
day this time of year. Yesterday we did twenty-three. We
could close up."

"Why don't you?" she said with mischief. "I wouldn't
mind having you home all day for a little while."

He smiled. They were having a good time together.
They had taken an apartment on top of one of the high-
rises overlooking the lake and were taking pleasure in
doing very little to it. Karen simply painted it white, or
most of it, and they combined the paintings they owned
and thus had walls done by some of the better young
artists of the world. Meanwhile, they were entertained.
Endlessly.

"The thing that baffles me," Karen said, "is their endur-
ance. After all, no matter who gives the party, you see the
same faces."

"So far," Louis said. "This is the *crème de la crème*
entertaining you. And they have to do it and we have to
do it because they're all good customers of the store.

156

Eventually, you'll start meeting people who've never set foot in Starr's."

"They exist?"

He laughed. "You haven't even really met 'Texans' yet. I know at least four writers, six or eight artists, three of the greatest chili cooks in the world and at least fifty sensational yarn spinners who wouldn't be caught dead in the store. What we're doing now is our duty dances. So, in case you're impressed with our desirability, are our hosts."

Karen made a face. "And I thought we were so devastating."

"You are."

At most, though not all of the parties, Adam and Claude were present, at some of them Bernie and Becky. Adam, Karen thought, was superbly gracious; and said not an honest word to her during her first months in Texas. Claude she grew to like immensely. She had underestimated her at the beginning and was prepared to admit it. Becky she felt to be gay and honest and funny, and Bernie she absolutely adored.

"What is it about Bernie?" she asked Louis. "Is it just that he's so damn sweet?"

Louis thought for a moment. "You know I think if Bernie could, he'd do something nice for every single person in the world."

"I think you're right."

BUT BERNIE could not do as well by himself, and it became necessary, one January day, for Adam to summon him into his office. Bernie sat in one of the three straight-backed chairs in front of Adam's desk, and, when he had done so, Adam rose and closed the door.

"This must be serious," balding, plump Bernie said with a grin. "We must be more overbought than I thought in my department."

Adam shook his head. "You're all right there," he said. "At least as all right as anyone else. If this weather keeps up, the whole store is overbought."

"Then what's the idea of the closed door?"

"Because you're my brother and I love you and I don't want the world to hear what I'm about to say. It's not pleasant."

Bernie's face looked suddenly frightened.

"Did . . . did Abe Weinstein talk to you?"

"No. Abe would never do that. I talked to Abe."

"Why?"

"Because the people who did talk to me, or rather to Bill King, were the people from the bank. They told us how much you owe them—one hundred and thirty-seven thousand. Practically all of it gambling debts."

Bernie looked relieved. "That's all collateralized."

Adam said, "Bernie, the biggest part of your collateral is Lone Star Electronics. And, of course, some of our own stock. Now, it isn't on the street yet, but Lone Star is shaky."

Bernie looked perplexed. "You saw their last quarterly statement, Adam. Record sales, record earnings. The stock went up."

Adam looked out of his window. "Creative accounting. Get out now, Bernie. Pay off the bank. Stay out of Vegas. Now that brings us to Abe. When I found out about the banking situation, I called Abe to find out how you stood in the gambling around here. You owe him fourteen thousand, Bernie."

"He shouldn't have told you that," Bernie said.

"He didn't want to. I forced it out of him. He won't press you. He's too good a friend. But if your name weren't Starr you'd have both legs broken by now."

"I went to the bank . . ."

"I know you did. And they wouldn't lend you any more. You can't cover any more with the collateral they want now. They want four dollars for one, and you haven't got it."

"When the stock goes up . . ."

"Or down. That's the point. Now, I have a proposition for you."

"Which is?"

"The store will cosign the fourteen thousand. That way, Abe gets paid. He's got his pressures, too, you know. You sell Lone Star and pay off the bank. We'll take the money gradually out of your salary. Over, say, one year." Adam smiled. "Unfortunately, we can't take it out of your bonus because you already owe that on your store charge account."

Bernie did not speak for a few moments. Then he said, quietly, "Well, it's damn nice of you, Adam. Damn nice."

Adam rose, walked around the desk and came up behind his younger brother. He put both hands on his shoul-

ders. "We all love you, Bernie." Then removed his hands.
"But for Christ's sake, stay out of Vegas. You drink too
much to shoot crap with those boys . . ."

Bernie said, sharply, "You know damn well drinking's
never kept me away from work."

"I know, though some days it doesn't seem so easy for
you to light a cigarette. But up to a point . . . that's your
business. I'm simply trying to say that over the long pull
you can't stay with the house sober, never mind tight."
Bernie was again silent for a few moments. "Is that all?"
he asked, finally.

Adam nodded. "Sure." He paused a moment as Bernie
was rising. "Look, Bern . . . I haven't hurt your feelings,
have I?"

Bernie shook his head. "As I said, what you're doing is
damn decent. As for old Bernie . . . I guess born the baby,
always the baby."

And he left. And Adam realized that he had indeed
hurt his brother. But when a man couldn't handle his
affairs properly and he was your own brother whom you
loved, what could you do? And Bernie would get over it.
And would at least be solvent. It had been the right thing,
the only thing to do; as Bernie had said, decent.

BERNIE FROM defiance, from defensiveness, from pride,
from whatever, waited six weeks too long to sell his stock
and pay the bank. When he did, he was wiped out. He
came that night to the big, rambling Colonial house he
and Becky had, and she kissed him as usual and went to
the bar to make him a drink, as she always did. Their
house was comfortable, unpretentious and had in it a good
many expensive things but nothing of any real value.
Becky was the sort who would spend two thousand dollars for a handsome sofa and hang a couple of two-hun-
dred-dollar prints over it. The bar was in the library and
was done in pickled pine with white trim. The shelves
held Book-of-the-Month-Club selections and *Reader's Digest*
condensations and such. There was a huge color TV. They
spent much time in front of the TV, very little reading,
though Becky plowed through a best seller now and then.
They had three servants; a cook, a maid and a butler, all
black. There was a pool table in the basement. People
liked to go to Bernie and Becky's house. It looked as
though the couple liked living in it and liked each other.

"You can make that a triple, baby," Bernie said. He sank heavily down on the sofa.

"That's what I usually make it. For the first one. Tough day?"

He said, slowly, "Yeah. Pretty tough."

She brought him his drink and only then did she notice that his face was very pale.

"My God, honey. What is it?"

He looked up at her, this boy in a man's body who hurt no one.

"We're broke, honey. That's what."

She almost whispered: "Broke?"

"I'm afraid so. I failed to take my older brother's advice. Lone Star Electronics blew it. I hear some people may go to jail. The hell with them. Anyway, the bank's paid, and the store bill will be. But they're going to be taking fourteen thousand out of our income this year. That's after taxes. And we barely make it as is, the way we live."

Becky sat down next to him. "I suppose it was the gambling," she said.

"Mostly. And parties. And presents. And our store bill. And the fact that we've been living like millionaires and we're not." He took a long drink. "And also booze."

Becky looked for a moment as though she might cry. "Oh, Bern," she said. "Will we have to sell the house?"

He laughed without pleasure. "That's so mortgaged we wouldn't get much for it. And Starrs don't go broke that way. The store'd save the house. Buy it, if necessary. Which they may have to do."

Becky was in a light pink pair of hostess pajamas which she liked and so did he.

"Bern," she said.

"Yeah, baby."

"Put your drink in your other hand and hold me." So he did.

"I don't care what we have to do," she said. "I don't even understand what happened. I don't know about Adam's advice. I don't know what happened about Lone Star Electronics, and I don't know about the fourteen thousand. And I also don't care what we have to do. We'll fire everybody and I'll do the housework. We'll never set foot inside that hateful store. I don't care. Anything. I just want you to know one thing. You've taken me a long way from when I slung the booze. And I've liked that ride. Now if we have to stop dead in our tracks . . . it's all right, honey. I love you so much. So much. Does that matter to you?"

He kissed her cheek.

"I love you too, baby. We'll make it. We'll cut down. Economize. We'll do it together."

"Then it's all right."

"Yeah. Okay. Let's have another belt. Before the liquor store cuts us off. And then we'll cut down on him, too." And they cuddled together like two hurt bunnies.

But they had had no practice in cutting down and it is a hard thing to learn.

BILL KING sat across from Adam. In front of him on Adam's desk were piles of books and papers with rows of figures to which King had been referring since four o'clock that afternoon. It was now nearly seven. Outside, the city was dark and heading into a cold January night. The secretaries had left for the day, as had most of the executives. Even Louis, who often left with Adam, had gone home a few minutes before. He had not been a part of this meeting. Neither had anyone else. King had done most of the talking for three hours, interrupted by Adam's questions and comments. He had done this in response to a request from Adam for the most complete review of Starr's business which had been done since he, Adam, had come to the store. King had submitted the written report two days before. Adam had spent two nights studying it, and this meeting was the result. The faces of both men were drawn and pale.

"So," Bill King said, exhaling with a kind of finality. "What it comes down to is that we come out with under two percent net profit on eleven percent increase in sales. What it also comes down to is that the increase in sales is dollars, which, of course, reflects further inflated prices. Transaction count is up four percent. In one of the fastest growing cities in America."

"It's all about in the neighborhood of what we did last year," Adam said.

"Not quite. We were over two last year and nearly three the year before. Also . . ."

"I know," Adam interrupted. "Transaction count. We aren't adding enough customers."

"And . . ." King paused and then looked hard at Adam. "We're fat," he said.

Adam did not reply for a moment, but looked out into the darkness.

"How fat?" he said, finally. "Three percent, five percent, ten percent?"

"Figure ten overall. Personnel, expense of doing business including advertising, catalogue, mailers, travel, etcetera. On an averaged-out sales-to-bodies figure, we have twelve percent more bodies than Saks. We'd go higher, of course, if we compared ourselves with Bloomingdale's or some other Federated or Allied store."

"The new suburban store," Adam said, as though he were talking to himself, "should help with transactions. Too many people right here in Ramsey simply are not going to come downtown any more. The twelve million we've been projecting for that store may be conservative."

"But we also aren't sure what that twelve or fifteen or whatever it turns out to be . . ."

"Will do to downtown sales. I know."

King spoke gently. "Adam, what it is, we're making less than half the profit a first-rate outfit like Federated would consider satisfactory."

"We always have lesser margins."

"Not in the early days. Not for the first twenty years. In those days, your father brought in twelve percent pretax. Sometimes more."

Adam laughed without amusement. "That was before the salaries of his three sons," he said. "And their expense accounts."

"And fewer markdowns. What he had, he had exclusively, so he bought strong. But he didn't have so much. Any time a new designer makes a success, even a flash, we think we've got to have his stuff exclusively, so we do. And we don't cut out anybody. And we mark too much down and at the end of the sales we sell too much to Filene's basement at seventeen or twenty cents on the dollar."

"We haven't really discussed the divisions individually. But I've gone over those figures in a preliminary way. I have everything at home and by the end of the week I'll know exactly what I'm talking about. But besides so-called couture markdowns, we're slow in Shoes, Children's, Men's . . ."

"Accessories," King cut in. "We're nowhere near where we should be in Accessories. Accessories are poorly merchandised. Too much overbuying, too many markdowns . . . Cosmetics is nowhere near as profitable as it is in other stores."

Adam was grim. "That's because we let the manufacturers stock it and, for that matter, merchandise it."

Both men were silent. Adam tapped a pencil against his desk and examined this movement idly.

King said, tentatively: "For those departments, maybe Louis needs an assistant."

Adam shook his head. "Won't do," he said. "Louis understands some businesses, not others. We need a second general merchandise manager. On Louis's level. Reporting to me, not to Louis."

King did not speak.

Adam smiled. "Don't we, Bill?"

King also smiled. "Of course. I just didn't want to spoil your dinner."

Adam was thoughtful. He spoke slowly. "If we cut personnel seven to ten percent across the board . . . Do you realize who goes, Bill?"

King shrugged. "Sure. Some of the ones who've been here twenty, thirty years and are still living back then. I'm not saying you can do it. I'm saying that's what ought to be done."

"The overall store markdowns were at twelve percent."

King nodded. "Should be eight or so."

Adam slumped back in his chair. "I'd settle for ten," he said. "If I didn't have to do the things I've got to do."

"I know," Bill King said. "Blood . . ."

"And marriage."

"What's marriage got to do with it?"

Adam shook his head. "I don't know. Maybe nothing. But Louis just got married, and I'd rather the first thing that happened to him was not that I cut his authority in half." He rose and stretched luxuriously. "I have some more homework to do," he said. "And I don't know when I want to announce all this. Maybe not for a few months. Or a year. Maybe gradually, maybe at once."

"You know the retail business, Adam. You can't waste too much time."

Adam looked at his closest associate for a moment, and then strode over to his window.

King broke a long silence. "I think you have to hit 'em with it all at once," he said. "Then fight out the para--graphs."

"But then, they're not your blood," Adam said, shortly. "Come on, let's go. I feel like a drink."

The two men left the office and walked briskly to the service elevator. All the customer elevators ceased running at six, but a maintenance man was available to run the service elevator all night.

"To give you one other thing to think about," Bill King said, "Riley Clark and Cullum Roberts each called within the last couple of days. They want to meet with you. Have you given that much thought?"

"I've thought about it. It hasn't kept me awake. It has a lot of minuses, running for the Council."

"Mayor. As the end result."

"Okay, Mayor. Still, it means time. And you and I have just spent three hours outlining what I'm going to be doing with time for the next hundred years or so."

"Most of the Mayors of Ramsey have been working businessmen."

"What are the pluses?"

They had reached the first floor. Outside, the night was cold and windy, and they walked briskly across the street.

"Well," King said, "as a practical man, senior vice president of Starr's and all that, I'm not so sure there are any pluses. The Council meetings kill your Tuesday afternoons, and, knowing you, you'd do your own study on the matters that came up instead of leaving things to the City Manager. So it's some work, though not quite like being Mayor of New York. But, and I may sound like Joe College here, frankly, I think it's quite an honor. For God's sake, Adam, this isn't some wide space in the middle of the road. This is a city of a million and a half and growing. It's an important goddamn city. Being Mayor of Ramsey is—something."

Adam was silent, after signaling the garage boy to get their cars.

"There's another thing," King said. He was perhaps one of the very few people who knew he could say what he now did. "You'd be the first Jewish Mayor in this city's history."

"I know. I looked it up. Oddly enough . . . I'm not really sure I know why this is true . . . that appeals to me more than anything else. The trouble with Ramsey is it's such a hell of a tight town. I wouldn't mind loosening it up. Just the fact I'm a Jew would do that. Somewhat, anyway." Adam suddenly grinned. "Of course, I might also lose."

Bill King shook his head. "You'd have to be trying. The Charter Association really does have clout and they've got both newspapers in their pocket. As well as money. The campaign wouldn't cost you anything."

"I haven't even listened to that black guy's show yet. But I will, of course."

"Riley and Cullum tell me he has no organized backing at all. At least, as yet. Not Urban League, not NAACP, not anything. But he's the biggest thing on radio. And he has more listeners than any other disk jockey in the state. He's probably the best-known black man in Texas. So he can use his program . . . And he's bright, they say."

"Which worries our friends."

"They don't want to go after him with a nobody."

Adam's Rolls came down the runway and to a halt in front of them.

"All right, Bill, set it up," he said, walking around to get into the car. "Maybe we should do lunch. The four of us. Or whoever they want to bring."

"What about Louis? Or your mother?"

Adam shook his head. "Not their decision," he said. "I'll talk to them, of course. See what they have to say."

He brought it up to Claude that night while they were having a drink, and she looked as though she had been struck. "My God," was what she said. And rose and left the living room to have Rivers make her another drink. Startled, Adam followed her out into the liquor pantry. He drained his glass and handed it to her. Rivers seemed to be busy in the kitchen, so Claude was making the drink herself. "How about making me one, too." She took it silently, made both drinks and handed him his. They walked slowly back into the living room.

"Why does it bother you?" he said, gently. She sat across the room from him on the long sofa and looked for a long time into her vodka martini.

"It's very selfish, I'm afraid," she said, not looking up.

"Well, we're all that. Go ahead."

She thought out as best she could what she wanted to say and then said it as carefully as she knew how. "I often think, even now, that I'm in the zoo," she said, quietly. "In a cage. Or else that . . . I'm a piece of merchandise. Quite expensive. Being inspected. That's always been what being Mrs. Adam Starr is like. I . . ."

She was having difficulty, and he tried to help.

"I've been aware of that," he said. "I know how hard it often is for you. And I'd give a lot to change it. But I can't. It's something we both have to live with. And you handle it fine."

"Sometimes. Sometimes not. I'm not always up to it. And there's no point in saying anything, Adam, because I know better than you do when I'm handling it well, and when I'm not . . ."

He started to say something, thought better of it and stopped. A surprising thing happened to him. He had begun by being sympathetic. He understood very well, he thought, the problems of Claude's life. Throughout their marriage, this understanding had produced within him the feeling that he was consistently just slightly in the wrong. In the wrong because he was Adam Starr, and being Adam Starr presupposed a certain type of life, a certain amount of visibility with which Claude was uncomfortable. So it was all, to his eyes, his fault. And now a deep wave of resentment passed into him. What, in fact, was *wrong* with being Adam Starr? What was wrong in leading the life he was supposed to live? He had been Adam Starr when he had first met Claude and he would be Adam Starr until he died. That was what she married and that was what she had got. The world was filled with women who would very happily trade places with Claude Starr.

And he thought of Karen. Whenever she entered his thoughts, he pushed her away as he would a physical presence. When he saw her, he was, to all outward appearances, perfectly controlled, affectionate, jocular and a fond brother-in-law. Inside, he was upset and fragmented, and suspected that she was, too. So he spent the proper time with her at parties and avoided being alone with her. Talking with her alone, he would find someone to call into the conversation, anyone. If he could not quickly do this, their kiss at the St. Regis burned his tongue and there were stirrings in his loins. At these times, he was certain she knew what he was feeling. It seemed to him that something in her face and her unwavering eyes was amused; lightly mocked him; not for feeling as he did, but for the fact that he would certainly do nothing about it. Such thinking horrified him. Most of the fear he could usually push aside, but there were times when he waked during the night and thought these thoughts. And now, as he talked with Claude about becoming Mayor of his city, he could visualize the excitement and enthusiasm Karen would feel if she were his wife; and the sudden anger he felt directed him to be unkind.

"I've told you," he said to Claude, "that I understand some of your problems. I cannot, however, bring myself to weep about them."

She looked up quickly, startled. "I didn't ask you to," she said.

"Sure you did. Are. Poor, dear Claude. Plenty of money, a fine house, fine children, travel, love, a loyal husband, the respect of the community and a thousand ways to pass the time usefully . . . but it's all not sufficient. Poor, sad Claude."

Her face and body were rigid. "That's enough," she said, quietly.

"I doubt it," he said, angrily. "It's time somebody said how very good you have it. A concept that seems to have escaped you."

"Please stop," she said, and now she was begging him. Her face was very set, her back rigidly straight. Her eyes looked harmed. Adam had never spoken to her with sarcasm before. As he realized this, his anger evaporated as quickly as it had come. In its place came waves of guilt and sadness. He had actually compared his wife to his sister-in-law. At no time, in his conscious mind, had he ever sincerely compared his wife with any woman. It was unthinkable. He rose and sat down next to Claude on the sofa. He put his arm around her and kissed her cheek. She was stiff and unyielding and her skin was cold.

"I don't know what got into me," he said. "It must have been a worse day than I thought."

"It's all right," she said, looking straight ahead.

"Of course it isn't. Please forgive me."

She was silent.

"Please, let's not carry it on," he said.

She stirred, more or less shaking off his arm, and looked at him. In the paleness of her face, there were two pink spots on each cheekbone.

"You don't understand," she said. "It's not that you were angry . . ."

Puzzled, he said, "What then?"

"It's that you're mostly right."

"Nonsense. It was a quick, silly flareup."

"As you said, I have it very good." She leaned forward and had a sip of her martini. "I'll try to keep that in mind. By all means, be Mayor of Ramsey."

After a moment, he said, "I haven't at all decided."

Without hesitation, she said, "That's what you will decide."

"What makes you say that?"

"You go wherever the lights are."

"That's not very kind."

"Not quite true either," she admitted. "You bring your own lights. I'll give you that. You'd be very unhappy in obscurity."

"You see," Adam said, slowly, "I'm not sure there's anything wrong with that. Accomplishments and notoriety have a way of going together."

Claude nodded. "No argument. As you know, I admire greatly what you have accomplished."

He then said something he possibly had never said before, and he found it difficult to get out: "And love me?"

She looked at him with surprise and then amusement. "Oh, yes," she said. "There's no help for that."

Later in the week, they dined at Karen's and Louis's apartment, the first family dinner Karen had set, and Adam, before he had made a decision, brought the matter up to all of them. When he had described the plan the Charter Association was offering and its reasons for doing so, he stopped, and Bernie said, "Well, I call that damn fine. Mayor Starr! That's one hell of a thing for this family. Hell, Adam, you might be Governor some day."

Adam smiled. "I'm afraid one has very little to do with the other."

The others at the table went on eating. Adam watched them and thought, Why am I surprised? What did I expect? And said, "I'm delighted at your enthusiasm."

Jenny looked at him steadily.

"Partly, it's a matter of confusion of interest," she said. "Arnold always found heading the store full-time work."

"Everyone on the present Council has a full-time job," Adam said. "All the past Mayors have had full-time jobs."

"No doctors and no retailers," Louis said, calmly. "One of your favorite sayings, Adam, is that retailing is the most time-consuming job there is except medicine."

"That would be my problem. I wouldn't consider this if I thought it would detract from my work at the store."

"I'm curious about one thing," Karen said, slowly. "Isn't the Mayor of anywhere supposed to take political stands?"

"To some extent," Adam said.

"Well, in the months I've been here, both from talking to people—or rather listening to them—and reading the newspapers, I'd say this is one of the most reactionary cities in the United States. But these aren't your politics at all, Adam. If, as Mayor, you start saying a lot of things you believe, isn't that going to make you very unpopular in the city? And wouldn't that hurt the store?"

"The Mayor isn't expected to make statements about national and international policies," Adam said. But he realized he was on the defensive. His back stiffened.

"Karen has a point," Louis said. "It's not just one thing. It's a whole outlook. You've been shooting at the political system around here most of your adult life. Complaining that ordinary people are never heard. Now, suddenly, you become the symbol of that system."

Adam shook his head. "I don't disagree with most of what the Citizens Council has done. I've often helped them do it. I've been critical of the private club atmosphere. As Mayor, I'd be in a position to let a lot of air into that club."

"Then why do they want you?" Karen said. "You sound like trouble to me."

"They think on most serious things we'll agree. That we have the same basic interests. Assured growth, new hotels, the new airport, the merchandise marts . . . In such matters, we do agree. So do all of you."

"It's a principle," Karen said. "How this is done."

"No one seems to have brought in the idea that this is public service," Adam said. He was now angry. "Something good people have always aspired to."

Bernie, looking bewildered, said, "Well, that was my point. Look at the Rockefellers. That was what they trained their boys to do. So I've read. We've never had a Mayor in this family. Or a Councilman. Or a dogcatcher, for that matter."

Jenny looked at her youngest son. Her eyes were bright. "That's very important, Bernie, what you said. There is much truth in it." Bernie sat back in his chair, looking pleased. Jenny looked at Adam with a hard smile. "You could honestly say, Adam, that this is something your father never did. I can make that even better for you. He was never asked to do it."

Adam's face felt hot. He supposed he was flushing. Before he could speak, Karen continued the attack: "Do you know anything about the man you'd be running against?" she asked.

Adam shook his head. "Not yet. Just that he's a very popular disk jockey. With a big following."

Karen was leaning back loosely in her chair and the mocking expression was in her eyes; something like the look she had at the times when he wanted her, but now there was no relieving, answering want in her face. "That's his job, not him. Do you know what he thinks?"

"Obviously not," Adam snapped. "Nobody's started campaigning yet. He's said nothing publicly. I've never met the man."

"Why don't you?" Karen asked. "It's at least possible he'd be better for the Council than you. For your own reasons. Letting in some new voices. Airing out the place. He might even be brilliant." After a moment's silence, Claude said calmly and clearly: "Adam has never touched anything he hasn't improved. If that is wrong, will one of you give me an example? Just one."

To this there was silence.

"Thank you," Adam said. The heat had left his face and his anger was now controlled. "I seem to have given the wrong impression," he said, quietly. "I seem to have given the impression that I am asking my family whether I *may* run. That is not true. I'm discussing the matter with you because I'm always interested in your views. Interested. Not directed. Emphatically not. Now, I gather, with the exception of Bernie, you're all negative. I confess that dismays me. I should have thought you'd be pleased. It is an honor. The highest, in fact, this town can give. What I'll do about it, I haven't decided. When I do, I'll do you the courtesy of letting you know."

Karen laughed. "Oh dear, Adam, we've upset you!"

"Surprised me," he interrupted.

"Whatever. Of course you'll do what you want. And

I'm sure it will be the best thing for you." She added mischievously, "And for the city. But this is my first family dinner and here we are arguing. Couldn't we change the subject?"

They did easily enough, but the sourness in the air never really disappeared and the dinner party broke up earlier than would be normal. Jenny was the first to leave. Adam would not have left first if his life had depended on it. Before he did leave, he found himself momentarily alone with Karen at the bar.

"Why are you so against this?" he said.

"Because it's an ego trip." There was no mockery in her eyes at this moment. "And you know it."

"What if this had been offered to Louis?" Adam said.

She smiled. "I would have scratched the eyes out of anyone who stood in his way."

Adam now also smiled. "You don't lack the competitive spirit," he said.

"Neither do you. If you're worried about yourself, don't be. Your last little speech was vintage Adam. Fuck off, brethren, you said. Very properly, too. As you know, not one of us except Bernie was being honest. Jenny was thinking of Arnold, I was thinking of Louis and Louis . . . I imagine he was thinking of me thinking of him."

Adam laughed. "I will go and meet this disk jockey," he said. "That much I promise."

"What's his name?"

"He calls himself Tiger Kirk. Real name's Stacy."

"Then call him by his name. Either one. Not 'that disk jockey.' Your arrogance is one of your charms, but not that much of it."

His good humor remained. "Sorry," he said.

She looked at him steadily and he did not turn away.

"We're off and running, you and I," she said, unsmiling.

"Yes, we are," he said.

Claude now came over and took his arm.

"It's getting late," she said.

# 2

BEFORE CALLING Stacy Kirk, Adam listened to his program. He discovered quickly that to refer to Kirk as only a disk jockey was erroneous. It was true that he played records, but he seemed to use the music as filler. The rest of the time he spent talking. He read excerpts from newspapers and magazines aloud and commented on them, sometimes humorously and sometimes seriously. He also read aloud passages from books and then reviewed them, briefly and intelligently. A great deal of time was also consumed by answering telephone calls from listeners. Often, the calls were from people who just wanted to talk; lonely people who wished to hear another voice in response to their own. His own voice and laugh rasped into the microphone like those of a man who's never had a cigarette out of his mouth. Yet the tone of the show was gentle. He would be a habit with his listeners, Adam felt; he was good company during the sad hours.

When Adam telephoned him, Kirk seemed stunned at the sound of his name. But he agreed to meet for lunch a couple of days later.

"You want me to come down there?" Kirk asked.

"Not necessarily. Why don't I come out your way? It's been a long time since I've been west of the Viaduct."

"That's funny. I been east of it lotsa times, but it seems like I always gotta come back. Jus' like a magnet was drawin' me."

"I'll see you at twelve-thirty at Red's Charcoal Pit," Adam said, shortly.

The Viaduct crossed from downtown Ramsey into the broad western suburbs of the city over a diffident stream named by optimistic early settlers the Great Fork River. Now and then, after a few days of rain, it vaguely resembled a river, but for most of the time it was a trickle, and nearly dry in the hot summer months.

Once across the Viaduct, one arrived almost immediately at Red's Charcoal Pit. No investment had been made for decor, except that the charcoal grills were exposed behind a semicircular low wall of red brick. There were tables in the middle of the room and booths around the perimeter. As Adam entered, the restaurant was nearly full. Most of the clientele was white, but here and there, Adam saw a table of blacks. There were few women in the room. It seemed to be a white-collar workingman's lunch place. He asked an official-looking fellow at the door if Mr. Kirk had come in.

"Tiger?" The thin balding man pointed over to a booth in a corner. "Over there."

"Thanks."

Adam walked over to the booth. A thick-set black man wearing a short, neatly trimmed beard was reading some papers. He had short, curly hair peppered gray and black, and he wore a green jacket, tan pants and an open-necked green-and-white-checked shirt. Adam had seen pictures of him in the advertisements the station placed for his show. In these pictures, he seemed to be laughing maniacally and his arms were always raised in what appeared to be a kind of victory salute. The headline was always, "Stay Up with Tiger"; obviously many people did. When Adam arrived at his table, he was studying some typed papers and smoking a cigarette.

"Stacy Kirk?" Adam said.

Kirk looked up and smiled. His eyes were set close together and rather squeezed by the pudginess of his face and his smile gave his wide, thick-lipped mouth the look of a quarter moon.

"Well, hello there, Mr. Starr," he said in the trade-marked rasping voice that seemed to be one of the points of his appeal. "I am truly honored." He half rose from his position and offered his hand, which Adam took. "Please sit down."

Adam did so, saying, "I'd heard of this place."

"Pretty good barbecue," Kirk said. "And the best hot fudge sundae in town. With whipped cream and nuts." He patted his stomach. "With a tire like this, there ought to be a law against me eatin' 'em, but I do. And you can, acourse. You have no weight problem." He looked down

at the typed papers in front of him. "I just been lookin'
at some new commercials we got. Apartment houses. You
know how they sell apartment houses these days, Mr.
Starr?"

"What kind of apartment houses?"

"The kind that looks like Miami Beach from the outside and has a pool that's full of beer cans every mornin'
and that calls itself the Beachcomber or the Luau. In five
years it's fallin' down. No quality. Well, the way you sell
this kind of apartment, you promise anybody who takes
one—indirectly, of course—he or she is gonna make it
with every other soul in the apartment house. You are
practically guaranteein' that this will happen."

Adam smiled. "Does it?"

Tiger Kirk shrugged. "Some places, I guess it does," he
said. "But you know, it's a funny thing. It's part of my
contract in some of these commercials I got to make PA's.
Like when they open the pool. Or the club. They all got
clubs so at least you can know the name of the people
your lease guarantees you're gonna ball. An' what I see in
some a these projects, they get all the winners. Beautiful
young people who I guess spend every night fuckin' up
a storm, jus' like my commercials says they will. And
others, they get the losers . . . the thin an' the fat, the bad
skin, the no-hair, the sad faces and the fake laughs, the
talk too muches and the talk not-at-alls. It's like radar.
And I tell all these fucked-ups it's gonna be a new life,
and for most of 'em, it's not."

"Does that make you feel guilty?"

Kirk looked thoughtful. "In a way it does, yes. Those
folk are the ones that call me most during the show. All
the beautiful ones, they may listen, all right, and the sur-
veys show a lot of 'em do, but they got better things to
do than call me up in the middle of the night. It's the
fucked-ups that do the callin'."

"You handle them well."

Tiger Kirk's little eyes widened. "You listen to the
show?"

Adam said, "I've listened to pieces of it. Sections of
shows. It goes on a little past my bedtime. You do a
good job."

Kirk nodded. "What I'm doin'," he said, "I'm makin' a
place for people to be. Not just a sound, a place for 'em
to be. See, anybody who's got the radio on late at night

listenin' to me, well, you can bet wherever they are they'd rather not be there. Whoever they're with, they'd rather be with somebody else. If they're alone, they can switch on the dial and they're with me. And I'll stay up with 'em till they fall asleep. See, they don't *know* anybody else'll do that. You oughta see my mail."

"You get a lot of it?"

"A whole lot. Mostly grateful. Some kinky." Kirk laughed his growling laugh. "We got a lot of kooks in this world."

"And insomniacs."

"You fellas ready to order?" A faded blonde waitress in a soiled white uniform stood over them. She looked at Adam curiously, clearly trying to place him. She did not give Kirk a second glance. Apparently, she knew him. Adam looked at Kirk questioningly.

"Like barbecue?" the black man said.

"Sure."

"What I usually have is a barbecue beef sandwich and a barbecue ham, a glass of chocolate milk and hot coffee later. It's a good lunch an' it isn't too much."

"Okay," Adam said, looking at their waitress. "I'll have exactly that, please, ma'am."

"Tiger?" she said.

"Same. Like always." When the waitress had gone away, Tiger Kirk looked around the room. "In this part of town, it ain't too usual for a black man and a white man to sit down to eat together. Folks look up when that happens."

Adam almost said something. He almost said that it was no longer unusual for blacks and whites to sit down together in Ramsey. He did not, because while the races did sit down together in meetings, white and black men did not sit together casually.

Kirk now lit a cigarette and said, quietly, "Why'd you come out here anyway, Mr. Starr? I could prob'ly guess, but I'd kinda like to hear you tell me."

Adam did not at once reply. He picked up his knife and played with it. Then he said, "I was curious about your announcement. That you might run for the Council. We live in the same district, which maybe you didn't know."

"That's a big district. I knew you and your Pa were in it. It jus' goes to show what a mixed-up district it is. It's hard to believe the same dude could represent on the Council where you live and where I live. Considerin' the way we live is so different."

"The district is twenty-eight percent black, about eleven percent higher than the rest of the city," Adam admitted. "And nine percent Mexican-American . . ."

Kirk laughed. "And one millionth of one percent Starrs. Golden Starrs."

Adam said evenly, "I'm still curious about your running for the Council."

"Well, there really isn't any good reason I should answer your question, you know. Why I'm runnin', that's my business, wouldn't you say?"

The waitress brought them their sandwiches. Kirk began eating immediately. The restaurant had become jammed and noisy. On one side of it was a counter, and people, black and white, were three deep waiting to be served. The waitresses sang out their orders to the cooks. "I got two rib plates cookin'," one yelled. "Where's my rib plates?" "Comin' up," yelled out one of the black cooks, "keep your pants up, sister." But in general, the motions were fast and accurate and the counter people ate quickly and moved on. No lingering over coffee.

"Sure it's your business," Adam said. "You don't have to tell me a damn thing if you don't want to."

Kirk shook his head, chewing on his food. When he had swallowed it, he said, "I got nothin' against tellin' you. I'm just wonderin' why you care. But I reckon I can say it in a hurry. The City Council of Ramsey is a bunch of rubber stamps for a group of about a hundred businessmen who are very fat cats. An' outa that hundred is a dozen that really counts. Every man on that Council is owned by one dozen very big businessmen."

"There's a black man on that Council."

Kirk laughed. "Jus' sunburned, Mr. Starr. He's backed by business 'cause he's a builder, and he owes the white banks and the white insurance companies every damn thing he's got. An' he gets the zonin' he needs, why hell man, Tom Estes gets more zonin' variances than most of the *white* builders get in this town. He ain't a man, he's an ornament. So's Ramsey can say it's got a black Councilman. Lemme ask you—what'd Tom Estes ever do for black people?"

"You'd know that better than I would."

"Yeah, well the answer is, nothin'. Look, we're supposed to have integration in this town, right?"

Adam nodded.

"Then how come every school in the county is damn near one hundred percent white or one hundred percent black? Because the livin' places where the schools are, they're all black or all white."

"So what's your solution to that?"

"Busses."

Adam smiled. "That's a dirty word."

"An' it'll be a dirty word for five years, ten years, forever maybe, if nobody starts yellin' for it right now."

"You'd have demonstrations, maybe even riots."

"Maybe. I doubt riots. But somethin's gotta happen, Mr. Starr, or the kids'll grow up separated just the way I did. An' they won't have any education and no skills. Just like I hadn't. And they won't get the jobs, jus' like they don't now. I was lucky. Most niggers are not lucky. Fifty years from now, Ramsey'll be just like it is, only the fat'll be fatter and the hungry'll be hungrier."

Kirk looked at Adam steadily. He wiped his mouth nervously with his napkin. Adam had no doubt that the man felt what he said. His little eyes were bright; the emotion of his words was in them. "When I was younger, I worked at a lotta things from night watchman to bartender. I went to Ramsey College at night. I took English an' history an' accountin' an' elocution. Took me four years, nearly five, to do two years' work. I got so I could write and speak in different ways—educated enough and also back-country black. I ran the mail for that radio station for two years. I did part of a newscast. So they gave me a shot at the show I got now. Why? They thought a black would pull his own people. Well, I did, but I also pulled some of yours. And I'm successful." His face changed and he showed bitterness: "But I got the same black ass, Massa Adam Starr, and this town beats the shit outa black asses every day, just like it always has."

"So you want to run on race," Adam said quietly.

Kirk nodded. "Mostly," he said. "Not all the way." He put down his napkin and sat back in the booth. "I've been doin' the talkin'," he said, quietly. "Isn't it time you told me why you care?"

Adam did not hesitate. "Some people here want me to run against you," he said.

Kirk blinked. "I thought you'd just come to talk me outa it," he said, softly. After a pause, he chuckled. "Well, I reckon this is quite an honor. I guess they must figure I could get some votes, hey?"

"You must have thought so yourself."

"Yeah, well, I thought I'd get some votes all right. But I never expected to win. Hell, I ain't got no money for a campaign. A real campaign. They pay me pretty well at the station 'cause the show makes money. An' I expected to pay for some advertisin'. And acourse, I got the show itself. But I always figured the Charter'd find somebody who could beat me. You know, Mr. Starr, right now at least, some of my own people'd vote Charter. They wouldn't take a chance on me—I'm a nigger, no better than they are—I couldn't be good enough for the Council. I wouldn't've won. But they really thought they hadda get Adam Starr to run against me? Well, well. Are you gonna do it?"

"I haven't decided yet. That's why I came out. To help me decide."

At first, Kirk looked astonished. Then, he smiled. "Oh, I see. I'm bein' interviewed. Like for your butler." He laughed and, once again, he seemed bitter to Adam. "Well, pull mah pud, like those white crackers out in the little towns say."

Adam was silent for a moment, then spoke evenly. "Do you," he said, "for example, know what a bond issue is? When to call for it, what for and how much? And about interest rates? Do you know anything about land and air use, how you go about getting state and federal money, what for and how much? Do you know what the city's rights of annexation and condemnation are, how you go about building a new airport . . ."

"No," Kirk said, angrily. "Not yet. Not all of that anyhow." Some other people in the restaurant stopped eating and looked at them curiously. "But I'll tell you what I do know. I know that five years ago, when that old Northwest Highway was finished, it made so many twists and curlicues, it looks like a corkscrew on the map. But it touches every bit of property old man Carpenter owns. Old man Carpenter was president of the Citizens Council then. Funny coincidence, ain't it? And I know I was raised in Riverside. That's ghetto, Mr. Starr. And I had eight brothers and sisters livin' under one roof, so's we could hear our folks fuckin' and fartin' and we were listenin' and eatin' beans. And another thing I know is that I pull in about one hundred thousand a year and there ain't no place in this goddamn city where I can build a house 'cause they won't sell me the land."

"Yes, they will," Adam said, calmly. "You haven't looked in the right places."

"Why should there be any wrong places?"

Adam shrugged. "I'm a Jew. There are clubs that don't ask me to join. You seem to have the feeling if you got on the Council you could suddenly buy a piece of property any place you wanted."

"I could blow all over the Council meetings if they didn't sell me. I could give the newspapers and the TV people quite a show."

"You're an amateur," Adam said, flatly and unkindly. "The papers and the TV people wouldn't touch you. They're your natural enemies. They *are* the establishment."

"Then I have my own program."

Adam, expecting this, kept the harshness in his tone. "If you used your program to campaign, to attack your opponent, for instance, you wouldn't have a single local advertiser within two weeks. Because a local advertiser suddenly wouldn't be able to get a bank loan if he touched your program. And the agencies that place the national ads would be informed that it would be in the best interests of their clients to turn you off. You'd be well on your way back to those tar roofs, back into those shacks where in the summer time it must get to be a hundred and forty degrees. And left in peace to raise your own fuckin', fartin' children and feed 'em beans."

Adam stopped. He was not angry, though he had meant to sound so. He had simply wished to hit very hard early on. He had wished to take the wind out of his opponent, to shake confidence, to suggest fear, to instill the notion of disaster before the fight began. Now, as he looked at Kirk, he did not think he saw defeat in the black man's face. "Do you still want to run for the City Council?" Adam said, without compassion.

After a long time, Kirk nodded. "I'll run. More now than ever. Just so you'll have to. Just to get you into the muck of it."

"Muck doesn't bother me."

"I might just beat you, you know."

"You might," Adam said. "I doubt it. Too much going against you. Like you said yourself."

Stacy Kirk said quietly, "You'll get some of my voters, Starr. But lemme tell you, I'll get some of yours too. Some whites'll hate a rich Jew even worse'n they hate me. And I'll get more niggers than I'd thought. They *hate* rich Jews. And also *poor* Jews."

Both men were now silent. Adam sipped on his coffee and found that it had grown cold. He pushed it aside. Kirk drummed a spoon against the table. When he spoke, he did not raise his eyes.

"If you didn't run," Kirk said, slowly, "and the folk did elect me, would that be so bad? Why would it be so bad, Mr. Starr? It's not as if I did time. Don't molest little girls. Are you gonna tell me it's because I'm a nigger? Because I won't believe it. That ain't what they say about you."

Adam considered for a few minutes before he spoke.

"If I run against you, it'll be because I think I can be more effective than you. I grew up in this town and I was born knowing who to go to for what and all the buttons to push. I represent one of the city's major taxpayers. And one of its major attractions. You have no power base. And you have too much to learn."

"I'm not dumb, Mr. Starr," Kirk said, but he was tiring. "I can learn fast. And I can explain a lot on my show . . ."

Kirk stopped short: he seemed to know what was coming.

Adam sat back in the booth and examined the other man steadily. "Gordon McAdee, who owns your station, is, I'm sure, very happy with you. Gordon would be happy with anyone who brought in bucks. Gordon needs bucks. He has a mixture of business interests, from real estate to bowling alleys to an expensive and not very successful restaurant. All of his enterprises are in Ramsey, as are his bank notes and his mortgage . . ."

Kirk said, almost whispering, "You told me all that already. You got the money and the organization. I ain't got nothin'. Only my show. So you tell me if I use my show, you an' your friends'll lean on Gordon till I ain't got the show."

"That's it," Adam said.

"And the papers won't give me the space. And the TV."

"They'll give you space. They'll be against you in their editorials, but they'll give you space. Some space."

Kirk said, slowly, "You seem to be a real bastard, Mr. Starr."

Adam shrugged. And then, looking at the pudgy face in front of him and remembering it had been pulled from a black womb under a tar roof with eight brothers and sisters looking on, he did at last feel compassion. Adam knew he was capable of being as rough as he had to be, so his performance on this afternoon did not surprise or dismay him. But, as he looked at the bulky figure across the table from him, it seemed to Adam to have diminished. Kirk looked not only smaller, but he seemed to be slumping against the back of his seat as though it were the ropes of a prize ring. Adam had begun to leave but he felt suddenly that he was leaving the scene of an accident. He hesitated for a moment and then said, "There's some money in Ramsey you can get. There are people here who hate the men who run this town. Probably including me. They'll spend to hurt. They'll help you."

"Help me?" Kirk's laugh was weak. "I don't even know who they are."

Adam waited a few moments, thinking, doubting, then pulled a pad out of his pocket and a Mark Cross gold pencil. He wrote in his usual hurried scrawl. When he had jotted down a dozen or so names and business affiliations, he tore off the sheet and put it on the table in front of Kirk.

"Here are the names of some men who would do nearly anything to hurt the Citizens Council. By and large, they're rich men who could have been a lot richer except for the Council. What they wanted to do was either illegal, immoral or not in the best interests of the city. So the Council thought. They're bitter. If you can persuade them you've got a chance, they'll give you money."

The black man did not say a word, nor raise his eyes to Adam's.

"So long, Kirk," Adam said, rising. "See you on the stumps." He stuck out his hand, but Kirk did not take it. He was still staring blankly at the list of names when Adam rose and walked briskly out of the restaurant.

At home, Claude asked, "What did you say?"

"I said, they're taking a hell of a chance. A lot more chance than they usually like to take."

"Who?" Claude asked.

"I was thinking out loud," he said.

"What about?" She sat down on the sofa with her martini and again curled her legs under her.

"I probably think more like Stacy Kirk than I do like Cullum Roberts," he said. "When they make me Mayor, they'll be taking a risk. They don't control me."

Claude's eyes widened in mock astonishment. "Is that so? All night, you've been sounding like they did."

"Have I?"

"Talking about power. Burying Stacy Kirk. You know how to get things done and he doesn't. Etcetera."

"That's all true."

"All right, so it is," she agreed. "And you've admitted the ego involved. That's not an issue any more. It's just a fact. Which some people may not forgive. Just tell me one thing."

"What?"

"All the things you used to want to do about this city. Will you still want to do them when you're Mayor?"

"Yes."

"Will you succeed?"

"No. But I won't be ignorable. I'll establish beach-heads. I'll give the liberals—nearly half this city—a voice they've never had on the Council before. And, for whatever it may turn out to mean, it'll be the voice of the head man."

She did an odd thing for Claude. She reached over and took his hand and kissed it on the palm. And said, smiling, "Then I guess I'll vote for you, after all."

# 3

ADAM CALLED Cullum Roberts that night and told him
that he would run. Roberts sounded very pleased and the
two men agreed to meet soon, for the election was not im-
minent. And Adam had other work to do. With Bill King's
detailed analysis of the past-five-years business pattern
and his projections for the coming five years, Adam began the most exhaustive investigation of his own business
he had ever undertaken. He did this by himself, consulting no one. Since his days were filled with the usual
run of meetings, merchandise and advertising presentations, touring of prominent visitors through the store (and
selling them en route; Adam was expert at this) and
every-day paper work, most of this special project was
done at night. He had breakdowns made for him of the
productivity of every salesperson in the store, listed in
descending order, and short analyses made of their clientele books by the Customer Relations Department. He
compared bound copies of the advertising for one, three
and five years back with the store's present efforts. And
found of course that, as volume had increased, so had
advertising space; and to a greater degree. He pored
through the records not only of the main merchandise divisions, but of the departments within the divisions, so
that, on paper at least and allowing for what he knew
himself of market variables, he had a shrewd idea of the
skills of every buyer in the store. He analyzed selected
buys from individual vendors, especially in the high-
priced departments where markdowns were traditionally
high, and found that purchases varied little year after
year whether the particular line was outstanding, mediocre or terrible. Because of its desire to offer as much
merchandise as possible on an exclusive basis, the store

had trapped itself into buying heavily from so-so collections whose designers had done well before and might do well again. You couldn't simply cut them off in a bad season, was the theory. They would go broke or sell elsewhere. But the practice of this theory led to inflexibility and shocking markdowns. He also analyzed markup ratios. While the store maintained about a forty-eight percent margin, he discovered that on foreign buys, where much of the merchandise was exclusive in the entire state and where risk potential on high-priced goods was great, the markups were essentially normal; they should be much higher. The greater the risk, the greater the markup was the cardinal rule.

Nor was this the only area in which he must fault his brother. As King had suggested, a number of potentially profitable areas of the store brought forth nothing like the return on investment they should have. Louis's basic interest was fashion apparel for women. The other divisions of the store represented annoyances to him. The need for an aggressive, skilled independent general merchandise manager for these divisions was clear. Adam's study turned up no one then employed at the store who seemed ready for the responsibility. That meant a search on the outside. Mentally, Adam put aside at least one hundred and twenty-five thousand dollars a year for the man he wanted; high, but you always had to pay more to attract a first-class man to live in Ramsey, Texas. Starr's in itself was an attraction, but Ramsey, as a place to live, was still the sticks. So, he would have to pay. And that meant further cuts in present expenditures. The only nights when he did not work on all this material were the nights on which they had engagements. During those months, he had no relaxation, and he grew tired and looked haggard. For the first time in his life, he was not sleeping well. One night, Claude asked him, concerned, "Adam, what on earth are you doing every night? You're going to be sick."

"Preparing for war," he said, grimly.

The great difficulty was that his studies showed him, incontrovertibly, that major personnel changes had to be made. Arnold and Jenny Starr had built a small personal business into a large personal business. Veteran employees were not just employees, they were friends. Some of them had called Arnold by his first name and still did Jenny.

Emma Goldman was a case in point. Adam had known Emma since the days when he was in grammar school; as a child had called her Aunt Emma. She had always been a particular friend of Jenny's; now that Arnold was dead, she was perhaps closer than ever. Adam was very aware of this. But Emma was living in another era. Emma Goldman would have to go, as would all the other Emmas still hanging on at Starr's. He felt sick as he came to understand what he had to do.

As he considered this, the matter of his mother came to Adam's mind. Jenny Starr, as chairman of the board of Starr's, contributed nothing. It was difficult enough just to get her to the monthly board meetings. She was too busy in fitting rooms. There, she was a brilliant saleswoman. She was an extraordinary "loader." When a woman who had come to Starr's to buy a dress left with just that dress, Jenny considered she had failed. She was a genius at building a sales ticket; two or three dresses, a proper coat, shoes, bag and jewelry, often a fur when the traffic would bear it. Saleswomen with vacillating customers automatically brought her in to consummate multiple sales, even though they knew that she might well undo whatever initial sale they had built.

"That dress simply isn't yours," she might say to a wavering customer. It was the wrong collar, the wrong shape or it was not fitting properly. "Let's start over." And might end up selling a less expensive garment, then loading it with expensive accessories. But it would be, in fact, right. Jenny's credibility depended on unselling as well as selling, and she knew it. She kept in close touch with Bob Hardy, the credit manager, during the course of many major sales. Hardy guided her, sometimes after a couple of quick calls to banks, as to whether she was getting a woman in over her head. And she had an advantage no saleswoman at Starr's could match. If a woman said, "My husband will kill me," Jenny often simply asked for his telephone number. "This is Jenny Starr," she would say on the telephone. Men were flattered to get a call from Jenny Starr; instant status. "Betsy and I have picked out some things that we both think are absolutely beautiful on her. They're the basis for her whole fall. I'm convinced you'll approve or I wouldn't sell them to her. It's going to cost three thousand dollars and change, and Betsy is worried that it's too much. Is it? Tell me truthfully. We can do a good job for less, though not as good." The ego of nine men out of ten approved the sale at once.

When Jenny had to cut down, she still often came back to the customer with an allowed figure of double what the customer had expected to spend. She was a superb sales directrice. She made one hundred thousand dollars a year, not including her dividends; more than double what a great sales directrice was worth.

There was, of course, nothing to do about that. A more serious problem was perhaps her influence in the markets. She covered religiously the high-priced markets in New York and Europe, skipping California because she considered that market beneath her. While she bought nothing herself, her conservative taste influenced all buys to a greater or lesser extent. The younger ones were probably helped by her in that they learned quickly about quality standards and good taste. They did not buy gimmicks, flash fads or gussied-up merchandise. In almost any good store, the acute fashion eye would spot a percentage of merchandise which is mediocre in style and quality. Starr's had little of this. What was missing in the stocks was a strong enough sense of contemporary flair; news; excitement. All these elements were present in the store, and they were shown in the windows and the advertisements and the fashion shows. Starr's *looked* as contemporary as any store. But Adam did not feel that the look was backed by dollars. As he prowled through the stockrooms, he kept coming away with the feeling that the power of the store's fashion position was in what had sold well yesterday. All big stores, he was aware, are plagued by the same problem. It is insane to be putting millions of dollars into what you think will be good tomorrow. All bets must be hedged. Only the little boutiques can afford such a luxury, and many of these will die after a single lost bet, one bad season. It was a matter of balance; certainly adjustable. But it was Adam who would have to adjust it. Louis was too like his mother; too much the child of yesterday.

When he had assimilated all the information he could in Ramsey, Adam prepared to go to New York. Before leaving he did an interview with *Newsweek* on the theme of second-generation takeover of a world-famous institution. Scrupulously, he referred the reporter to Louis and to his mother with regard to their responsibilities; even arranged that he dine with Karen and Louis. Then he left. He spent the business part of a week in New York, nearly all of it talking with vendors in most of the areas of the store's business. When it was clear he was seeking frankness, they were frank with him. Allowing for old friendships or suspected personal animosities, the broad picture he got of the Starr's merchandise people could be very closely equated with the information he had dug out of the figures. When he returned to Ramsey, he hired an outside graphics firm to prepare some graphs for him and worked with these people for the better part of another week. When this was done, he was prepared, as well as he ever would be, to enter into the first battle of what he was well aware might prove to be lasting war with his family. But he did nothing for many months; months during which time marked them all with the strife of another year.

"Why not?" Bill King asked him.

"I keep hoping," Adam said, "that Louis will come to me."

"He won't."

Adam looked out his window. "It's just so . . . goddamn sad, you know?"

Bill King looked at him with great kindness. "Take your time, then, Adam. Maybe Louis will come to you. And maybe it will snow this July."

## 4

AT FOUR o'clock on a cold, gray afternoon, Adam walked into the Eatwell Cafe. Five men sat at the counter drinking coffee. They were workingmen on a break or non-workingmen killing time. None of the booths was occupied except the one nearest the kitchen, where three black waitresses sat, smoking and talking listlessly. In an hour they would be busy with the early beer crowd, and then dinner; it was the kind of place which closed at nine o'clock because it attracted only lower-middle-class people who lived somewhere around it. It held no attraction for the visitor.

Adam sat down in one of the booths, far enough away from anybody, and one of the waitresses came and took his coffee order. Just as she went to get it, Abe Weinstein arrived and seated himself opposite Adam, shaking hands with him absentmindedly as if he had forgotten that one shook the hand of a friend. He also ordered coffee, and when each man had his cup and the waitress had gone back to her gossip, Adam asked: "Why didn't you just call me?"

Abe shook his head. "Wasn't as simple as that," he said.

"You said you found him. Positively identified him. You had the money . . ."

Abe interrupted: "Adam, I don't reckon you ever did anything like this before and won't again. But when you do it at all, then you have a responsibility."

"Which is what?"

Abe said, wearily: "To know exactly what happened. Don't always come around the way you planned, see?" He reached in his pocket and pulled out a small newspaper clipping and handed it to Adam. It read: "The body of an unidentified black man was found last night beaten to death in an alley near Lamar and Houston streets. Police have no clues, but theorize that the motive may have been revenge since the sum of twenty-two dollars was found in the dead man's pocket."

When Adam spoke his voice was not much more than a whisper. "That's . . . what I said shouldn't happen."

Abe nodded. "Couldn't be helped. We found this guy through a friend of his here in Ramsey. Goes by the name of Chigger. My boys, they was quite a time even findin' this Chigger, who ain't no bigger'n one, they say, and he chirped out . . . after some persuasion . . . where his friend was. Which was New Orleans." Abe gave a half-smile. "New Orleans draws a lot of queer ones, Adam, I don't know why. Always has. Well, they tracked him right to the address Chigger had said, and got to look at him. Then, one night, out on the streets, they as't him if his name wasn't Donald Duck. When they said, 'Donald Duck,' that nigger turned white. So they had him. But he was big and strong, Adam, and there was a tussle. Very mean, and it's good we had three men on him. Now that's what I mean by responsibility, Adam. You got to take into account the human element. My men was havin' this hassle, and gettin' hurt themselves. They just plain didn't know when to stop. Or didn't wanna, or whatever." Abe shrugged. "So that's it."

"Police . . ." Adam began, and suddenly found himself unable to continue.

Abe looked at him with his icy eyes set in the improbable kindness lines around them and his mouth. He smiled. "The body of an unidentified nigger in New Orleans don't make much of a never-mind, Adam. And even if somebody can put a name to him, my boys is long gone and, for that matter, ain't nobody knows they was there in the first place. We're all safe, Adam." And then suddenly, Abe's eyes lost their coldness. "Adam, don't you lose no sleep over this, hear? You had the best reason there is in this world to waste a black man. The very best."

And Adam, going slowly from horror to puzzlement that such a strange occurrence as murder could have been a part of his life, came to the conclusion that an even stranger one had been, indeed, the rape of his daughter: the rape of the daughter of Adam Starr. And he began to understand better that there is nothing, nothing at all, a man can count on. Accepting this, after a time, he did begin to sleep again.

# PART FOUR

# 1

As DIVISIONAL merchandise manager of the Men's Store and of furs, Bernie never overruled his buyers. He often questioned them, in his studies of their figures and of their stocks, but he did this only to learn as much as he could about their operations so that he would not be totally blank if Louis or Adam asked him a question. Understanding this, the buyers were kind to him and taught him as much as they could about their businesses. They were all fond of him. In the case of the Men's Store, Bernie was sometimes even helpful. He had taste and a good eye for putting ties with shirts and handkerchiefs with ties. He knew the difference between flair and vulgarity. He understood quality and he was a good salesman to his numerous friends.

In furs, Joe Fox was especially thoughtful of him because in this merchandise category, Bernie was helpless. He did not even have the knowledge of the educated consumer that he had in Men's. So Joe Fox taught him. He took Bernie into the New York market and let him watch while he made his decisions and then went into the complicated financial finaglings involving rebates, merchandise and promotional allowances, rancher tie-ins, consignment shipping and other factors which seemed to enable Joe Fox to buy for less than most other stores would have to pay, but to sell at premium markup. Not that his manufacturer ticket price was any lower, but there were all those allowances that other stores did not get. As far as Bernie could tell for a long time, the power and influence of Starr's in the volatile fur industry was such that any manufacturer would sell the store on an overall break-even basis, just to get his merchandise accepted by Joe Fox. Since Fox then turned around and sold the furs at top retail prices, it therefore followed that Starr's must often be making nearly one hundred percent markup in its Fur Department. Bernie was fascinated by Joe Fox's machinations in the market, a factor which persuaded Fox, a man of sufficient ego, to allow Bernie to be present at nearly all of his triumphs. It also did not hurt to have a Starr present at the negotiations. With family blood sitting next to him, Fox could press even harder than he had before. Bernie's presence, unperceived by Bernie, took away a bleeding manufacturer's last resort: appeal to the Starrs. Bernie watched all this with awe.

"The funny thing is," he said to Fox one night, "they all seem to like you."

"Sure. Why not?"

"Because every time you come into a show room, those guys go on the rack. When you leave, they haven't got a gold filling in their head."

Fox grinned. "Sure they have. They also have big Cadillacs and swimming pools in Great Neck. Or they're in Chapter Eleven, depending on what year it is. That is the fur business. But even in Chapter Eleven, they usually manage to keep the swimming pool. Then times get better. Don't forget, they use me all over America."

"How do you mean?"

"What Joe Fox buys, everybody tries to buy. Where Joe Fox goes, everybody goes. Me and a few other guys —Bergdorf's, Magnin's, Saks, Marshall Field—we're the signals. We direct the market. Stick with me, baby, and I'll make you a star. Ho, ho, that's a good one."

Bernie and Joe Fox grew so close that Bernie became one of the few people at Starr's (and the only Starr) to know about Fox's double life. Bernie not only knew about it, he participated in it. Joe's women always seemed to know other women and the four of them spent many nights on the town. A good deal of drinking was done. On some mornings, Bernie found totally unfamiliar faces on the pillow next to his. He also found himself shaky and in need of a restorative. Such mornings were nearly always Saturday or Sunday; on the week nights, the two men were more circumspect in terms of both hours and drinking. For the bad mornings, Fox usually had a bottle of vodka in his room. When the girls had awakened, a gathering would take place at which, over screwdrivers or Bloody Marys, nerves were quieted and good humor restored. Brunch would follow, after which, the party would disperse until that evening. Joe Fox paid all the checks, all the time. Bernie assumed he somehow finagled this money out of his manufacturers, too. He had nothing but admiration for Joe Fox; loose, sharp.

One night, shortly after one of their trips, Bernie mentioned Joe to Louis, as they were both walking out of the store.

"He's got to be the best fur buyer in the world," Bernie said.

"I wouldn't be surprised," Louis replied, without much interest. "That's his reputation."

"The deals he makes."

"What deals?"

"With his vendors. When he gets through with his twisting and turning, we must make a hundred percent net profit."

"I wish we did." Louis was still unconcerned. They were crossing the street now to the parking lot, and the wind was chilly, blowing down from the North. Their breath came out in white steam puffs.

"Well, we must make a hell of a profit. Counting promotional allowances and everything."

Louis shrugged. "About normal for a store like ours. About the same ratio as other stores of our type. We do a better volume, of course, and a lot of it is in high-priced goods. So it's a good operation."

"But the expenses must be very low against it. I mean, advertising, fashion shows, windows . . ."

"Well, I imagine the other top stores get advertising allowances. As far as fashion shows and windows go, I don't know what you're talking about."

Bernie had heard in the market sums of money guaranteed by vendors in return for use of their merchandise in major fashion shows and window banks. He said nothing. In a few moments, Louis's car was driven up. "Good night," Louis said.

"Good night." Bernie waved absently.

He was slow but not catatonic. With the bits and pieces of information he had, he began to study the figures for cost of goods versus the retail prices. He checked what he had heard of the promotional allowances against the advertising which actually ran. He figured space cost and the highest production figure that was remotely reasonable. He looked into national advertising, of which the Fur Department did a good deal. He found that the store had been paying half the space cost of such ads, at least half of the production (photography, models, engraving, etc.) and sometimes the entire cost. In other words, the Fur Department was getting about the same amount of vendor participation for promotion as other departments of the store. It was a perfectly reasonable operating procedure. No one would question it. The only thing was, it did not check with what Fox had told him, what he had heard and seen and what he had therefore assumed to be true. By the time he had finished his work, he knew solidly that much of the money he had assumed to be coming back to Starr's was instead going into Joe Fox's pocket. No wonder Joe picked up all the checks. No wonder about the Cartier baskets with the large bills in them. No wonder about the swimming pool and the tennis court on his property. Bernie could not figure how much Joe was taking, but it was clearly a lot. He also could not prove absolutely that he was taking anything. He did not know how the vendors kept their records, but he assumed Joe took his cut in cash and paid no taxes on it. Whatever he took was therefore roughly double in value to the actual amount. Bernie was quite aware that kickbacks were a part of the retail business, as they were of many other businesses. He took no moral stance on this. Bernie did not take moral stances. Whatever people did was all right with him, so long as other people were not being hurt. Kickbacks, so far as he could see, hurt no one. It was a part of the manufacturer's cost of doing business. Nobody had to kick back money. When people did, the business was worth it to them. That was the world, in Bernie's view. If somebody had explained to him that substantial kickbacks create a false price structure on the net and retail levels so that the eventual loser is the consumer, he would have said that that price structure was actually the real one. What was prevalent was right; everybody did it.

So Bernie had no criticism of Joe Fox. He simply wanted in.

He wanted in because he and Becky could not live on what he now made after the subtraction of a thousand dollars a month off the top to pay his debt to the store. In real after-tax pay, he now had less than $2300 a month. $680 went for mortgage payments and taxes. $400 went for cook, maid and gardener, another $600 for groceries and nearly as much for liquor and wines, for they gave a lot of parties and would not have known how to live had they not. This was all before Becky had bought a blouse or Bernie a tie; before they had had a single meal in a restaurant, a single drink in a bar or lost $50 in a poker game. Prior to the sale of his Lone Star Electronics stock, the dividends from it plus the dividends from the store stock had left them about even for a given month. With the exception of the heavy gambling. After the payment to the bank, they no longer took the trips to Vegas. He explained to his friends that he now had too many business pressures, and they believed him.

But other things—liquor, restaurants, clubs, giving parties—he could not have escaped had he wanted to. He had his end to keep up. No more, but never less. He was going into the hole more than a thousand dollars a month. The bills now had the word "Please" on them, underlined. He got phone calls. There would be no more bank money. He had no real market for his stock except for his own family. That, of course, was unthinkable. He continued therefore to move inexorably toward bankruptcy. He did not know how to change his life. It was the only life he had ever lived. He did not know people who were poor. The minimum standard of living for Bernie was the millionaire's standard. He might actually be a millionaire someday if his stock came to have true market value. That was off in the haze of the future. He could use the word "broke" about himself to himself, but it had no real meaning. Starrs were not broke. They were not broke because they were blessed. But he could not pay his bills. Nor could Becky help. She had come too far from a single-girl apartment to go back. She was as trapped as Bernie. She had forgotten how not to spend money.

So Bernie wanted a piece of Joe Fox's action. He told Becky what his study of the Fur Department operation had revealed. She laughed. "Old Joe!" she said. "Good for him. What would happen if anybody found out?"

"He'd be fired."

"Why?"

Bernie shook his head. "In a store like ours, it's like breaking all Ten Commandments at one time. My father might have forgiven stealing from the store. Like for temporary insanity. But he fired two buyers during the time I'm in the store for kickbacks."

"How'd they get caught?"

"Vendors squealed. That's two buyers in nearly twenty years got caught."

"Do you think many of them do it?"

"I don't know. More than two in twenty years. Parts of the fashion market are used to payoffs. They're a cost of doing business. Also in the fur industry. Not everybody. Some people."

"What are you gonna do?"

"Talk to Joe."

Becky was silent. They had had dinner and were sitting in the den having a nightcap. Normally, they would be watching television, but Bernie had said he wanted to talk about something. Now that he had, she only stared down into her drink until he said, "Why so serious?"

"I'm scared, Bern."

"Right now, as of this minute, the only one to be scared is Joe."

"You wouldn't do anything to Joe."

"He doesn't know that."

Her eyes opened very wide. "You mean you'd threaten him? Unless he lets you in?"

"He may think that. But I can explain it to him."

"Don't let him think you're threatening him."

"I won't. I promise."

"Will it be a lot of money?"

"I don't know. I don't know how much he takes. I don't know how we'd split. I'll just have to talk to him."

"He might be mad. Even after you explain to him."

"Maybe. But I'll tell him if he can't do it . . . really can't . . . then we'll forget about it. Forget we even talked. But if he can . . . we can use it."

Again she was silent, and he did not speak himself. Then, to his astonishment, he saw that tears had squeezed out of her eyes and rested on her cheekbones. He went over to her on the sofa and hugged her. "Don't cry, honey, please."

In a tight voice, she said, "It's only that we never did anything bad before. Not really bad."

"I don't know how bad this is. Half the world seems to do it."

"It's breaking the law. You read about it in the papers."

"Maybe I won't talk to Joe. Just let it go."

"Suppose Adam found out."

"Joe must have been doing it for years. After I figured it out, I thought of the kind of money he spends. That home of his. The bread he puts out on the trips. Nobody's ever found out. In the industry he's king. And Adam thinks the world of him. I know that because he told me so when he gave me furs. He said he thought Joe Fox was the best fur buyer in the country. Joe must have been on the take then."

Becky's tears had stopped. "Can you talk to Joe, and then if it doesn't sound good, back off?"

"Sure."

"Maybe you can't. You have to make it very clear you're not threatening him."

"I can do that. Joe and I get along. Buddies. What I'm doing, I'm really doing him a favor. I can put it that way. He can't be mad at that. And if he can't work it out, he can't. That's all. Or won't. I guess that's all right, too. I guess . . . he'll know I won't blow any whistles."

"God knows we can use the money."

"We have to do something. I don't know if this is it but we got to do something."

On the fifth floor of Starr's, Bernie's office was perhaps thirty feet from Louis's, no more than fifty from Adam's. No art hung on Bernie's walls. Instead, there were pictures of celebrities, many of them photographed with Bernie, some at the store, some in Vegas, a few in New York. There were people in show business, some at the top, some in the middle, and they were all autographed. Bernie scarcely knew many of these people, but he had met them all; been with them for an evening, part of an evening, a few moments, long enough for a picture. These pictures and autographs were important to him. Bernie Starr would never be a celebrity, but he had met a few and that helped some. Otherwise, his office was very plain; solid walnut and black vinyl chairs and a long vinyl couch with tweed cushions on it. On the credenza behind his desk were photographs of his father and mother, Adam, Louis, Claude, Bobby and Nancy, the latter two at ten and twelve respectively. He would soon ask Karen for a picture and it would go up with the others. Bernie was proud of his family.

In this office, with all the Starrs staring at them, Bernie closed the door late one afternoon, after he and Joe Fox had been through a session on open-to-buy, sat down on the sofa across from Fox, stared at the floor a moment, and said, quietly: "Joe, I need money pretty bad. Can you help?"

Joe Fox looked at him in astonishment. When something surprised him, Joe's eyes seemed to widen innocently and often with his vendors. Like Bernie, Joe Fox figured Starrs did not need money. And he was certain that Starrs did not borrow money from their employees. To give himself time, he nevertheless said, "If you mean you want to borrow a little bread, well, hell, Bern . . ."

Bernie was looking at him, and Joe Fox could see nothing in his face but the same old Bernie. No calculation, no trickery. Joe Fox was a poker player. He read eyes well. Bernie's eyes said he didn't have much of a hand.

"Wouldn't be any good, Joe. And I couldn't pay it back anyway."

So now Joe understood. And his mind raced while his eyelids dropped a fraction.

"Whaddya got on your mind, Bern?"

Bernie took a deep breath and exhaled through his mouth. "All that stuff about allowances, rebates, all that shit I been hearing in the market . . . Well, I figured it out, Joe."

"What did you figure out, Bern?" Joe Fox's voice was steady. Within him, his pulse was now very quick and he thought Bernie must hear his heart beating. Because, of course, it was possible that he was sitting still in this office to be murdered. But not probable. Not the way it had started. He just had to play it very cool.

"I know you're getting a cut."

"A cut of what?"

"The business we do with our manufacturers. You get a percentage. You're on the take."

Joe Fox was looking at him steadily. The thought that he might be wrong flooded over Bernie and terrified him. But he was in it now; no way to turn back.

"What kind of cut you figure I'm taking?" Joe Fox said in his steady voice. He had not even blinked.

"I don't know."

"You have proof of this?"

Bernie shook his head. "No clear proof."

Joe Fox nodded. "Bernie, you know I like you very much. We've had a lot of good times together. So why don't we forget you ever said anything like that and go on like it was before."

Bernie shook his head. "What the hell, Joe, it won't stand up, you know that. If the store . . . Louis or Bill King or Adam himself ever got into it, it'd fall apart. It'd be wide open. It'd just take one push on one domino and they'd all fall down."

Joe Fox hesitated. "That what you have in mind to do?" he said, finally.

"Of course not."

"Why not? It's kickbacks. Kickbacks is illegal, immoral and whatever. It is possible to serve time for kickbacks, giving or taking. Or at least big fines."

"Joe, for Christ's sake, I'm not the cops. I don't care, understand? If I thought it was hurting the store, well, that's one thing. But you're running the best fur operation in this country . . ."

"The best. Volume and profits. In high-priced goods. An honorable business. We don't rip off customers. Somebody buys a fur here, it's the best. Half the fur operations in this country, they're ripoffs. Not Starr's."

"I know all that."

"So, why are you mentioning this, Bernie boy? This is a big fire you are playing with . . ."

"I want in."

Joe Fox looked suitably shocked. "Want in? Bernie Starr wants in on the take? From our sainted vendors?"

"I need it. And I know it's possible."

"Possible, possible," Joe Fox said, irritably. "What's possible? I don't even know what you're talking about. What if I said that?"

"It's not true."

"Who's saying it's not true? You are. Bernie Starr is, but Bernie Starr has got no proof. Bernie knows about the fur business exactly as much as Joe Fox told him. No more. Bernie Starr could possibly be sued if he brought charges like this out in the open because they are certainly slanderous. Bernie is a very good example about how a little bit of knowledge ain't worth a shit."

But now Bernie was getting angry. "Listen, Joe," he said, "I'm not interested in all that crap. You're the buyer of furs and I'm the merchandise manager. Every order you write up I initial. I think Louis doesn't even look at these orders and I know that Adam doesn't. With furs, you and I are like on an island where nobody comes. My brothers don't wish to embarrass me by checking everything we do, you and I. I'm supposed to be checking that myself. Now this business is doing very well, which is why nobody pays any attention to it. We are a team. I didn't know much about the fur business when I came into it, that's correct. I will never know as much as you do. But I know when everything isn't kosher. Which it is not."

Joe Fox interrupted him. "What you are telling me, Bernie, unless I'm reading you wrong, is that unless you are getting some skim from this operation, you're going to call in your brothers. And we will have a big Scotland Yard investigation."

"I didn't say that."

"Is that what you mean?"

Bernie took a big breath. He remembered that he had promised that he would not threaten Joe. But he said, because he was pressed and unsure, "Maybe. Maybe not."

"Do you think your brothers would believe you instead of me?" Joe Fox said. He immediately regretted saying it. He had overplayed his hand. He started to speak, but Bernie, sighing, was first: "They'd have to. I'm their brother. The only way they could not believe me is they'd have to prove me wrong. I wouldn't have to prove me right. You see, Joe? See how it is?"

Joe Fox rose and walked over to Bernie's window. Looking out of it, he said, "How much do you want?"

"How much is there?"

"I might be able to skim fifteen thousand. Maybe twenty."

"Whatever there is."

"Would that help you?"

"Yeah. A lot."

"You'll have to go to the people with me, you know."

"Why do I have to do that?"

Joe Fox turned back to him, seemingly angry. "Because

I want that you should get your hands dirty. This will mean that the percentages will change. I do not wish that my friends think I'm simply taking more for myself. I want them to understand that I'm not lying to them when I tell them we're cutting in our friend, Bernie Starr. I want Bernie Starr in the flesh to be sitting there with me. So there is no doubt."

"Okay."

"We will be in New York in three weeks. We'll go and call on our people then. Okay?"

"Sure."

"So there is nothing more to talk about now."

"Well, one thing . . . Whatever you said, I was not going to Adam. It was never in my mind to shoot you down."

Joe Fox shrugged. "You see, Bernie, that I have to believe. I have no choice. You understand, we both know, that you cannot prove what you say. You have only suspicions. You could be trapping me into this. When we go to our friends, you would have your proof. Then poof, goodbye, Joe Fox."

"Why would I do that?"

"To make points, maybe. It doesn't matter, I have taken what you say on faith and our friendship. What you're referring to is not unheard of in the fur industry. Also in the ready-to-wear industry. And construction. And purchasing of any kind. You are now in the fur industry and it's probably right that you should get what there is to get in that business. So be it. Good night, Bernie."

"Good night, Joe."

"He says it will work out," Bernie said to Becky that night.

"Was it bad?"

"Not so bad, no."

After a pause, Becky said, "Bernie, if we didn't need the money and you knew this about Joe, what would you do?"

"Nothing."

"You wouldn't blow the whistle?"

"No. It doesn't hurt anyone. Joe is good for the store. He's also my friend. I would never have mentioned it. Which, Adam would say, is also a crime . . . I know, but I don't tell. So I'm committing a sin either way."

"I'd like us to be very careful about money. Like now, we still don't go to Vegas. We leave Abe Weinstein alone, too. We can cut out the gambling. We already have. Maybe we can get a little ahead with this help. And you can get out and leave it all to Joe. In a year, maybe, tell him he did us a favor when we needed it. Now we don't. That'd please him very much. And me."

"I like that, honey. I would like very much to get out as soon as we can."

"I know," she said. "I love you and I think you're very brave. You hated to do it, you're not built to be a gangster, you lie lousy, even, but you did do it and it'll help us. I'm proud of you." Becky laughed. "Now that you're a crook, you're even sexier."

On the following morning, Joe Fox called Samuel Rosengarden from his home, and explained what had happened.

"This news does not please me," Samuel Rosengarden said. "I don't like it."

"Listen, Sam, look at it this way. This man's name is Bernie Starr, Sam. Not Harry Schlotz. Starr. You own a Starr, Sam. That is money in the bank."

"Joe, the more people who get into the act, the more people can sprain an ankle so the whole act falls down."

"Bernie isn't gonna sprain an ankle, Sam. The day the axe falls on Bernie, that's the end of his life, not just his job. All he's got, he's a Starr. For a Starr, there's no such thing as disgrace. Caesar's wife or whatever it is."

Joe Fox could hear Samuel Rosengarden's sigh over the thousand miles. "There is also the matter of the money," Samuel Rosengarden said.

"I expect our buy to be up in terms of dollars, Sam. In dollars, not garments."

"So your own prices . . ."

"I will have no problem. Everything is going up, Sam. We are not talking about major increases, anyway."

"You are already running the highest sales ticket in the country."

"I have plenty of company in that league. You know my company, Sam, those buyers are all your friends, just like I am. I will bring Bernie in to see you in three weeks, when we are in New York."

"Why does he have to come in?"

"I want him in the water with us, Sam. Right up to his neck."

"That is sensible, Joe. I will see you in three weeks."

Joe Fox then called the four other vendors who paid him money and told them the same thing. They had no serious objections. He expected none. In the fur industry, Joe Fox was God. And now he was God with a Starr in his pocket. Which was also Joe's way of thinking. A man on the take lives always with the fear that a giver will squeal. Most of the time it does not happen because the giver is in as much trouble as the taker. But it can. Somebody possibly could squeal on Joe Fox. Nobody in his right mind was going to squeal on Bernie Starr. Because the Starrs would kill to protect their name. Or at least Joe assumed they would, and so would the people of his market—a thought that had occurred to Joe Fox on the day Bernie entered the fur business. If he was going to have to be working with an idiot, he might as well be working with a useful idiot. Which now, he was.

## 2

ONE OF the reasons Nancy had selected Taunton College in Massachusetts was that there had been few blacks at the school she had attended in Texas and a strict quota of Jews. All forms of injustice infuriated her and had all her life, and so she had gone East, where she expected to hear the liberal, caring voice more clearly than she had ever heard it in Ramsey. So the recurrent dreams she had that winter were ironic, as well as terrible; chase dreams. Sometimes it seemed to her that she had committed a crime and that the people after her represented the law. They were hooded figures, like Klansmen, and she could never see their faces. The evidence against her was apparently overwhelming. There was no question of her guilt; she was aware of it herself. But of what, she never knew. In the dream the pursuing posse drew closer and closer, sometimes from one house to another, through back streets unlit except by the moon, across bridges, up hills and down into valleys. She was running like the wind, but they were catching up. She awoke just before they reached her. At other times the dream was basically the same, but the people pursuing her were familiar and they were the lawbreakers, not she. She simply owned something they wanted. It was a trophy, or a piece of paper, or a secret. As the chase went on, the familiar faces, school friends, professors, people from the store all turned black. Before the end of the dream, the familiarity had gone from their faces and they were only unknown black people. In this dream, they were not in hoods, but in exotic costume: buccaneers, armored knights, cardinals in red robes and circus aerialists. They were villains and she the chased princess. Or a nun, perhaps. It did not matter. When she awakened from either dream, she was terrified and shaking and afraid to go back to sleep. Sometimes, she moaned, and she would wake in the arms of her roommate, Jennifer Martin.

"It's all over now, honey, Jennifer's here," she would say and hold Nancy's head to her breasts until the shaking stopped. Then she would sometimes make them both a cup of hot chocolate and they would sit and talk a while in their pajamas. On some occasions, when Nancy's fear would not go away, Jennifer would climb into bed with her and hold her until they both slept. Jennifer knew about the night six black men with funny faces had raped Nancy. This, Nancy's junior year, was their second as roommates at Taunton, a smallish (twenty-five hundred students) college in the Berkshires. There was little they didn't tell each other. Jennifer was the golden girl of the campus. She was nearly six feet tall, quick, funny, energetic, tawny and bright, which made her fellow students, male and female, envious but impressed them and also the faculty. She had come from Los Angeles, land of golden girls, and had crossed the country to escape it. Her father was a motion picture and television writer. "One night," Jennifer had explained, "I must have been about seventeen, we were out at Chasen's for dinner. The most repellent, pockmarked, sleazy, sinister, subhuman ape stopped at our table. He had a redheaded girl with him who was falling out of her dress and so bombed he was half holding her up. 'I may vomit,' she was saying, trying to sound like Tallulah Bankhead or somebody. She was his wife. When they left, my father said, 'Great guy, Manny, a real sweetheart.' My mother said to him, 'That was the most horrible thing I ever heard you say, Harry.' But she really didn't get through. He'd forgotten the difference. I thought maybe I would, too, so soon as I could I got out."

Yet Jennifer wished to be an actress. "If I'm any good, I'll end up right back where I started," she had laughed. "And think Manny is a 'real sweetheart.' But never fear, Nance. Ever since Gary Cooper died, all the leading men in Hollywood are five foot two. The best they could do is paw at my navel. I'll never make it."

But she worked stock every summer, painting scenery and sewing costumes, and, once, owing to the star's illness, had played Amanda for a few performances in *Private Lives*. Nancy had seen her and she had been electrifying; brilliantly stylized and funny; but a head taller than the Elyot. Anyway, did it matter? It was their junior year in college. One had The Goal. But perhaps not the final goal. There was time. Nancy wanted to be a lawyer. Or did she? There was time.

They were an impressive pair, the one all bright and smiling, the other dark, serious and with a snapping mind. Nancy stood at or near the top of all her classes and Jennifer could have done nearly as well had she bothered to study the subjects which did not interest her, such as mathematics. At the end of every semester, Nancy sat up with her by the hour, cramming into her head enough information to pass her math; which she just barely did. But in English literature, American drama, political science, philosophy and French, Jennifer needed no help. Neither girl went out much with Taunton men on dates. Jennifer had a friend in the Yale School of Architecture and sometimes went to New Haven for a weekend with him. Once or twice, Nancy had gone along to be with a friend of Jennifer's friend. But it was awkward because Jennifer and her friend slept together and that left Nancy at the end of the evening saying no to young men and feeling rather left out. Or, once or twice, yes, which left a bad taste in her mouth. In her previous life, Nancy had slept glancingly with two men, one over a period of weeks, the other over one weekend; the first, when she was seventeen, the assistant conductor of the Ramsey Symphony Orchestra, married with two children, who could see her after certain rehearsals and always have her (and himself) home before one o'clock; the second, a young writer she had met on a weekend in New York and had never seen or heard from again. Neither had been a particularly scarring experience. Worried during late adolescence that she might be indifferent to sex, aware that her peers indulged in it more often and much more casually than she did, she had been pleased to find that she enjoyed it, but did not seem to be obsessed by it. She was, she thought, a cool girl in the modern sense of the word. She had not been sad when the young conductor left Ramsey for the same job with the Pittsburgh Symphony. He had initiated her into something for which she was grateful, he had been gentle and considerate and careful, and he apparently cared for her. But he had no excuses to be out after one o'clock and neither, really, did she, though she supposed she would have had the guts with her parents to do anything he wanted, had he been free and had she wanted to enough; neither of which was true. The young writer had been disappointing. On Friday night he had seemed irresistibly funny, self-deprecating and intelligent; by Sunday afternoon he only seemed lackluster and his conversation had gone flabby. She had smoked a lot of marijuana. She had been glad to get back to college.

After the days of shock and hysteria following the rape, Nancy had seemed to recover. For most of the year, she herself thought so. Back at school, rooming again with Jennifer, working hard, laughing a lot, in the main enjoying herself, she was unaware of any continuing trauma. But then, so long afterward, the dreams started. "Everybody has chase dreams," said Jennifer. "Original sin or something. We're all running away. We're all guilty and we all want to be caught."

She sat on the bed, smoking. Jennifer smoked incessantly; three packs of Pall Malls a day, smoked through a long green Dunhill holder. "When you're six feet tall, you have to gag it up," she had explained. She also wore men's buttondown shirts open at the collar, and expensive slimline slacks. Most of the students wore jeans, so Jennifer never did. "And you should wear skirts, Nance. Soft, full skirts, below the knee. And silk blouses and at least two sweaters and ninety-dollar shoes. You should *be* the daughter of a merchant prince. We'll look like a pair of knockout Lizzies. Every man who sees us will go mad with his fantasies." The prospect had amused Nancy. She had bought a few midcalf skirts, under and over sweaters and long scarves, all designed and made in Paris. Looking at her with approval, Jennifer had bought a short sheepskin coat and a couple of warm windbreakers to go over her pants. Often, they walked around the campus arm in arm. "Let the jocks slaver," Jennifer had said with relish. They had read Friedan and Millet and Doris Lessing, and halfheartedly believed that all men were jocks. They would be free women; an actress, a lawyer; or maybe not. There was time.

It was spring and Nancy's dreams had begun to change and they puzzled her. They became highly sexual. The pursuit was no longer simply justice pursuing the outlaw or the outlaw pursuing the innocent. Now the creatures who were nearly catching up to her were sexual assassins. Not always masked or hooded, they were yet somehow faceless. Once or twice, they had turned into animals; horses or bulls. And her flight became more desperate than ever. She knew that her pursuers meant great harm to her. Sometimes, but not always, she was naked. Inevitably, she awoke with sweat on her forehead and she was moist between her legs. And so, when the shattered parts of her consciousness had come together, she masturbated. Jennifer, across the room, never paused in her deep breathing. With masturbation Nancy reached great heights of orgasm and found herself gasping as she finished, while simultaneously looking furtively at Jennifer's sleeping form. Nancy told nearly everything to this girl, but was horrified at the idea that Jennifer might have waked and be lying on her side, propped up on her elbow, watching. She was ashamed of her masturbation, not because of anything evil associated with it, but simply because she had started at fourteen and had long since considered it childish. And this sudden obsession with sex worried her greatly. After masturbating she would go back to sleep and wake at the morning's alarm with a brown taste in her mouth, a muddled head and a feeling of apprehension. She suffered anxiety attacks. Her armpits grew wet, her vision blurred and she had difficulty concentrating on what was being said to her. At these times she became quite frightened. She felt alone and remote even from Jennifer. In her small classes, whose success depended on active student participation, she was often caught paying no attention. Her withdrawal from the sense of the discussion was especially noticeable in Nancy since she had always been active, even argumentative, in class. One of her teachers was Alexander P. Witherspoon, a stocky, florid-faced man in his forties, who sported a short, trimmed gray beard below a crewcut. He taught a course in the Age of Johnson, and one Friday he gave her back a paper on which there was no grade, but only a note: "Make an appointment to see me." She did that and went to see him one night in early spring after the evening meal. "Tempt him," Jennifer, who also took the course, advised. "They say he's gay. I think he's not."

"It's only that he's a bachelor," Nancy said. "Everybody not married has to be gay. Typical."

"Strike a blow for reason. The freedom to unentangle. Force him to make a pass at you and we'll announce to the whole school his frenzied heterosexuality."

Nancy laughed. "I'll never know. All he wants is to tell me how rotten my work is."

Now serious, Jennifer said, "Why is it, Nance? All of a sudden?"

Nancy shook her head. "I've misplaced my mind. Can't find it. Or my patience. I want everything to be done. I don't want to do it."

Maybe, she thought, walking slowly across the newly greening campus early that evening, it's just the forsythia. To be followed by the dogwood and the tulips and then the wisteria. An early spring after a leaden, cold winter. Spring fever. Lethargy, which causes everything to appear static and living to offer no more than unending sameness. To hear another alarm bell in the morning; another brushing of the teeth; the same faces at table in the dining hall; showering, the washing of the hair; the dinners at the Pizza Palace or the Iron Kettle where the Taunton students drank their beer before settling down to sliced beef sandwiches with glops of A-1 sauce and the stupid jukebox blaring out Dylan or Baez or whoever had the newest hit, all seemed too much for her, wasted time.

"You should have been here for the marches," Witherspoon said to her. They were sitting in his study, each in an identical brown leather wing chair. He had a faculty suite in Rogers House, a white clapboard house, one of several like it which had been bought from estates by the school to complement the brick, ivy-colored dormitories. The suite had a small living room decorated in austere Bauhaus, a tiny kitchenette, a bedroom with a queen-sized bed and posters by Chagall, Miró and Dali on the walls. In the study, most of the shelving was for his books, but there was also space for his stereo on which he had been playing a Schubert trio when she had arrived. "Just a few years ago," he continued, "bored students—like you—had the protests, the marches, the rallies, the singing—the anger. It was quite stirring. And, of course, they were right."

"Did you take part?"

He nodded, emphatically. "A number of us did." He smiled. When he did, his face, rather heavily lined around the small eyes and fleshy mouth, looked gentle to her and vulnerable. "We needed our releases, too. But there was genuine fury at what our government was doing. However, more people believed the government's lies than did not, so the war protesters were called radicals. The hawks were the radicals, of course. They believed in ravaging, pillaging, destroying, all in the name of victory."

"Victory is hardly a radical idea."

"But it is. One of the definitions of a radical is an extremist. Victory is an extreme notion. It alters the status quo. Anything which alters the status quo is radical. When a prizefighter knocks out his opponent, that is a radical solution to a problem. The most radical solution possible. Except, of course, murder."

Nancy laughed. She had noticed that his eyes underneath his heavy brows were dancing. He had a way of sinking his round gray beard into his chest and cradling his head against the knuckles of one hand with his elbow on the arm of his chair so that he appeared to be looking at her over spectacles which he wore only when reading.

"But the status quo was gung ho to beat the Communists," she said. "By protesting, you became the radicals."

He nodded. "So it might appear. We, of course, were only trying to impose rational thought over maniacal pursuit of folly."

"But you got very emotional about it."

He smiled. "That was the music. Play a song and people cry or go to war. We will all follow the sound of a tune to hell. Shepherds know that. You'll never find a shepherd without his pipe to blow into."

When Nancy had arrived, the professor had lit a small fire in his study, and now he rose to put a log on it. When he had done this, he took the poker and shoved the wood around until the new log caught. Nancy watched him silently. Not more than five foot eight inches in height, he looked very strong. A gray shetland wool sweater stretched tight over his wide square shoulders and the solidity of his chest and stomach. Thickset, he did not look fat. The flesh around his middle, she thought, would be solid as would his thighs and buttocks. It occurred to her that he probably exercised regularly with weights. The pinkness of his complexion was attractive. He had none of the exposed purply blood vessels of the heavy drinker; even though he now hastened to pour her and himself a splash of Martell. He simply looked like a man in his mid-forties who was flushed with good health. She sipped her cognac, feeling warm and pleased to be where she was.

"How is lovely Jennifer?" he said, slumping back into his chair.

Surprised, she said, "I'd have thought you'd hardly know her first name."

"Do I seem so impersonal?"

"Miss . . . Mister . . ."

He nodded and sighed. "In fact, I don't know many first names. Few of my students write one interesting sentence during the course of an entire school year. When one does, I note his first name and what he looks like. Or she. In the Johnson class, you and Jennifer have written and spoken many—well several—interesting sentences since September. So have four boys. Everyone else in the class is Mister or Miss. Since you and Jennifer are inseparable, and picturesque, you are highly visible."

Warmed by the cognac, Nancy said mischievously, "Jennifer wants me to make a pass at you. Or vice versa, I guess."

He grinned, eyes bright with pleasure. "Why?"

"To prove you're not gay."

"Am I supposed to be?" He no longer seemed so pleased.

"Nobody knows. Most of the faculty are married . . ."

He made an impatient move with his hand. "Marriage guarantees nothing. Haven't you silly students gotten past that yet?"

"Well, at the least, it's a disguise."

"I was married for a few years," he said matter-of-factly. "Shortly after I got my Master's degree. I married a girl who was studying to be a psychiatrist. I found our constant exploration of motives wearing. It was difficult to do or say anything casual. It had to be examined. So," he waved his hand carelessly, "it ended."

Nancy was silent. She looked into the fire and thought it might be the last of the season. Already, she and Jennifer slept with their windows wide open and explored the woods for fresh flowers to cut for their room.

He said, "Why have you lost interest in your work?"

"Is that why you didn't mark my paper?" His question made her suddenly nervous.

He shrugged. "It's a sound enough paper. It's simply uninvolved. As though you had no interest in what you're saying."

"Well, I haven't," Nancy said, defensively.

"In my course." He smiled gently. "That I can't pass off. It must be my fault."

She took a deep breath. It seemed important to be very clear. She found that her fists were clenched, and forced them open. "It's not just your course," she said. "I seem to have gotten very sunk . . . depressed . . . I feel . . . scared and anxious sometimes, as though my hands should be shaking but they're not. Everything seems too much trouble. Deciding whether to wash my hair or not is a major thing. I feel . . . paralyzed. I see people laughing and I don't see how they can be. What on earth are they laughing about? Nothing is funny . . . nothing is gay."

As she was speaking, her voice quite steady, the most terrible tension was curling up in her stomach. And her shoulders suddenly began to shake. She caught them by pressing her arms over her breasts. But now her teeth were chattering and she felt cold. She began to try to say something else, but the words stuck in her throat. Her eyes and nose were running now, and she brushed them with her sleeve. In fury, she picked up her snifter and, rising to her feet, flung it against the wall where it shattered and fell noisily to the wood floor. A little cognac had been left and it ran down the dark brown wall like a tiny stream. And

then, sinking back into the chair, she began to sob helplessly. Professor Witherspoon disappeared into his bedroom. When he returned, he put a box of Kleenex on the
table next to her. He poured himself another cognac and
left the study so she could be alone.

Later, she had no idea how long she had sat there sobbing. "Close to an hour," he told her. When she did stop
she felt nauseated. He showed her to his bathroom and
left her there. On her knees in front of the bowl, she
vomited up her supper and the cognac. Even after she had
done that, the retching continued so that when it was over
she was soaked with sweat, her black hair plastered
against her temples and the nape of her neck. Her face,
she saw in the mirrors, was chalk white. She took off her
sweater and doused the top of her body and her face with
cold water. She rubbed a towel all over her torso and into
her hair. She took his toothbrush and brushed her teeth
fiercely, then found an after-shave lotion in his cabinet
and splashed it over her. Finally, she slipped her sweater
back on, took a brush from her pocketbook, gave her hair
a few strokes and came back into the study. He was sitting in the same leather chair reading *The New Yorker*,
but he dropped this to the floor as she came in, rose and
took her hand. At first she stiffened, but almost immediately he grasped her in his arms and pressed her against
him and forced his mouth down against hers. Stunned,
for a moment she was motionless as his hand began to
curve toward her breast. She did not scream. She mus-
tered her saliva and spat in his face. As he recoiled, she
struck him with all her strength and a grunt came from
him. He retreated, his eyes bright and terrified. Scream
and I ruin his career, Nancy thought. She walked slowly
to the door, out of it and started back home. On the way
Professor Witherspoon became confused in her mind with
a madman: The madman who had put on a Donald Duck
face. And must be crushed in turn. Donald Duck, Witherspoon. And this, she realized at last, she expected her
father to have arranged. If he was God, the bridegroom
as he had silently professed to be all her life, then it was
his responsibility.

"WHAT I think we should do," Jennifer said to her when
she had told what had happened (nearly in tears again as
she did) "is get out of here. Before we perish. Smother

'neath the stately elms of Taunton. Cut some classes. Especially cut Witherspoon's class. The button pusher. Shake him up. Shake us up."

And suddenly Nancy had an idea. "I'd like to go to Cambridge," she said. "To see Bobby. And I'd like you to meet him."

Jennifer slapped her knee. "Good show. To Cambridge we'll go and bring Harvard to its knees. God help the Radcliffians, if that's what they are. Poor lumpy wretches with bad complexions. I hear they always have a cold. The entire student body. Red noses and runny eyes."

But when she called Bobby, he was not going to be in Cambridge. "I go to New York on weekends," he said. "I play cocktail piano at a bar. Friday, Saturday and Sunday, five to nine. So come to New York instead."

"Well, where do you stay? Can we all stay together?"

His voice sounded thin. "I stay with a friend," he said. "Not quite big enough for all of us. But I'll tell you, he knows somebody at the Algonquin. I'll get you and Jennifer a room there, which isn't far from where I play. Have you got money?"

"I'll call Mother. I probably don't have enough. Unless you plan to pay for everything. Like a gentleman."

"Horseshit. Call Mother."

"Oh, well," said Jennifer, "the hell with Radcliffians. We'll destroy the Barnardites instead."

They cut their Friday classes and arrived at the Algonquin Thursday night in time for dinner, Jennifer with seemingly endless canvas satchels and tote bags, and Nancy with two Vuitton cases her father had given her. Since transportation from Taunton involved a combination of buses and trains, they had hired a car and Nancy had driven down. They both knew New York well. Jennifer's father had worked there for a while in television in the early sixties. "He also wrote a novel; it was published and remaindered practically simultaneously. It was not very good. Daddy is a hack, God bless him." And Nancy had visited the city often with her parents and once, as a little girl, with Jenny and Arnold. Their room was small and frayed and offered them a double bed instead of two singles. No twin-bedded room was to be had. "I flop a lot," Jennifer had said, dubiously. "Oh well, so we won't sleep," Nancy answered. "Here," Jennifer said, reaching into her big patent leather tote. She handed Nancy a large number of bills. "There's three hundred dollars. Pay everything. I hate fiddling on scratch pads, dividing up. Spend every cent. When it's gone, use your money."

"We'll be mugged and it'll all be gone," Nancy said.

"Darling," Jennifer said wryly, "I am six feet tall. I remind people of a white Muhammad Ali. My knee to the balls is lethal. We are all too safe."

The weather was glorious in New York. Cool enough for a sweater at night, warm and sunny during the day. On their first night they charged over to Avery Fisher Hall and heard Leonard Bernstein conduct Strauss's *Four Last Songs* and Mahler's *Fourth Symphony* with Yvonne Minton. Nancy knew more music than Jennifer, mostly from Bobby, but Jennifer was suitably excited at watching Bernstein even if they were far back in the balcony. They had supper at the Ginger Man close by Lincoln Center and allowed two young men who turned out to be out-of-work actors to buy them a drink. One of the young men had a gimpy leg. "Vietnam," he explained, then humorously, "If anyone can explain to me what I was doin' in Vietnam, I'd be glad to hear. Of course, it was last century."

"Too long ago to worry about," Jennifer said. They were standing at the bar and Jennifer stood over nearly everyone. She wore semi-high heels when she was dressed up. "I'm too tall, I'll just be too tall," she explained. "Flats is copping out."

"And you never cop out?" said one of the young men with mischief in his eyes.

"Never," Jennifer said, firmly. "For example, you're both unemployed, my friend, and I will spring for a drink." At the packed bar, she reached over the man in front of her and tapped the bartender on the shoulder. "Four more, my good sir, the ladies are paying."

"Personally, I have very good vibes about Women's Lib," said the Vietnam veteran. "Are you Women's Libbers?"

"Of course," said Jennifer. "Militant. Deeply committed. Also lesbians."

"Oh, Christ," said the protestor, but he was grinning. "Well, it doesn't matter. We're both impotent."

"We protest the heterosexual tyranny in America," Jennifer said.

"And we protest sex in general. Sex is dirty."

"Let's all go to a motel and plot," said the Vietnam veteran. They did not do that, but the girls allowed the young men to walk them back to the Algonquin. It was a long walk because of the bad leg.

"My name is Harry," said the veteran. "And this is Pat."

"Veronica," said Jennifer. "Called Slim."

"Mildred," said Nancy. "Called Snooky."

Harry smiled. He had light brown hair down to his shoulders and a ragged blond moustache. His sweater had a hole in it and his khaki pants were unpressed. The walk had been difficult for him and he was breathing hard. Pat was taller and he wore a green jacket over a yellow, open shirt and dungarees. His hair was black and kinky. He looked like a white Negro.

"Why don't you want us to call you?" Harry said.

"Our fiancés are upstairs waiting for us. When they get jealous they kill," Jennifer said.

"We're harmless," Pat said.

"It's a matter of time," Nancy said, kindly. "We're involved."

Harry shrugged. "So be it. Take care." They shook hands briefly and parted.

"No involvement," Jennifer said upstairs. "Freedom time."

Though it was after three in the morning, the two girls, each lying carefully in the big bed so as not to disturb the other, did not sleep. Nancy, having been gay and optimistic all evening, now felt a queer letdown, as though liquor had worn off. But she had had little enough to drink. It could not be that. Nevertheless, she was suddenly nervous and ill at ease. Irritably, she turned from her side over on her back and stared up at the ceiling. Her eyes were now accustomed to the dark. Roaming from the ceiling, they could make out the forms of chairs and bureaus and lamps. All the objects seemed harsh and angular; unfriendly. She turned her head toward Jennifer, whose back was to her and whose long hair cascaded over the pillow.

"Asleep?" Nancy whispered.

"Not close."

"Why do you suppose we told those two we were lesbians?"

"Oh—shake 'em up. They didn't believe it, though. We're getting unconvincing. It's too much a joke."

"We did it to shake people up. When we started. I mean, we sort of let people think it. To laugh at them. To put them down."

Jennifer turned over and leaned her head on her hand. "That was me," she said, very seriously. "I seem to have to put people down. Except the ones I totally, absolutely trust. Right now, in all the world, that means you. I'm afraid to be hurt. To be a joke. I'm so goddamn tall, you see, and I always have been. Compared to the other girls, I was always a basketball player. So I became one. I had to quit. Every night after practice or a game, I cried myself to sleep because I scored so many points. The other girls complained about me. They said I should play with the boys. So I stopped playing at all. And the boys . . . I fell in love every month. Slavering in love, like you can when you're twelve or thirteen. In dancing class they'd grab me around the knees and off we'd toot. I embarrassed boys. They ran from me. I got very flip and sassy and then they were scared of me. I didn't stop crying at night until I was eighteen. By that time, I'd decided to let it be known I couldn't be hurt. I was granite. Nothing was serious. Everything was a kick. Put everybody down so they couldn't damage me. I often upset people badly. Not meaning to. I hated that, but did it. When you came along, we made such a pair. My, how people looked at us. And still do. So I wasn't so alone anymore. And not so mean. But I thought if we don't separate ourselves from all of them—get away up on a hill and look down—they'll destroy us. Or at least me. So I got you into it. It's always me that takes your arm on campus. I know you love me and I flaunt you. 'This girl is brilliant, attractive and rich, and she adores me. What have you got, you boring, normal-size, pea-headed apes?' "

Jennifer stopped and flopped down on her back. There was a silence. Then Nancy said, "From the first time I ever saw you, I thought you owned the world. For a while, it seemed amazing to me that you even remembered my name."

Jennifer laughed. "People don't forget your name, Nancy. It's rather well known."

"I suppose. It doesn't impress me because I don't relate to that store. I just shop in it. I never think of owning part of it. I might as well be shopping at Saks except I get a forty percent discount. It's really a trap, you know. Long ago, my mother forgot who she was, whatever that was. Pieces of that former person are always struggling to get out of her, but she stuffs them back in. My father . . ." Nancy stopped.

"What about your father?"

"I think if Adam had been born with nothing, he might have been a great man."

"They say he's a great merchant."

"That's not the same thing. When Adam first started to walk, he was carrying that store around his neck. He might have been a great—effective—humanitarian. But his whole purpose is to sell more things to people than they need at higher prices than they should pay. He's the absolute symbol of everything that's wrong with this world."

"Oh, that's pretty heavy."

"Well, I try not to think of it that way most of the time . . . I feel funny tonight. Destructive."

After a silence, Jennifer rolled over on her stomach and cupped her chin in her hands. "I feel better," she said.

"Because I was glad you remembered my name?"

"Mm-hmm. I thought any day now you'd marry a Bloomingdale and I'd be alone again. Like a totem pole in the desert."

Nancy turned on her side, raised up on an elbow and put her hand on Jennifer's hair and gently began to stroke it. She thought it was the softest substance she had ever touched and envied it, for she considered her own hair coarse. Neither of them spoke. After a while, Jennifer folded her arms and rested her forehead on them, so that Nancy's hand following the hair down its length now touched the tall girl's body past the pajama top she wore to the small of her back, where the swell of the hips began. She was suddenly very frightened. She wished to allow her fingers to follow over the naked hips and was afraid to. Jennifer gave no hint; did not move. In all the wildness of her dreams since the rape, in the waking hours, deprived and empty, in the frantic masturbation, in the blackness and lethargy of her days and the apprehension that crept after her wherever she went, the single constant in her soul through all these months had been, she was certain, anger. At this moment, she realized, there was no anger in her. She was nearly crying with relief. An intense and thudding pressure seemed to have been removed from her brain. It was replaced by the most extraordinary flooding of love and sympathy and desire and need, all mixed together, so that, drunk with it, she scarcely knew what she was doing as her fingers traced a gentle line over Jennifer's slim hips. When this happened, Jennifer turned on her back. Her eyes somehow looked twice their normal size. Her lips were slightly parted. She looked puzzled. But she put up one of her long arms and her hand touched Nancy's cheek. Her touch was very warm. Unsure, tentative, Nancy bent down over the other girl until their lips were nearly touching and each could feel the other breathing. Jennifer's hand circled the back of Nancy's head and the dark girl felt, or thought she felt, pressure. Their lips came together, grazing them firmly, and their tongues touched and explored. Jennifer suddenly withdrew. Her eyes never left Nancy's as she threw the covers down and removed her pajama top. Mechanically, dazed, Nancy slipped out of her cotton nightgown. And the two girls drew back together and looked at each other, at the familiar nakedness so known, so frequently observed, and it was as though neither of them had ever seen the other before. Each of them, nearly simultaneously, began to touch the other with great gentleness, horrified of a false move, looking at the other's body, then quietly, guiltily, into the other's eyes. They were inexpert and afraid; had either pulled away an inch it would have been over. But Nancy, reckless with the love and desire in her, now sank her lips against Jennifer's and the girls kissed hungrily, sucking at each other. And Nancy stroked the silken fleece of her roommate and felt her legs spread and sent her fingers down until they were drowned in the liquid heat of Jennifer; and Nancy, safe now and exultant, felt that nothing in her life would ever be the same again.

They made love all night, experimentally, full of wonder at the pleasure they could give each other, in love with themselves as with each other, uttering many lovers' words of endearment and more.

They often laughed at an unexpected response of one or the other. They did sophisticated things without knowing it, for they were children in a new house where all the corners and corridors were unfamiliar and to be explored.

Through all that they said to one another during the long night, through all that they did, through all the sensations they brought to their bodies and the happiness they recognized with their minds, a single benediction saved them from tears: and this was trust. Whatever they said, more important was what they did not need to say. Once, when light was beginning to sift into their room, Nancy's eyes focused on the gold velours-covered wing chair across from the bed and the standing lamp next to it. The velours was faded and ripped at one corner and the grime of the city had imbedded itself in the white lampshade, so that the pieces of furniture were sad and graceless. She shuddered and laid her head against Jennifer's shoulder, and was grateful when Jennifer pressed her closer. Witherspoon was gone and so, for now at least, was all the anger in her life.

After a time, Nancy raised her head. Jennifer's eyes were closed. She was asleep. Silently Nancy rose. She looked at her wristwatch on the bureau. Quarter to eight. She walked to the window and looked down on Forty-fourth Street. It was another fine clear day. A few people were up and about on the sidewalk and the Algonquin doorman was unloading some luggage from a taxi while a stout, middle-aged couple watched him. It occurred to Nancy that she was stark naked, and she flinched back from the grimy window, nearly giggling. She pulled down the shade and sat for a moment in the wing chair and looked at the girl lying in the bed. Then she rose and lay down next to this girl and pulled the covers up over them both. She turned on her side and put her arm over Jennifer, who, in half sleep, curled up with her back to Nancy, and took her hand and pressed it to her small breast. And in this way, their bodies mingled, they both slept.

Later that morning, the sound of the shower spattering down awakened Nancy. She lay quietly, letting her mind come together slowly. The room was bright with the sun and a light breeze was wafting in through the open window. It felt late to her, and after a few moments she got up. Her nightgown was still on the floor where she had dropped it. She picked it up and, feeling that she had decided something, slipped it on. Then she looked at her watch. Nearly one-thirty. She could not remember the last time she had slept so late. She was also hungry, so she called down and made them a luncheon reservation in a half hour. She asked for a table in the Oak Room where Adam liked to lunch when he was spending a day in the Seventh Avenue market. She had been there often with him. Now and then she had seen familiar faces from the Broadway stage or the movies and once she had seen Sir John Gielgud and Sir Ralph Richardson, in town to do a play, lunching together. And Adam, who had never met either of them, had brought her over to their table and said, "From two generations, let me say what a pleasure it is to have you back in New York. And how much we look forward to your opening." And Sir Ralph had smiled and Sir John had said, "What a lovely speech. It changes the weather, words like those." And at seventeen Nancy had been so impressed that her father could do a generous, likeable thing without even using his name.

Now, she went into the steamy bathroom and called out over the noise. "Hurry up, we'll miss lunch."

"Coming."

Nancy walked over to the window and again gazed down at the street. She felt gay and optimistic. Perhaps they would do some galleries that afternoon, since most of them would be jammed on Saturday. Then on Saturday and Sunday they could visit the Museum of Modern Art and the Metropolitan. She would get a *Cue* and check out the theaters. Because of his piano job, Bobby would not be able to join them for a play, but they could meet him for supper afterward. She realized suddenly how much she was looking forward to seeing her brother. They never corresponded, she had no idea about his job, but they had been so close all their lives that when Jennifer had suggested getting away from Taunton, visiting Bobby had come to her mind instantly.

She turned from the window and there was Jennifer, standing behind her, wrapped in a towel. Their eyes met. For a moment Nancy felt panic coming on. Now, she was thinking, something must be said. But she had no idea of what it was, could never have said it and was frightened of whatever Jennifer might say. But Jennifer was smiling and her face was glowing and eager. "Look," she said, "what He's done for us."

"Who's done for us?"

"God. It's the most beautiful day in the history of the world. In the most sublime city. Just for us. Isn't it?"

"Oh yes . . . yes," Nancy said, softly, panic gone. Their eyes met for a moment and it seemed that one of them must speak. But the moment passed and suddenly Jennifer was darting to the closet. "We must look very elegant today," she was saying with her back to Nancy. "It's absolutely vital that New York know we're here. We'll be just late enough for lunch so we can make an entrance. Sweep in. Stop all conversation. Cause mouths to hang open." She was shuffling around in the closet. "People are still wearing pants, of course, so we won't." She wheeled around and placed a long, gored skirt at her waist. It was camel colored and would swing as she walked.

"Perfect," Nancy said.

"With my white ribbed turtleneck. And you should wear that marvelous plum Ungaro you have. So hurry up and let's go show off."

Downstairs in the Oak Room, they did indeed take the eye of the people in their half of the room. They brought the sunshine inside. They looked happy and relaxed and seemed to have much to say to each other. They ordered white wine and toasted each other, and Nancy thought she had never tasted wine so good though it was just the bar wine. Before they had even ordered, the maître d'hôtel, a good-looking man with a British accent, came over to their table. "Miss Starr?" he said.

"Yes?"

"Telephone call. You can take it at my desk."

"That'll be Bobby," Nancy said. "I'll be right back."

She went to the desk at the entrance and picked up the phone. "Hello?"

"Oh good, I caught you," came Bobby's voice. "I had classes all morning and couldn't call till now. How are you?"

"Sensational. We're swilling wine."

"Good. Have you got a pencil and paper?"

"Wait a minute." Nancy found a pencil on the desk and the maître d's notepad. "Okay."

"I play at a place called The Little Room. Madison Avenue and Thirty-eighth Street, east side of the Avenue. It's just what it sounds like. Gets a lot of youngish people from around Turtle Bay. Come after five-thirty. I'll reserve a table when I get there and join you between sets."

"Will we have dinner there?"

"No, it's not much for food. Have a lot of hors d'oeuvres, because I don't get through until nine so it'll be close to ten before you get anything substantial in you. Guy will meet us at nine and go to dinner with us."

"Guy is the friend you stay with?"

"Yes." There was a short silence. "You know him, as a matter of fact. Guy Racquette. He was down for the Gala."

Nancy felt a quick, hurting feeling. And suddenly laughed. "I remember him," she said. "The makeup man."

"He's a vice-president now. Marketing. I wouldn't ask him about famous people he's made up lately."

"That's all behind him, is it?"

"Yes. He's a bit sensitive about it."

"And . . . you stay with him every weekend?"

"That's right." Again, there was a pause before Bobby said, quietly, "Nance, you remember when you told me to tell you anything? No matter what it was?"

"Yes, I do," she said.

"Well, I just did. All right. Go back to your wine and have a good time, and I'll see you tonight." He clicked off.

Nancy put down the phone slowly. In spite of the portion of her mind that told her to be amused, she felt a certain sadness. Whatever she and Jennifer might have done, it was their own private concern. Racquette was a clear, unmistakeable homosexual. No one would see Bobby with Racquette and doubt that her brother was, too. That would include Jennifer. Well . . . She wandered slowly back to their table. Jennifer had not come to New York to fall in love with Bobby; only to enjoy herself. And he would see to that. She wished only that she had liked Racquette more. But perhaps she had been harsh on him. It seemed quite a different age when she had met him. These days, she had no wish to make harsh judgments. Or perhaps any judgments. Still, she was unable to shake off a slight feeling of apprehension as she approached their table.

"Bobby?" Jennifer asked.

"Mm-hmm. We're to meet him sometime after five-thirty. And then a friend of his—of ours—in the cosmetic business is going to join us for dinner."

"Very good. Off to the art galleries, then. Maybe we'll pick up a Modigliani or two."

LATER ON, when she looked back on it, the weekend seemed to Nancy to have been a series of events at which she had been an onlooker rather than a participant. Always excepting the first night, of course. Bits and pieces of Friday, Saturday and Sunday came back to her, often out of sequence and blurred. They had done many things and had been many places, the four of them, but the things and the places were indistinct and only the snatches of dialogue or lack of it were vivid; and occasionally the look on someone's face.

Jennifer's look when she saw Bobby sitting at the piano was startled.

"I had no idea he was so beautiful," she said, sitting down at the table he had kept for them. Bobby, seeing them, smiled and waved. He was playing "I Get a Kick Out of You," and doing all kinds of rhythmic and melodic variations on it. Nancy regarded her brother with interest.

"I guess he is, isn't he?" Nancy said, pleased.

"And he plays so professionally. I mean he's not even twenty, is he?"

When he rose from his bench to join them between sets, Nancy realized something else that hadn't occurred to her. He was tall enough for Jennifer. So later, when they were dancing at the Pierre, they looked very good together. And since Jennifer was a good enough dancer for him, they danced often and for long periods. Whenever Nancy looked at them, they seemed to be laughing. She was doing some of that herself with Guy, who offered acerbic comments on the products he marketed as symptomatic of the civilization which had given birth to them. She supposed he was being entertaining and laughed at what she hoped were the right spots. He meant nothing to her; Bobby and Jennifer everything.

At one point, Guy seemed to be talking about feminine hygiene products; or, as he called them, crotch sprays.

"I mean, the whole point is there's not one inch of the human body we don't exploit in my business," he said. "Think of it, not a square inch."

Nancy was thoughtful. "It scares me sometimes."

"Crotch sprays?"

"No, advertising. Selling. The foundation of our country. The enormity of the lies. Our acceptance of them. Or lack of indignation."

Bobby and Jennifer had sat down in time to hear the last of this. "We all know nobody wants to hear the truth," he said with a slow grin. "Tell the truth, you're an instant leper." He was flushed, as Jennifer was, from dancing.

"I think we should make a bargain," Jennifer said. "No matter who else we lie to, we'll never lie to each other."

"I'd be for that," Nancy said, quickly.

"All right," Bobby said, still smiling.

"Impossible," said Guy, lightly. "I don't know how to tell the truth. It's like asking me to speak Latin."

Bobby laughed. "That at least is honest."

"Well, it's all silly," Nancy said. "Governments lie to the people, corporations lie to the people, the military lies to the people and the people lie to each other. All words are lies. The only truths are violent. Murder is truth. All violence is truth. It's what we want and we can't say it. We can only do it."

This brought a silence.

"A bit heavy, Nance," Bobby said mildly.

"When two teenagers rob and kill an old woman on the subway, what do you want?" Nancy went on, stubbornly. "To arrest them? Of course not. You want to kill them. Personally. And slowly and painfully."

"They always come from broken homes," Guy said, after a silence. "And ghettos."

"I don't care," she said stubbornly.

"I've never heard you speak like that, Nancy," Jennifer said, slowly. Nancy only shrugged. She was surprised at herself and embarrassed. More and more, lately, it seemed she had been doing and saying unexpected, angry things. At this moment, however, she had no special reason that she could fathom to be angry.

Or rather, she had an old reason and a new one . . . that the men who had raped her had not been executed; that nothing had been said between Jennifer and herself. And absolutely *had to be*. She did her best through the evening, and eventually they came back to the Algonquin and prepared for bed silently. Jennifer had been gay and chattering all night, but now she only turned on her side away from Nancy and was soon asleep or seemed to be. Perhaps she will never wish to speak of what happened,

Nancy thought. And because there had been such trust and sweetness between them the night before, she was greatly saddened. I can stand it, however, she thought. She was not at all sure herself that she wanted ever to make love to Jennifer again. It was quite possible . . . probable . . . that for them, once was right and more would be wrong. The thought that saddened her was that they might never be able to say that to each other. But she could stand it, or anything. So she told herself and lay awake most of the night in bitterness and despair while Jennifer slept.

Bobby rang the next day early.

"What about breakfast?" he said. "It looks to me about the only time we can have to be alone. To catch up."

So she was on her way to the Plaza before Jennifer was awake. Bobby was even earlier and had gotten them a table by the window.

"I never much think of this place for dinner or even lunch," he said. "But breakfast at the Plaza is so wildly extravagant it has a sort of chic."

"You're an extravagant young man," Nancy said.

"All Starrs are extravagant. As retailers, we're our own hungriest customers. We don't know what it is not to have the best in the world."

"Do you like that?"

"Sure. Don't you?"

"I don't think I care much."

"You wear Paris clothes."

"Not often. Usually much cheaper. But not jeans. That's because everyone else does. I can't stand being one of the sheep, I'll admit that."

"You'll never be that. Starrs are not sheep."

"You're awfully big on Starrs this morning," she offered.

"They're roots. As is the store. As is Ramsey. I'm very big on roots lately. I seem to meet a lot of people lately who're looking for them and I have them."

"That sounds rather smug."

"Well, look at Guy. Whatever and wherever his roots are, he's long since lost track of them."

She was silent while their breakfast arrived. Identical orders of scrambled eggs and sausages. With tips, this breakfast would cost in the neighborhood of fifteen dollars.

"How did you get involved with Guy?" she asked.

"I ran into him in New York during a holiday," Bobby said. He spoke evenly, but his eyes searched his sister's intently. "One night he took me for a drink at the place where I play. He knew the owner, who is also homosexual, though it's not especially a gay bar. After a number of drinks . . . quite a number . . . Guy sat me down to play. The rest, as they say, is history."

"So you see him every weekend. Are you fond enough of him for that?"

"We wrote to each other a lot—well, still do, really. He writes an amusing letter. He's a great change from college and home. For a while I thought I loved him." Bobby paused. "Nancy, we can stop this any time if it's bothering you." His eyes were kind.

"I'm all right. Not shocked if that's what you meant. I'm just trying to place everybody where they belong. In my little world. But you haven't really answered my question. Do you still think you love him?"

Bobby looked away. "He can be mean at times. Especially when he drinks. To waiters even. Other people. Once I saw him working with his salespeople at Bloomingdale's. When he finished with them they must have felt . . . degraded. He seems to need that."

"Does he do it to you?"

"Never."

"Why not?"

"He knows I'd leave him that minute. He's terrified that I'll leave him."

"How do you know?"

"He's told me so. Drunk and sober."

"I think you should. The whole thing sounds unhappy."

"I'll leave him, Nance. Sooner or later. I learn things from him, especially about art. He has a good eye. He can make me see. But I discovered something I'm glad to have discovered. I do not wish any extended gay relationships. That part of my life—which is half of it, incidentally, since I seem to be bisexual—I want to treat in episodes. A long way from home."

"Because of the roots you mentioned."

Bobby laughed. "And also Adam. I can't think of much that would destroy Adam, but my being partly gay . . . even maybe preferably . . . would come closer than anything I know."

"So what? It's your life."

"I don't want to hurt him, Nancy. What for? He never did anything against me. Except I guess to try to make me into him."

"That's enough."

"Not really. As far as parents go, we could have done a lot worse."

Not being able to quarrel with this, Nancy sipped her coffee and was silent. The Edwardian room was quiet that Saturday morning. It did well during the week with business people staying at the hotel, and was packed always for Sunday brunch, a New York tradition. Saturday was weaker. A waiter came and poured more coffee for them, and a captain wandered indolently by from time to time, eyeing them in case they should decide on a Baked Alaska for breakfast, which would add to their check and to his tip. Outside on another pleasant day, the gaily decorated hansom cabs with the drivers, both male and female, often in top hats, were available for customers.

"So after I've been in the store a while, I'll marry appropriately and get ready to run it. And be the soul of propriety."

Nancy was astonished. It had never occurred to her that her brother, whom she loved but considered fragile, would conceive of a life as president of Starr's. She had associated his future with music, playing it, composing it, writing about it. Even more shocking to her was his blandness: "marry appropriately"; "soul of propriety." He could not have found two expressions which would so astonish and enrage her. But now as she looked at him prepared to jump all over him, she saw that what he said had not been bland. It had been hard and tough. His eyes, which she had always considered soft, were unblinking and cold. On certain occasions, she had seen her father's face just so set. Always when he was talking of problems at the store.

"My God," she said, "he's done it."

Now this hard face broke into a smile.

"Who's done what?"

"Adam. He's made you him."

"I could do worse," he said calmly. "Anyway, don't worry. I'll never have a good seat on a horse, the way he does."

Nancy's next words broke from her before she had had

time to think what they meant. "What on earth am *I* going to do?" she said, lost. And recovering, said, "I didn't mean that. What nonsense."

But he took her up on it. "Struggle, I think. And resent." He paused and smiled. "Or maybe change. Either way, I'll always love you. But for me . . . I want to take what the world's going to give me, which in my case is quite a lot. And do the best I can with it."

"What happened to you?" Nancy asked, without anger.

"I grew up. Part way."

"I . . ." she stopped.

He laughed. "Liked me better before? Well, Nance, I spent too many years considering all the things I couldn't possibly do. I now find I can do them. As well as most other people anyway. It's interesting, though . . ."

"What is?" she said softly, not expecting to be interested.

"You could do it all better. You'd make a much better president of Starr's than I would. Intellectually, you're brilliantly equipped for it. And you and Adam are more alike than you think. You both will always do what you want."

"What will you do?"

"What is feasible. So in the end I may make fewer mistakes than either of you. But I won't be as interesting to watch."

After a moment, Nancy said: "I suppose you will become 'Robert'?"

"Who knows?" He was enigmatic.

She looked at her handsome brother in his dark blue blazer and his gray slacks and his solid burgundy tie and saw that she had counted too much on him, had felt that he too was as much an exception to the rules of his life, the Starr life, as she. What was feasible; his blazer, tie and slacks were feasible. Guy was not. Farewell to Guy. All his nonconformities would now be nasty little secrets that people could choose to ignore, as they did Claude's drinking and Adam's eyes closed to it. There would be no fury in him. He would accept. He was—would be— the establishment, the same old establishment. He would accept it and sneak his life. He was suddenly not a young man at all. He was already, at not quite twenty, middle-aged.

So where was she, Nancy—bearing all her anger, directed for years against injustice in general, now honed to injustice against herself—to take it? There had been Jennifer. She was not so sure now of Jennifer. There had been her brother. But her brother was gone.

"Long thoughts, Nance," Bobby said, without reproach.

She supposed she had seemed in a trance.

"It's a surprising morning," she said. She smiled. "That's all."

It was ten o'clock in the morning and she felt weary.

"I think of you a lot, though. I was awfully glad when you called me."

"I needed to get away. The only person I could think of was you."

"I hope that's still true."

"I hope so too," she said flatly.

"Jennifer's marvelous. I adore her."

"Good. I hoped you would. I do, too."

He laughed. "And Guy won't bite."

"Oh, I guess he's all right." Nancy shrugged. "Not my type is all."

"Well, as I've explained, not really mine either. What are we up to today?"

They decided to hit the museums, after which they would have a drink and a snack at Bobby's club. The two girls would then go to the theater and they would all meet for supper afterward.

"I'll take you to '21,' " he said, gaily.

" '21.' You're a madman."

"You know, when I hit eighteen, I got a letter from them. Adam had opened an account for me and put away a case of wine in my name in their cellar."

"Well, damn him! He never did that for me."

Bobby grinned. "Girls are supposed to be taken to '21.' Not to take . . ." He leaned back in mock horror. "Don't hit me. This is the *Plaza*."

"I'm serious. It makes me furious."

"I know. Take it up with Adam."

"When was the last time you took anything up with Adam?" she said, confidently.

"Never," he laughed. Expected.

"Or Claude."

His face became serious. "Well," he said, slowly, "that has happened."

Not expected. But, though he seemed to wait for her to pursue it, she did not. She had been sitting at the Plaza too long. She needed to be in motion. He used up most of a twenty-dollar bill getting them out of the room.

At "21," as they were finishing, Bobby suggested they go down to the Village and pub crawl.

"If you absolutely promise it'll be evil and exotic," Jennifer said. She had been gay and energetic all day. Beside her, Nancy felt lethargic.

"Neither, I'm afraid," Bobby said, smiling. "But you should hear some better music than mine."

"Saturday night in the Village, everyone's from Dubuque," Guy said sourly.

Bobby shrugged, but Jennifer said pointedly. "Well, if we follow them, maybe we'll hear something good. Tourists know more about what's happening here than New Yorkers. All New Yorkers do is get on subways."

"I'll pass," Nancy said. She honestly did feel tired and headachy. Two drinks and the wine had only sunk her.

Guy looked at her and smiled. "Oh well, children never do want to go to bed," he said, conferring conspiratorial adulthood on her, which she resented. Then turning to the other two, "Just don't forget to brush your teeth with Colgate, children. Right before you kiss goodnight. Cavities are catching, you know."

Nancy, startled, saw that Jennifer was laughing. But Bobby, signing his checks, said, "Why, suh, it'd be mah honah to catch Miss Jennifer's cavities. Ah intend speakin' formally to huh fathuh first thing in the mornin'."

And Jennifer, equilibrium restored, said, "Come early, Mistah Stahh. Don't forget Daddy's always drunk by nine. So am Ah, for that mattah."

"Your brother Bobby likes to flirt," Guy said, walking Nancy back to the Algonquin down the glass paradise of Sixth Avenue.

She laughed. "That is absolutely the last word in the language I would apply to him," she said.

"He does, though. I see him more than you do these days. He struts and flirts his way down Fifth Avenue, his eyes darting out like a young kitten's, his little claws clicking on the pavement . . ."

Nancy felt her muscles tense from anger, but she only walked faster.

"Just needing to be petted," Guy Racquette added, bitterly. "Little, cute kitten, preening . . ."

"You have it wrong," Nancy said, controlled.

"What wrong?"

"He isn't interested in being petted."

"No?"

"He wants to fuck."

Aware that he was staring at her, she walked on. The vulgarity pleased her, but the tension remained a steel band around her. She realized that Racquette was no longer walking beside her. "Bitch," she heard from behind her. "Miss Marjorie Morningstar bitch." It did not bother her. Instead she thought of what she had just said and realized that she might have stated the truth quite inadvertently. If she had, what she had said was that her brother wanted Jennifer. And this irony made her smile so that people who passed her looked at her oddly. As she turned up Forty-fourth Street, a chunky, bearded man wearing a cap on backward and an old blue cloth jacket with all the buttons buttoned over shapeless trousers, was listing toward passersby. "Puleese," he was croaking, his hand out. The people passed him without looking, their pace imperceptibly quickening. He was moving forward a half step at a time, swaying from side to side. He had just awakened in some dark doorway, the wine bottle empty. As Nancy drew near him, she saw that his eyes were focused on her. She was at that moment alone near him. His eyes, in all their rheuminess, looked sneaky to her. She averted her face as all the others had done and stepped more briskly. "Puh-leese," he bleated. And then, as she was passing him, she felt his hand on her shoulder and his fingers seemed to be trying to grip her. She gasped in horror, turned and was facing him, and he seemed to be clawing at her and it was a gargoyle face she saw and she felt the weight of her large, sharp-edged patent leather bag in her hand and swung it with all her might in an upward through downward arc so that it thudded into his face just to the side of his left eye. Off balance anyway, he fell like a stone to the street. He landed on his elbows and blood came from where the bag had struck him. For a second, she was unable to move, even to cast her eyes away from the blood. Then, her heartbeat striking against her skin, her legs suddenly unsteady, her breath coming in short gasps, she began to run to the hotel. After a few yards, she could run no more. She walked carefully, taking deep breaths. It was not far to the door. When she had reached it, she saw that the doorman was looking at her curiously. He said nothing. She made herself look back. The man was on all fours. Four people, together, circled him just as they would have done had he been on his feet. She entered the lobby and saw that the little bar to the right of the entrance was still open. She went in and sat at a table and ordered a vodka on the rocks.

Fifteen or twenty minutes later, she was astonished to find that she felt exultant.

Upstairs, she could not sleep. After what seemed like hours of tossing, she got up, sat down in the old wing chair and tried to concentrate on a "What's Going On in New York" kind of magazine which she noticed was a week out of date. She had no idea what she was reading. She sat in the chair and stared in front of her, cursing Jennifer for not coming back, Bobby for keeping her out and herself for caring. Her eyes fell on the television and she snapped it on. The reception was blurred and jumpy, but there was Errol Flynn in a British World War I fighter pilot's uniform. And David Niven. And Basil Rathbone. She stared at them all, toasting and singing and going romantically to death with tight lips and brave hearts and "England Forever" expressions on their faces and wished that it were still so; wished even that it had ever been so. She watched, listening for footsteps or the door-knob turning, and wishing that she had known Errol Flynn or even David Niven or Basil Rathbone and that it were now 1914 or 1944 or 1650 or anytime at all except now. Errol Flynn, deceiving his old friend David Niven, flew off at dawn to his death, looking pleased with himself. *Dawn Patrol* was the picture. And she turned off the television and the lights and crept back into bed, thankful for *Dawn Patrol*. She must have slept, because she was dreamily aware that when Jennifer came in, light was entering the room. She was too exhausted to think about it.

SUNDAY WAS rainy and the three of them went to a movie.

"Guy is tied up today," Bobby said briefly. But later, when for a moment he was alone with Nancy, he asked, "What happened?"

"He was nasty about you. Because of Jennifer, I suppose. I was nastier back."

"Good for you," he said. She did not tell him about hitting the wino and the satisfaction it had given her. When they went for the last time to Bobby's Little Room, they sat mostly in silence while he played his first set. When he joined them at the finish, Jennifer said, "Nancy, I suppose we ought to be thinking about getting back. It's a bit of a drive and I should at least open a book before tomorrow."

"I guess you're right," Nancy heard herself say.

"Too bad," Bobby said, lightly, looking around the room. "You're about half my audience tonight." They weren't really. As they left, people were coming in. Bobby kissed them both alike.

Jennifer said she would drive back. As she did, she told Nancy about the places she and Bobby had gone in the Village, about singers and musical groups they had heard, about eating at the Brasserie, which had been full of people, about sitting over cold coffee and talking endlessly and about walking down Fifth Avenue as the dawn was coming.

"It was clear then," she said. "We thought it would be another good day, but it failed us. Rotten luck. But then we had some coming, didn't we, Nance?"

"Yes, we did," Nancy answered.

"Did something happen between you and Guy?"

"No. Not at all." She thus broke quickly their truth oath. "He can be amusing."

"Now and then. He has this feeling he has to shock you." Nancy laughed. "That's hard on his humor. We're all so unshockable, aren't we?"

After a while, her eyes fixed carefully on the road, Jennifer said: "It's all going to be just the way it used to be, isn't it, Nance?"

"I don't know what you mean," Nancy lied.

"You and I. I mean . . . I mean, we go into our old act again, right?"

Nancy felt an overpowering sense of relief; so much that she could not, for a moment, speak. Then she said, "Of course we do."

"Because I couldn't stand it if it weren't the same as always. And I turned into that totem pole in the desert."

After a long silence, Nancy said, "I don't want to forget what happened, Jennifer. I know what you're trying to say and I guess I wanted to say it, too, because one of us sure had to. But it was . . . you know . . . something. It was rare. Or whatever you want to call it. What I'm trying to say . . . Jennifer, please say there was nothing wrong with it." She had a dreadful feeling she was getting teary. But then, a thing happened which saved her. Jennifer was slowing down and finally she pulled over to the right of the highway and stopped.

"I'm crying, Nance. I can't drive. Can you drive?"

"In a minute."

After a while, the stronger girl got out of the car and they switched positions and Nancy drove them back to college. Jennifer stopped crying soon and put her hand at the back of Nancy's neck. It was very much as it had always been between them. But not quite. Something had happened that neither of them would forget. In the months that followed, Nancy thought she felt a tenderness that had not been there before. An episode was done. They did not remember it harshly. It would not be repeated, probably, certainly. But it had happened, and they were grateful.

DURING THE next week or so, Nancy got a letter from Adam. It was his usual letter, containing news of the family, of the store and of the city. He told her that he might run for the City Council, and that if he won, he would then be appointed Mayor of Ramsey. He hoped that she would approve this idea. In truth, as she read about it, she neither approved nor disapproved. She did not think it made much difference. As always, his letter was dictated. She would have liked, sometime, to see a handwritten note of five lines from him, but she never had. At the end, he wondered whether anything was bothering her.

"We had your last report," he wrote. "The fact that your grades are down doesn't bother me, but I suspect it may you. So is anything worrying you? Let me hear."

After some thought she answered, describing their weekend in New York.

"And there are other pleasant happenings. As you can see, I'm having too much fun to work. That's all. It'll stop soon."

It was all she wished to say at that moment.

And he wrote back in effect that she should not stop having fun.

As time went on, she was happy to note that her obsession with sex had left her. She never went to Witherspoon's apartment again, though he wrote twice on her papers that he would like to see her. She saw him both times, feeling cool and tough, and he said some minor things and got some minor comments and he stopped writing notes. Jennifer was her superb companion. Nancy was amused that Jennifer and Bobby exchanged letters regularly but had small curiosity as to what was in them. She worked hard and with brilliance. The anxiety fits seemed to have gone. She still dreamed the chase dreams but was not shaken by them in the morning. Once or twice she dreamed of the wino at her feet, but even this did not bother her much. But once, when this dreadful man's face turned up to her, it was not his. It was Adam's. That night, she awoke in terror and for a while was afraid to sleep. But this dream did not recur for a while. At the end of the term, she was invited to stay on as a tutoring aide, grader and seminar leader for the summer school students. She accepted with surprise and pleasure. And Jennifer got a job in a stock company in northern Connecticut. They would see each other on weekends. And as the term ended, Bobby wrote that, through his father, he had a job as a trainee at Bloomingdale's, and would also be able to get away on some weekends.

It was all good. But then the dream of smashing Adam's face with her handbag, drawing blood, did recur. More than once. Again and again. In a fury, late one night, she scrawled a letter to him: "Dear Adam: If those men who (she crossed out 'raped' and put 'hurt') me *thought* it was your fault, then it *was*. If you *didn't* make the decision, you *should* have. Or *cancelled* it. And after it happened, you should have *punished* the one man. I know I said no police, but you should have *made* me. Or done something else. Anything. You only looked sad. It wasn't enough. I have too many dreams."

She simply signed her name. She felt no love.

In a week, she received a letter from her father in his own handwriting. She was so unused to it, she found it hard to read, but managed: "Dear Nancy," it read. "I should not do this, but I am your father and too proud not to tell the truth. Proud, I mean, of me, as well as you. 'Your father' in the sense that I—no more than you—could have let it go. Through private means, I have had the man who hurt you punished. He will hurt no one again. If you wish to know more about it, you can ask me and I'll tell you face to face. I hope you won't. Best love, Adam."

She read this letter with fascination, understanding what it must have cost him to write it; and also, for she was his blood, how much more it would have cost him not to write it. She called him at the store.

"I forgot to sign my letter, 'love,'" she said. "I meant to."

"That's all right," Adam said. "I wrote it in."

And so the summer began for her in some tranquility. And the dreams did stop.

# PART FIVE

# 1

DURING THE first six months or so of her married life, Karen Starr learned much about her husband, not all of which pleased her. He was good to her; unfailingly kind and generous, often bringing her unexpected presents for no reason. She was not impressed with the idea of presents in the peculiar land of Ramsey, Texas. She had met too many women who showed her jewelry or furs or snake-skin handbags which their husbands had given them, also for no reason; sometimes, she was sure, from simple generosity and often from guilt. But Louis's presents were unassuming. They were chosen from the store or the marketplace with flair, and when occasionally they were expensive, they never looked it. He had an acute eye for things she would like and this pleased her, because they were things he liked himself. So they had that in common. And other things. They enjoyed their quiet dinners together, they enjoyed going to the movies, they enjoyed the concerts of the gallant Ramsey Symphony Orchestra, they enjoyed going out to dance at ten o'clock on a whim, they enjoyed a good dinner with a good wine, they enjoyed entertaining and, depending, being entertained and they enjoyed each other in bed. They had enough to talk about.

Her background at the gallery in New York and her private collection became the basis of a newspaper article. And, to her surprise, she was asked one night to be a director of the Ramsey Museum of Fine Arts.

"You could chair the acquisitions committee," said a Russian named Paul Rodovsky, who had made millions in oil and was known to have one of the outstanding contemporary art collections in the nation, at about two o'clock in the morning.

"Zo, Karen, why not? Maybe trust, you would be president. It could happen."

She was stunned. Said nothing.

"Or Louis," somebody else suggested. "Either one."

Rodovsky laughed. "Ve haff zo many men chairing things. Ve could use a beauty one time."

She found her voice. "Well, of course, it has to be Louis."

That would have settled it except that Louis then said, "I agree with Paul. First of all, I have enough work now. Karen has the time. Second, she knows more about art than I do. Third, she'll attract more interest than I will. I'm too familiar. Karen's the new girl in town."

Later, home, she was furious.

"Why, why, why?" she said, trying not to scream at him. "You could be president. They all said so."

"I said why. You'd be better. You have the time."

"So have you."

"Not really. It's going to take a lot of work, if you do it right." His calm drove her far beyond what she wanted to say.

"You absolutely refuse to be first-rate."

He was sitting in the armchair in their bedroom in his pajamas. She was on the edge of the bed. He did not change expression, but his eyes flew from hers for a second, then determinedly returned. He said nothing. She was aware that an apology would simply hurt him more. "The problem is," she said, quietly, "I've met nobody in this town who is more first-rate than you are. All of them use it. To build themselves. Call it glory, if you like. A better word would be . . . well . . . recognition."

His eyes never wavered from her own.

"I don't suppose I really care so much about all that."

Angry again, she said, "Nobody in the world cares about it more than you do."

"I doubt that."

Evenly, but attempting not to be cold, she said, "Your whole situation in life . . . where you are in the damn store, in that damn family . . . cries out for it."

He was silent a moment. He had scarcely stirred and his tone of voice had not varied. "What you mean is you cry out for it," he said.

"Well, if I do, it's not for me, it's for Louis Starr, the man I married. Of course I want you to be recognized."

"As what?"

"As a major person."

He now stood up, stretched and, to her fury, smiled. "That's an essential difference," he said. "My thought is if I'm a major person to you, I'm major enough."

He had her there and she knew it. "But," she said, quietly, "I simply want you to make the most of yourself, not the least. I want this whole city to say Louis Starr is one of the most important people we have. Not that Louis Starr is kind to old ladies and cats."

"Old ladies, yes. I don't much like cats. Hadn't I ever told you that? I'd rather we never had a cat."

"I hate cats," she said, truthfully. And grinned. "I wouldn't want to be tested on how much I like old ladies, either."

"Think ahead. You'll be one."

"I hope not."

"Stop it."

She thought for a minute. "I've never really liked the idea of being old. Very old. Not remember things. Not be able to control my bladder."

He looked at her in surprise. "You're very odd sometimes, Karen."

"I know," she said, honestly. "From recognition and glory to bladders. I never told you I wasn't . . . erratic."

"You're not erratic. Your mind just bounces around some."

She was thoughtful. "My mother thinks I'm erratic," she said, slowly. "And so do some of my friends." She smiled. "And my father thinks I'm perfect, so that's the balance. Why are Tuesdays bad for you?"

Startled, he said, "Tuesdays?"

"On Tuesday mornings, you leave here uncertain. You look gray. You look as if you don't trust your legs. Some Tuesday nights, it's all gone when you get home. Some it's not, and you don't talk much and sometimes you have an extra martini."

He sat down again, wearily. "Tuesdays are advertising meeting days. All the merchants present what they want to advertise. There is a jury, including Adam. Things can get rough, if the jury doesn't like what you're presenting. All my buyers hate Tuesdays. I hate them because I'm responsible for what they present."

"Adam being the whole jury, I gather," she said, nastily.

"Oh, no. Peter Shaw, Jennifer Martin, the ad director, the art director, the copy director, Mindy Minsky, the PR director . . . Promotion departments and merchandise departments live in uneasy truce."

"Can things get nasty?"

"In a civilized way."

"Does Adam get nasty?"

He laughed. "Never. He just says what he thinks quite objectively. And when he's finished, you feel nine years old. It would be much easier if he were nasty. Adam is never nasty, Karen. However, I am. Sometimes."

"Which loses the game?"

"I have my people to defend."

She was silent. "Do your people trust you?"

"They can't. They don't know what Adam will decide. About what I've decided."

"I see. I want to meet what's-his-name," she said, surprising both of them.

"What's-whose-name?"

"The man Adam's running against in the city election."

"Why?"

"Because I do."

Louis shrugged. "You do bounce around. Okay, I'll call him and ask him for a drink. After he picks himself up off the floor, I guess he'll accept."

With the lights out, Karen said, "I'll take that chairmanship."

"You can't avoid it. You've been elected."

"But I still wish you would."

"They didn't really want me, you know. They wanted you." And she knew it was true. Which was what happened on one occasion to Adam's hopes for the promotion of his brother.

The *Newsweek* article was a valentine to the corporation. Mindy Minsky, the store's Public Relations director, was ecstatic. Adam was sunk in gloom.

"Why?" Mindy asked him.

He read aloud: " 'Adam Starr has two brothers, Louis and Bernard, both in the store, both with merchandise positions. But the brother who calls the shots is Adam. It is, and has been for many years, Adam who initiates those things which have made Starr's a famous name and unique specialty store and it is Adam who will supervise the expansion of this famous name into profit pockets throughout the country. He is the epitome of the modern merchant, carrying within him his parents' sense of quality with promotional talents that were not in them and sophisticated marketing abilities that would perhaps have shocked them. In an old phrase, he is America's shining "merchant prince." ' "

Adam stopped reading and put the magazine down slowly on his desk. "So what is anybody going to do about it?" Mindy asked.

Adam was looking out the window. "I don't," he said, "know what to do about this sort of thing. I sent the writer to Mother. He had dinner with Louis. They come out like spear carriers."

Mindy lit a cigarette, not speaking. Then she said lightly, "The trouble with you is you can't win for winning . . . Look, throw it back on me. I'm PR director, it's all my fault. What's gonna happen, anyway? What can?"

The telephone rang and Adam picked it up. "Yes?" he said to his secretary. "Mrs. Louis Starr?" He grinned at Mindy. "Thanks. Hello, Karen. Of course . . . tomorrow, if you like. Not in the store is okay. What about the City Club? Top floor of the Republic Building. One o'clock. Fine." He put down the phone. "What can happen? That can happen. Also my mother's face can turn very chilly. Between them, she and my father have about five lines in this story. It's written so that they don't seem to have really figured, not for years . . ."

"It can't be helped, Adam." Mindy spoke quietly and seriously.

"Well, yes, it can."

"I didn't seek out that story."

"I know you didn't. And I didn't turn it down. Well, that's going to change."

"How change? People are always wanting to do stories on Starr's. Or on Texas, or on Ramsey, or on something where Starr's will figure."

"Maybe. But I don't have to figure."

Mindy smiled. "You're going to be 'unavailable for comment'?"

Adam also smiled. "For the time being. I should have handled this one in absentia."

"You can't do that to *Newsweek*."

"Why not?"

"Because it's lousy public relations, that's why. And

that's what this store's built on. You simply can't turn into an instant Howard Hughes."

Adam did not answer for some time. He was looking out the window, drumming his fingers against the blond wood of his desk. When he did speak, it was as if he were thinking aloud. His tone was scarcely above a whisper. "I don't think it's so bad if we get quiet for a while," he said. "There are things to do . . ."

"Like what things?"

"Hard things. Unpopular things. See—the world's changed and keeps on changing. We don't. Not enough." He seemed to remember suddenly that Mindy was with him. He spoke briskly. "I have some difficult times with my family ahead, honey. Also, with me. You'll see what I mean. What I don't want, repeat *don't* want, is publicity about what is happening here. This piece is our swan song. For a while. Until the suburban store opens. Even *Women's Wear*—who are going to have some questions as time goes on—I want everything to be carefully planned between you and me. Everything we say will come from Louis. Personnel changes, anything at all. Any interviews we have to give, and I want them to be few, will be with him. I want to go into hiding."

"All right," she said, shortly. "I gather you're not going to explain this."

"Not yet."

"In any firm, one man gets most of the publicity. This is not peculiar to Starr's."

"They are not all family run, as we are. We have a different problem. We are special . . ."

KAREN WAS waiting for him when he arrived at the City Club from which one could look down on the remarkable things men can make from nothing: all of Ramsey, Texas. She was wearing a beige knit dress, and she looked as though she had been painted into the club by its designer.

"Hello," Adam said. "I'm sorry you're here for the reason you're here."

"What makes you think you know the reason I'm here?" she said, smiling. He also smiled.

"I'd make book," he said. "You're drinking wine? Yes, I'll have a glass of white wine, too, waiter."

"I'm surprised you're drinking at lunch. That's imperfect of you."

"Very imperfect. I sometimes issue memos against this. Not one executive pays any attention to them. They read them aloud over their luncheon martinis, and laugh. I don't know why I do it. Father used to be serious about it, but they didn't pay any attention to him, either. And nobody gets plastered. You're looking very well."

"Thank you. So are you." She paused and sipped her wine. At the same time, the waiter brought Adam's. He raised his glass. "Cheers," he said.

"Happy days." Impulsively, she clinked her glass against his. "Oh, Adam, we're so hopeless together."

"Hopeless?"

"Proper. Distant. As though nothing had ever happened. Between us."

"Nothing has," he said, stiffly.

"Of course. And won't, dear Adam. Won't. I suppose you think I've come to complain."

"Haven't you?" he said, surprised.

"Not really. You can't help these things. We had that man for an evening. We hardly talked about the store. We talked about our pictures, foreign automobiles, the oil business, Texas real estate and the news magazines. By the time he got to us, he'd already written his story. What will you do for Louis?"

In astonishment, he did not answer. So she laughed.

"You must have thought of that," she said. "He works ten, eleven hours a day and the public doesn't know he exists. But you do. A story like this comes out and it crushes him. He says nothing. I do all the saying. He is silent. But he is crushed. And you know this. So . . . well, haven't you planned to do something for him?"

Adam shook his head. "I hadn't."

"You really should."

"Like what?"

"Some extra title. Some new bonus arrangement. Something that says you know he's there."

Adam shifted in his chair. He wished to tell Karen that not only was he prepared to do nothing for Louis but that instead he would be doing something against him. If, of course, he won against his mother. He wished to state honestly that he was about to cut Louis down, not elevate him. If he had already spoken to his mother he would have done this. Instead, he said, "I'll try to work out something. I have been thinking . . ."

"Of . . ."

"Increased bonus tied to profitability. Which could be worked into deferred income. Or at least a share of it. Salary won't help him."

"We don't need money."

"I know that."

"What I mean is, we wouldn't need money if I had none. I've spent none of my own since I've been married. Louis is a good provider. But . . . I intend to spend some."

"Oh?"

"On Stacy Kirk's campaign for Councilman. We've met him. Had him for drinks . . . I'm hopeful that he will make a good showing against you."

Adam did not speak.

"If he does, perhaps they won't be able to make you Mayor. As I understand it, it is customary to appoint the man who has won with the most votes Mayor. To go against custom would be dangerous for the local politboro. I like Stacy Kirk. He wants nothing this disgraceful town should not have. He's a perfectly acceptable candidate."

"And I am not?"

"Of course you are. You're a superb candidate. But your ego suffocates me. I can't build Louis to match you, so I must tear at you. In the ways I can, anyway."

"I thought we were going to be friends—or at least friendly enemies."

"You're too impervious. I have to see you . . . wounded and in need."

"Not of anything from you, I think."

She laughed. "It's already worked. You're hurt."

He started to retort, and thought better of it. He drank his wine, called the waiter and ordered another glass. "You're right," he said, finally. "You've hurt me."

"I'm going to continue to try to do that," she said, quietly. "Somehow, if I'm going to cope with you—which means coping with Louis, the marriage, the city, Texas— this whole strange life I've chosen at this time—I've got to know you as a wounded human being, like Claude, like Louis, like me."

"I am that."

"Don't be Mayor."

"You haven't hurt me that much. I only have to fight you. That's all. I can do that."

"Not forever."

"We'll see."

She was silent. Adam wished to slap her, to kiss her violently, to run away with her, to do anything but sit across from her impassively, which he did.

She said, "Don't you want to know what Louis will do? About the race?"

"I was going to ask you."

"He will support you. It will be well known in the city that we have disagreed. Shocking to every Ramsey woman I know."

"That it will."

"Are you relieved about Louis?"

"Yes," he said, truthfully. "That would hurt worse. Or maybe it wouldn't."

"I'll try to change him. But I expect to fail. I have hired David Smolley to help Kirk."

"Smolley. He runs gubernatorial elections, not councilmen."

"He handles anything for money. I want to be sure that Kirk still has his radio program when this is all over. And during it. And if something should happen to his show, he just might win the election. That's how nasty it will be, Adam. Don't think I'm so smart. I talked to my father, who thinks I'm crazy. But knows about political and economic pressures. Those will do no good with Smolley here."

"I would never have used them."

"No, but you wanted Kirk to think you would. Now he knows you can't."

"Why does your father think you're crazy?"

"He doesn't . . . he didn't understand about you and me."

"What is there to understand?"

She looked at him steadily. "The one thing you can't do is lie to me. Not about us. It's impossible. I know exactly how you feel. At all times. And how I feel. Nothing is going to happen, all right, I'm prepared. But you cannot lie to me."

Adam looked down at his wine. He twirled his glass slowly.

"Sorry," he said. "Of course. I do know that."

No ONE else in the family mentioned the article to him, though his mother seemed remote. But this conversation remained in Adam's mind. He wished to push it away, but he could not. He told himself that what Karen was doing was simply the expression of a supremely ambitious creature cutting at him to build up her own husband; while admitting, as she had, that this husband had had his chances and had flubbed them; and knowing, as she must, that he would flub other chances. Simple enough. Adam liked to pierce to the heart of a matter, eliminating the extraneous. It was, he considered, his greatest business talent. He did not normally oversimplify, he simply talked essences and reduced problems to manageable proportions. In the case of Karen, he was aware that he was lying to himself. He lied to himself about her feelings for him and about his for her. Adam, accustomed to directness, found it difficult to say the unsayable, even to think the unthinkable. He could face the fact that he found his sister-in-law the most challenging woman he had ever known. The memory of their kiss at her wedding had never left him. He did not remember feeling the same way sexually about a woman since the early days of Claude; and even then? He knew he could have his sister-in-law when he wished it; he never saw her without wishing it.

All these things he knew, fought and tried to push out of his head. When they met at parties, he continued to be stiff with her. She only smiled. She did not know any more than he did, perhaps, but she accepted more. "For Karen," he thought, sometimes, "all things are possible. They always have been." For him, he was sure, this thing was not.

HE SCHEDULED the executive committee meeting for a Saturday morning at ten o'clock. He considered ordering lunch for them all and decided against it. He could finish what he had to say before lunch. His colleagues could do what they wanted after the meeting. He was not sure they would wish to have lunch with him. For a week before the meeting, he reviewed his charts and graphs with Bill King. He rehearsed what he had to say so many times he was in danger, he felt, of speaking by rote. His palms were often damp, as he discussed endlessly with King everything he planned to present to his colleagues, his brothers and his mother. There was no question in anyone's mind as to the importance of the meeting. Each Saturday, half the major executives were off. On this Saturday, no one was off. Adam had made it clear to his mother that she must schedule no customer appointments for that morning. Louis and Karen had planned a trip to Austin for the weekend. This was canceled. Normally, a secretary took notes during executive committee meetings. Adam did not invite one. He did not wish notes on this meeting. On the Friday night before the meeting, he was so short and brusque with Claude that she challenged him.

"For one thing, you've had three drinks," she said, "and you look as if you mean to have a fourth. What is it, Adam? I've never seen you so nervous."

He sat down heavily on the sofa opposite her.

"I was meaning to have another drink," he said.

"Well, all right. It won't make you drunk. I'll get it."

While she went to the pantry to mix his drink, he wondered how much to tell her. He decided a little. He took his drink from her and put it on the coffee table.

"I'm going to hurt people tomorrow," he said. "Some of them badly."

"Who?"

"Primarily . . . Louis and my mother."

Claude looked at the floor. "Do you have to?" she said. "They're already not pleased with you. With us."

"Just me. You're not included."

"I defend you. I did in that terrible dinner about running for Mayor."

"You're expected to. Right or wrong."

"Why do you have to hurt them?"

"Things have to be done. In the store. Unpopular things. Major changes. People . . . familiar people . . . loved people . . . will have to go."

"Like who?"

"Emma Goldman for one."

Claude looked as though she had been struck. "That's impossible," she said. "She's . . ."

"My mother's best friend. My own Aunt Emma. It's still necessary."

"Fire Emma. My God, Adam."

"Well, not fire. Some other arrangement. Something can be worked out. There are other things, too."

"Adam . . ." Claude picked up her glass. He noticed that her hand was shaking.

"What?"

"Your mother will not stand for that. She will not stand for it."

And it now struck him for the first time that perhaps she wouldn't. He took a sip of his scotch and leaned his head back against the pillows. For a moment, he closed his eyes.

"What then, Adam?"

He took a long time to answer. "She will accept it," he said, slowly. "In the end."

Claude spoke angrily. "The silver tongue, the great persuader! Adam, who can do anything! If keeping Emma is wrong, then your mother has a right to be wrong. It's *her store*, Adam!"

"It belongs to a lot of people," he said, wearily, not returning her anger. "Stockholders . . ."

"Who never heard of Emma Goldman."

"It's the right thing to do," he said. "It symbolizes the whole thing. What's wrong with the store."

Claude was silent for some time. Then she said, "If, for once, the great persuader doesn't persuade, then what happens?"

While he thought, Claude watched him intently. When at last he looked at her, he thought he had never seen her face so serious. He smiled, "Well, I guess it'll be a test," he said. "Mother and I may go to the mat."

"And she has the stock."

"And she has the stock." He paused. "As a matter of fact, you've just convinced me of something."

"Of what?"

"I may as well do this all the way. Get into the Houston store, Fort Worth, the whole expansion program. Maybe even . . . if it comes up . . . the eventual sale of Starr's."

Claude shook her head. "Gently is better. Over a period of time."

He laughed. "Always the gentle Claude. You would be a terrible businessman. You would be a rug."

She drew back, stung.

"But then you aren't a businessman. And never will be. And gentleness becomes what you are." Adam stopped speaking. His eyes left Claude and gazed, unfocused, on the big living room and the scores of paintings. "It's necessary," he said, finally, "to find out who's running this store. If I am—or I'm not."

Claude said sharply, "Adam, what if you lose?"

Again he was silent for a time. "I don't know," he said quietly. "I've made no provisions . . ."

Rivers, the butler, entered the room. "Dinner is served, Madam," he said.

They spoke little during dinner and retired earlier than usual. After a couple of hours, Claude got up and went into the bathroom. When she returned, she carried a glass of water and a pill.

"This may make you sleep," she said. "I just took one."

"I don't want to be groggy in the morning."

"It's very mild. You'll be groggier if you don't sleep."

He took it, and after a time, did sleep.

ADAM WENT to the conference room shortly before nine that Saturday morning and set up his visual aids on easels. He then distributed typed copies of his report, containing all the information he had gathered so laboriously over the months. It was complete. In the case of personnel, it named names. He had not capsulized. He had even had it typed in New York so that no Starr's secretary could know its contents. At nine-thirty, Bill King joined him.

"You really haven't told me how much you expect me to do today," he said.

"I don't know yet. It depends. I'll call on you and you'll know what to say. I'm going into the expansion as well."

King whistled. "The whole bag. Well, why not?"

"Exactly."

"We should have some coffee. They should have something to fool with."

"Or throw."

One of the secretaries brought in a large pot of coffee and distributed Royal Crown Derby cups and saucers at every place. And well before ten o'clock, the members of the executive committee began to arrive. Bob Hardy, the rumpled credit manager, was first, then Matilda Johnson, the personnel director, then Eli Goldstein, who ran operations, then Peter Shaw, sales promotion, then Mindy Minsky, public relations, then Louis and Jenny Starr together. The "good mornings" were formal. Ordinarily, the executive committee met with some joviality. In general, they were fond of each other. It was an organization surprisingly free of political infighting. Arguments there were and jealousies arose at times; but usually they were soon gone. Today, they were silent. The calling of the meeting had signaled something important. That none of them except King (and the others did not know that King knew anything more than they did) had been informed of the purpose of the meeting seemed ominous. They sipped their coffee and the smokers lit cigarettes.

Adam began to speak at five minutes past ten. At first, he remained seated.

"I've called you together for what I consider to be our most important meeting in many years," he said, speaking quietly and calmly. He was no longer nervous. The sound of his voice always gave him the feeling of authority and direction. As he spoke, he shifted his eyes from time to time to one or another of them, being sure he left no one out. He did not, for the moment, concentrate on either Louis or his mother. That would come later. "I've spent the last months making an exhaustive study of our store. Probably the most exhaustive that's ever been made, at least during my days here. I've done this personally, calling on none of you, precisely so that I could learn for myself where we stand—and where all of you stand in your respective divisions—and where we are going. This is not a meeting to criticize any of you specifically—at least any more than me. We've got where we are gradually. Because we are all living well and the store is not losing money. When that is true, things happen to businesses. Hard decisions are not made, alertness is blunted and signs are ignored. When this happens over a long period of time, businesses fail."

Adam paused. "We are not failing," he said. "But we will be in three or four years, maybe five, unless we take some steps. We are currently making a four . . . less than four, right, Bill?"

King nodded. "Under four."

"Under four percent pretax profit, not even a two percent net. If we were a Federated store, that would mean a complete change in management. It is unacceptable. What is more, under present circumstances, those profit margins will not increase significantly. The new store will help but will subtract business from downtown, will add staff, and will still leave us with the weaknesses of the downtown operation. There are some storeowners who never learned how to make a decent profit until they sold their stores and somebody told them how. I don't wish to be one of them. I'm sure none of you do. My findings are not pleasant. My proposals are not pleasant. My facts, however, are correct."

Adam then outlined in general terms everything he had found and what his proposals were: the ten percent cut in the personnel budget; the necessary cuts in advertising, but the addition of more seasonal catalogues mostly vendor paid; the lower amounts of dollars spent in buying expensive, couture clothes, the increase in designer appearances and the resulting special order business; the cut in the number of buyers' trips and the length of the trips; a major charge for men's alterations (always done free) and higher charges for women's; and half a dozen other matters of a general nature. When he had finished this part of his discourse, he paused.

"Have any of you anything you'd like to say now?" he asked. "These are only the generalizations. I will also get into specifics."

"If you cut the initial buys from couture houses—forget special order—we'll lose some exclusives," Louis said.

Adam nodded. "Some. But when we lose an exclusive we'll cut the line out. Throw it out of the store. And let them try to sell it somewhere else in north Texas. They can't and they know it."

"That will be very hard on some houses," Jenny Starr said. Her face was calm and thoughtful.

"Not any harder, as you'll see, than we'll be on ourselves," Adam replied.

"We make more money on foreign goods than on domestic, yet you want to cut trips," Louis said. "That doesn't add up."

"I didn't say to buy less foreign goods, I said to buy them quicker and not stutter and stammer along," Adam said, snapping. "If we haven't the buyers to do that, then we'll get them."

Louis flushed and was silent.

"I don't know about the other divisions," Peter Shaw said, slowly, "but I can't see that sales promotion is over-staffed. Advertising is crying for more help now."

"I never heard of a department head who thought he was overstaffed," Adam said. "It's in the genes. Look into freelance help for the new catalogues. Mail order is only when the costs are kept down. And it's seasonal. You don't need people on staff polishing fingernails half the year. Does anyone here feel he's overstaffed?"

No one spoke.

Adam smiled. "Then you all have the same problem. How to be understaffed and also more effective than you are now. Matilda, you know the Saks figures and you know our body count is appreciably higher than theirs. In proportion to volume, square footage and any other mea-suring stick."

"It's a different operation," the shapeless gray veteran said, defensively.

"More profitable," was all Adam said.

"Adam, one thing," Bob Hardy said. "You haven't men-tioned charge account promotion. We need to do much more charge account promotion in cities like Houston and Fort Worth. We don't do anything like the business with those towns we should."

Adam was silent for a moment. Then he said, "Bob, we're doing about all the business now with Houston and Fort Worth we're going to do. Until we're there."

Hardy shook his head. "But we can do more than we're doing. Especially through the mails."

Adam shrugged. "We need to be there. We need to be there now."

The silence was suddenly very heavy in the room.

"What are you saying, Adam?" his mother said quietly.

Adam sighed. Now he rose from his chair. "I was going to do this last, but since it's come up, I'll do it now."

He went to one of the easels and pulled off the top couple of sheets which indicated volume and transaction activity over a ten-year period. Under them was an ar-chitect's sketch of a store.

"This," he said, "is a preliminary sketch of the Houston store. In six months, I will have one for Fort Worth. The land is available in Houston now, the developer will build and it is my thinking that we begin the work of drawing up contracts. In Fort Worth, there remains the matter of

site. There are several available, and we'll have to decide.
Fort Worth is not quite so immediate. In Houston, we're
already very late. We should have done this years ago."

"Adam," Louis said, "we haven't even finished our new
suburban store here."

"Nothing in the Bible says we can't work on three stores
at once. Opening at different times, of course, but not more
than a year apart, maybe less."

In the silence which followed, Jenny's whisper sounded
like an organ. "It's mad," she said and her face was white.

"Are there any money problems, Bill?"

King shook his head. "All the lending institutions think
we're a cinch in those areas. They'd stand in line to finance
us."

"That's pretty ambitious, Adam," old Eli Goldstein said.
"We're not even staffed . . ."

"Exactly," Adam said. "We're not properly staffed.
That's my next point. In the reports I've given each of you,
you'll see a breakdown of the performance of each department within the store over a ten-year period. Sometimes
under the same buyer, sometimes, of course, under different ones. Certain divisions are a disgrace. Accessories,
Shoes and Intimate Apparel. We make nothing like what
we should. We don't make the profit on Men's we should.
And on certain women's departments, we've fallen behind
the times. I'm going to take one example—Emma Goldman."

And carefully and without emotion, Adam went through
Emma Goldman's performance. When he had finished, he
said, "As you can see, this does not measure up. Not only
is the department itself not producing, but it hurts other
departments because people go to other stores to find what
should be in Emma's department. When we find sicknesses
like this, we have to cure them."

No one spoke. Adam's eyes were on his mother. Though
her face was still colorless, she gazed at him levelly, not
dropping her eyes. Nor did he.

"What is the cure, Adam?" she said, finally.

"I'm afraid, Mother . . . the cure is to replace Emma,"
he said, slowly. For the first time, he felt he might not be
able to continue. His mother did not look as though she
would cry but he suddenly felt that he might. "And all the
Emmas of the store, Mother."

"I never realized you could be so . . ." Louis began, quietly, "so . . . goddamn cruel."

"Fire Emma?" Eli Goldstein said. "This store was built on its Emma Goldmans, Adam. They're the rocks we stand on."

"Have been," Adam said. "We're on different ground. Emma's not."

Jenny's voice came as though something was sticking in her throat. "So long as I'm alive," she said. "Emma Goldman will never be fired from Starr's."

Adam shook his head. "I didn't say fired," he said. "Replaced. How old is Emma, Mother?"

"Sixty-one."

"She could retire now. Or we could give her some other position. Sales directrice. A special salon of her own. Something to *get her out of the buying.*"

Jenny said nothing. She examined her fingernails.

Matilda Johnson spoke: "Adam, if all your recommendations for personnel changes are like this one, it's a blood bath. That will absolutely kill the morale of the store."

"Some of them are the older girls. Some younger, nonproducing ones. And I'm not expecting everything to happen overnight. What I envision is a two-year plan to streamline this store and make it sing again."

"There are some public relations problems here, Adam," Mindy said. "You can't just execute the people who built you just because they've developed arthritis."

"I said a two-year plan. With a humane solution for all the older people. We do have a perfectly adequate retirement plan as stores go. I made Father put that in years ago."

"You made your father do nothing," Jenny said, viciously. "He did what he wanted to. *When* he wanted to. If he had done everything you wanted to do when you wanted to do it, this store would have been bankrupt years ago."

Furious, Adam said, "Under my father, this store went from an eight-and-a-half percent pretax profit to well under four percent."

"Your own goddamn Foreign Fortnight, Fashion Galas, and all the other extravaganzas you pull," Louis said, as angry as Adam.

"Bill?" Adam said, quietly.

King pulled out a looseleaf notebook. "These are the studies of the periods of the Fortnights and Galas both before and after we began them. They are both profitable. Have added profitable volume. They can't be questioned. I prepared these over the last month because I wondered myself. In the future it will depend on costs. One day they may prove unprofitable, but we'll have a hell of a time replacing that volume."

After a silence, Adam said, clipping off his words: "Since you're angry now anyway, I may as well tell you that I feel we must add a second executive vice-president and general merchandise manager. On your own level, Louis. Responsible for Shoes, Accessories, Men's, Intimate Apparel and Furs. To leave you free to work with the fashion departments, where you are most comfortable."

Louis looked at his brother in disbelief.

"Reporting to you?" he said.

"To me."

"Why not just GMM," Matilda Johnson said. "Why executive VP?"

"Because then he would report to Louis. As I've said, I want to free up Louis for the work he does best."

"That's a hundred thousand, Adam," Matilda objected. "At a time when you're supposed to be economizing."

"The man I want will make that back and much more in a year or so. That's how bad the productivity in those areas is, Matilda. That's how bad."

No one spoke. Adam was through. Suddenly, he was exhausted. He reached to sip his coffee and realized it was stone cold. He looked around the room. Oddly, no one was looking at him except Louis. And Louis said nothing. After a time, he pushed back his chair and silently left the room. Adam wished above all things to call him back. He could not do it. And he knew Louis would not have come. But his mother took this matter into her own hands.

"Excuse me," she said. "I'll be back in a moment."

She knew that Louis absolutely must not leave the room; a personal disaster. She went to his office and found him there, sitting on his sofa with his head in his hands. He had shut the door, but she did not even bother to knock.

"Come back to that meeting," she said without emotion.

"I have no desire . . ."

"I didn't ask you about your desires. I told you to come back to that meeting. You are not a whipped dog. You are Louis Starr."

He looked at her for a moment, rose and followed her

back into the conference room. They took their seats silently and were surrounded by silence. Adam wished they had come back separately. It was too much as though Louis had returned holding his mother's hand. "Judgment," he said to himself. "Poor judgment."

"Consulting architects about the Houston store without our knowledge is at least a breach of good faith," Jenny said.

"I knew about it," Bill King said.

"Then it is also a conspiracy. This is an important matter which we should all have known about."

"I wanted to show you something visual," Adam said. On this point he was defensive. His mother was right.

"I'm sure you did," she said. "It is, however, slightly unusual and possibly unethical."

"Nonsense," Adam said. "So far the expenditures are well within the president's own budget. We are not into detailed plans."

Jenny was silent. "I do not agree with the concept of a second executive vice-president," she said. "The store should have a secure second in command, and he should be a Starr."

Adam shrugged. "When I am away, Louis would still be in charge."

"Not by rank within the organization."

"No. By name. Because he is Louis Starr. When I am away, on general store matters, the new man would consult with Louis. Not on matters connected with his own divisions."

"I would be totally ignorant of what half this store is doing," Louis said. His tone was bitter. "After more than ten years of running the show."

"We're probably the only store our size which still has a single GMM. We're out of date."

"The effect is to leave me with half my job."

"The half you do best. As we grow, it will consume more than enough time for you. I can guarantee that."

"You have been putting me down—and Bernie too—all our lives, Adam," Louis said, his face white. "I wonder if you know the damage you've done."

Bernie spoke for the first time. "Oh, I don't know about that," he said. He might have had more to say, but Louis broke in: "You *might,* in fact, understand, Adam. You just might. What is so appalling is that you don't give a damn."

"I've never meant to put you down," Adam said, believing himself to be truthful. "All I've wanted is that we are all doing what we do best."

"You're a goddamn liar," Louis shouted. "The only thing that'll ever satisfy you is when we're all gone—including Mother—so that it's really your own personal empire at last. Emperor Adam Starr. How grand it sounds. Emperor Adam Starr, Mayor Adam Starr, President of the United States Adam Starr—Adam Starr, ruler of the whole goddamn world! . . ."

"I've been instructed by Adam, many times, to play down his public image," Mindy Minsky said quietly. "And to build up yours."

"With him winking the whole time." Louis seemed close to hysteria.

"Stay out of it, Mindy. Thanks, but it's between us," Adam said, quietly.

Jenny Starr took a deep breath. "Well, of course, it isn't at all," she said, so quietly the others had to lean forward to hear her. "It's between Adam and me. Because, in the end, I control this store. That is incontestable. Would you agree to that, Adam?"

It was Adam's turn to flush. "Of course," he said.

"And I will make the final decisions regarding all these matters." She had been looking down at the table when she spoke, but now she looked Adam straight in the face. To his astonishment, he saw that tears were running down her cheeks; his mother's, who had not cried at her husband's funeral.

"Emma Goldman is coming for dinner tonight," she said. "Am I to tell her she's too old . . . out of date . . . through?"

"Tell her nothing," Adam said. "Until . . . until we have decided what to do with her."

"What bone can we throw her, you mean, Adam? What do you think we are doing to this woman's life? I use her as an example. There will be others in this report of yours."

"Financially, we'll be sure she's taken care of . . ."

"I am not speaking financially. I would see to that myself, if necessary. I'm speaking about the fact that Emma's life is one thing: Starr's. When we take that away, we have killed her just as surely as if we had put a bullet in her head. Many people in our store, all they have is that store. Our store. Your father and I always knew that."

"They will be compensated within the bounds of the store's abilities."

Jenny stared at him a long time. The tears continued to course down her cheeks, and when she spoke her voice caught occasionally. Adam thought that it must be with a great effort of will that she held back the sobs.

"I wonder, Adam, if Starr's is the right job for you," Jenny said. "It seems to me you would do well with some faceless, multinational company where the people are numbers in a computer. Where you can cut and juggle and tear apart and you are dealing only with paper and machines . . . That was not the business your father and I built. Ours was a flesh-and-blood business. Everyone here was a human being. We took care of our own. We were careful hiring so we had to do very little firing. We had a large family because it included everyone in this store. Anyone could talk to us, confide in us. And many did. We *know* these people. They are *not numbers* . . . You may, Adam, be *misplaced* in life."

No one spoke. Jenny took a lace handkerchief from her pocketbook and dabbed at her cheeks. "It would occur to me, Adam, that I am considerably older than Emma. Have you a bone for me, too?"

"Don't be silly, Mother."

"I can see no reason why that is silly."

"What you do," Adam said, carefully, "you do matchlessly."

"You mean that I have a certain influence with a good number of customers. What will you do when I die, Adam?"

"This talk is getting ridiculous," he said. "No one's thought of that."

"You have. And I have. What you will do is nothing. And in a month or so, it will be as though Jenny Starr were never here. So quickly do things change . . . It has been nearly two years since I have heard Arnold's name mentioned. His ghost has not haunted us. We wish to rid ourselves of his memory. It is uncomfortable to new management. It will be the same with me. Would you like me to retire with Emma, Adam?"

"Of course not."

She smiled, but it was a bitter smile. "Louis is right.

You are a liar. If I retired and did not vote my stock, the directors would give you a free hand. And that is what you wish. You were encumbered by your father and now you are encumbered by me. You are tired of encumbrances, Adam . . ."

The old lady suddenly stopped and once again stared down at the table. Her hands dropped on it. She had looked at no one but Adam. She did not now. She looked not for support or opposition, not even from her other sons. It would be Jenny and Jenny alone, who would decide.

"What will you do, Adam, if I decide against you?" she said, at last.

He did not speak for some time. "I would have to resign," he said, quietly.

Jenny nodded. "I agree," she said. She rose to her feet. "I will let you know my decisions on Monday," she said. "And now, if you will excuse me . . ." But it was difficult for her to rise and Eli Goldstein had to help the old lady with the wet face. She was steady by the time she reached the door.

When she left, no one spoke. Bob Hardy stubbed out a cigarette and immediately lit another one. Louis stared at the ceiling. The others examined their fingernails or the table. Eli Goldstein riffled through Adam's report, reading nothing of it. Adam himself felt weaker than he could ever remember feeling. It seemed to him that there must be things for him to say, things he must say. But he did not know what they were. Eventually, he gave up.

"This meeting is adjourned," he said. He rose and strode from the room. King followed him immediately and the two men went back to Adam's office.

"Would you shut the door, please, Bill?" Adam said.

King did so. Adam took off his coat and shucked it carelessly across his desk. He then sprawled out on his couch, staring glassily in front of him.

"That was the most insane thing I've ever heard you do," Bill King said, angrily. He sat on the edge of Adam's desk, looking fiercely at the lanky form in front of him.

"Which part of it?"

"Threatening to resign, of course. It was totally unnecessary and you're not going to do it, anyway."

"Maybe I am."

"Of course you're not. This store would go to hell and so would you. For that matter, so would your mother."

"I never realized," Adam said, almost dreamily, "the depth of Louis's hatred of me. I had no idea."

"Bullshit. He was just angry. Out of his head. A little boy spouting off. He'll get over that."

"He's never been over it. That's what's so clear. He's been living with this all his life."

"By Monday, he'll be used to it. Louis is a second man, not a first man, and nobody knows it better than Louis."

After a time, Adam said, "You know, Bill, I never in my life saw my mother cry before."

"Not really cry," King said, weakly. "Just a little watery."

"Oh yes . . . I didn't know it was possible."

King said boldly, "Well, I didn't know it was possible for you to be so stupid. We both knew this was going to be tough. Maybe it was a little tougher than we expected. Not by very damn much. And we have time, Adam, time."

"What do you mean?"

"I mean, if your mother decides to go along with some of it, all of it or none of it, nothing has to be done tomorrow. In the old days, it was sometimes years before you got what we needed from your father. Eventually, we'll get it all from your mother."

"If she turns it down, Bill, I'll have to quit."

"You'll have to hedge. You *cannot* quit, Adam. You lost your head in there. For the first time since I've known you, you lost your head."

"I put myself on the line before the whole executive committee. If I lose to Mother, I lose to all of them. There isn't any president of Starr's. I had no choice."

"You still have choices. Everything in there was said in anger. No thought. Zero consideration. That is no way to run a business and you know it. So, leave it lay. Your mother will give in on some points, maybe, and, if she doesn't now, she will soon."

Adam rose to his feet. "I'm going home," he said.

"Sleep on all this tonight. Call me tomorrow."

"Maybe. We'll see. Do you suppose they'll read the report?"

"They'll read it."

"So long, Bill. Thanks."

But Adam did not go home. He did not feel like talking

to Claude about what had happened. He did not wish company. Instead, he drove out to the ranch, saddled up one of the horses and rode slowly across the prairie he and his father had owned together. The basic feeling he had was an obliterating sadness. If he had been a different man, he might have cried. He was not able to recover from the sight of the tears running down his mother's face. Somehow, Louis's bitterness was easier to take. He could deal with anger, his own and that of other people. He could probably also deal with tears, but not his mother's. Adam had never questioned the fact that he loved his mother. It had never occurred to him that he might not totally understand what he meant by this. He simply loved her, as he loved his wife, as he loved his children. He had known there would be an argument, serious dispute. He had simply not expected tears. And, long after the fact, they stayed in his mind and flayed at him.

He never even trotted the horse. Just walked him slowly across several miles, scarcely getting his business suit dusty.

Resignation? And what would that mean? Oh, there were other jobs. During his father's lifetime, Adam had often been felt out for store presidencies. He had, of course, never considered one of these offers. He was a Starr, as much as they all were. No matter what else he was, he was a Starr. His own family might fight him, but he was one of them; their leader, in fact. One could not cease to be what one was. He could not, he thought, become some strange man named Starr in some strange city . . .

"Of course I can," he said aloud. "I can do anything I have to do."

He drove home slowly. He really did not wish to talk to Claude. It came to him joltingly that there was but one person in the world to whom he wished to talk and that was Karen. And he, who had just told himself he could do anything, could not do that; could never, he was certain, do that.

IT WAS Louis's way to bury his anger. It sank into him like poison, settling down in his body; a physical thing, there to remain through the months and years and bringing on black depressions and self-disgust. He had spent thousands of dollars on psychotherapy, but the psychiatrist had never been able to bring forth from him the screams which were in him. He had sat across from the old gray-haired psychiatrist and been reasonable.

"You always come wearing armor," the psychiatrist had said.

"I can't help that. I'm always in armor."

"There is a solution, you know. A practical solution."

"Which is?"

"To leave the store. And your brother. Since you can not defeat him, abandon him."

"I'm not sure . . ."

"What are you not sure of?"

"Who else would want me."

"You don't know. You've never tried. Never investigated."

"The family. The store. I don't visualize life without them."

"Perhaps we should discuss fear. At greater length than we have discussed it. What do you fear?"

"Each day."

"Do you specifically fear your brother? What your brother will say and do?"

Louis had hesitated. "I suppose I do."

"Yet, he will not fire you."

"That's not the point."

"He diminishes you."

"Yes."

"What else do you fear? In each day."

"Being wrong . . . because Adam is right."

"Adam is always right?"

"Always."

"You will have to learn how to do without your armor. Perhaps eventually you will scream. At least in this office."

But Louis never had. Until that morning, he had not shouted at Adam. Now he had. The experience left him weak and with his hands shaking. Like Adam, he did not wish to go home. Instead, he went to the City Club, changed into swim trunks and swam in the huge indoor pool. He swam thirty laps, slowly and steadily. When he was through, he was exhausted. He lay on one of the chaises and took long deep breaths until his heart had stopped pounding. Several people he knew stopped by to say hello, and he was polite but did not wish to get into conversation. He closed his eyes so that they then would not stop by his chair. When he got up, he went directly to the sauna, where he spent twenty minutes and allowed the sweat to pour off him. Then he took an ice-cold shower and dressed. It occurred to him that he had not had lunch. He barely made the dining room before the kitchen closed. He ordered lamb chops, but fiddled with them. He was too upset to be hungry. There was plenty for him to do that afternoon. In retailing, the masses of paperwork always provide things to do. Though he did not wish to do it, though his palms broke out in a sweat as he came to his decision, he forced himself to go back to the store. He went to his office, closed the door, picked up his Dictaphone and began to work. He worked the rest of the afternoon. On Saturdays the phone seldom rang and no one knocked at his door. Normally, one of the other executives who was working would have dropped in. Saturdays were informal at the store. No one did. They would, he reflected, have no idea what to say. And he had nothing to say to them. At dusk he left the store and got into his car to drive home. He dreaded telling his wife what had happened. He dreaded this because the things that happened to him in life would not happen to Karen. The only way diminution of Karen as a person could take place was through him. As he skidded, by accident of marriage, she skidded with him. *Accident* of marriage. He wondered sometimes whether that was how she considered it. Was it indeed how he himself considered it? He did not at all understand why she had decided to marry a tentative man; unless, of course, that was what she needed in her own definiteness. He did not believe this. Like most people, Karen did not say everything she thought. But she said enough. He knew what she wished him to be; and that he was not. Sometimes, very occasionally, he woke up in the middle of the night and looked at the sleeping body next to him and wondered if this body had been placed there by chance. Temporarily. And it occurred to him that if it were taken away, he would be destroyed. For of one thing he was sure. He was totally in love with his wife. He did not expect her to return his love in degree; had never expected this. He simply wanted, above all things in life, to keep whatever feeling in her had brought her to marry him. To keep her with him.

She came home late, after playing tennis. When she had changed and he was making their drinks, she said, "Why are you putting off telling me about the meeting?"

"Because it wasn't pleasant."

She looked at him steadily.

"That," she said, "is no reason not to tell me about it."

"I know. I thought I'd have a drink or two first."

"Go ahead."

"How was your tennis?"

"All right." She smiled. "Have your drinks and tell me when you want to."

After dinner, when he told her about the meeting, she was gentle.

"So it means they would cut your job in half. I mean Adam would do that."

"In effect."

"Leaving you with one leg. And of course, the new man will be Adam's property."

"Obviously."

"How do you feel now?"

Louis considered for a moment. "When I was shouting at Adam, my main feeling was surprise. I couldn't believe what I was hearing. Then I went for that swim and everything. I suppose it calmed me down."

She was silent for a long time. "Do you know how I would feel if I were you?"

"I think so. You would want to kill him."

She smiled. "I might have done that long ago. No, I was thinking I probably wouldn't be here tonight. I would be at your mother's."

"You'd be making a mistake. If she'd wanted me, she would have called."

"I wouldn't have waited for that. I would have fought early on."

"I promise you, that would simply be in Adam's favor."

"I see." She looked at the bulky report on the coffee table. "Is that what Adam prepared?"

He glanced at it.

"Yes."

"Have you read it?"

"Not yet. I'll read it tomorrow. I know what's in it. He explained that pretty clearly."

"The work that must have gone into it . . ." Her voice trailed off.

"Adam has never been afraid of work. And he's careful. I'd be amazed if there were the smallest mistake in that thing."

After a time she said, "I should think you *would* want to kill him."

He looked at her in surprise. "You almost sound serious."

"I'm completely serious. You said *I* would, and I would. I can't understand why you don't."

He said awkwardly, "It's just a joke, that's all."

"I don't mean you would. Or I would. I mean want to. Seriously wish to."

"I would rather . . . defeat him."

"And that you can't do. Only your mother can do that. And you feel you shouldn't talk to her. You feel you shouldn't do anything at all."

"There's nothing to do."

"Whether it's wrong or right, there's always something to do."

"Let's put it this way: There's no right thing."

"My father always believed in action. He said it distracted his enemies. He said to sit still was the only impossible thing."

"Can we stop now?"

"Of course we can. There's a revival of *The Magnificent Ambersons* at the Coronet. Would you like to go to that? We just have time."

"Why not?"

That night when Louis made love to his wife, she seemed absentminded and responded mechanically. It was not a great success. Later, when he was long asleep, she rose and went downstairs. She turned on a lamp and read Adam's report from beginning to end. When she had finished, she read it through again. He is good, she thought. He is really good. She went back upstairs but slept little that night.

When she announced the next morning that she was going to visit Jenny, Louis said seriously, "I'd much rather you didn't."

"I have been promising to go and see her by myself. We have a good relationship."

"This is not the time for it."

"I don't expect we'll get into affairs of state. We won't unless she wants to."

"But you don't want me with you?"

"No. I'm just a young woman calling on her mother-in-law."

When she called Jenny, the older woman sounded pleased.

"Do you want lunch?" she said.

"Of course."

"There's a good bit of salad niçoise. We can have that. I'll be glad to have company."

"You see," Karen said to Louis. "She was pleased."

He shrugged.

Jenny greeted her in the enormous living room. "Sherry or a little cold champagne?" she said. "It's Sunday."

Karen laughed. "Then champagne."

Jenny nodded to Maitland, who returned in a moment with two glasses of champagne.

"What is it?"

"Taittinger. Arnold preferred this to Dom Perignon. He said automobile dealers drank Dom Perignon."

"He was a snob."

"Oh yes. Like all self-made men, he became one."

Karen hesitated. "Are you accepting it better? His death, I mean?"

Jenny looked away and her eyes seeming vague. "Mourning has not been the usual thing with me," she said, slowly. "I have had no wailing and gnashing of teeth."

"But sadness."

"A certain . . . emptiness is always with me. There are vacant spaces in life. Questions do not get answers. There are times when I need him badly and then sadness creeps up on me like a mugger." She looked vacantly around the room. "The house, of course, is too big."

"I should think it would be a comfort," Karen said. "You have plenty of help to run it."

"It is somehow obscene to live in this mansion by oneself."

"I can't see you anywhere else."

"I can. I have been seriously thinking of selling it. I would have to be careful. Zoning is one acre through here, and if I sold through a blind to a developer, I would kill the value of the land. Including Adam's."

Karen sipped on her champagne.

"I wouldn't know how to deal with grief," she said. "It would scare me."

"I don't deal with it. It deals with me. Treats me as it wishes. Very erratically, I must say. I find myself remembering many bad things as well as the good. That may be unusual. I'm told one remembers only the good, but I have not found it to be so. Arnold and I were not perfectly happy, you know." Jenny looked at her daughter-in-law with a half-smile on her face. In slacks and a silk shirt, she looked younger than her years and extraordinarily like Adam, it seemed to Karen.

"No, I didn't know."

"He was . . . more sophisticated than I in some ways. Of course, in others, I taught him all he knew. We did not, however, quarrel often. We do not like to quarrel in this family, as you may have noticed."

"It must happen."

"Oh yes. We do not like it, though." Once again, the half-smile appeared on Jenny's face. "I assume you know we are quarreling now."

After a moment, Karen said, "Yes, I know that. If quarrel is the word."

"It was the word yesterday. It was the word last night when I went to bed. I was in a rage when I went to bed. Do you know who was the object of my rage?"

"I suppose so. Adam."

Jenny shook her head and took a small sip of champagne. "Oh, no. Arnold Starr. For not being here. This, you see, is what he did in life. He dealt with these matters. I lack practice in this. I was viciously angry with him for deserting me. Have you read Adam's report?"

"Yes," Karen said.

"I thought you probably had. And what did you think?"

"I thought it was brilliant. Unfortunately, I thought it was brilliant."

"Unfortunately because of your husband, of course."

"Yes."

"Why did he not come this morning?"

"He thought it would be wrong."

Jenny nodded. "He was probably right," she said. "Shall we have our salad?"

They sat in the dining room, Karen to the right of Jenny at the enormous table. "Normally, I would have had two trays. Arnold and I often ate from two trays. This room is a trifle formidable for two. When the children were home . . . with their friends and dates . . . it was noisy and joyous and argumentative. I had the most peculiar feeling yesterday. I kept seeing Adam as a small boy, as a young man.

Once he came down from Harvard in spats. He was rather a dandy for a couple of years."

Karen laughed. "He's hardly that now. He always looks slightly askew."

"Askew, yes. And Louis looks immaculate. And Bernie sometimes looks like a golf pro." Jenny paused. Maitland came in bringing the demitasses. "I expect you know I cried."

"Yes."

"It was a shock to me." Jenny laughed. She had a low, tight laugh. One did not imagine her finding anything uproarious; only mildly amusing. "Think what it must have been to the others."

Karen did not speak. In the silence, Jenny suddenly looked at her sharply.

"Have you come to plead your husband's case, then?" she said, sharply.

"No."

"What then?"

"I've come to tell you I think Adam must not resign. Whatever has to be done, Adam must not resign."

Jenny's mouth opened slightly. "I must say," she said, "you astonish me. You—who are actually helping his opponent for the Council."

"I dislike that because it is ego . . . Adam and Starr's . . . that's a different matter."

"What would happen to Starr's if Adam resigned?"

Karen looked and was flustered. "Bad, sinking things," she said, finally.

"It would mean your husband would be president," Jenny said. "I should think you'd want that more than anything in the world."

"I . . . had thought so, too," Karen said, hesitantly. "But not at such a cost. Perhaps not at all. Certainly not now. Louis . . . is not ready."

"Will he ever be ready?" Jenny's eyes were cold.

"I don't know," Karen said, almost whispering.

"People do grow in jobs," Jenny said.

"He is not prepared. For the store, things are complicated now."

"Adam's report impressed you."

"He must be right. His evidence was clear."

"Shall we go back to the living room? Or would you rather take a swim?"

"I don't feel like a swim."

"Good. Neither do I."

They sat down together on the huge sofa and Maitland brought them more coffee.

"You are very ambivalent about Adam," Jenny said. "Do you realize that?"

"Not ambivalent. I simply remember all the things my father has said about business. He made a huge success. He did many unfortunate things to other people. But many more people are employed and reasonably happy today because of the growth of his company. Because of the unpopular things he did."

"Adam does not feel flesh and blood around him. He sees only numbers. You do not feel that?"

"No. I think he feels the flesh and blood and takes harsh measures to be sure it is kept safe."

"You are also ambivalent about Louis, my dear," Jenny said, softly.

"I love him—But I am realistic." Love him, she thought. Well, in her way . . .

"I see. Well, I was realistic about Arnold, too. And the marriage lasted. I will not ask you whether your marriage will last because of course you don't know. I will pass that." Jenny finished her coffee, rose and walked to the huge window overlooking the back property. All her trees were green now, and mountains of forsythia were everywhere. The willows bent gracefully in tribute to the graceful pond on which ducks floated. "What a lot of land we seemed to need," Jenny said. "It comes from having been poor once. Arnold had to be reminded he no longer was." Jenny turned around and faced Karen. "I made up my mind last night about this," she said, quietly. "Perhaps I had made it up at the meeting and didn't know it. With certain minor provisions . . . with which Adam will have no trouble, I am accepting his proposals. His report. In its entirety. If you will call Louis and ask him to drive over, I will explain the matter to him myself. I will also telephone Adam and have him call another executive committee meeting for tomorrow so that this can be announced. I will do the announcing. There is one thing I might tell you, Karen."

"What is that?"

"All that you have said here today is . . . unusual. There are those who would call it betrayal."

"Do you?"

Jenny shook her head. "It was, as Adam would say, the proper thing. You were honest and thoughtful—and correct. I shall say nothing to anyone about our talk. Or any talk we ever have. There are layers within you that are not in most people. So there are in me. Let us keep those layers private unless we wish to express them to each other."

Karen nodded. She said nothing.

Jenny looked away. "I suppose," she said, quietly, "you may as well call Louis. Since . . . as we have decided . . . I seem to have no choice."

ADAM, LOUIS or even Matilda Johnson could have told Emma of the change in her status. By agreement, she was to be made assistant to the chairman and sales directrice of the second floor. Her salary would remain the same, and there would be bonus opportunities involving sales increases on the floor. But Jenny told her.

"I will have her at the house for a drink," she said to Adam. "She is my friend and I owe it to her."

"If you like," Adam said. "I do want you to know I'm not afraid of it."

"That is not the point. You are not the point. Emma is the point."

Emma, sitting in one of the wing chairs across from Jenny, who was on the sofa, took only club soda. Jenny had a sherry. When Jenny had finished explaining what would happen, Emma cried as Jenny had; no sobs, but tears running down her cheeks. Old people often cry like that, Jenny reflected; perhaps we have grown too feeble to make noise.

"I personally asked for this," Jenny said. "I personally wanted you for my assistant. We will still make the New York trips together."

Emma shook her head. "Do not tell me this was your decision," she said, in her heavy voice, the only kind of voice that could come, somehow, from such a massive face, such a massive body. "This was the decision of Adam Starr. It is the beginning of the slaughter."

"There will be no slaughter," Jenny said. "That is silly."

"The old mares will go out to pasture. Young colts will come in and make terrible mistakes because they will not know what Starr's is. But that is what Adam will want. He will want dollars and he will move people around like

Chinese checkers until he has the dollars. Do you know what that job has meant to me, Jenny Starr?"

"I think so," Jenny said. She was sad and weary.

"I do not like aeroplanes. They make me nervous. I think they are going to crash. But it was my mission to get on aeroplanes and undergo this fright. It was my mission to spend long nights in lonely hotel rooms, making up my papers . . ."

"But you will still go to New York, as I said," Jenny interrupted. "Maybe not to Europe . . ."

"But only to look," Emma said. "To look at what the others have decided. That was my life. The decisions. My decisions made money for this store for more than twenty-five years. Lately it has not been so good, but it is the period we are going through. Fashion and quality are not fashion and quality—they are junk. I will not buy junk and sell it to Mrs. Morrow from Amarillo and Mrs. Christian from Corpus Christi who trust me. Quality will come back . . ."

Jenny broke in. "Maybe it won't. I worry about that myself."

"Why . . ." Emma looked now as though she might sob. But she set her mighty jaw and did not. Nevertheless, it took her some time to get the words out. "Why didn't Adam just fire me?"

"He had not the slightest thought of that," Jenny said, firmly.

"Oh, I think he had."

"Never."

After a pause, Emma said, "Don't you find it hard, Jenny Starr, that you will never have your store again? The store that you and your husband built?"

"Starr's will exist and do well. Adam will be a fine president."

"It will not be Starr's. It will be another store. Around the country, great old names are becoming just . . . stores. With columns of figures and no flesh and blood. Starr's is one of the last."

"I will always fight that."

Emma was silent. "You could have fought this, Jenny Starr," she said, bitterly. "You own this store. You did not have to allow them to put me away. Hide me."

"I had no choice," Jenny said, almost whispering. "I would have lost Adam. Adam is my son."

"First he's a president, *then* he's your son . . . a long way down the line."

Both women were silent. Emma seemed to have forgotten Jenny was with her. Her eyes were off somewhere in the far reaches of the room, but they saw nothing. "I have money," she said, at last. "I never spent much. I do not wish this position you have offered me. I am sixty-one years old and I will retire from Starr's."

"Emma, please don't," Jenny said. She was begging.

"I will do that, Jenny, because it is all over anyhow. I'll take my retirement pay and move to New York. I'll get a part-time job with one of the buying offices. My manufacturers will see to that. Nobody knows the market like Emma Goldman."

"I will have no friends left," Jenny said. She was close to tears herself now.

Emma looked at her for a long time. Under the steel-wool hair and the vast forehead, her eyes were still misted with tears. "You let this happen, Jenny."

"I couldn't help it."

"You will have no friends left. You will not even have your family left in the end. They will be interested in other things. The old have no one. Poor Jenny. Poor Emma."

"Then stay."

"You can call me in New York. We can go to the movies."

And so Emma left Starr's. There was shock one day, acceptance the next, little memory that she had ever been there within a month. A woman in her thirties from Bonwit Teller took over. She was handsome and toughminded. She began with a special markdown sale of much of what Emma had bought. The store absorbed the losses to give her a free hand.

Adam's whole plan, by compromise with his mother and Matilda Johnson, became a three-year project instead of two. The Houston and Fort Worth stores were approved. All announcements of these moves were made through press releases from Louis, and curious newspapers were referred to him. He handled himself competently and with grace. To questions concerning the lessening of his own influence, he simply pointed to the projected growth of Starr's and the necessity for senior manpower. And so, Louis Starr finally got publicity. It did not help him. He sank deeper into depression. Karen could not rouse him from it and often grew impatient with him. About her own visit to Jenny, she felt no guilt whatever. She had done the right thing. She was convinced of it.

In midsummer, a 37-year-old divorced man from Famous Barr in St. Louis was named to the second executive vice-president's post. This announcement came from Adam. His name was Neal Adams. He was considered to be a rising star in retailing. He cost $125,000 a year, plus certain bonus arrangements.

And Adam, purged, his business in motion, was free to throw himself into his campaign for city councilman and eventually for Mayor of Ramsey.

# PART SIX

# 1

"I DON'T even know what's involved in a political campaign," Claude said to him one morning at breakfast.

"Neither do I totally. TV, meetings, many speeches before many groups. For councilman, the whole campaign's only a month."

"You don't expect . . ." Claude stopped and looked down at her plate.

"What?"

"You don't expect me to campaign with you, do you?"

He spoke kindly. "There might be one or two occasions when you should at least show up. I just don't know. But you won't have to make speeches."

"Will I be interviewed?"

"I doubt it. This is only a City Council election. Not Presidential."

"Because . . . that sort of thing would really be torture for me. I think you know that."

"I do, yes."

He had lunch with Cullum Roberts, the lanky president of the Citizens Council. Roberts was in his sixties. He was not the only powerful man in Ramsey, but what he said carried weight. He was persuasive because he was shrewd. He said to Adam:

"The fact that someone hired David Smolley to help Kirk will mean all the television he can afford because Smolley believes that's where boys become men."

"My sister-in-law hired Smolley," Adam said, grimly.

Roberts looked astonished. "I don't believe it."

"There are family jealousies. And other matters," Adam said.

"That should not come out."

"It may."

"This is Karen, I assume?"

"Yes."

"What about Louis?"

Adam thought for a minute. "I don't think Louis will campaign against me," he said. "That would be against his nature. And it would be anti-family. Karen may not campaign either. I doubt she will. But it's her money. I want to ask you: How many of the present council do you control?"

"Out of eleven, we own six. Two owe us, but don't always vote the way we think is right. Three beat us. And nearly always vote against us."

"The Mayor is your man, of course."

"Henry Stevens'll jump six feet if one of us belches."

"I won't, you know."

The older man smiled his cold smile. "Adam, we ain't gonna have no trouble. We got plenty of private rooms here in Ramsey where differences get settled. Not in the newspapers."

Adam also smiled. "We'll see," he said.

"There is one issue you don't want to get mixed up in. If you can avoid it."

"Busing."

"That's it. That's in front of the Fifth Court of Circuit appeals and it'll stay there until after this election."

"Then what? If they rule, we've got to bus."

Roberts shook his head. "More private schools. Whatever, we got to keep things cool. This has always been a cool city and it's got to stay that way. Now—somebody's got to do the dirty work in this campaign. Get out the direct mail, place the ads, get the free TV and radio time. We propose to lend you Ira Newcombe for that. As you know, he's done that for years, and he can set up your storefronts and get you organized. That suit you?"

"Fine. I know Ira."

"Everybody knows Ira. He was a city hall reporter when I hired him for the Charter Association thirty years ago. There's nothin' he don't know about city politics."

Adam pulled out some folded yellow paper and scanned it. "What I'm going to talk about is crime—the crime rate in my district is the second highest in the city; housing—there are bad pockets of slums to be cleaned up; the new airport bond issue—the jobs it'll provide, the transportation center it'll make of Ramsey; and mainly—expertise. The fact that I can get things done and Kirk can't."

"Crack hard on that one. People'll believe that."

"I think so, too."

"Taxes, too, Adam. Hit on taxes as bein' too high."

"They'll be higher soon."

"You don't have to tell 'em that."

"For the other things I'm recommending, we need more funding. That's more taxes."

"People don't tie them things together. Just say you're against higher taxes. God's against higher taxes and so is Mother. No reason you can't be."

Adam grinned. "You're a cynical old bastard, Cullum."

Roberts gave a deep chuckle. "I been around all this a long time, Adam. You run into any little problems, you just pick up the phone. Uncle Cullum can spit a long way. Even into the wind."

October is the pleasantest month in Ramsey. The air has at last turned cool, the women are in fall clothes, the football season is at its peak and little rain falls. Adam plunged into his campaign as he did into all things with all his energy. He opened his storefront in a shopping mall not far from his house and Ira Newcombe, a little, almost totally bald man in his sixties ran it. Young volunteers, white and black, were recruited, and the direct-mail flyers, with a huge picture of Adam and the legend "The Man Who Can Get Things Done" imprinted on them, were finished and mailed. Billboards went up in strategic parts of the city and the TV and radio paid spots were done. The spots were second nature to Adam. He memorized them and delivered them without script. He came across as warm, caring and capable; and relaxed. By contrast, Tiger Kirk was tense on TV. He read from cards and looked it. He seemed uncertain. He was good ad lib when he was saying whatever came to his mind, which was the success of his radio show. When he was harnessed to a script, he tightened perceptibly. His theme was "New Blood for a Tired City." He pressed hard on the de facto segregation that still existed in Ramsey. He did not mention the airport. He spoke of police harassment of blacks, but never mentioned the crime rate. His billboards were sparse, his advertising irregular. He did use his program and used it well; unseen, in front of his own microphone, he was at his best.

Two weeks before the election, Newcombe had a poll

done. It showed that Adam would win by nearly two to one and had an edge among the black voters as well as, overwhelmingly, the white ones.

"This one's too easy," the veteran politician said. "It scares me."

So Adam took no chances. He spoke at shopping malls, shook hands at football games, addressed church rallies and civic clubs and appeared on every interview program he could get on, which was most of them. Several times he came face to face with Kirk. Once was in a studio at the public-service station. All the candidates had been invited on separate evenings to debate each other and be questioned by a moderator. Kirk went first. He delivered an emotional and, Adam thought, moving diatribe against segregation. But again, working from a script, his delivery was uneasy. Adam, sitting down the table from him, worked from notes. By this time, he could do his spiel in his sleep; as always, he did it well. When he had finished, the moderator asked some polite questions, and then Kirk turned to Adam.

"They's more than a third black people in our district," he said. "What you got in mind for them, Mr. Starr?"

"Improvement," Adam said, easily. "Better housing and better—and more—jobs. That's one reason I'm hitting the airport so hard. Which you have never mentioned. That's thousands of jobs."

"Skycaps," Kirk said. His face was hard and one eyelid was twitching.

"All kinds of jobs," Adam said, stung. "The trouble with you is you don't think things out. You want blacks to be able to buy a house in North Ramsey, and so do I. *When they have the money.* You have no program to get them the jobs that will get them the money. What it comes down to is, you have no program at all. For anything." Now Adam was as furious as Kirk.

"I'm just a dumb nigger that wants to get uppity, right?"

"Well, that's a dumb enough statement. Nobody in all my life has ever faulted my record on civil rights, Kirk, so don't try it. Your own people won't swallow that. Just as they won't swallow you."

"I'm black like they are. No honky can ever understand that, Mister."

"You're calling your own people stupid. They won't vote for a man who's black just because he's black. Only if he has ideas. Practical, workable ideas. And can get them carried out."

"I'll ask you people out there in the audience," Kirk said, facing directly into the camera. "Do you really want this rich, honky son of a bitch to represent you on the council? Do you really? . . ."

Of course he was immediately blacked out.

"If that happens again, Mr. Kirk, the program will be ended," the moderator said. "This is live television."

When he came back on again, Kirk said: "Folks, you'll jus' have to excuse that slip. I get a little angry now and then at this man across from me. He's spent four, five times as much money as me on this campaign, and he could spend ten times that if he wanted to. He got it all, folks. He got it made. But I tell you what you don't know. I ain't got an awful lot of money to spend but part of what I got comes from a member of Adam Starr's own family. *That's what his own family thinks of him.* You got somethin' to say to that, *Mister* Starr?"

Adam, stunned, was silent. And a buzzing started. So he said, uncertainly: "My family does what it wishes to do . . . I suspect . . . it wanted a fair race."

"From his own family, folks. At least my own mother ain't votin' against me." And the buzzing continued and the people in the audience were whispering to each other.

"Neither is mine," Adam said, fierce. "That money came from a relative by marriage. With her own reasons, having very little to do with this race."

From out of the studio audience, Karen rose to her feet. She walked down the aisle and said something quietly to the moderator.

"Mrs. Louis Starr, Mr. Starr's sister-in-law, wishes to say something. In view of the circumstances, I think we should hear her."

Karen took the moderator's microphone.

"I gave that money to Mr. Kirk," she said, quietly. "I didn't think it fair that a man with so many resources at his command should compete against a man with none. In the spirit of fair play, I helped Mr. Kirk financially. I would not do it again. The fact that Mr. Kirk has used it against Mr. Starr is against our agreement and shows that he is not a man of his word. If I lived in his district, I should vote very confidently and happily for Adam Starr. Thank you."

She returned to her seat. The auditorium of the studio, about half full, was now crackling with conversation. No whispering now. The moderator banged his gavel a number of times before he could quiet things.

"Have you anything to say, Mr. Kirk?"

Tiger Kirk shook his head. "No," he said, quietly.

"Mr. Starr?"

"Nothing."

"This is the fourth in the series of broadcasts bringing you the views of all the candidates in this month's city election," the moderator said. "Next week . . ."

Adam was quickly out of his seat and walked over to Kirk.

"You kicked it there, Tiger," he said.

Stacy Kirk shrugged. "It was already kicked," he said. "I pulled an ace. If she hadn't've been out there, that ace might've won."

"Do you want to withdraw?"

"I'll go through with it. It's almost over. You kin have your big night when the votes come in."

Adam thought as he had so often of the tar roof under which this decent man had grown up. "One day, Tiger," he said, quietly, "you'll run for something and I'll be one of the first to vote for you." He put out his hand and Tiger Kirk shook it. "Good luck, Adam," he said.

Adam walked quickly and then started running out of the studio and around to the parking lot. He raced up and down the lines of cars looking for Karen's Volvo. He found it, just as she was backing out. "How about giving me a ride?" he said.

She smiled, wearily.

"Where to?"

"Anywhere we can have a drink. We're downtown. The City Club?"

"All right."

And so, soon they were once again high up in the air, looking over the lit-up skyline of Ramsey. The lounge was dark, lit only by candles and soft, indirect light at the tops of the walls. A waiter brought them drinks.

"It was very brave of you to do that," he said.

"I have courage."

After a silence, he said, "Why do you always fight me?"

"I felt I had to," she said. And smiled. "I'm getting tired of it, Adam. Very sick of it."

"Are you? I'm glad."

"I can't win for losing." She laughed. "The silly thing is I don't want to win."

Adam looked down at his glass. "I know you don't."

Karen looked at him rather sadly. "You know so much," she said. "So do I. At least I think so. And nothing can be done."

Adam shifted around uncomfortably.

"From here," he said, looking out the huge windows, "this city looks major. Well, of course, it is major. Sometimes we think of New York as the city. Everything else is a town."

"And soon you'll be Mayor of this city. This major city. How will that feel? Please do not tell me of the contributions you can make."

They both laughed. "You know my lines," he said. "Why do you come to so many of these meetings and rallies? They're just stump speeches. They're all the same."

"Not quite. Each one is a little different. The Rotarians are not the same as a black Baptist group. I like to hear how your language changes. Sometimes even your voice. I like to watch you work, Adam. Your report—your report on the store—was brilliant."

He looked at her in surprise. "I didn't know you'd read it."

"Oh yes. That Sunday I went to see Jenny."

"You did what?" he said, in astonishment.

"That's what I did. I said, whatever happened, she couldn't let you resign. Partly selfish, of course. She may have suspected that. She said some funny things about ambivalence. Anyway, she agreed. I knew you had won before you did."

"Won is not the right word for that situation."

"So I come to hear you because I like to watch you work. Sometimes I wish I were in the store."

He was silent. Then he did something which astonished them both. He leaned forward and kissed her softly on the lips. It was a long, gentle kiss. When they separated, neither of them spoke for a long time.

"Why didn't you go to New York with Louis this time?" he asked. "Normally, you breathe in that smog like perfume."

"I wanted to follow your campaign. I told Louis that. He didn't take it very well. He was surprised and . . .

miffed. Not really angry. I suppose he thought I wanted to protect my investment in Stacy Kirk."

"Did Louis contribute to Kirk?"

"Oh no. I think he felt that would be treason. He hates you and also loves you and is terrified of you . . . I also didn't want to miss tonight . . . Obviously, I'm glad I didn't. Oh hell, Adam, I just didn't want to leave you right now."

He looked at her steadily for a long time. At last, his head stopped swimming with confusion. He came to the decision to do something which was wrong, indefensible; for which there was no moral nor intellectual justification; something for which he would not forgive himself. And at this moment, he was willing not to forgive himself; to live with it.

"Will you excuse me a minute?" he said. "Or first, would you like another drink?"

"All right."

He beckoned to the waiter and ordered them two more brandies. Then he left and went to the telephone.

"I feel like going to the ranch," he told Claude.

"The ranch?"

"I need to clear my head. I want to ride and be alone. Did you watch the show?"

"Yes. Very dramatic. Was Karen planted?"

"I had no idea she was there."

"That's unlike you. You're normally too careful for that."

"I wasn't careful at all."

"Then you're very lucky."

"That's true. Anyway, all that's why I want to go to the ranch."

"Then go there."

"Go to bed. I'll try not to wake you when I come in."

"All right."

He made a second call and returned to the table.

"I've reserved a suite for us next door at the Sheraton," he said, quietly. As he looked at her, it did not seem that her face changed. In the soft light, she looked marvelously beautiful to him, and her eyes seemed larger and deeper than he had ever seen them.

"Is that . . . all right?" he finished.

She spoke as softly as he had. "Oh yes, Adam. Yes . . . yes." Then her eyes fell from his to the floor. She gave a small laugh: "I'm so afraid I might cry," she said, and her voice was shaky. "Because I'm so . . . whatever . . . the word . . . or . . ."

Again, he leaned over and kissed her softly.

"We can finish our drinks and look at the sky," he said.

"But not change our minds . . ."

"No . . . not that."

They could not go together. He went to the suite first, while she remained in the club. In thirty minutes, she joined him. It was any hotel suite: imitation French furniture and second-rate abstract paintings on the walls.

"I ordered a bottle of champagne," he said, awkwardly. "It goes with brandy."

She stood next to him. "I think it would help if you kiss me now," she said. "Standing up, like this."

So he did. "I remember how it felt at the St. Regis," he said. "I've been fighting that out of my head ever since."

She walked to the sofa and threw her coat over one arm of it. She was wearing a simple white sweater and a full suede skirt. "I haven't fought it," she said. "I must have fewer principles than you, Adam."

"It doesn't seem so."

"Well, it will. Sometime or other."

When the champagne came, she disappeared tactfully into the bedroom, returning when the waiter had gone. He poured two glasses and gave her one. They clinked and drank, saying nothing. Shyness was so new to both of them, they could find immediately no way to deal with it. He sat down next to her on the sofa and they sipped their champagne without speaking or touching. Eventually, she laughed.

"What?" he said.

"I'm wondering which one of us is the more terrified."

"I'm pretty nervous," he admitted.

"I've done things that I thought were wrong. Even while I was doing them. But not evil. What is happening . . ."

"We can still stop it," he said.

"Do you want to?"

"No."

"I wouldn't let you. I'm too close now," she said, looking away from him.

"Too close to what?"

"The reason I'm here at all. Here in Texas. Married.

Mrs. Louis Starr . . ." She paused. "Why don't you not comment on all that, okay?"

"Okay."

After a few moments, she said, "Adam, I'm going to leave you now. I'm going to bed. Would you not come in until I call you?"

"Of course."

She left him. Sitting alone, he had the fierce temptation to call it off. He wished to call to her, "Stop it, it's impossible. Stop it now before we smash up our lives." But with this thought came the full knowledge that he was doing what he wished to do; what, perhaps, it was necessary for him to do. Necessary: that was the key word. He had always done what was necessary. Now, for the needs of his life, the betrayal of his wife and brother and the risk of destroying everything one family had built were necessary. I am, he thought, in love with this woman. I have been from the first. And I have fought it. I have done everything in my power not to have it so, and it is so. And it is so for her. We have tried and failed, and now we must do what is necessary.

"Adam," she called.

"Yes."

"I'm . . . all right now."

He threw his jacket over hers and went into the bedroom. It was pitch black.

"I'm sorry about the light," she said, nervously. "Later on, I promise there can be all the light you want. I'm just afraid now, is all."

"So am I."

He undressed quickly and soon was lying beside her on the narrow bed. He held her and they were silent for a long time. He did not immediately feel his sex rising, and he had a moment of panic. But then, he turned to her and kissed her, long and hard, and all his normal force and energy came to him, and he touched her breasts and kissed them and ran his fingers over all of her and marveled at how firm she was and how ready for him she was. After a while she used her own fingers, and said, "Adam, we should take more time, but I can't seem to wait. Come into me now, please, Adam. I don't want to wait."

He entered her and felt her close in around him and knew at once that it would all be over too soon. He told her so.

"I know. It's all right. Later on . . . Oh, Adam, do it hard and fast and pick me up and . . . fuck me, Adam, please, hard and come when you want, don't hold back . . ."

They spent hours discovering each other. Adam learned about Karen in that time certain things he did not know about his wife and some things about himself. He and Karen did something of everything to each other. Their shyness gone, they fell in love with recklessness.

From the bed he called the operator and asked to be called at three o'clock. Then he took her in his arms, and they were soon asleep. When the operator called, he did not for a moment know where he was. When the realization came to him, he was disconnected, frazzled. It was Karen who got up first and began calmly to dress. As he was watching her, she came over to the bed and kissed him lightly on the forehead.

"It will be all right," she said.

After a time, when he was dressed and they were ready to go, he felt himself again.

"Will you have to check out?"

"Yes. You go ahead. I'll come down later."

"Could you come to see me tomorrow, even for a cup of tea."

"Of course."

"Good night, Adam."

He took her in his arms and kissed her gently.

"Good night, my dearest," he said.

He waited about for a half hour or so, and then went downstairs and checked out. No one looked at him oddly. Only a single clerk was on duty. He did not seem to recognize Adam.

At home, as he crawled into bed beside Claude, he moved silently and tentatively, hoping not to wake her. But he did.

"It was a long ride," she said.

"I was thinking a lot. I may have ridden twenty miles or so. You haven't been awake all this time?"

"I've dozed on and off."

"Do you want a sleeping pill?"

"I'll get one."

She rose, naked as she always was when sleeping, went to the bathroom and ran some water. After a time, he heard the toilet flushing. It was all completely unfair, he thought.

Returning to bed, she said, "I should think the election would be over after tonight."

"He didn't help himself."

"How amazing that Karen was there."

"Protecting her investment. Seeing it go down the drain."

"She was good to do that."

"Yes. She could have remained silent. I don't think she liked him bringing it up. You know she had told me all about that."

"Oh yes, I know. She's an odd girl. She still makes me uneasy."

He did not reply. She lay on her side and put her arm across his chest. In dismay, he realized that she wished him to make love to her.

"I'm very tired. Drained. Do you mind?"

"Of course not."

After a while, she fell asleep. He got up and took a pill himself. It did not help. He lay awake and watched the sun come up . . . he was filled with horror. He could not believe that he, Adam Starr, had committed such a crime against right, even against reason. But even as these thoughts came to him, he knew that he would go on down this new path. And who would block his way? He looked at Claude in the early light and his eyes filled with tears for a little while; she was lightly snoring. She almost never snored.

KAREN WAS dressed in slacks and an open silk shirt and her hair was bright and glistening as if she had just washed it. A maid showed him in. This branch of the Starrs had no butler.

"Hello," she said, sounding shy.

"Hello." He kissed her softly and quickly on the lips. "How are you?"

She laughed. "Nervous again."

"What about?"

"You. How you feel . . . how you felt when you woke up this morning . . . and how it is now."

"I didn't wake up. I never went to sleep."

"Were you filled with guilt and horror?" There was an edge to her tone.

"No. I'm not saying those things weren't there. They weren't dominant."

"What was dominant?"

He said simply and quietly, "That I'm in love with you."

She was sitting in a black leather armchair, he on a small sofa across from her. She was looking at the floor.

"Are you sure of that, Adam? It was only a night."

"It's been all these months, well over a year. As you know."

"What are we to do?"

"I have to ask you what you want to do."

She looked up at him with a half-smile. "Not stop. Whatever happens, not stop. But I have the least to lose. There's no comparison. Your life could collapse. Just . . . collapse."

"I have to take that chance."

"You'll be Mayor of this city. You might even lose that."

"Well, look, we have to protect ourselves. We can't meet here. Or at the Sheraton."

"Then where are we going to meet?"

"I'll have to get an apartment. It won't be very grand. Just a furnished apartment. Somewhere obscure."

She shook her head. "Adam, you can't just lease an apartment in this town. Adam Starr leasing a furnished apartment? It would be known at every dinner party in Ramsey."

"I've thought of that. You can."

Her eyes widened. "Me? How?"

"In Sam Houston Heights. As Karen Woodward. They don't know a thing about Woodwards in Sam Houston Heights." He looked at her steadily. "I'll tell you the places to look. You write the check and I'll give you cash." He paused. "Can you do it?"

She looked back at him just as steadily. "Of course," she said. After a pause, she added: "I can do something with a furnished apartment. I can do something to make it possible."

"Well, we can't very well take it unfurnished and go around pricing furniture."

"No . . ." She hesitated and looked back down at the floor. "Of course, we'll have to see each other at odd times. At lunch. Matinees . . ."

"Don't put it that way. No negatives. We can't afford negatives. We'll just see each other when we can. Don't go on so many trips with Louis."

"He won't understand, but I'll arrange it."

"As Mayor there will be many places I'll have to go that I won't go to. Or will go for five minutes. Ceremonial things."

They sat in silence for a few minutes.

"I forgot to offer you a drink. You mix it yourself here, you know."

"What do you want?"

"A glass of champagne. There's some there in the bucket. I got it out for us. I wasn't thinking about furnished apartments."

"What were you, then?"

"I wasn't thinking at all. Just feeling."

He poured the champagne and handed her a glass.

"Are you thinking it's sordid?" he said.

"I was. I'm not now. We won't let it be sordid. I'll fill the place with flowers and books and magazines that we'll never read. I'll buy a picture or two. I'll buy some linens. Some glasses and plates. Some marvelous wines. A stereo and some records."

He frowned. "You'll have to be careful," he said. "Having things delivered there."

"Nothing will be delivered. I'll carry the stuff there myself."

She rose and closed the door to the study. Then she sat next to him on the couch and put her head on his shoulder.

"Nothing has happened to me like last night, Adam. I want to say that."

"Nor me."

"There's something else I want you to know. I'm not . . . a conventional girl. But I've never in my life done to a man what I did to Louis last night. I don't think you've ever done that to Claude . . . I'm going to be living with a lot of guilt. I can do that. I think it is in me to be treacherous. Is it in you, Adam?"

He did not speak for a long time.

"So far," he said, quietly, "it is."

She was silent for a time. "I suppose," she said, finally, "there'll always be another shoe to drop."

"We just can't think about it."

"No," she said, positively. She straightened herself up. "Do you want us to come over and watch the election returns with you next week?"

It was his turn to be silent.

"I gather you don't," she said.

"I'd just as soon not see you and Louis . . . when it's just us . . . any more than we can help."

She nodded. "All right."

"Do you understand that?"

"Of course. When will they elect you Mayor?"

"A couple of days later. They just pick up the votes out of a hat. I won't get all of them, incidentally. There'll be two non-Charter Association votes. Then, of course, they'll make it unanimous."

"It's getting late. You'll have to be going."

"I know." He kissed her strongly and passionately.

"I want you," he said.

"I do, too. I think of that all the time. It's frightening." She smiled. "But then, not many things frighten you, do they, Adam?"

"Not many," he said, slowly. "This does."

HE AND Claude watched the election returns by themselves. He won by better than two to one, gathering by far the largest number of votes of any district candidate.

"That's good," he said.

"Why?"

"It just makes it easier to elect me Mayor. Since I got more votes than anyone else. It wouldn't have been disastrous the other way, but this it better."

Two hours or so after the polls closed, he got a telegram from Stacy Kirk. "It is okay, Adam," it said. "Stay well."

"I got to like him, you know," Adam commented.

"But you won fairly."

"Oh yes. No dirty tricks."

"I'm pleased." And so she seemed.

All his family and many friends called until quite late. That night he knew he had to make love to his wife. He was awkward and unsure and not like himself. God, he thought; it can't be like this. But it was the first time since Karen and he blamed it on that. It did not really bother him. She put it down to preoccupation. It did not bother her either.

2

ADJOINING THE main City Council chamber, which was in effect a small auditorium with a dais to accommodate the eleven councilmen, was an anteroom containing a large oval table. In this room, the Council met two hours before its two o'clock meetings on Tuesday to deliberate in advance the questions on the agenda, to vote informally on what action would be taken, and to eat corned beef sandwiches. As a result, very little that happened at the public hearings which followed these meetings came as a surprise. When there were to be protests, the Council was forewarned. Expected arguments were countered in advance and the language to be used was carefully considered. In spite of these precautions, an occasional protest developed into a shouting match, but in keeping with the calm spirit of Ramsey, the Council tried to keep this unpleasantness to a minimum. Even in executive session, the tone was mild. The two young non-Charter Association Council members often were at variance with the prevailing views, but they knew they would be outvoted, and after stating their cases, resigned themselves to making public statements which would be received well by their constituents during public session; and to being defeated. The other Councilmen ranged from early forties to late sixties and were all Charter backed. With rare exceptions, they voted as a bloc. They had all been advised in advance how the Citizens Council felt about the matters on the agenda, and this advice was never ignored.

The Mayor was chosen simply by the Council members' submitting envelopes to the City Manager, one Elgin Crowell, a former City Hall newspaper reporter who had been managing Ramsey for twenty years. He was a long, lean man, with a saturnine face and a low, careful voice. Carefulness was his great virtue. He carried out his mandates with precision and efficiency.

Adam and others had often suggested the need for a more innovative, forward-looking man in the City Manager's job. These suggestions had always floated on the water for a few days and then sunk out of sight. But they did not make a friend to Adam of Elgin Crowell.

On the morning before he was to be named Mayor of Ramsey, Adam arrived at executive session promptly at noon and was surprised to find that all his colleagues were already there. So were three members of the Citizens Council: Cullum Roberts, its president, Sam Wrather, a banker, and Seth Brody, a lawyer. Wrather, a stout man with a florid face, was chairman of the second biggest bank in the Southwest, and Brody was a partner in one of the largest law firms of the area. After Roberts himself, they were two of the most powerful men on the Citizens Council. Adam knew them well, and shook hands cordially.

"Fine race you ran, Adam," Wrather said. "Tell you the truth, I thought that boy'd do better than he did. But every time he opened his mouth his foot went in."

"Silk purse, sow's ear," Brody said, smiling. "Old story."

"He's all right," Adam said. "He'll always be a useful man."

"Do you know all these men, Adam?" Elgin Crowell asked.

"I've met most of them, but I'd like to shake hands with you all."

Adam went around the table, shaking hands, exchanging pleasantries, giving and receiving congratulations. At some time or other, he was certain to be in conflict with most of them. But for now, he was smiling and at his most gracious. When he sat down, it happened that his chair was next to Cullum Roberts, who was smoking a big cigar.

"We have," Crowell said, in his dry voice, "four new members of the Council replacing men who have retired. For their benefit, I'll just say these sessions are informal and always closed to the press. So everyone can be quite open in what he has to say."

"Shouldn't we have an agenda?" one of the new men said. "I don't have any idea what's comin' up today."

"Normally, you will have an agenda," Crowell said. "Today, there is none. Today is largely ceremonial. It simply marks the election of our Mayor. There is no public hearing. Those begin again next week. We usually meet Fridays at nine and I present those things which I expect will come up the following Tuesday. So you have the weekend to study them and discuss them before we meet again Tuesday."

"You mean call each other up?"

Crowell nodded. "Sure. We only have two hours in these informal sessions, so you have to do your homework. At the public meetings we find out in advance who will present what to the Council. And then who will answer what of the public's questions or reply to the public's statements."

"And reject them," Adam murmured.

"Not always, Mr. Starr, not always."

"Elgin," Adam said, carelessly, "the people who come to open sessions are ninety percent against the Council. On something or other. The ones who are in agreement with the Council don't come because they know they've won in advance. The newspapers have told them."

"The newspapers don't know in advance what the Council will decide, Adam," Cullum Roberts said, looking mildly amused.

"Amazing how their advance editorials and Council decisions resemble each other. You'd almost think there'd been prior consultation."

"There is, Adam," Seth Brody said. "You know that as well as I do. The newspaper publishers are indispensable. We'd be insane not to take them into our confidence. In many cases, it's one of the publishers who comes to us."

"Do you suppose they'll ever disagree on anything?" Adam said, lightly. "Sometimes I think they Xerox each other's editorials. Which usually come out sounding just like something I heard Cullum here say at lunch or dinner."

Roberts looked annoyed. "You give me too much credit, Adam. You always have. And that causes little bits of friction that shouldn't oughta happen. Well, now, Elgin, we might as well get on with this."

Crowell pointed to a pile of envelopes on the table. "Here are the votes," he said. "As per my mandate, I've opened them and tabulated them in the presence of the city attorney and the controller. Of course, as you all know, they are signed. Anyone at this table can inspect them, but they are privileged. Not to be released to the press. Only the final result. That's in the Charter."

"Okay," Roberts said, pleasantly. "Who's our new Mayor?"

"We don't have a new Mayor," Crowell said, evenly. "The vote was eight to three for Henry Stevens to continue as Mayor. There were three votes for Adam Starr."

Adam could not for a moment take his eyes off Crowell. The City Manager drummed his fingers against the desk and gazed down at the envelopes.

"Well . . . congratulations, Henry," someone said.

"Thank you," said Stevens.

When the first shock had passed, Adam looked carefully at each face around the table in turn. Only Cullum Roberts looked back at him. There was a faint smile on the old man's face. The others looked somewhere else.

"I would like to see the envelopes," Adam said, his voice just barely shaking. His face was white with anger and he realized his hands had formed two fists. Every muscle in his body was taut. He opened each of the envelopes slowly, reading the signatures. He did this slowly to give himself time to regain control. He had got his own and two non-Charter councilmen's votes. The others were unanimous. He looked up at Roberts.

"You double-crossing son of a bitch," he said, in a quiet voice.

"Well, like I told you, Adam, we couldn't *promise* nothin'. Nothin' at all. The Council acts as it sees fit. Personally, I'd hoped they might vote for you. I thought you'd make a mighty colorful Mayor. But I guess they decided a mite too colorful."

"You're also a fucking liar," Adam said, still quiet.

"We don't use those kinds of words in here, Mr. Starr," Crowell said.

"Shut up, you little prick," Adam shouted. "I'll say any goddamn thing I want to."

"The newspaper boys are outside, Adam," Seth Brody said. "They'll hear you."

"They will soon enough."

"That won't do you any good," Roberts said. "As you surmise, we talked with those boys, and I might tell you, Adam, they were in agreement. Look, son, you always been a peck of trouble around this town, and you will be as a councilman. But you woulda been a hell of a lot more as

Mayor. That's the story, Adam, and you can take it or leave it, except, when you come right down to it, you got no choice. We did what the Charter for this city says we can do. You dead, son."

Adam was silent.

"I'd like to work with you," Henry Stevens said.

"Shut up," Adam said to him. "What you ought to be doing is vomiting. You're a man with a foot on his neck." He pointed to Roberts. "His foot."

"Adam, people always call you a civilized human bein'," Sam Wrather said. His face was redder than usual. He was angry. "You ain't actin' too civilized right now, I'd say. You sound like a little boy who didn't get the ice cream."

"Crowell," Adam said, evenly, ignoring Wrather, "will you give me in writing the exact procedure for getting the City Charter amended?"

"I can tell you it takes fifty thousand signatures on a petition and then a referendum."

"I said in writing. As a councilman, I have the right to demand that, have I not?"

Crowell flushed.

"You have," he said.

Adam looked around the room at the silent faces. "All right, you bastards. Now we're really in for it. I'm going to take this public. I'm going to the people."

"How do you mean, Adam?" Roberts said, but he had paled.

"I mean I can get fifty thousand signatures. And I can force a referendum."

"On what?" said Crowell.

"On how Mayors get elected in this town. On why the people don't elect them, as they do in practically every other town this size in the world. That can be a very popular issue, Cullum, by God. It might just shake up the people around here. The proud people of Ramsey might just *like* to be able to say themselves who their Mayor's going to be."

"It'd break you," Cullum Roberts said. "This time *we* got the money."

"I can get the money. If I force the referendum, the city pays. I just need campaign money. And money won't beat me, Cullum. You run this dead ass against me—and now you've got to since you've already named him Mayor—and I'll crunch him."

"You're crazy, Adam," Seth Brody said. "You're takin' on the whole power of this city."

Adam nodded. "And what's more, I can beat it," he said. "And when I do, you won't have a Mayor who cuts ribbons and kisses asses. You'll have a *Mayor* . . . And God help you bastards if that Mayor's me."

HE ANNOUNCED what he would do in a press conference that night at his home. He was measured and calm, but he did not avoid the word double-cross. He would endeavor, he said, to put both the issue of whether the people would elect the Mayor and who that Mayor should be on the same referendum to save the city money. He would employ the help of the David Smolley Organization, which had recently worked for his opponent in the Council election. And he named certain other people who would be working for him.

"Mr. Starr," a reporter said, in amazement, "those are Senator Calhoun's men."

Adam smiled. "I imagine you'll be wanting to get a statement from Senator Calhoun," he said. "He is backing my campaign all the way."

Adam had called him that afternoon, and the old man had cackled like a hen. "You can't lose," he had said. "Of *course,* they ought to elect their own Mayor. You can have a lot of fun about how cities are not private clubs. Well, here are my boys. They're all good and know the ropes, and they play dirty if that gets needed. If you win this, and you should . . ."

"What?"

"You might have a good future, Adam. This'll make *Time* and *Newsweek.* It ain't just local. You can make it into you against Fascism, if you work it right. How long you got?"

"I'm going to try to make it sixty days."

"Time enough. Any more, you'll just bore people. I'll call all my boys and get the word out. You tell your press conference Hayden's organization is workin' for you. Ain't nobody who's gonna ignore that."

The newspapers ran heavy headlines the next day. The day after, they ran equally heavy editorials denouncing Adam's plan. But he had his fifty thousand signatures in less than ten days, owing mostly to the efforts of the Smolley group. Smolley himself was obese, always seemed to be perspiring and never wore a tie. He had once been a newspaperman on the Austin *American-Statesman*, but had shifted into political organization twenty years before. He was usually on the winning side. This was partly because he was good and partly because candidates who stood to win hired him to insure their success. Smolley could pick and choose. He had no political convictions whatever, at least that were discernible. Like Calhoun and other successful politicians, he talked a country lingo understood by all kinds of Texans. Too much obvious education was bad politics.

"Why did you work for Stacy Kirk?" Adam asked him at their first meeting in Adam's living room.

"In my business, we look for things to do durin' slack times," Smolley said. He had tiny eyes set in folds of flesh and they seemed perpetually amused. "We didn't have nothin' big, and the pay was good. Besides, it didn't do us no harm."

"Why? Your man lost badly."

Smolley waved his hand. "Don't make no never mind," he said. "Everybody knew he had to lose unless he could pin murder on you. Hell, Mr. Starr, he might nota gotten *any* votes except for us." Smolley laughed. "Might've been the first shutout in election history."

He seemed to overflow the armchair. A cigarette dangled from his lips and once or twice he caught the ash in his hand before he could reach the ashtray. "You know," he said, "we're talkin' 'bout two elections here. Ain't no way you can get them both on the same referendum. You can't amend the charter *and* elect a candidate at the same time."

Adam frowned. "I'd hoped we could."

"No way. Hell, there might be five or six candidates for Mayor if all you need is three hundred signatures and fifty bucks, like for councilman."

"Can't we get that changed?"

"Might get it up a thousand signatures and a thousand bucks. That'd keep the freaks out, anyway."

"In time . . . what are we talking about?"

"Four months minimum. Two for the amendment, two more for the election. We'll have to get it on the first ballot that we're gonna have a special election for Mayor right now. That can be done. Once they've voted to elect their own man, they're gonna want to elect him."

"What's the fee?"

"Five thousand dollars a month plus expenses. So double that."

"All right."

"It won't all come from you. We can raise some money. Calhoun's boys can help. They own some money in this town. Now, your platform . . ."

"Is that this is a big city. Little towns appoint Mayors. Big cities elect them."

Again, Smolley waved his hand. "Oh, that's okay," he said. "Appeals to civic pride and all. Look, Mr. Starr, we're gonna win that Charter amendment. We're gonna win that one easy. I don't even want you to get much involved in that campaign. Shouldn't seem too personal. We got plenty of people to handle that part of it. Now when it gets down to who's gonna *be* the Mayor—that's a different ball game. Just how popular are you in this town, Mr. Starr?"

Adam shrugged. "I don't know. More popular than Stacy Kirk."

"That was no trick. But here, citywide, we're buckin' the Charter Association, and they been electin' most of their men for a long time. They ain't bucked Adam Starr who's got a very familiar name and who's done a lot for this town which nobody can question. After we get the amendment, we'll start takin' our own polls. See where we have to do the work. But . . . I think we'll win."

Smolley lifted his great bulk from the armchair. "Tell you what," he said smiling.

"What?" Adam said, also rising.

"I ain't even gonna ask for the first month in advance. In all politics, you get your fees in advance. But, Mr. Starr, I figure you're good for it."

JENNY HAD the family for dinner one night. It was the first time they had all dined together in some months. Some wounds had not healed, would never heal, but Jenny had a purpose which she stated at the table.

"We have had our reservations about this Council matter," she said to Adam. "You know that. I have asked everyone here to announce a decision I've made. I shall support the Charter amendment and your election as Mayor. I shall do that because you were treated treacherously. Quite objectively, you are in the right. Subjectively, no Starr should serve as just another councilman. If he is to serve the city, it must be in the leadership position. We are not used to subsidiary positions. You are free to call on me for money and all necessary support. I should like to know now whether the rest of you are joining me in this?"

"Of course," Bernie said.

"Yes," Louis said. He spoke almost under his breath.

Jenny looked at Karen, who simply nodded. Becky said, "Well, thank God we're a family again."

"We were always a family," Jenny said. "Families have disagreements. They are put aside at certain times."

"I'm very . . . appreciative," Adam said, slowly. "I'm glad you're all with me."

Within the week, he met Karen at the furnished apartment in Sam Houston Heights. It lay in a complex of garden apartments, each with its own entrance. There were no doormen, no elevators. Everything was on ground level. An enormous pool lay in the center of the complex. The apartment was furnished in second-rate Danish modern and the pictures on the walls were reproductions of Van Gogh and Cezanne. But there were bookshelves which could be filled, the furniture was comfortable and the kitchen was adequate.

"We can make a small wine rack out of that shelving," Karen said. "There are things we can do."

"Pretty bad," he said, gloomily.

"No worse than a hotel. Magazines, books, wine . . . I'll buy a few graphics instead of those ghastly reproductions."

"It'll work," he said with force.

"Anything will work. I don't care. Anything at all. Does it bother you, Adam?"

"Yes," he said, truthfully. "But it's all we can do."

She was silent. "Treachery."

He was startled. "What about it?"

"Your mother used the word."

"It's a word that now has to be eliminated. Purged."

"I know. How long have you got?"

It was lunch hour. "Not more than an hour and a half."

"Hold me for a while. Don't make love to me just yet. Only hold me."

After a while, they felt better; and eventually they did make love and when Adam saw Louis at a meeting that afternoon he did not flinch, but when he saw his wife that night he was greatly saddened and wished that he had never met Karen Woodward Starr. But he had.

In the half year that followed, Adam often thought of himself as having lost his flesh and blood and, to an extent, his intellectual processes. Many of the things he did and said were the reflexes of a mechanical man. His training was such that, even reactively, his decisions made sense and were probably the correct ones. He carried himself as loosely as he always had, spoke as forcefully and gave no outward sign that he had abandoned the difficulties of sustained thought and carefully planned action. He had not the time for such things. He was engaged in what were really two simultaneous political campaigns, he was running the store, he was visiting or being visited by the architects and interior planners for the new stores, and, most of all, he was coping with his obsession with Karen. Things were happening during this time of which he took reactive note. Nancy graduated from Taunton Summa cum Laude. The whole family went up for the graduation and Bobby came down from Cambridge. They all stayed at a Colonial inn some miles from the campus, and Adam gave dinner to the group. It was gay and pleasant, and, for the first time, they all met Jennifer and fell in love with her. She was also graduating, though not with such high honors.

"I had it planned to sit next to Nancy in the calculus exam and crib," she explained. "But two terrible jocks beat me to her—for the same purpose. I sat behind her and couldn't read enough over her shoulder. I got a C. It was Nancy's fault. She should have taken me by the hand and led me to the seat beside her. Or thrown the jocks out."

But Jennifer had As and Bs in everything else, and an essay of hers on Coleridge as plagiarizer won a prize. She had never looked more beautiful, and the striking contrast between the two girls delighted the Starrs as much as it had delighted the campus. Bobby was also at his best. In another two years, as he was progressing, he would also graduate from Harvard cum Laude. He seemed confident and happy. He laughed easily and his good humor made them all smile.

"There is something between Bobby and Jennifer," Claude said to Adam in their room after dinner.

"Good," he said. "She's enchanting." He spoke absently.

"He's very young. Younger than she is."

She was lying in the huge four-poster bed, a specialty of this old inn, while Adam sat in a faded armchair, removing his shoes. "A year or two," he said, not looking at her. "That means nothing now. Probably never has. Anyway, nobody's mentioned marriage."

"I hope not. Bobby seems very cool these days. As though he's very sure of himself."

Now he did look up at her. "Well, isn't that good?" he said. "After those years of shyness. I used to worry about him. Too noncompetitive. Withdrawn. And now he's doing well at Harvard. God knows, better than I ever did. So he has confidence."

"You're pleased by the competitiveness?"

Adam nodded. "He has to compete. Even when and if he comes to Starr's."

"You'd expect more from him?"

"I'd have to."

"That's not true of Bernie."

He shrugged. "Claude, nothing much has come to Bernie. He runs nothing. He's protected. People understand that. I'm talking about real responsibility."

"Like . . . Bobby being president of Starr's someday."

"I would hope so. Personally. But the important thing will be whether he wants it and is good enough for it."

"But you'll make the final decision?"

He took off his shoes and slipped out of his trousers, standing up in his shorts and shirt. "Not necessarily," he said, shaking his head. "Or at least not completely. As Starr's grows, more people will be involved in that kind of decision."

"Who?"

"I don't know. The public. Other owners."

Claude looked at him in surprise. "Sell the store?" she said.

He shrugged. "Anything's possible. Someday. What pleases me about Bobby is this self-assurance. He seemed so tentative. Now he doesn't."

Claude looked at her husband carefully. She had an insane desire to blurt out that it was she who had given Bobby his confidence; and how she had done it. She wished to stun Adam; to shock him out of his distraction. She said nothing, of course. But certain things puzzled her. His tenderness, for one. Adam had never been so tender toward her during their marriage. Now, he often sent her flowers for no reason, or bought her small presents. Whenever he came back from New York from a meeting with the architects, he brought her something. She did not know why. Perhaps it was because they now made love so seldom. She blamed that on his preoccupation with his avalanche of responsibilities and so did he when she mentioned it one night.

"My mind is frazzled," he had said. "All of me is. It's temporary."

She was willing to accept this, knowing that it was true. But she missed him in bed.

"Would you like to work in the store this summer?" Louis said to Nancy on the morning following Adam's dinner. They were sitting in the dining room having breakfast. "I'm looking for an administrative assistant—would you object, Adam?"

"Not at all. I'd be all for it."

"Come to Bloomingdale's instead," Bobby suggested. "Adam can pull his strings with the brass over there and we'll be together."

"Do," said Jennifer. "I'll be in summer stock again and we'll have our weekends."

That is what Nancy finally did. "I'd like to have some training before I come to Starr's," she said to her father. "If I ever do . . ."

"All right," Adam said.

"Next year, we'll buy Bloomingdale's," Bobby said, grinning.

"I wish you would," Louis said. "I'd like to do their business per square foot."

"Is it my imagination, or are you mellowing?" Bobby said to his sister later when they were momentarily alone.

"Maybe I am," she said, smiling. "Do you call that growing up?"

"You might," he said.

"I don't dream as much. That helps."

"Then it's wearing off." Now he was quite serious. "Thank God for that."

She kissed him quickly on the cheek.

Karen was quiet during the weekend, though she did and said all that was proper. She and Adam were restrained together, even awkward. No one took note of it. They always had been. Jenny, on the other hand, was effusive.

"I hope someday to see you both at Starr's," she said to

the young people. "At my age, continuity is . . . well . . ."
She did not finish.

"What about me?" Jennifer said. "Couldn't I even model?" Her parents had not come East for the graduation. "Father's in one of his broke periods," she explained, carelessly. "It happens every other year. It was a question of tuition or the trip. I opted for the tuition." So she spent her time with the Starrs.

"You would be a great model," Jenny said. She smiled. "One way or another, we will not lose touch, Jennifer. I have that feeling. I'm glad people don't call you Jenny."

Adam was secretly relieved that his children would not be home. He had sufficient people with whom to cope. He had one pleasant surprise. His new executive vice-president, Neil Adams, proved tactful and immediately receptive to the Starr's techniques. He also went out of his way to seek out Louis's thinking on some matters, though not all. He did not always follow this thinking, but he took it into account. He was young-looking, even for his thirty-seven years, and he knew what he was doing. His presentations for advertising had point and offered legitimate fashion stories, and his merchandise editing and interior display were the work of a gifted merchant. He was sure but not cocky and not abrasive. Louis was cool to him, but scrupulously fair. Jenny rather warmed to him.

The store had momentum. It was improving.

SUMMER PASSED and a new autumn arrived. Which meant the elections. Smolley organized storefront headquarters and teams of volunteers for the Charter amendment referendum. Leaflets poured out, but the major thrust of this campaign was newspaper, radio and television advertising. He and Senator Calhoun's men raised the money. Adam was present at all meetings and met and talked with the entire volunteer force of several hundred people, most of them young, in their late teens, twenties and early thirties. But publicly, he was in the background.

"This can't look like a personal vendetta," Smolley said. "This is procedural. Personalities are not involved—yet."

The newspapers editorialized against the amendment, calling it the beginning of one-man rule. But they were surprisingly mild, though they did not hesitate to put forward Adam Starr's ambition as the major reason for the referendum.

"They're weak 'cause they're gonna lose," Smolley said. "They won't be weak when it comes to who's gonna *be* the Mayor. But newspapers don't win elections. Organization and TV win elections. We got more organization than we need for the amendment 'cause it's the nucleus of your own campaign organization. That's why you gotta be around all the time. I want you should charm their ears off. I don't want to lose one of 'em. This is Adam's Army."

Adam worked until he thought he would drop.

KAREN DID all she could think of to make the apartment what it was not. She filled it with books and magazines and good wines, and there were always fresh flowers. She loved daisies, and they were everywhere. And she was smiling and loving when he was there. Adam thought her efforts gallant, and he was touched and moved by them. He could see her two or three times a week during the day, driving to and from the apartment in a rented Chevrolet he parked in an open lot five blocks from the store; and on some nights when Louis was in California or New York and he could invent some political excuse for Claude. But, at the end of a couple of hours, three at most, he always had to leave her.

"I have the best of you," she told him one night. "I'm sure of that. I can stand the cruddiness as long as I know that."

"For now," he said.

"I think of nothing but today. I never let myself think any more ahead than one day. I'm like an A.A. alcoholic."

He rose from the bed, slipped on a silk bathrobe she had given him and sat in a chair at the far end of the room.

"I have to admit . . ." He stopped, shaking his head.

"Admit what?"

"The thought of you and Louis together . . . childishness."

She was silent for a while. She lay, propped up on the pillows and looked out the window. "I'm very sharp with him," she said. "Whatever he says, I bite at him. It's terribly unfair. I resent his talking to me. What can he say? That matters, I mean. That is interesting. That is worth hearing. I can hardly stand for him to touch me."

"What is happening to him?"

"He's bewildered. I think he must be very unhappy.

Well, of course he is. He was depressed anyway . . . when you made all those moves in the store. Now he is very withdrawn. Silent for long periods. I'm ashamed to say . . . I'm grateful for his silence even though I know it comes from his suffering."

"His work is slipping."

She shrugged. "I'm sure it is."

"Listless. No drive."

"Is yours?"

"Probably. I seem to be doing mainly the right things, without always knowing what they are or why I'm doing them."

After a long silence, she shook her head. "I'd rather not talk any more about this," she said. "It will lead to things I'd rather not discuss."

"I know." He took a deep breath. "And I have to go anyway."

She smiled. "Of course you do. You've given me thirty minutes extra that you shouldn't have. You don't know how grateful I am when you keep people waiting because of me. I know that you don't normally keep people waiting." She sat up straight in the bed and ran her fingers through her hair. "I'm going to wash my hair. I wash my hair every time you leave. I call it therapy and I don't want to know what Freud would have said."

# 3

THE REFERENDUM on the election of the Mayor by the people was won almost as easily as Adam had beaten Stacy Kirk. No suspense attached to it. The Charter Association slogan, "Our System Works, Let's Keep It," was no match for Smolley's "Adult Citizens Elect Their Own Mayor." The polls had shown well in advance that the amendment would be an easy winner.

"The trouble is," Smolley pointed out, "it poses some problems for the election per se. The Council will now be thirteen men since the Mayor cannot represent a single district. That means . . ."

"Four elections," Adam interrupted. "A third councilman at large, someone to replace me and someone to replace Stevens. Besides the Mayor."

"And the Charter Association will win Stevens' place and may win yours. They may or may not win Councilman at large."

"So Charter people who want to vote for me will have to split their ticket."

Smolley grunted. "We got some work to do, my friend."

But Adam did have a sound organizational nucleus. And he, Smolley and Senator Calhoun's men added to it. From scores the numbers went to hundreds, and they mailed flyers, rang doorbells and piled up telephone bills. "A Leader All His Life," was Adam's phrase for himself. He had that advantage: Stevens was only a partner in the law firm. "Has Brought More Business to Ramsey Than Any Man in Its History" was a subsidiary theme. This could be questioned, but Adam had certainly been a major participant in these business-getting efforts, and he had, without question, brought more publicity to Ramsey than any other man. That much was unarguable.

"Acourse, the Charter wishes to hell they could run somebody else," Smolley said with a grin. "He's a weak fish, that Stevens. But they're trapped since they already ran him and appointed him. They can't dump him without lookin' like stupid fuckin' assholes."

And so Adam debated his opponent before any forum he could find. Stevens stuck to the prosperity of the city and its calm. "Leave it alone," he said in effect, and not very forcefully. "Leave it alone and it goes backwards," Adam replied. "There's no such thing as standing still." He hit on crime, education, housing for lower income groups and the need for the new airport to make Ramsey the transportation hub of the Southwest. His speech, given over and over again, was a recording in his head. But the feel of an audience or the sight of a microphone gave him the adrenalin he needed. Exhausted, he sounded fresh. Face to face, Adam had it all over his opponent. But the Charter had money, and, of course, the newspapers; which pressed on Adam's unseemly ambition and the beginning

of boss rule should he win. Their tone was often bitter.
This slowed Adam, but he went on working. In addition,
despite all his financing efforts and those of Smolley and
Calhoun's men, Adam could not match the Charter's spending in the media. "One-man rule," this spending proclaimed. "What Ramsey has always fought." Adam countered that the Mayor would still only have one vote, but
it seemed that the Charter ads appeared at least twice as
frequently as his own. He tried to make up for it by personal appearances. He appeared at coffees for fifty and at
the policeman's ball, shook hands at football games and at
every bus stop. He spent twenty thousand dollars of his
own money and ten each he got from Louis, Karen, Jenny,
and, to his astonishment, Bernie—in cash.

"Where did you get this?" he said, incredulous.

"We don't go to Las Vegas any more, Adam."

"But still . . ."

"I got it. I want to give it to you."

Adam hugged his younger brother.

A week before the election, a combined newspaper-tele-
vision station poll showed Stevens with a hair's edge.
Karen gave him five thousand more dollars. He spent another five of his own. On the eve of the election, he appeared with Stevens on a news show. Stevens repeated all
his slogans. Adam said: "Our city does well. As we do
well, we become complacent. We ignore our problems.
Sweep them under the rug. When a city does that long
enough, the problems fester like wounds and become in-
fected. I am running to prevent infection. I ask you to believe in me. As I believe in the future of Ramsey."

And Senator Calhoun issued a statement from Washington. "Adam Starr is the obvious choice. Ramsey has
badly needed a gifted and inspirational leader. Throughout his adult life, Adam Starr has proved he is exactly
that."

"Won't that help?" Claude asked him as they got ready
for bed the night before the election.

"I don't know," he said. "I don't know what would have
helped. Anyway . . . it's too late for anything more."

Election day was crisp and sunny. Adam and Claude
voted early and she returned home while he went to the
store. Their precinct was crowded. It might be a very heavy
vote. The hours of the employees had been staggered so
that everyone had plenty of time during which to vote. He

did a day's work without knowing what he was doing. The years of training got him through. The Starr for Mayor organization had reserved the Grand Ballroom of the Sheraton that night for the celebration or the wake. He walked over there late in the afternoon. A cheer went up as he entered the room. There were hundreds of people in it, and he had met and talked to them all. He stood near the door and smiled and clapped back as Russian performers do. His banners and giant blowups of his picture filled the room. He walked up to the stage, took the microphone, switched it on and said: "However we come out, I love you all. Someday one of you will be standing here and I'll be voting for him or her. I look forward to that." The cheering was very loud. He went to a phone booth and called Karen at home.

"Louis is in a meeting that'll last a couple of hours," he said. "Can I come by?"

"Here?"

"What the hell. Yes, there."

"Of course."

He kissed her decorously on the cheek when he arrived, noting that her black maid was in the living room and said, "I don't know why I'm here really, since I'm going to see you in two hours or so."

"Well, not really see me. We'll be like strangers as always. Come in. Do you want a drink?"

"I think so. No, on second thought, I don't. Can you produce some iced tea?"

She went to the kitchen and ordered it.

"I don't know any other way to act," he said. "In public, I mean."

"I'm the same way. Don't blame yourself. But sometimes I think we're so distant we're suspicious."

He shrugged. "Well . . ."

"Well, it can't be helped . . . I can't tell you how glad I am you came."

"I feel better myself."

"Yes, but I have something to say." She spoke softly and carefully. "You might lose this election. I know the polls say you might. But whether you do or not, you have been superb. You've been effective, strong, dignified, but very powerful—I'm sure there's no one else in the city who could even vaguely threaten the Charter on a citywide election. Not in this damn Fascist city. As you know,

Adam, I'm deeply . . . crazily . . . in love with you. But I'm more admiring of you than I've ever been. And I know you're exhausted, but it's been worth it. You are more . . . than even I thought."

He accepted his iced tea from the maid and gulped half of it. "I think a real drink would have put me unconscious," he said. "My bones ache. Thank you, my dear, for what you just said. Now tell me how to lose."

She laughed. "That will be a problem. You're not very accustomed to that."

"Not very."

"Oh well, you'll be gracious."

He smiled. "And angry. And bitter. And cursing myself for getting into it at all."

She looked away. "Oh well, Adam . . ."

"Oh well, Adam, what?"

"I adore you my dear, but you'll never turn your back on glory."

"You really think that?"

"I'm sure of it. I love and hate it in you."

"Why do you hate it?"

She looked at him steadily. "It might come between us some day."

He shook his head. "It would have already. When we took the apartment . . . I was not aware what could happen to me. In this election, I mean."

"That was the beginning of us," she said, quietly. "It was a time when neither of us could stop. We were half-mad. We still are. Will we always be so mad?"

He smiled. "One day at a time," he said.

After a pause, during which she stirred her tea and did not look at him, she said, "I suppose the whole family will be there tonight."

"Yes. And prepared to go to the Sheraton. Win or lose."

"In case you lose . . . remember what I said."

"I will. It was very important."

THE POLLS closed in Ramsey at eight o'clock so Claude served dinner promptly at seven. The guests were the immediate family, Smolley and Bessie Goldsmith, Jenny's sister. Bessie was not always asked to family gatherings since the members all had in common that they were bored by her. But for this occasion, it was deemed appropriate that she be present. Everyone had dressed rather properly since they would be making an appearance at the hotel later. Even Smolley, whose usual uniform was a boldly printed sportshirt worn under a loud jacket and over brilliant trousers, was in a gray business suit. Adam was surprised. This figure did not resemble the Smolley he knew. In addition, his normal machine-gun speech pattern was muted. At dinner, he scarcely said a word. In truth, it was a quiet dinner, even awkward. In some ways, it reminded Adam of the night after his father had been buried when, for a time, no one had found anything to say. He was bemused by this. They were, he realized, thinking of him; considering that his nerves must be raw. Actually, he felt unnaturally calm. He had had a couple of drinks before dinner and, for the first time in many weeks, he felt a sense of peace and relaxation. There was nothing, absolutely nothing, he could do now. All the strife was behind him. He would win or lose. For these moments, at least, with his mother on his right and Aunt Bessie on his left, he scarcely cared. From time to time, when Claude spoke, he noticed that her words were just slightly slurred. So she had been drinking; but was nowhere near drunk. It occurred to him that whichever way the election went, Claude would lose. If he won, she would be the First Lady of the city, which she would loathe. And if he lost, she would be relieved for herself, but sad for him. He felt, as he had through the years and especially lately, great tenderness for her. To see her eyes too bright and her cheeks slightly flushed depressed him. It would not be long before they would be married twenty-five years; and had loved each other, within the limitation of their characters, for all that time. Now, of course, he knew that his own ability to love did not carry the limitations he thought. Feelings were possible that he had not believed were in him. But, he felt he did not love Claude any the less for these. The fates had simply brought something to him which he had never expected but could not do without. Adam had not been a great believer in the accidents of destiny. He had believed that, except for death, a man made his own destiny. No god had decreed it. And so, of course, there was guilt in him; guilt when he worked late in his study to allow her to go to sleep before he came upstairs at night; guilt when he lied to her. Guilt and immense distress because such things were new to him. He knew that many men lied to their wives and were unfaith-

ful to them; and that to most men, such things came easily.
And he assumed that such men found it not a problem to
make love simultaneously to two women. He envied them.
But, as well as he could, he buried guilt; just as he buried
the fact that there must someday be an outcome to what
was happening between Karen and himself. He would not
face that. In his life Adam had faced all things; not this.

He was aware that Nancy, who after her summer at
Bloomingdale's had come home to work at Starr's at least
temporarily, had said something to him.

"I'm sorry. What, dear?"

"You're far away, Adam," Nancy said. "I said, when
will we know actually what has happened?"

Smolley answered her: "Unless it's a walkaway—and if
it is, the poll people will kill themselves—you'd have to
say nine-thirty to ten. Unless some voting machines break
down, which happens every election, as a matter of fact."

"Let's not turn on the television until nine then," Jenny
said. "Wouldn't it be too much—vote by vote?"

"I'll need your study telephone," Smolley said to Adam.
"I want to keep in touch with my people in the precincts.
I'm interested in the early totals, but I'm more interested
in where they're comin' from."

"You can take over the study," Adam said. "You'll have
it to yourself."

"Oh, it's all too exciting," Bessie Goldsmith bubbled. "I
can hardly stand it."

"Bear up, dear," Jenny said, dryly. "Like the stoics."

Claude laughed, waved her hand and knocked over her
wine. "Oh dear," she said, looking at the spreading red
stain, "how clumsy." She rang the dinner bell and Rivers
came in. "I've spilled some wine," Claude said, "would
you cover it with a napkin, please."

"Yes, Madam."

"What I meant to say," Claude went on, "is will *we* all
survive? I mean if Adam loses. What an impossible
thought, after all."

"Not impossible," Adam said, cheerfully. "And I'll survive either way. So I expect all of you will."

"I wish Bobby were here," Karen said, suddenly. "He
could play for us."

"Do you feel like singing?" Louis asked, smiling.

"No, just listening with my eyes closed."

After a silence, Nancy said, "I want to tell you that

being an assistant buyer at Starr's is the lowest of the low."
She smiled. "I say that to change the subject and make
conversation."

Louis laughed. "Well, you have a point. There's a lot of
paper work and detail. Are you learning anything?"

Nancy shook her head, still smiling. "Nothing I want to
know. I don't think it's my kind of life."

"Did you know we were building a tennis court?" Becky
said, after another silence. Bernie looked at her quickly,
then shrugged and turned away.

"*I* didn't," Adam said, genuinely surprised.

"Regular exercise," Bernie said, rather too quickly. "Live
longer. Not as expensive as I thought."

But they all knew what tennis courts cost. Both Louis
and Adam looked at their brother curiously. But then Jenny
said, "It's eight o'clock. The polls have closed."

"We'll have coffee in the living room," Claude said. She
rose and was steady, Adam noticed. He was relieved. One
thing she could not avoid was making an appearance at
the hotel. If his whole family was coming, so was his wife.
She would not, however, have to say anything. In fact, he
had no idea what he himself would say. He would think
of that later.

"Have you worked at all with our new man, Neal
Adams?" Jenny asked Nancy.

"A couple of times. He's very nice." She smiled. "He's
asked me out for dinner next week."

"Has he?" Jenny said, startled.

"He's practically an old man, Nance . . . for you, I
mean," Becky said. "Not for me." She giggled. "I think
he's pretty cute, actually."

"Fifteen years," Nancy said. "It's only dinner, Becky.
Not an engagement."

"The boss's daughter," Bernie said. "He's not losing any
time."

"He wouldn't have done it for that," Adam said. "He
would have done it in spite of that. So it's a compliment,
my dear."

"I did the complimenting," Nancy said, with a laugh. "I
said yes."

They talked aimlessly in an improvised circle around the
television set. They drank coffee and Louis and Bernie had
brandy. Adam now felt that his hands were cold. He rose
and took some brandy for himself, gulping it down. When

he turned back to the group, he saw that Karen's eyes were on him. She gave a little smile and turned away. Silence had fallen on them.

"It's nearly nine," Adam said, clearly and decisively. "I think we can turn on the set."

Nancy turned it on the local NBC outlet. This station's principal newscaster was acting as anchorman with three or four associates at their desks, shuffling papers. The newscaster's name was Douglas McCullough. Behind him was the electronic board containing the changing totals, but the camera was focused on him, not it, and they could not read the numbers.

". . . no precedent for this kind of vote in a non-Presidential election," McCullough was saying. He was a pretty, blond young man with a lock of hair that kept falling over his forehead which gave him something to do with his hands. "Reports from precincts that normally show light returns even in national elections indicate heavy turnouts. This is in sharp contrast to the light vote on the Charter amendment which actually authorized this election. That, of course, according to the prereferendum polls, was something of a foregone conclusion. This election, with the turnout as heavy as it appears to be, may confound the pollsters . . ."

"Okay, beautiful," Smolley growled, "so what's the score?"

"They're all like movie stars, these news people," Nancy said. "Look at him fooling with his hair."

"And weak on news. Good with hair, bad with news. He probably wears a corset."

"A heavy vote may be good for you, Adam," Louis suggested. "The Charter usually gets its vote out, no matter what. The extras should be independents."

"It might," Adam agreed.

But when the camera eventually did turn to the tabulating board, Stevens had 97,000 votes, Adam 94,000. Charter candidates led easily in the councilman-at-large and in the two district elections.

"Not so good," Adam said, calmly. He felt chilled but not anxious. He felt as though he had taken a bottle-full of Valium.

"Not so bad, either," Smolley said. "They're splittin' the ticket. They don't split the ticket, we're dead."

"These are very early returns," McCullough was saying.

"Much too early to indicate any probable winner in the Mayoralty race. Charter candidates do seem to have the other races well in hand . . ."

"That's what I mean," Smolley said.

Claude got up, went to the sideboard and poured herself a brandy. Adam rose and went to her.

"Would you do me a favor?" he said, softly.

"Of course."

"Will you not drink that? We absolutely have to go to the hotel."

Without a word, she carefully poured the brandy back into the bottle.

"Waste not, want not," she said. She suddenly kissed him on the cheek. "I'll have nothing more," she said. "You deserve that."

Smolley got up from his chair. "Telephone time," he said. "We need to know who's not in yet."

By nine-thirty, Stevens was ahead by fewer than a thousand votes and more than 300,000 votes had been cast.

"Starr's personal vendetta—or at least that's what his opponents have called it—has certainly caught the imagination of Ramseyites," McCullough was saying excitedly. He checked with one of his colleagues who said that the eventual number of voters might come to within seventy percent of the eligible voters. "That's much higher," he said, "than in Presidential elections."

Smolley returned from the study. He looked grim. "There've been breakdowns in three precincts in North Ramsey, two in West Ramsey. No funny stuff. My people are there to see to that. Just breakdowns. It may be an hour before we get those results. It could even be tomorrow."

"North Ramsey," Adam said. "Charter territory."

"Yeah," Smolley said.

By ten o'clock, Adam had taken the lead. He had 297,000 votes, Stevens 293,000. But the missing precincts were still not in. Smolley went back to the study. The family sat in silence, watching with glazed eyes. Adam felt curiously light-headed. Once, catching Karen's eye, he smiled. She smiled back and it was as though they had touched.

For half an hour, nothing happened.

At five minutes before eleven, Smolley reappeared in the room. His face was covered with sweat.

"They got it on the TV yet?" he said. He sounded as though he were gasping.

"Got what?" Adam said.

"The machines are fixed. The votes are in." Smolley looked Adam straight in the face and suddenly burst out laughing.

"What is it, man?" Louis said. "What the hell . . ."

"Adam," Smolley said, wheezing, "we fuckin' *won* this election. You took the North Ramsey precincts nearly two to one. You beat 'em on their own ground, Adam . . ."

"West Ramsey . . ." Adam began.

"Fuck West Ramsey," Smolley said, almost snarling. He did not even make a motion to apologize. "West Ramsey's in the bag. You always had the jigs and the Chicanos. I don't give a shit if it takes a week to straighten out that fucker—Adam—you're the Mayor."

Almost immediately, it was on the air. "Astonishing," McCullough was saying. "A great personal triumph for Adam Starr in traditionally Charter territory. We now project that Adam Starr is the new Mayor of . . ."

"Adam," Louis said, standing before him, "Congratulations." And then his family was on him, the women and Bernie kissing him, Smolley pumping his hand as though he could not stop. It was possible now, and so Karen threw her arms around him and he pressed her hard. And finally, Claude came to him.

"I'm very proud," she said. The tears were rolling down her cheeks. He brought her close to him and held her a long time. She was crying softly and he held her until she stopped. The telephone was ringing.

"I'll handle the phone," Smolley said. He picked it up. "Yes, Dave Smolley here . . . no, we've received nothing yet from Stevens. No, we won't go to the hotel until we get the concession wire. Then we'll go and see you there . . ."

And the phone kept ringing, the media people calling and Smolley gave them all the same answers. "Why doesn't that son of a bitch concede?" he muttered, after hanging up for the ninth time. "We got it by thirty thousand votes, maybe forty, minimum. Jesus Christ could Come Again and He couldn't help that bastard now . . ."

At quarter to twelve, with Adam's vote 422,000 and Stevens's 374,000, almost a seventy percent turnout of eligible voters, Henry Stevens's telegram arrived. Smolley answered the phone and handed it to Adam. "Here it is," he said. "A copy will be delivered soon."

Adam immediately wired back his congratulations on a good, hard race and his desire that the two men work together for the good of the community. When he had finished with this banality, he laughed. "I'll never even see Stevens," he said. "The Charter drops losers like hot charcoals."

"We got to go to the hotel," Smolley said. "Now when we get there, I'll lead the way. My people'll pick us up and clear a path to the stage. Then the family, except Adam and Claude, who will be last. Then Adam takes the mike and says his piece. Then we leave. No hangin' around. It's gonna get drunk at the hotel tonight, and the Mayor can't be there for that."

THE HOTEL was bedlam. At least a thousand people were in the Grand Ballroom, far more than the number of Adam's campaign workers. "Everybody's aunt came down for the fireworks," Smolley muttered as he located his people and lined them up to clear the way. The crowd was predominantly white and young to middle-aged, but there were plenty of blacks and even some Mexican-Americans. A high school band had been imported and were playing "Ragtime Cowboy Joe," as the Starrs entered. They were in purple jackets and white trousers, and drum majorettes twirled batons, and dropped them as they were jostled in the confusion. People were pouring beer on each other as after a World Series victory and hugging and kissing and starting impromptu cheers. Others sang with the band, and still others danced, crashing up against the bodies all around them.

"I can't take this," Claude said, grasping hard onto Adam's arm.

"Yes, you can," he said, grimly. "If I can, you can. I'll make it short and we'll go home and let them have their children's hour."

"So this is politics," she said.

"When you win."

At the sight of Adam, the band switched to "The Eyes of Texas Are Upon You," as he followed his family down the aisle Smolley's men had more or less cleared.

"Smile," he muttered to Claude.

"I am. It's frozen on," she said.

People clawed and grabbed at them. Somebody inadvertently ripped the shoulder of Claude's dress and she was forced to hold it up with one hand.

"My God," she said. She sounded very frightened. Adam put his arm around her waist and held her fast. Her shoulders were quivering.

But they were almost on the stage now. The rest of the family was already there and had fanned out behind where Adam would speak. Smolley, beet red and still perspiring, came up to him. "Here's a wire from Calhoun. You wanna read it or you want me to?"

"You do it. Then get me introduced and get us out of here."

It was minutes before Smolley could get the attention of the crowd. When he did, he was fairly screaming into the microphone. "First a wire from Senator Hayden Calhoun," he said. "Congratulations to the citizens of Ramsey for having elected a superb man as your Mayor. The future is heartening with such men as Adam Starr at the helm of our cities." Cheering. Then Smolley yelled out, "Ladies and gentlemen, the new Mayor of Ramsey, Texas, Adam Starr." The band, somewhat to Adam's horror, struck up the Presidential anthem, "Hail to the Chief." The yelling and cheering continued for at least ten minutes. There were snake dances all over the huge ballroom. Adam did everything he could think of to quiet them, to no avail. If they were against me, they'd kill me without a thought, he was thinking. Mobs. He looked at Claude and saw that she was deadly white. "Please," he yelled into the microphone. He waved and smiled, and beckoned again and again for silence. At last, though silence never came, there was enough quiet so that he could speak.

"We have scored a great victory tonight," Adam said. "For which I have all of you to thank. It might have been a narrow victory, which would have been good enough. But it was decisive. And that gives us the mandate to carry out the necessary steps to keep Ramsey moving—and improving. We have the backing. We can do it. We *will* do it. And this will be a greater city for our work. I have here the following telegram." Bulbs were flashing in his eyes and the TV lights were on him so that he found it hard to read Stevens's wire. When he had finished, another enormous cheer went up. "And now, I want you to meet my family." He went down the line one by one, each of them drawing cheers, even Aunt Bessie. When he reached Claude, he pulled her to him and kissed her on the cheek and hugged her like any other veteran politician. Roars of approval. "And so I say to you, we have just begun," Adam yelled. "Tonight ends nothing. It begins years of hard, tough work. I am filled with humility. Join with me. I need the help of all of you."

He stepped back, took Claude's arm and led the way off the stage. Microphones were shoved at him, but he said only, "No more tonight, boys. Tomorrow we'll talk as much as you want." And they fought their way through to the door. Smolley's people got them to the cars, but even there people crowded around so that the cars could not move. Only when the police moved in did the crowds begin to move back into the hotel. Jenny, Nancy and Claude were in Adam's car. Rivers was driving.

"God," Adam said.

"That was very frightening," his mother said, quietly.

"I thought I was going to be sick," Claude said. "I'm still shaking."

Nancy was silent. Then she said, "I don't think Ramsey has much future. Not if those are the citizens."

They all gathered again at the house for a nightcap, but it was soon over. Everyone kissed Adam and Claude once again and left together.

"I think I'll go to bed," Nancy said. "I'm still a little shaken up." She kissed her parents goodnight and left them alone.

"Now I will make a very stiff drink," Claude said when they were alone.

"You can make me one, too."

Adrenalin poured through him. Power was bursting out in his whole body. He made love to his wife that night with something like his old zest. But at three in the morning, still wide awake, he crept downstairs, went to his study and called Karen. He had no idea on which side of the bed their phone rested. But she did answer after only two rings, and her voice sounded fresh as if she had not been sleeping either.

"Just say wrong number, but I had to say I love you," he whispered. "And need you."

"I'm sorry, you have the wrong number," she said.

"Good God—at this hour," Louis grumbled.

"Yes," she said, lying back with a cat's grin.

So Adam Starr had risen to the top of his world; and was simultaneously aswarm with the seeds of his own potential destruction; and was aware of the dichotomy in himself. He poured himself a scotch and stared at it, drinking nothing, until the dawn sent him to bed.

# PART SEVEN

# 1

THE TWO new stores opened within ten months of each other. The first one, in North Ramsey, was an instantaneous success. Bill King's initial highly conservative projection of ten million dollars in volume the first year was revised quickly to twelve million.

"And downtown volume hasn't slipped as I expected," he told Adam. "We're getting the best of all possible worlds. At least so far."

"That's because of the merchandising. We were right to keep jewelry, furs and couture clothes out of the suburbs so people have to come downtown for them."

"Well, that's part of it. So is the fact that this is the best convention year in Ramsey's history. We get ninety percent of that business."

"That'll only get better. In two years, we'll have two new major hotels. By that time, this town will be ready for the American Medical Association, anybody."

"You're sure of the hotels?"

Adam laughed. "On the Council, I don't even have any opposition to that. We have all but one parcel of land. We have to put the screws to the owner, but he's into the banks. He hasn't got a chance."

King smiled.

"Good work, Mr. Mayor," he said, without sarcasm.

Houston was slower, though there was no question of its eventual success. Surrounded by good entrenched Houston retailers, King calculated it would do no more than the ten million he had projected for the first year. "It's blood and guts down there," he said to Adam.

"It's also some new buyers. Neal Adams wants to make some replacements. For people who don't know how to buy for multiple stores and never will. Or at least until somebody else trains them. We haven't time."

"Louis has the same problem, you know."

Adam was silent.

"So what are you going to do about that?" King asked.

"Give him time," Adam said. "He needs time himself. It's all new to him."

"He needs to be pricked, Adam," King said. "He's going through the motions."

"You prick him."

"He doesn't report to me."

"You're the financial man. You have the right to intervene."

They were sitting in Adam's office, and King contemplated his next remark. When he made it, he was direct: "He's dead on his feet, Adam."

Adam looked carefully at his old friend. "Do you have any idea why?" he asked.

"I think he's having trouble at home."

"Oh? What makes you think so?"

"When I see them out. They're careful as burglars together."

"I . . ."

"You what?"

"I can't do anything about that," Adam said.

For in truth, it was not Louis who brought him the guilt he lived with; somewhere, deep in his mind lay the thought that it was up to Louis to hold his woman. Intellectually, he was appalled at what he was doing to his brother; emotionally, he was only lightly affected. Karen lived with the problem of Louis, as Adam saw it; he lived with the problem of Claude. This was enough for him. He continued his small tendernesses, but they could not disguise the rareness of real intimacy between them which had always been their sex together. Once, she took the initiative.

"I'd like . . ." she began, tentatively, whispering to him in bed.

"What, dear?"

"To . . . suck you. Like a French whore."

He was astonished and appalled. She had not said anything like it in their years together. And he did not wish it, did not think he could rise to it, was overcome with guilt and remorse and a sudden attack of nerves.

"That's very sweet," he said, hoping a miracle would happen.

"Shall I?"

"I'm awfully drained," he said. "There'll be a better night."

She turned away from him. After a while, he was aware that she was crying.

"What on earth . . ." he began.

"Do you know . . . what it took . . . for me to say that?" she whispered.

"I think so." He was silent. He decided to gamble. "I don't know . . . how it will be . . . but let's try it," he said.

She shook her head, buried in the pillow. "Don't be silly," she said. But she cried softly for a long time, and the sound grieved him so that he could not stand it. He went downstairs and sat on the couch staring at walls. He stayed away long enough to give her a chance to sleep and then lay awake himself, thinking black thoughts.

IN THE year and a half it took to open the two stores and roughly since the night he had first made love to his brother's wife, his marriage and Louis's were held together largely by the presence in them of so many people. Adam, as Mayor, had to entertain or be entertained more than ever. Five or six nights a week, he had something to do. He was by no means simply a ceremonial Mayor. He had pushed through considerable civic opposition on the airport bond issue of nearly $440 million, helped secure a $54 million federal commitment to the enterprise and thus assured Ramsey of one of the largest, most modern airports in the world. He had taken on the police chief on the subject of black harassment in the matters of both minor and major crimes and, to his own surprise, falsification of figures regarding crime in black neighborhoods. This, after a fight with his Council colleagues and the Charter Association, he had taken to the people through paid time on radio and television and unpaid news conferences. The police chief had been forced to resign. And Adam, encouraged, had made monthly television chats with the people on civic affairs a regular feature of his administration. He was, in truth as well as by title, the most powerful man in Ramsey. And, in this popular power, he sometimes had the exultant feeling that if he were one, and the rest of the Council were banded against him, he could still beat them.

He knew that, behind his back, he was a radical kike to many of the right-wingers in the rich suburbs and perhaps even to some of his peers on the Council. But it could not do him real harm, and he found pleasure in grinding out his policies over their opposition. The store lost a little business, but may have gained more as the affection less affluent people felt for him persuaded them to give Starr's a try; once there, they were often pleased and the store's transaction count was actually up.

But many of his duties *were* ceremonial. He was present for all the significant openings, whether of the symphony orchestra, a new housing complex or a relocated manufacturing plant which would give jobs to people. Sometimes, whenever absolutely necessary, Claude was with him. She was of course present at all their home entertainment, which was more extensive than ever, and for which she had had to hire a secretary for detail work. She handled it all with her usual grace, but she was now drinking more than she had and it showed to him and perhaps to others. She neither staggered nor misbehaved. She simply seemed vague and inattentive. After planning what would happen, she allowed it to happen around her, taking little part in the occasion itself. Nancy knew what was happening and took an active role in these public evenings at home. She had quit the store and was studying at the University for her M.A. in English literature; she had several good prospects for teaching at good secondary schools in the East once she had written her thesis. She saw Neal Adams for dinner several times a month and enjoyed it, especially since he did not at the moment seem to wish to press anything. Nancy could find nothing to fault in her father's conduct. She noticed it when he sent flowers, when he touched her mother's cheek softly when he came home and when he spoke tenderly to her. She could not understand why her mother was drinking, and asked her about it one night. Claude was honest enough not to avoid the question.

"I don't like my life very much," she said.

"But why not? It is the life of the Mayor's wife. It may be a bore sometimes, but he spares you as much as he can."

"You are like him in many ways. You would be a good President of Starr's. Or Mayor. Both, I think."

"He seems so kind to you. Even loving. And, Claude ... you don't to him."

Claude looked at her daughter steadily. "I no longer believe him," she said.

"Believe what?"

"Anything. The presents he gives me are from his guilt."

"I don't believe it. What has he got to be guilty about? He's doing his best."

Claude did not wish to hurt her daughter; did not even wish to surprise her.

"There are two parts to marriage. Public and private. Mostly the private part is bigger. Never in ours. The private part was always small . . . but important. It made up for many things we did not do well." Claude laughed. "Like be alone together."

Nancy thought she knew what her mother might mean.

"As the years go on . . ." she began, but Claude stopped her with a wave of her hand.

"I'd rather not go on with this." She smiled. "It is after all, the private part we are talking about. That is my problem . . . and his . . . and not yours. However, I would appreciate your making me a nightcap. To sleep on. I'd make it myself, but I'm tired."

"I don't think . . . Of course, I will."

That night, one of very few, Nancy had to help steady her mother when she rose to go to bed.

"Your father will either be asleep or he won't," Claude said, bitterly. "I will not know."

And, of course, when she and Adam were alone, there were long silences at dinner, and much reading Adam had to catch up with after they had left the table. He usually retired to his study, leaving Claude to the television.

"Eventually, you will lose your looks," Nancy said to her mother once.

"I already have, dear. I'm thickening. I don't care."

And Nancy, grieving for her mother, instinctively took her father's side. She was impressed by him. He was on the right side of matters and winning. She was quite aware that it does no good to be on the right side if you are losing. She was a Starr. She did not believe in heroes of lost causes. Starrs won. She had not forgotten, would never forget, the exhibition of raw power her father had mentioned to her . . . only the one time, she had inquired no further . . . concerning the man . . . men? she did not know, but at least the leader who had raped her. Power was in Nancy's blood, as it was in her father's.

Louis and Karen also had their share of evenings with people. Karen had thrown herself into the work of the art museum. She had a secretary, and a good deal of correspondence as she and her colleagues on the board began work long neglected of building a permanent collection. And this activity was loose enough to provide time to meet Adam when he was able. For Louis, she filled as many evenings as she could with dinner parties, theater, the symphony, lectures and literally anything she could find which would provide something to look at or other people to be around. But they did eventually have to come home. There, she sank into books and magazines and even as she looked at the pages, she was aware that he was looking at her with bewilderment and sorrow.

"Have I done anything?" he said once, in despair.

"No. Of course not."

"Then what is it?"

She became angry. She was often angry. "What is what, for God's sake?"

But Louis never showed anger. She would have given a great deal if he had. She would have wished to fight bitterly with him, but he gave her no chance.

He made his mouth form a half-smile. "We just don't seem to have much communication."

"Then tell me some jokes."

He was silent, and she was immediately remorseful. "I'm sorry," she said. "That was a silly remark."

"Karen . . ." He stopped short.

"What?"

"Would you like to go away?"

"Me?" she said, astonished.

"I mean together. I could take a couple of weeks. Mexico. Paris. Anywhere."

The thought was terrifying to her. Leave Adam? Go away with this man to a place where there would be no other people?

"I have too much to do," she said, abruptly.

"Not really. Not that can't wait two weeks."

"I said, not now. Sometime, all right? Not now."

Again he was silent. He sat in the wing chair with his hands resting on its arms. His face showed little. It was one of the things that infuriated her about him. She hurt him daily and he would not show hurt. She angered him daily and he would not show anger. His face was impassive. She thought she saw helplessness in his eyes, but she could not be sure. He must, she was certain, be torn to pieces inside but he could not cry or scream or beat the air. Her own voice rose and fell and was waspish and abrupt and shifted tone without warning; but his remained quiet and reasonable. He had shouted at Adam. Why on earth could he not shout at her? That he could not only irritated her more. But often, too, she was ripped at by guilt. At these times, she kissed him, spoke tenderly to him, listened carefully to whatever he had to say and submitted with all the grace she could to his lovemaking. She sought his opinion on whatever was in the newspapers, what she was doing with the museum and anything else she could bring to mind. She could do this, she found, for days, sometimes. But, in the end, his gratitude sickened her and she would turn on him for the slightest thing, for nothing at all.

"My God," she thought, "he must think I'm schizophrenic."

And she was to an extent. She was consumed by Adam; not just by their hours together, but by the sense of him; the public man, what he was, what he was doing; the private man, how he touched her and spoke to her and made love to her. She raged over the hours and days when she was not with him at all and was baffled and even hurt when they saw each other at parties and she received a brother-in-law's kiss on the cheek and not even a finger's touch.

Louis, having no one else, spoke to his psychiatrist.

"Have you thought of a separation?" the doctor asked.

Louis shook his head. "I'm deeply in love with Karen."

"In love? Addicted?"

"I don't know the difference."

"There is, however, a difference. The thing that bothers me, Mr. Starr, is you are too reasonable. You have the right to be angry. I don't see that."

"Not angry. I can't be angry at how she feels. Sad."

"Angry. She is treating you badly. She has turned against what you have always been and therefore were when she married you. That's unfair."

Louis smiled. "I haven't felt that life is particularly fair."

The psychiatrist did not smile. "I see . . . Well, our time is up. I hope you will become angry one of these days. Perhaps we would begin to learn something."

And at home, thinking over what the psychiatrist said, Louis, for the first time, accepted bitterness. Within him, he accepted it. To the world and his wife, he remained bland.

## 2

ADAM AND Karen had had the apartment a year and a half when Karen said, sitting across from him, fully dressed, "Will you still be going to New York as often as you have been?" She had seemed nervous on his arrival that afternoon; pale, shaky; totally unlike herself, though she had been sometimes like this lately. The time was coming for him to leave.

"I'll have to go," he said. For his meetings with the architects and interior designers, he had been in New York one week out of every five. "We've barely started Fort Worth . . . I'm sorry . . ." She was always sad when he was leaving. Instead she said, "Then, I'll leave him." Her voice was flat, matter of fact, and her words were distinct. "And go back to New York."

Adam sat silent, stunned.

"There's no other way," she said, her voice rising. To his astonishment, he saw that she was close to hysteria. "I can't stand doing this with you . . . and I can't not do it. I can't live with your getting up and leaving me, but worse than that, I am watching this . . . other man disintegrate before my eyes. We hardly talk. I am sick when he touches me. *I* am disintegrating."

"You can't leave him," he found himself saying.

"What else is there to do? God knows I can't live with him. Maybe I couldn't have sooner or later anyway, I don't know . . . but with us . . ."

Adam Starr buried his head in his hands.

"What will he do?" he said, his voice muffled.

"*I don't know,*" she said, nearly screaming. Looking at her he saw that her face was contorted, as though in physical pain. Her mouth was twisted, and the knuckles of her hands, clasped under her chin, were white. And then she said, quietly, "And I don't care. Adam, it's not your fault, oh, I suppose it is, and mine . . . I can't *stand* him. And I can't stand another minute of us. The way we are. Us. This squalid apartment. The squalid leavings. The squalid glances in public . . . My God, can you?"

"No," he said. He went further than he had ever gone. "And it's impossible at home."

She became quiet. With an effort that he noticed, she made her hands unclench and sat back and took a deep breath.

"Every time you leave me, you dislike yourself," she said. "Every time you don't . . . make love to Claude you dislike yourself. If she drinks too much . . . it's your fault. Now for me it's the same. I put Louis down, keep him away from me, don't talk to him, don't respond to him and it isn't him I dislike . . . it's me." She stopped, looked at him imploringly. "Adam, I've never loathed myself. I'm afraid of that. I know people who do. They're alcoholics or in mental institutions."

He waited to be sure she was through. Then he said, as calmly as he could, "If you leave Louis, I will see you one week in five. Even though you still have the apartment, I won't be able to stay in it because everyone in the building knows Louis. What would you do? Move to a hotel when I'm in town? In a week, forty people would have seen us together."

"Take a house," she said.

He did not follow her. "What kind of house? Where?"

"Anywhere. Connecticut. Long Island. I can rent and you can commute to it. Every night, and go into the city in the mornings for your meetings. When you're in Texas, I would go back to the apartment."

He thought for a long time. "Would that be better for us?" he asked.

She shrugged. "We'd have all of each other one week in five. You could stretch it now and then. There's practically no chance we'd be found out."

He said, deliberately, "You have never mentioned the possibility that I should leave Claude, too."

She looked down at the floor. "I've thought of it," she admitted. "Many times. I think we were meant to be, you and I. I really think that's true." She looked up at him. "I'm compromising for now. You and Claude, my Adam . . . you've had twenty-five years. Louis and I less than three. Louis and I . . . we've been an interlude in each other's lives. You and Claude are the entire investment of your adult lives."

"I could leave her," he said. "I would have to set it up. Properly."

She shook her head. "I'm not even thinking of that seriously now," she said. "You are the Mayor, there are the children . . . many things. That can come later."

He rose and went to the bar and mixed himself a scotch and soda. "Do you want anything?" he asked.

"Nothing."

He sat down where he had been and took a sip of his scotch. "A month totally without you would be a long month."

"I could call you now and then on your private wire. Or you me, better. When the office is empty. And I could write you to a box here. I would love to write to you. I would like to see in writing all the things I feel about you."

After a while, he said, "A few minutes ago, you were close to hysterics. Now you seem very calm."

She nodded. "Relieved, maybe. Oh, Adam, it's been so degrading . . . such bad style."

He said, slowly, "I've been thinking mostly of Claude all this time, you know. Now I'm thinking of Louis. What I've done to Louis."

"No. What I did. I should never have married him. Perhaps there's an excuse. I was fond of him. I was not sure of . . . what I became sure of. That I only wanted to be close to you. And perhaps that's no excuse. But Adam . . . leaving him is better than what I'm doing to him. You don't know that. You don't see it. I promise you it's true."

He suddenly laughed. "Being a former Starr involves some formalities. Seeing Mother, for example."

Karen's hands became clenched again and she bit her bottom lip. "I hate the thought of that," she said.

"Mother's very strong. She won't collapse."

"It's not that. I think she sees through me."

He was shocked. "You don't mean about us?"

"Oh, no. Not yet anyway. I think I puzzle her, though. I'm in a fraudulent marriage. How did I get myself there? I'm too intelligent for that. These are things I think she feels. For Louis's sake, I suppose she'll try to hate me, but I don't think she really will."

"She might, my dear, she might."

"Then I will have to accept that."

There was a long silence between them. He felt inexpressibly sad. She did not seem to; only thoughtful. He knew that this was the point between them he had never faced. It saddened him and surprised him that Karen had. He was, as it were, not leading but being led. He vaguely resented this. They were stepping out of limbo, and he was the follower. Yet, he thought, she was right. What she was suggesting was possible. They could live with it. Clearly, they could no longer live with what they had. Just as clearly, they had to live with something.

"When will you do this?" he asked.

"Soon. I don't know. Tonight. In a week. When I think I can trust myself to do it well. So, I guess I won't tell you beforehand because I won't know. I'll have to tell you after."

"I go to New York in ten days."

Not looking at him, she shook her head. "I can't be ready for you then. I will be by the next trip." Suddenly, she smiled. "Adam, what time do you have to be where?"

In sudden fright, he looked at his watch. "Oh, my God, half an hour ago. At a City Manager's meeting."

She continued to smile. "Go quickly. Do you want to call?"

"I'd better." He called and made his excuses, telling them he would be there in twenty minutes.

"Hold me very tight," she said, rising.

And he did. She was trembling. He was too, he discovered, and the shakiness and the fast pounding of his heart persisted all day and came and went for many days afterward.

On the following morning, Karen called Adam on his private wire at the office. "Call me back when you're alone," she said.

When he did, in an hour or so, she said, "I've looked through our date book and there are many things to do these two weeks. There are things to do after that, but they are far off and I can cancel more easily."

"Then wait. Don't tell him until you're ready to pack your bags."

"That's what I mean. Adam . . . I don't want to go back to the apartment. I'm going to pay off the lease."

"I understand that. I'll get the cash . . . "

She broke in: "Never mind that. As you pointed out, I'll have to go see Jenny. Should I come to see Claude?"

He considered that for a moment. "Write her. You'd better do that. And Bernie and Becky. The less conversation the better."

After a pause, she said, "Adam, I probably won't see you again for a while."

"I know. Nearly two months. Can you handle everything . . . the house . . . in that time?"

"Of course."

Adam took a deep breath. "The Fifth Court of Circuit Appeals," he said, "handed down its decision on busing today. The city will have to start busing kids next fall to achieve real integration in the schools, which is going to be a very bad trip for a lot of white people in this city. And maybe black. I'm going to start having neighborhood meetings right away. I may be pretty much alone in this. The damn thing is so explosive, the other councilmen won't get involved any more than they have to. So I'll be busy. I'll be out many nights. Fighting rednecks. If you have to go, this is a good time for it."

She laughed. "Adam Starr. You'll never have the problem of filling up the hours." She hesitated. "But I guess I will . . . Well, anyway, goodbye, my love, for a while."

"Goodbye, Karen."

"I do feel better."

"So do I."

As the tension which had been so taut within her lessened, she was kinder to Louis than she had been in two years. He did not understand it, but he certainly did not question it. They went to their dinners or gave them and actually seemed relaxed together. In bed, she was still passive, submissive, but at least she did not turn him away. He felt that things were improving.

He did not, of course, know of the engagements Karen turned down. After a certain date, their calendar was relatively empty. She invented various excuses. She did not wish to embarrass him any more than was necessary; to cancel things (or go) and explain that one's wife has left one is too absurd. She was aware of this and tried, in advance, to spare his feelings. It occurred to her that he might wish to go away somewhere. She left him the time to do it.

And then, one night in the late fall when the night outside was chilly, they dined alone, and after dinner went into the small study where two Marcel Breuer chairs, each with its own goose-necked reading lamp, faced their white linen-weave sofa. On the coffee table facing the sofa were the liqueurs, and the silver coffee service with the two Meissen coffee cups they drank from every night they were home. She always sat on the sofa, he on one of the chairs and she poured him a coffee and a cognac and the same for herself. On this night, she did everything as she had during their marriage. And he slipped back into the chair waiting to carry on the conversation about Adam and busing which had begun at dinner.

"I think it can mean real trouble for him next fall," he said. "It's all right now. It's almost a year off. But when those buses actually arrive . . ."

"You think there could be violence," she said, curling her legs under her. "What a city."

Louis shrugged. "Maybe, maybe not. If he's smart, he won't get into philosophies. He doesn't have to. All he's bound to do is enforce the law."

She looked at him fiercely. "Which is what you would do."

Startled, he did not answer. She arose from the sofa and wandered to the bookshelves. She was wearing Chinese red silk pajamas and black and gold slippers. He passed off the sting of her last remark and thought how lovely she was. She had worn this same costume many times. It was Karen's luck to be able to wear clothes over and over; yet, somehow, they never looked used. She was aware that when something is right, it can be repeated. She did not look back at him as she spoke: "Have you thought much about this marriage, Louis?"

In his astonishment, he did not immediately reply. She turned and looked at him, and he saw that her face was pale; and it seemed to him that her eyes were frightened. "Did you hear me?" she said, softly.

"Yes," he managed.

"Well . . . have you?"

His voice sounded stronger than he had expected. But he put down his cognac because he discovered that his hand was beginning to shake.

"I've thought about it a great deal," he said. "I suppose . . . in one way or another . . . it's in my mind most of the time."

"Have you reached any conclusion about it?" she asked. Her voice continued to be quiet and kind.

"I'm often puzzled," he said. "You know that. I've wondered if I've done anything wrong. So much has changed in . . . a year and a half or so, I . . . don't know what changed it."

She lied with ease. "Nothing changed it," she said. "Nothing you did, I mean." She looked at him without blinking. "Will you understand me, dear Louis, when I tell you I cannot do this kindly. There is no way to do what I'm going to do that is considerate of your feelings. And . . . I care very much about your feelings."

"Do what?" His voice was leaden. He was still in the chair. He was afraid he might be sick to his stomach.

"I'm going . . . to have to leave you, Louis." These words came in the same soft tone. They did not immediately impress him. They were the words, or words like these, he had been expecting. He realized, of course, that he had not just been expecting them for these few minutes but for months. He had lived in dread of them from waking to sleeping and in the middle of many nights. It occurred to him, oddly, that he had never actually told his psychiatrist that he expected his wife to leave him. He wondered why. Nor had the doctor asked him this specifically. He wondered why. An experienced professional should have anticipated this turn of events and prepared him for them. Well . . . of course, there was no way to be actually prepared for them. It would be like a psychiatrist telling a man to prepare for his wife's death someday. Not a doomed wife; just a loved one. "Prepare, for someday she will die," he would have to say. Or, "Prepare, for someday you will." The doctors would have to concern themselves with the matters at hand, not with eventualities. Louis had a sudden urge to call the doctor and ask him what the proper method of coping with the present problem might be. Instead, he leaned forward and, unsteadily, drained the glass of cognac. He rose and poured himself another one. This he also drank, dimly aware that Karen was continuing to speak.

". . . a mistake I will regret all my life I made," she said. "For both our sakes. I know I've been cruel to you."

"Cruel?" he said, for she seemed to pause.

"I couldn't help that. Could not. It was never you, my poor Louis, always my dislike of myself for making the mistake . . ."

She was continuing. The words had something to do with love; about the feelings she had for him not being enough, never having been enough. That she should have known that. This thought struck him as a true one.

"Yes," he said, blinking. To his horror, he realized that there were tears in his eyes. He was crying. He felt the tears on his cheeks. "You should have known that." His voice sounded choked. He resolved not to speak again until he had regained some control over these tears. I will, he thought, drink nothing more. He looked at Karen carefully. He could see no sign of weakness in her. Even her eyes did not look frightened now. He supposed that they had been frightened before because she had not said what she had to say, and now she had. He now looked down at himself. He was standing, slightly bent over, with his arms hanging down like those of an ape. He had the feeling that his eyes were half-closed. And he realized that his mouth was slightly parted and that there was saliva on his lips. He was subhuman. His degradation was complete.

"Excuse me," he said. "I'll be back . . ."

He went to the bathroom. There he washed his hands, and then his face in cold water. He dried himself thoroughly, took out a pocket comb and ran it through his hair. He looked at himself carefully in the mirror. He wondered whether strong emotion dilated the pupils. He looked to himself like a man on some kind of drug; and the fluorescent lights on either side of the mirror heightened his sallowness. He would have to ask the doctor what the physical manifestations of strong emotion could be. When he walked back to the living room, the outlines of the furniture seemed blurred to him. Karen herself, standing near the books where he had left her, looked blurred.

"Do you feel better?" she asked. Her tone sounded genuinely concerned.

"I feel all right." His voice pleased him. It was steady. But he felt that his hands might begin to shake, and, in fact, one eye seemed to be twitching. This angered him. He wished to be physically fully in command of himself.

"I haven't . . . slept normally, in a long time," Karen was saying. "I wake up wondering. Wondering whether it might work itself out. For a long time, I thought this might happen. I thought I could pull myself together and become accustomed to this life. Feel natural in it . . ."

She continued to talk, but he only heard bits and pieces of what she was saying. All that had sunk into his brain was that she was leaving him. This creature whom he adored was leaving him. *Leaving* him. And he was conjuring up in his mind what this meant, and it seemed to mean a kind of death. Death robs; he would be robbed. Now if true, this was the most unfair thing that had ever happened to him. A parade of unfair things that had happened to him became visions in his eyes. He saw Adam in advertising meetings, saying, "Louis that presentation looks like what you sold last year. It has no life. I think you and your people will have to start again." He saw the nods of approval when Neil Adams presented his promotional merchandise; and he felt his presence next to him, Louis Starr, on an equal level at meetings of the executive committee. He heard the thousands of small and large criticisms of his operation he had heard over the years. He saw Peter Shaw standing in front of a thousand people in evening dress, commentating the biggest fashion show of the year, speaking from notes; in place of himself, Louis Starr, who had written and rewritten his entire commentary five or six times, only to be replaced as the physical symbol of the store's fashion image. He felt, all at once, the thousands of defeats he had suffered over the years.

As he walked over to Karen and struck her in the face as hard as he could with closed fist, he thought he heard a faint squealing sound coming from his own mouth before he heard her cry and saw her fall back against the books. This cry brought her into focus, and when he hit her again, he could see her clearly. He avoided breaking her nose. He hit her on the jaw, on the side of the head, in the stomach, but not in the breast or nose. She bled, however, at the mouth. When she sank to her knees, he opened his fist and slapped her across the face with all the strength he had. The blow spun her head around and her soft hair flew as if a sudden gust of wind had engulfed her. It also knocked her off her knees and she was now lying on the floor with her face down. He became aware that she was sobbing. He also felt drained of all strength. He left her lying where she was, went to a chair and sat down. He poured himself a cognac and his hands were shaking so badly he spilled some of the liquor and had to raise the snifter to his lips with both hands. He was aware of the moaning sound coming from where she lay, but was unmoved by it. All that concerned him was that his hands would stop shaking and that the paralyzing weakness would leave him. Concerned with these feelings of his own, he looked straight ahead and not at Karen.

How long they were like this, he did not know. But after some time had passed, he was aware of an absence of sound in the room and he realized that she had stopped crying and moaning. Curiously, he looked at her. She was sitting on the floor, holding her head in her hands; sitting crosslegged. Blood still dripped from her mouth and some of it had gotten on the light beige carpeting. Hard to get out, he thought; might leave a stain.

"I think . . . you better call Dr. Fry," she said, slowly. "I feel very dizzy. I'm afraid to get up."

"Yes. All right," he said.

"Tell him I fell down the stairs," she said. "Please tell him that."

"Of course."

He walked over to the library desk and called Dr. Fry at his home.

"My wife has fallen down the stairs," he said. "She's banged herself up quite badly and feels dizzy. Shall I bring her to the hospital?"

"Not until I see her. I'll come there."

"The doctor is coming here," Louis said to his wife.

"I wonder if you'd help me to the sofa . . . and perhaps you'd get a washcloth for my mouth."

He helped her to lie down on the sofa, dampened a washcloth and brought it to her. She cleaned her mouth as well as she could. He could see that both lips were bleeding. One eye was also closing, and there was a cut on one cheekbone. This seemed minor. The sight of Karen's damaged face did not sadden him, nor touch him in any way. He felt no remorse. He sought no excuses for himself. He simply sat and waited in silence for the doctor to arrive.

Dr. Elias Fry was a short, thin man with white hair and spectacles.

"How long ago did this happen?" he asked Louis when he arrived.

"Just a few minutes ago. Maybe it was a half hour."

"I see."

The doctor who had attended to the medical wants and needs of the Starr family for better than a quarter of a century sat next to Karen on the sofa and examined her for a long moment before touching her. After his first look at her face, he turned to Louis. His face was angry. "You told me on the telephone she fell down the stairs," he said.

Karen said, "That is what happened. I did fall down the stairs. I tripped."

"Let me be absolutely sure of this. You are both saying that Karen has fallen down the stairs? You are both going to say that?"

"Yes," Louis said. "As Karen has told you."

"I see." Doctor Fry felt for a long time around Karen's head. Everything hurt her, but there was no special source of tenderness.

"I'd like for you to try to get up now and walk around the room with me," the doctor said.

She did this and seemed fairly steady on her feet.

"All right. Lie down again." He turned to Louis. "I want her in the hospital tonight and tomorrow," he said. "I want to be sure there's no concussion. There's no special indication of one, but it's always possible. You can drive her. I see no need for an ambulance. They'll give her a thorough examination in the hospital."

"All right," Louis said.

"I'll see you in the morning," the doctor said. "If anything's wrong I don't see, they'll call me. But I'm sure there's not. And . . . there's nothing to scar."

"Thank you, doctor," Karen said.

When he had gone, Louis said, "I'll pack an overnight bag for you."

"If you would."

In about half an hour he drove her to the hospital, checked her in, and put her in charge of the interns and the nurses. Luckily for the middle of the night, she had a private room.

"I'll come back in the morning," he said.

"I suppose you'd better." Her tone was dull.

So he left the hospital and drove home. It occurred to him that he should telephone his family. He looked at his watch. It was nearly eleven o'clock. Nothing seemed seriously wrong with Karen. The phone calls could wait until the morning.

But he could think of nothing else to do with himself. He was too tense to read or watch television or even listen to music. He sat in the black leather and chrome chair and stared at a Ben Shahn drawing he had owned for years and did not see it. He was startled to realize that he could not remember what day it was. This bothered him enough so that he went to the kitchen and burrowed through the trash until he found the morning newspaper. It was Thursday night. What had they planned for the weekend? He riffled through a few pages. Most of them were blank. Little seemed to have been planned for them. He supposed she had allowed this to happen; this seemed intelligent to him. He considered making himself a drink, but drinking was not really his way and he did nothing about it. What he was feeling now, he realized, was a crushing kind of sadness. He was feeling, in advance, the grief of loss. Though he had never persuaded himself that Karen had been in love with him, still she had been *with* him. She was at breakfast, at dinner, at whatever they did in the evenings, across from him, reading and lying by his side in their bed. She was on his arm when they were out and he could be pleased by the admiring glances she brought. He could read something aloud to her, or she to him, and this often happened. When something was funny and she laughed, it always seemed to him that she lit up the land. He loved the way she dressed and was pleased by those occasions when she called him down to a fitting room to look at something she was considering. He was very pleased when she brought home for the apartment an antique box, a new lamp to replace one she had never liked, a pillow for the chaise in the bedroom, or, occasionally for him, a hand-kerchief or tie which had caught her eye.

Even after so short a time, he could not conceive of his life without her. He began to cry. At first the tears simply dropped from his eyes to his cheeks, but soon he was giving way to wrenching, exhausting sobs and they continued for a long time. He wished to stop but could not. He was helpless. During this period he did not regret that he had beaten her so badly. He did not even think of this. And he had lost his rage for the time being. He was grief stricken, bereaved; and no one could help him.

When the sobbing eventually calmed, he still sat in the chair. He could not face the bedroom. He did not feel sleepy, though he was bone tired, but he stretched out on the sofa and looked at the ceiling. Sometime or other, he fell asleep and woke only when the maid came in the morning.

KAREN STAYED in the hospital forty-eight hours. Dr. Fry was taking no chances. Her eyes closed completely and parts of her face grew purple. When Louis came to see her (he had come briefly in the morning, saying little, as did she) on the first evening, she said: "Jenny called and I told her what we decided had happened and asked her not to come because I looked a mess. She understood that. All the family have called and I've told them the same thing. I have made a plan."

"What is it?" he asked. He was sitting in the only chair by her bed.

"I will go home as quickly as possible. I will take very little with me. I can come back and pack the rest of the things when you are away in California next month. You can ship the paintings and the books that belong to me, if you will."

He nodded. "Are you going to . . . divorce me right away?"

"I'll talk to a lawyer. I suppose so."

"I guess it doesn't make much difference."

"Jenny will come to see me at the apartment. I'll tell her what I've decided to do. I don't want to get involved with Claude and Adam and Bernie and Becky. Or any friends. I will write a lot of letters later. I simply want to leave as quickly as I can."

"All right."

She looked at him and her face was kind. "It's all right about the other night, Louis."

"I'm sorry I hurt you," he said. He had said nothing of the kind before this moment. "I didn't know I could do such a thing."

She was silent.

"You will heal, however," he said. He could not disguise the bitterness in his tone, though he wished to.

"I'm sorry I look such a sight," she said, evenly. "Women should be pretty in hospital beds. Or does your heart break that I look this way?"

He shook his head. "Only that you are leaving," he said. The phrase struck her in the face like a club. She said nothing, and soon he left.

SHE WOULD not let Adam come to the hospital. "I don't want to see you. I don't want you to talk about what has happened. Please try not ever to let it come up. It was the punishment for us both, and please God, it is all the punishment we will have. But I doubt it."

"I won't come if you insist. Can I call again?"

"No. Nothing. I'm only anxious to be gone. To begin our plan. That consumes me."

"And me."

"It's all right that my face is banged up. It's all right that I hurt."

"But you see . . . it should have been me."

"It has happened to both of us. It doesn't matter which one of us is in the hospital. Don't you see, Adam, I feel freer than I have for a year and a half. Now, hang up and call me in New York with your box number so that I can write love letters to you. Goodbye, my darling."

And she hung up.

JENNY CAME to the apartment at three o'clock the Monday afternoon after Karen had gone to the hospital. Her face was still swollen and tender, but the purple of the bruises was turning to yellow. She was dressed in a sweater and skirt, Jenny in a black silk dress with a high mandarin collar. Karen had seen the dress many times. Jenny was another woman who did not mind repeating herself. They sat together on the sofa.

"Will you have anything?" Karen asked.

"Nothing, thank you."

"I feel somehow that this is wrong. I should have come to the house."

"The fewer people who see you like this the better," Jenny said. And added, bitterly, "Perhaps someone will believe you fell down the stairs."

Karen, startled, said nothing.

"Dr. Fry is a very old friend," Jenny said. "He could not possibly lie to me. I want to tell you something, Karen. My sons are my sons. When they are right, I am happy and when they are wrong, they are normally still right. They are my blood and my issue and I defend them to the end. However, I do not forgive Louis this."

Karen looked down at the sofa. "He was . . . temporarily out of his mind."

The old lady looked at her fiercely. "Starrs do not go out of their minds. We are controlled people. We may raise our voices but they quiet. Everything is smoothed over. We do not do . . . serious damage to each other. That is not our way."

Karen shook her head. "Not serious," she said. "I won't have a scar."

"What is serious is not that you will or won't have scars. It is that he beat you. Louis Starr has beaten his wife like a drunken Irishman."

Karen found this amusing and smiled. In a moment, so did Jenny.

"So I am a bigot, then," she said. "What an interesting thought."

"Louis had his reasons," Karen said.

"There are no reasons for such a thing. None."

Karen was surprised. "Surely some . . . infidelity . . ."

"None. I repeat that. If you have been unfaithful to him . . . and he minds it so much . . . he can divorce you. He cannot raise his hand."

"I am divorcing him, Jenny."

Jenny Starr grew pale.

"Not because of what happened," Karen went on. "Louis lost his head . . . after I told him that. This is what made him crazy. I had just told him that I was leaving him."

Jenny still did not speak. She looked as she looked sometimes when she was unusually tired: Haggard and old and drained.

"You will tell me . . ." she began, and stopped. She could not seem to find words. Her eyes darted around the room as she sought them. "Can you tell me why you are doing this?" she said, finally. "Are you . . . are you going to another man?"

"I cannot go to another man," Karen said. She went further: "There is no other man."

"Then why do you do this?"

"Because I'm . . . unhappy. Because I don't love him enough. Because I am hurting him. Because I demean him when I don't mean to. Because I dislike Texas, our friends, this life, but mostly, me. I want to get out before I've sunk too far. And Jenny, I'm sinking fast. I'm becoming another person. It's . . . much, much better for Louis that I leave him."

Jenny was silent for some time, and in that time, a trace of color came back to her face. She seemed to be making a great effort to regain her composure. Since she was Jenny Starr, it mostly did.

"I did not think," she said, "that you and Louis were perfect for each other. You are too ambitious for him. This is one thing. He may bore you. This has occurred to me. I suspect you are easily bored. So may we all bore you. So may Texas. Even offend you. There are still rough ways down here, and backward people that one sees. Until one is old and sees few people at all, like me. I am not innocent of the fact that divorce is the modern solution to such problems. I am not so blind as not to know that it can happen in our family. But to Bernie. Only poor Bernie. Not to Louis. Not Adam. Not to Arnold Starr. Not to Jenny Starr. We stand for stability in the face of anything. Anything at all." Suddenly Jenny's voice rose. "My God, Karen, I stood for anything for *years*."

"Why?" Karen asked, quietly.

"Because it was a marriage. Whatever bad things happened, we had a marriage. That is not a trifle."

"Jenny, what did you have mainly?"

"Each other."

"I mean, honestly."

"Each other in the end."

Jenny was now silent. Her posture on the sofa was slumped. She looked straight ahead.

After a time, Karen said: "Jenny, can you forgive this?"

The older woman shook her head. "I suppose not," she said, at the moment not unkindly. "Which is not entirely your fault. We have all hurt Louis, myself included, and recently at that. But you have hurt him the most and at the wrong time. I see no way for us to be friends, my dear. Subjectively. Objectively, I find much to admire in you. I always have. That will continue. However, I should think it best if you leave him quickly. With as little fanfare as possible."

"I intend to."

"And . . . remain away from our family." Jenny rose and looked down at her daughter-in-law. And this look was bitter cold. "We will want no part of you."

In three days Karen was on a plane to New York. In three weeks she had rented a house in Darien, Connecticut, within walking distance of the Sound. On the day after she rented it, she bought five thousand dollars worth of furniture at Bloomingdale's.

"At least," she wrote Adam to his box number, "the bed should be here when you arrive." And, as she wrote this, she was happy.

LOUIS PACKED and shipped everything belonging to Karen to her apartment in New York. With her pictures gone and her books, the apartment looked very bare. He did nothing about that. Like a robot, he awoke each morning, brushed his teeth, showered, shaved, dressed immaculately and went to work. No one but his psychiatrist knew the superhuman effort that went into accomplishing these daily exercises. At the store he sometimes lost the thread of what people were saying to him, but they knew he was under a strain and forgave him. He slept poorly, but his doctor gave him only the mildest kind of sleeping pill. "I have not yet had a patient who dies from lack of sleep," he explained. "People do die from Seconal."

## 3

THE COURT ruling that school children would have to be bused to schools outside their normal school districts to achieve real integration caused a predictable outcry. The newspapers editorialized fiercely against the decision, the letters column was filled with denunciatory outbursts, and the people protested agitatedly in interviews on the television news programs. Adam's fellow councilmen did not help. Each of them spoke out against the decision and predicted great difficulties in carrying it out. Adam himself, when confronted by the necessity of speaking publicly on the issue, said simply, "It is the law. This city has always

been law abiding. I'm certain it will continue to be so."
He actually said as little as possible publicly on the matter.
He did not wish to fan the flames. What he did was meet
with church and PTA groups. He met with them in the
evening and made a short talk which in essence was an
explanation of exactly what the new law meant. He explained, explained, explained: his patience was inexhaust-
ible. Then he opened the meetings to questions and fielded
the hostilities good-humoredly. Over endless Cokes, Dr.
Peppers and cups of coffee, he usually managed to shake
hands with nearly everyone in what were often crowded
gymnasiums or churches. These meetings never became un-
ruly. It was far too early. That was Adam's purpose. He
wished, quite simply to make busing a foregone conclusion
and a boring issue before it actually started in the fall. He
knew he could not possibly prevent isolated incidents of
noisy defiance. He wished to minimize these and to have
them controlled, not by himself and the police, but by the
rest of the citizenry.

What pleased his audience most was that he would stay
with them all night if they wanted him to. His sincerity
was obvious and convincing. He ate many pieces of home-
baked cake and endless cookies. Some of the black neighborhoods where he appeared surprised him. They were not
much more enthusiastic about busing than their white
neighbors. But he talked to them the same way. They
seemed to like what he said.

He attended meetings like these once a week and sometimes more. He wished to touch every conceivable group
within the city. There was no question in his mind but that
the issue was the most important he had faced as Mayor,
and might be the most important he would ever face. At
óne point, he viewed television news clips of the disturbances in Boston, thinking he might use these as examples
of what Ramsey must not do. But, in addition to the rage
on the faces of the Boston people, there was glee in some
of them. There is always glee in a mob scene. He decided
against using the clips.

He did his best.

ONE AFTERNOON, Senator Hayden Calhoun called. "I'll be
down your way next week and I'd like to have lunch,
Adam," he said. "Some quiet place, out of the way. Make
it Wednesday. Pick me up in your Rolls—I like that car—

at noon at the Sheraton and take me where we can talk. Okay?"

"Sure," Adam said, puzzled. Hayden Calhoun did not often wish to be hidden out.

Adam picked up the Senator at noon, as promised. He hadn't seen Calhoun in a year or more and he was taken aback at how much older he looked. His face seemed to sag around the mouth and chin and his shoulders slumped. But his eyes were as lively as ever and his voice sounded the same. As they passed the high-rise apartments and the shopping centers, the old man said, "Hard to believe this was all prairie when I was elected to the Senate. When you talk about business progress, you got to hand it to that Citizens Council of yours."

"Not mine."

"You're on it. Your Pa was once president of it. They may be dictators, but they don't kill all the Jews and by God, they even elected one Mayor."

Adam laughed. *"They* sure as hell didn't."

"Well, it happened. Unexpected things can happen in Ramsey. You're an unexpected thing."

The club Adam had selected was mostly empty. Senator Calhoun had an old-fashioned. To keep him company, Adam had one, too.

"You obviously have something on your mind," Adam said, lightly. "You never want privacy. No politician wants privacy. It's his mortal enemy."

Calhoun nodded. He turned away from Adam and let his eyes wander through the club. "They got a bookie joint in the back of this joint?" he said. "It sure as hell ain't supportin' itself on lunch."

"It's a disco at night. Gets all the stewardesses who live around here."

The old man nodded. "Can I get a decent small steak here?"

"I guess so." Adam ordered for them and they talked idly of old times when the younger man had worked for the then young Senator, of Presidents, kings and dictators. The waitress brought their steaks and the old man ate with relish. "Not bad," he said. "For Texas, that is. Where you can never get a good steak though they grow the beef right here."

"But don't fatten it."

"Still seems wrong." When he had finished and had lit

his cigar, Senator Calhoun leaned back and regarded Adam. He was smiling. "You like bein' Mayor, I'd guess."

"Yes. It's plenty of work."

"I often think there's no limit to the work a man can do. If, acourse, he's that kind of man. And if he likes what he's doin'. I get four hours, five at most, sleep at night, and it's been enough."

"It doesn't seem to have slowed you down."

"Mmmmm." The old man cleared his throat. "Adam, in about two years, it'll be twenty-four years in the Senate."

Surprised, Adam said, "I know that. I was there at the beginning, as we've just been discussing."

"And six before that in the House. Thirty years. I'll be sixty-eight, Adam."

"Senators go on until they're ninety. Like conductors."

Calhoun laughed. "I guess I can still get it up when it has to be got up. But, it's enough, Adam."

In astonishment, Adam did not respond. He looked at the old man blankly.

"I'm quittin'. In two weeks or so. I'm announcin' that. To let the scramble start." He smiled. "My, what a scramble there's gonna be in these parts."

"But why? You're at the absolute top now."

Senator Calhoun was now deeply serious. "You know the newspapers reported I went into the hospital for a checkup a couple of months ago?"

"Sure. And everything was fine."

Senator Calhoun smiled. "I keep tellin' you, politicians lie about whether the sun's out. That was a mild heart attack, Adam. Mild, but a heart attack."

After a pause, Adam said, "I'm sorry, Hayden. But, hell, people live through five of those."

"Me, I don't want to try. And Babydoll and the girls don't want me to. And . . ." The old man paused and looked up at the ceiling. He blew rings of smoke into the air. They were very good smoke rings. He had learned that, Adam thought with amusement, in a thousand back rooms, stalling for time. "I got a feelin' for home. Suddenly, I want to go home. For good, Adam. I want the sky over me, and the stars at night, and the prairie and the river and horses and the brush. And . . . I got enough money now. To go home. They tell me I could even write a book."

"You could do that."

"Well, if I do that or not, I'm gettin' out of that town,

Adam. They say a man never leaves Washington 'cept he's fired or in a hearse. I'm gonna do it. I'm gonna leave with my head up and on my own two feet."

After a silence, Adam said, "I'll be goddamned."

"I thought you'd be surprised. So will a lot of people. Not even my staff knows yet. Nobody 'cept Babydoll and the girls and now you. But it'll leak out when the staff starts preparin' the announcement. I got an immensely loyal staff. Forty reporters'll know it before I'm finished draftin' what I got to say."

"I tell you, Hayden," Adam said, slowly, "I think it's bad for the country and I think it's bad for Texas. Texas . . . a lot of this state's dignity . . . prestige . . . nationally . . . was wrapped up in you. *Is* wrapped up. You quit, this damn state'll probably elect a John Bircher or close to it."

Calhoun nodded. "Unless they don't. Texas politics is often surprisin'. They'll elect a man they like."

Adam shook his head. "Who they like is Teddy Roosevelt."

Senator Calhoun nodded. "Theoretically. But a personality could get 'em. They'd buy a personality. Providin', acourse, he's not an actual Communist and will defend the oil depletion allowance and loves his Mother. Or at least don't beat her."

"Who are you thinking of, Hayden?"

The old man took a deep breath. "I'm thinkin' . . . just thinkin', mind you . . . of you, Adam."

"Me?" Adam almost shouted.

"You can tell me ten reasons why it's impossible, and I agree with all of them. You're a Jew, you're too liberal, you ain't even really in politics and never have been, you're rich—though that's not such a handicap—oh, there're others. But . . . *you are a personality*. You look good— sound good—on TV. I followed you as Mayor pretty close. People genuinely like you. And Adam . . . ain't nobody in Texas hasn't heard of Starr's. All the other candidates are gonna spend a year gettin' their names known. By God, that you already done."

Adam was silent.

"Two questions," Senator Calhoun said. "One, do you want to try? Two, can somebody run those stores? Because you'd have to take a leave of absence and then, if you won, you'd have to quit."

Adam thought for a moment. " 'One' I can't answer. I'm

still in shock. 'Two,' yes, in a year or so, there's a young man who could run the stores. If I won. But Jesus, how the blood would run."

Calhoun grinned. "Succession?"

"Mmm . . ."

The Senator became serious again. "Well, that's only in case you won. Lose and you're right back where you were. And . . ." The old man puffed on his cigar. "You'd probably lose."

"The junior Senator from Texas a Jew," Adam said, slowly. "That's the Arabian nights—" He laughed. "If you'll forgive the simile."

Senator Calhoun was serious. "Sure is. If your name was Weinstein or Rosenberg, this wouldn't even come up. But it's Starr. Some Jewish names ain't as bad as others. I'll tell you frankly, Adam, I didn't know whether you had much of a chance for Mayor, either. This town ain't never had a Jewish Mayor, as you know, but it has now. And that was personality."

Adam shook his head. "And a weak opponent. They were stuck with him."

"That may be true and it may not. We jus' don't know. Anyway, for the Senate, we'd place you middle of the road. You'd get a gaggle of geese on the right and some lonely liberals on the left. The conservatives'd shake each other out, the liberals'd drown and the center would look mighty like the place to be."

"In the Texas sense I'm not really middle of the road," Adam said, slowly. "In this state, I'm way to the left."

Calhoun waved that aside. "In your head, my boy, in your head. Not on the record. Far as the world knows, you're one of the builders of Ramsey, the business, conservative center of the universe, and the head of an enterprise so capitalistic it's obscene."

Adam laughed. "You must have just got your bill," he said.

The Senator grunted. "Them goddamn catalogues of yours. I keep owin' you a thousand dollars a month when I ain't even been in the store. Anyway . . . I would back you, if you announced. My organization would work for you. It is one hell of an organization which has got somethin' on nearly every son of a bitch in this state who amounts to beans. A lot of powerful people'd have to go my way—wouldn't be no choice for 'em."

Adam studied his old friend for a few minutes. "Why would you do this, Hayden? For me?"

The old man looked away. "It ain't for you, Adam. It's somethin' you said yourself a little while ago. I love this state, or I wouldn't want to be comin' back to it. And you're right. My office has given it a little prestige. What happens to the United States of America, Adam, has got something, not such a little bit either, to do with me. With what I decide. Now, see, I want this to continue. The junior Senator from Texas, politically, is backwards for Coolidge. He ain't never gonna be a major factor. But he will be the senior Senator when I retire and that's bad news. So I'd like to see a younger man comin' up I believe in. A man I can talk to. Guide around tricky corners. But who wants this country to stay in the twentieth century and don't believe, deep in his heart, that slavery was a pretty good thing. We could get that, Adam, and I'd rather not."

Adam was silent. The old man suddenly coughed and spat up some phlegm into his handkerchief. "So he tells me: 'Cut down on cigars. An' no more than four ounces of scotch a day.' Ain't no way a man can live on two cigars and four ounces of scotch a day. When I break them rules, I want to break them in Texas. So, if I curl up my toes, I curl 'em down there on the ranch."

Adam still did not speak. Senator Calhoun suddenly smiled and his leathery old face seemed to be cracking. "You'll decide to try it, Adam. You couldn't ever pass this one up. You was born for this. So let me tell you two things. You can't fuck up as Mayor, and you can't fuck up your private life. Far as I know your private life is okay, at least I ain't heard nothin' bad about it. But it's got to stay that way till you win or lose. If you win, you can screw every broad on the East Coast like the Kennedys and others, but not before. Now, as Mayor, you got one big thing and that's this busin' shit. You keep that calm, and that's a big plus. A lot of racket, and that's a minus. An' you shouldn't get caught stealin' from the treasury, either, I reckon. But the busin' is a hot one."

"I'm working on that now," Adam said.

The old man nodded in approval. "Get 'em used to it."

"Do you know who else is likely to run?"

"Oh, a couple of Congressmen, and the Governor might. But he's a feeble Governor and might not even win reelection." The Senator smiled. "I tell you one guy who you know who might."

"Who's that?"

"Cullum Roberts. He's talked to me a couple of times like he's tired of bein' the man in the back room. What do you think of old Cullum, by the way?"

"He's a double-crossing son of a bitch," Adam said.

"Well, aside from that . . . he got any sense?"

"Oh, sure. Thought he made a mistake with me. He and his boys personally made me more powerful than they are by getting me elected rather than appointed. He never thought I'd go as far as I did."

"A man should never underestimate another man's ego."

"Most of the time he's pretty savvy."

The Senator shook his head. "He couldn't touch you on TV," he said. "He's dusty and his hair's too thin. He ain't said nothin' definite to me yet, but my genes tell me he'd like it."

"When am I supposed to let you know?" Adam asked.

"You got plenty of time. You don't have to announce too soon. Let the scramblin' go on for a while. I ain't gonna play nobody up for a long time to come. I ain't bowin' out for nearly two years after all . . ." He became silent. Suddenly, he slapped his hand down against the table.

"You know, Adam, I'm gettin' so carried away by all this, I think I'll go back to the store with you and buy me a Stetson hat."

Adam laughed. "Not at Starr's. Not a Stetson."

The Senator shook his head. "Should be a John B. Stetson," he said. "That's what's in all the songs. But anyway, you got Western hats, still, I reckon?"

"Oh, sure."

"Le'ss go, son. An' after that, you can drive me to the airport an' I'll go back to Washington an' fix whatever got fucked up durin' the two days I been away. Which will be enough."

TOWARD THANKSGIVING of that year, Joe Fox walked into Bernie Starr's office and closed the door.

"Sam Rosengarden never woke up this morning," he said. His face was pale.

Stunned, Bernie waited a moment, then said, "What happened?"

"Heart attack. In his sleep. Way to go, all right."

Bernie's voice was unsteady. "What does that mean, Joe?"

Joe Fox shrugged his shoulders. "For openers, it means we don't get our regular monthly offering next month. Or maybe for a lot of months."

"I mean . . ."

"I know what you mean, and I don't know. I only spoke with Sam. Did all of my business with Sam. I don't know who he told what to. He had a couple of vice-presidents . . . like Harvey who used to drive his car . . . but I don't know how much they knew. No partners. At least, I don't think so. He owned most of the stock, except what he may have given to those officers. No wife."

"Joe . . ." Bernie, deadly pale, had to force his next words out: "What do we do?"

"What do you think we do, baby? Nothin', that's what. We sit it out and keep track. We fly up for Sam's funeral, which is day after tomorrow. I already got us the tickets. Next day, we call on the boys who're left. We say how sad we are. That nothing will change between Starr's and their firm. That we'll continue to be their good customers. We feel around, Bernie, feel around. Just the way I did with Sam, years ago. Far as I know, there'll be no change in the whole thing. Far as I know, the payments will go right on. I don't know very far, is the trouble."

"Is there anything you want me to do?"

"Say nothing up there. Any talkin' I'll do."

"Sure."

Joe Fox turned to go. Before opening the door, he turned and faced Bernie. "Oh yeah," he said. "You might also pray. That was a very successful business. Somebody might buy it. We—you and I—would prefer that nobody buys it."

"Christ," Bernie said.

# 4

LATER IN his life, Adam was never able to separate in his memory the trips to Darien. They ran together like a continuing dream. The interruptions, when he went home and back into his normal business, seemed like entries into another life. In fact, his life was divided: there was Karen, and there was the rest of it. At first, when his week or so with her was ending, he held resentment that he must give up this one life. In time he accepted it. In Darien he was happier than he could ever remember being, but his intelligence told him that there were limits to this sort of thing, that idylls were transient and not part of the real world outside, where there were problems to be solved, decisions to be made and irritations and frustrations to be suffered. In this sense, he felt he was earning Darien. In Ramsey he worked hard and effectively to earn his next escape. He did cheat in one respect. So that they would have weekends together, he extended the New York trips from five working days to seven, on the basis, as he explained, that he wished to expedite the preparations for the building of the Fort Worth store. He left Ramsey on Sunday mornings, arriving in Darien in time for dinner and returned Tuesday nights, giving himself nine nights and two full days with Karen. The architects and interior designers were hard put to manufacture enough work for him to look at. But he had always supervised every detail of the stores, so they accepted his omnipresence with good humor, especially since he was both creative with them and pleasant to them; and Starr's paid its bills practically by return mail.

Of course, he remembered his first trip north after Karen had left Louis. They had planned for him to take a taxi downtown and the train to Darien, where she would meet him at the station. But when he reached the terminal building, there she was. He saw her before she did him, and he stopped short for a moment, startled. She was in jeans and a sheepskin jacket against the outdoors chill, and she looked to him very young. Well, she is younger than I am, he thought. But in this moment, she looked almost schoolgirlish, and when she did see him, and rushed to him and threw her arms about him, standing on one foot with the other up in the air, he felt he had a colt in his arms.

"Oh, darling," she said.

Looking down at her, he saw that her eyes were filled with tears and this pleased him immensely.

"Hello, love."

She was in a rush to explain, as they walked slowly toward the baggage pickup. "I knew it was dangerous, and if you'd been walking with someone I would have disappeared. I hated the idea of that dirty old train on your first visit. And I didn't want to wait so long, chewing my fingernails."

"There wasn't a soul on the plane I'd ever seen before."

"But if there had been, I would've been invisible. I promise . . ."

He laughed. "What made you pick Darien?" he asked.

"I didn't. It picked me. There aren't that many houses to rent within commuting distance of the city. I found this one in the *Times*, rode up to see it that afternoon and had it rented the same night." Karen paused, giving him a fast glance. "Adam . . . it's only a house. It's not what you're used to. Or me. But it can be fine. For what we need. We can walk to the beach . . . we could even buy a sailboat in the spring. You can't see the Sound from the house, but there are trees and a nice terrace, and . . . I'll *make* it all right."

Again, she sounded like a small, determined girl and he was touched. "Of course you will," he said. "Anyway, it'll be fun doing things to it together."

Suddenly, she looked away from the road and into his eyes. "My God," she said, "I forgot the hotel!"

"What about it?"

"You won't have checked in. Suppose Claude . . . suppose you get calls?"

He smiled. "Forget it. I'll check in by phone. I've been staying at the St. Regis for so many years I know everybody there. I'll check in by phone tonight and stop by tomorrow with a bag. I brought an extra for that purpose. And then call in every night and return calls. And turn off the phone."

She looked amused. "You sound as though you'd done this kind of thing quite a lot."

"Never once."

She put her hand on his.

When they were almost at the house she said, "Oh, Adam, please don't be disappointed."

"I won't."

Instead, he was pleasantly surprised. From the outside the house was ordinary, but not dismaying. It was in white wood with a shingled roof and red doors and windows. The two-car garage was attached, and the short driveway was gravel, leading to a cobblestone path to the front door. A second path led to the rear, and, he supposed, the kitchen. The lawn in front was good sized and had been carefully tended. In the middle of it was a big apple tree and there were other trees spotted here and there.

"The apple tree gets sprayed every year so it doesn't give apples," Karen said, with a laugh. "That's so the apples don't fall off and have to be cleaned up. You can't eat them anyway, the owner told me, and they get to be a mess. It's a neutered apple tree."

"Does he maintain the place?" Adam asked.

"No, sir," she said, firmly. They were still sitting parked in the driveway. "*We* maintain it. When something goes wrong, *we* fix it. Unless the roof falls in, of course. Then it's his. But, for instance, come spring, you mow the lawn."

Adam said, "I did that for a living when I was twelve. I mowed eight or ten lawns around us for money, and at the end of the summer I knew all those people pretty well, right? And my parents knew none of them. So I gave a client cocktail party."

Karen laughed. "You did what?"

"It's true. I made up handwritten invitations and handed them out to all my clients for a Sunday afternoon cocktail party. So my parents could meet all those people I'd worked for all summer. Naturally, they all came. They were curious as to how Starrs lived. My mother and father were very good humored. Two of my clients got so loaded, Maitland nearly had to carry them out. That was because I insisted on mixing the drinks. And I was anxious that everybody be loose. They were loose all right. They were spastic."

"What a precocious young man. Client entertaining at twelve."

"All right, madame, take me inside."

It was a pleasant house. The living room was quite large and had a fireplace, and the master bedroom also had its own fireplace. There were two other bedrooms and three and a half baths. The kitchen was oversized and had plenty of room for a breakfast table which did not as yet exist. The inside of the house had been as well maintained as the outside. The paint and wallpaper looked new and most of it was not only inoffensive, but striking.

He looked around him, "I'm amazed at what you've done in two months."

"Dear old Bloomingdale's," she said. "They're expensive and a pain, but they have everything."

Against the plain off-white of the living room walls, she had a sofa and two chairs done in a smashing black and yellow floral print. There was a superb old wooden coffee table in front of the sofa, and sleek goosenecked reading lamps by the two chairs. A white shag rug set off the area. "That we can live with," she said. She walked purposefully into the dining room, "This we can't live with. And I've done nothing about it." Adam burst out laughing. In the very adequate sized dining room was a card table and two directors' chairs.

She looked up at him rather shyly. "I thought we might have a great antique dining room," she said. "I used to take fancy cooking lessons to kill time, and I've gone back to them. And you should put in a wine cellar."

He smiled, gently. "Cooking lessons?" he said, quietly. "I would have bet you couldn't scramble an egg."

"Well . . ." she said dubiously. "The lessons haven't absolutely taken yet. I've been practicing, but dinner, so far, is erratic. In other words, anything can happen. Now, the bedroom." But she stopped and looked at him nervously before taking him in. "Adam . . ."

"Yes, dear?" He continued to be amused.

"At this moment, the bedroom has . . . a bed."

And that, indeed, was all it had. But there were sheets and blankets and towels in the bathroom, and they could make do.

He took her in his arms and held her close. "I am so

very glad to be here," he said. "I've missed you like hell. In all my life, I've never missed anyone so much."

She pressed him closer and said nothing.

IN THE days and nights that followed, they did many things to the house. Or at least got them started. Much of what she needed, Karen was able to find in Stamford, nearby, so there was only one occasion when she had to go to New York. This was to order fabric for the curtains. She had engaged the service of a fey young decorator from Greenwich to help her with such things, but he came during the day and Adam never saw him. On their one day in New York, she drove him in and dropped him off at the architects' office.

"Can we have lunch?" she asked in the car.

"Sure. Within limits, there's no reason we shouldn't see each other. You left Louis, not me."

"Where would you like to go?"

"The most obvious place we can think of. '21.' "

She grinned mischievously. "I guess we shouldn't hold hands."

He laughed. "No. Friendly and suitably serious."

"Why not go somewhere out of the way?"

"Because that *is* suspicious. Nobody in his right mind takes the wrong girl to '21.' "

"Oh my dear," she said, glancing at him, "you still sound so practiced. You're such a fraud . . . really so innocent. So am I, for that matter. I've never had an affair with a married man. As you know."

He smiled. "Think of all the mistakes we can make."

On that day in town, she bought a six-hundred-dollar KLM sound system from Liberty and some two dozen records, from rock to Solti's *Goetterdaemmerung*. Her tastes in music were broad, as were his, but, somewhat to his surprise, she knew much more about it than he did.

"I never knew you liked serious music so much," he said. *"Die Goetterdaemmerung*. My God, that's five hours."

"It's for rainy days when you're in the city," she explained, arranging the records in the bookcases. "And, incidentally, there's a lot you don't know about me. A good deal Louis never did either. I was an only child and when I was eleven, I had a friend who liked opera. So did her mother and she took us. And I listened to WQXR a lot at night in bed. I've seen *Goetterdaemmerung* several times."

"Buy some old show tunes," he said, to his surprise. "Bobby Short, maybe, with all those old songs of his. Back to the days of my youth."

She laughed. "You're young enough for me, my dear."

"I often feel . . . very young here."

As he began to realize, a part of what he was feeling was a reversion to a long-ago time that had slipped by him before he could grasp and savor it. As long as he could remember, including during his school and college days, he had felt serious and purposeful. He had been voted into positions of responsibility by his classmates. He could not remember ever owning, even for a time, the luxury of carelessness. There had been the exception of Claude. When he had seen her on the runway, he had been enchanted by her beauty, by the depth of her eyes and by the languid movements by which she showed clothes; she had had her own style, quite different from the bolder, more positive modeling of the other mannequins. Meeting her, finding that she spoke English as well as he did, being half-American, he had lost himself in the sound of her voice, her carriage, her kindness, and eventually, her unexpected passion. With Claude, perhaps, in their very early days, he had been a youth. Even then, he had known that she had limitations of interests; that they would have little to talk about when passion had subsided. He had heard that she had had affairs, even been kept; and was, in those days, far more worldly than he. He had been jealous of her past, even resentful of it. But he had been a youth and had thrust these things from his mind and married her. For the first time and for the last, so far as he could foresee, he had been a foolish youth. And had lucked out since the marriage, as he understood it, had mainly worked. Now, with middle age upon him, he was a youth again. He took delight in Karen: in her voice, in her words, her look, her movements, her expressions, and, especially, in the touch of her skin and her soft hair. And she was gay and young herself. Now that their old adversary relationship was ended, she seemed much softer to him. She consulted him on everything she planned for the house and was earnest in seeking his approval. He went through books of curtain fabrics with her and enjoyed himself. She had brought out a few of her pictures and they visualized what colors would go best with the paintings. He hung these himself, cursing loudly when he made a mistake. He had never before personally hung a picture in his life. Nor had she cooked many dinners, as became clear.

"God *damn* it," he would hear, sitting in the living room while she struggled in the kitchen.

"What this time?" he would ask in amusement.

"The spinach soufflé is like chewing gum."

And so it would be. Nothing was ever done at the same time as anything else. More than once, they drove down the road to a steakhouse and ate there. Whatever happened, he always helped her wash the plates and clean the kitchen. He mopped the floor. She dusted the whole house. They were so meticulous about these things neither of them had ever done before that the cleaning woman, on her twice-weekly visits, had little to do.

"She talks about her 'lowers' a lot," Karen told him once.

"Her 'lowers'?"

"I think she means her bowels. Whatever 'lowers' are, she takes very good care of them."

"How old is she?"

"In her sixties, anyway. And quite deaf, so she talks loudly as well as a great deal. She thinks you're a traveling salesman."

"Why?"

"Because sometimes your suits are here and sometimes they're not. She also thinks we're newlyweds because we have so little furniture."

He did not reply. As she did from time to time, which always astonished him, she guessed what he was thinking.

"I've written Louis . . . about divorce," she told him. "I suggested he get it in Texas. It's quite easy there, if you're a resident, you know."

She was sitting on the sofa, sipping a glass of white wine. He was in an armchair with a scotch and soda on the coffee table.

"On what grounds?" he asked.

"Any. I suggested to him incompatibility, mental cruelty, whatever is grounds in Texas. Do you know?"

He shook his head. "No idea. Civilized, I suppose."

"I haven't heard from him yet."

Adam was silent.

"I don't think he'll be surprised," Karen continued. "I mean, that divorce has come up so soon."

"As a matter of curiosity, why has it?"

Karen shrugged. "I seemed to need to get it started. Does it bother you?"

Adam thought for a moment. "A little," he admitted.

Karen looked down at her wine. "I'm sure I would have divorced him someday," she said. "And if that's true, then better soon than late."

"If that's true."

She hesitated, then looked at him inquiringly: "Do you think we should talk about guilt, Adam? Or keep it to ourselves. Even between ourselves?"

Adam, who faced all things directly, did not: "Not unless we have to," he said.

"Well," she said, "if you should have to . . . I can. Whatever has to be done, I can do it as long as I have you even one week in five."

He rose and kissed her on the forehead. Each evening, late, he checked the hotel for messages. When he did this, she discreetly left the room.

Both of them read the *Times* book reviews and the *New York Review of Books* and they bought what sounded interesting. These were all current books, but Adam purchased also, somewhat to his surprise, sets of Hemingway, Faulkner, Fitzgerald, Dickens and P. G. Wodehouse, most of these in paperback. "I find I want to reread certain things," he explained.

But there was more to it than that. These were books that were a part of his youth, and he wished, partly unconsciously perhaps, to recapture this period he had only fleetingly experienced. He often read aloud to her and she did to him during their quiet evenings. He experienced rushes of pleasure when they did such things. Once again, they were things he had never done.

Because they were in love, their lovemaking was tender and frenzied and frequent. On the first Saturday they had together, he drove her to a seafood place in Westport and they purposely drank a little too much wine and drove back and made love all afternoon. That night, they went to see *Scenes from a Marriage* and found it too long but very good. On the way back, she said, "Was there anything in that movie you related to?"

"Nothing," he said immediately.

"She did all the right things and he left her."

He was brusque. "I've not left anyone."

"No, but I have. Louis did all the proper things . . . I suppose he did."

"Is this one of the times we have to talk about that?"

"No. Not really. That movie shook me up, I guess."

"Then we should keep Mr. Bergman out of our lives," he said.

For he managed as well as he did by keeping his two lives distinct and separate. References to one in the other bothered him greatly. Of course, there were none at home. But in Darien, there were from time to time. Playing the last side of *Das Rheingold* on their stereo, she shook her head as the music ended.

"There's too much sound for the machine," she said, thoughtfully. "Someday, we must get a really sensational sound system."

"All right," he said, automatically. But the "someday" stuck in his mind and would not go away. That night, for the first time, he slept poorly; even got up and warmed some milk. He did not know about "somedays." For the first time in his life, he was working without a plan. To his amazement, he rejected the whole idea of a plan. He wished to harbor no thoughts of the future. It was not just a matter of being content to live from day to day; in his present existence, it was a necessity. It occurred to him that he should explain this to Karen. But he realized he did not know how. He also did not wish to risk discovering what was in her mind. He wanted to know many things about her, but not that. He was therefore baffled one night when, after making love, she said, "I could still have children." He did not respond. "For several years still," she continued. "I wonder what kind of children we would have, Adam?"

"I have children," he said. He did not mean it cruelly, but the words came out sounding cruel. Yet he could think of nothing to add to take away the sting. She did not, however, move from his arms.

"Just hypothetical," she said, after a silence.

Relieved, he asked her something that had been on his mind: "What will you do when I leave, Karen? Go back to the city?"

"Part of the time. I like being alone here during the days when I know you're coming home. I might be lonely if you weren't. But I'll have appointments here—drapery people, carpenters, painters . . . I guess I'll be back and forth."

"What do your friends think? When you leave town?"

"That I visit friends in the country."

"They're not more curious than that?"

"Some of them are. They'll just have to go on being curious."

WHEN THE time came for Adam to go, she was very down. She was able to drive him to the city that morning, where he would work as usual and then catch a late-afternoon plane. At the last moment, she asked him to drive. "My eyes seem to be all wet," she explained.

"It's only a month."

"I know. And I'll write every day. Five lines, maybe, but every day."

"I like your five-line letters."

"I'll try to make them funny. But we must phone."

"Of course we will."

In the car he said, "I'm hopelessly in love with you, Karen."

She took one of his hands from the wheel and held it all the way to New York. When he got off at the hotel so he could check out, he kissed her lightly on the cheek and left her quickly.

BECAUSE OF the time difference, Adam arrived home in time for dinner. Claude met him at the airport and seemed glad to see him. He was also glad to see her. That night, she and Nancy talked a good deal at dinner. He was rather silent. On his mind was the fact that he and his wife would be in bed together. Normally, he always made love to her when he had been away. It was a kind of custom in their country. When they were in bed, he felt, to his astonishment, almost instant desire for her and made love at length and with enthusiasm. She was greatly pleased. So was he. Perhaps he was indeed leading two separate, possible lives. Perhaps the difference between them would give a lift to the old one. In any case, he fell asleep with his arm around her.

# 5

SHORTLY AFTER Thanksgiving, Bobby called Nancy from Cambridge one night.

"Have you been hearing from Jennifer?" he asked.

"Off and on. Sort of slap-dash notes. I know she's working with a theater company in Santa Monica. Why do you ask? She writes you. She said so."

"That's the point. She can take time off over Christmas. With that particular company I gather she can take time off anytime she wants. It seems rather loose."

"So?"

"So, my question is: Which one of us should invite her down to Ramsey for the holidays?"

Nancy laughed. "You should, of course. You're Young Lochinvar. I'm only an old roommate."

Bobby said, patiently: "Nancy, which one of us is most likely to get her is what I'm asking. You see I haven't got any idea whether she *wants* to come to Texas for Christmas. I don't know whether *anyone* wants to go to Texas for Christmas."

"She will. She's not all that crazy about life at home. Or wasn't. Anyway, you invite her properly. Write her a Young Lochinvar letter. Point out all the chaperoning she'll get . . ."

"She'll never come."

"Then avoid that point. Anyway, I'll call her up in a week or so and press the matter."

"Think she'll come?"

"Sure. She adores you."

"And you."

"And me. And Adam and Claude and the whole family. After all we *were* her family at graduation, and she had a very good time."

When Nancy called her, Jennifer said, "Of course, I'm coming. I've already broken the news to the parents. They were suitably distraught, but I said I would probably marry Bobby and they rather like that idea. Father's even springing for the plane ticket. Apparently, we're rich this week."

So that was settled.

JOE FOX called Bernie at home. "A niece and a nephew inherited Sam Rosengarden's business. She's married and lives somewhere in Ohio, and he's an engineer in California. They've put it in the hands of a lawyer to sell. Immediately."

Bernie said, "I don't suppose they'll lack for buyers."

"No. It's a good business. Can you raise—any way at all —say five, ten million?"

"You must be kidding."

"I'd like to buy that thing. So would you like to buy that thing."

"Joe, I couldn't raise a tenth of that."

"I'm asking, Bernie: Would the family stake you to your own business?"

"No," Bernie said, flatly. "Not a prayer." He could hear Joe Fox draw in his breath.

"Well, I didn't think so. But there's no harm in asking."

"Joe . . . is this thing gonna blow up, do you think?"

"I doubt it. We ain't the only people involved, son. There's other big names in this. New buyers won't want to cross some of those big names. Not if they want to keep on sellin' them. I think we're all right."

When he had hung up, Becky said to him. "I want you to know that if it does blow, I blow with you, Bern. Whatever happens to you happens to me. It's always gonna be that way, Bern."

Bernie smiled the sweet, kind smile people loved in him. "I dig you, too, baby." He paused. "You know, whatever happens, we'll still be able to fuck and drink."

"That's enough," Becky said.

CLAUDE STARR looked in the mirror one day and did not like what she saw. "Things," she said to herself, "are better. All men have mistresses, now Adam has a mistress. I have always expected that. But he has returned to me in bed. Somewhat. Nancy is right. He is very kind. Maybe from guilt, but he is so. My eyes are puffy. Soon my chin will begin to go. There is softness everywhere. Flab. I am Claude Starr. All this is not possible."

She announced to Adam that she was going to the Golden Door, the health spa, in California.

"All right," he said, surprised. "Why?"

"To recapture my youth," she said.

He smiled. "If you like, darling."

"It can be my Christmas present. It's very expensive."

"I think we can handle it."

She lost twelve pounds in two weeks at the Golden Door. Of course she did not drink. When she returned, she drank Perrier water. No one commented on this. She looked marvelous.

ONE DAY in New York, Adam and Karen had a festive luncheon at the Café Richelieu. They had venison and a bottle of wine and went to Tiffany's, where he bought eight wine glasses and eight crystal dessert goblets.

"When are we going to have six people to dinner?" she asked.

"Never, probably. These are to look at in the cabinets."

Arm in arm and laughing, they entered upon Fifth Avenue and nearly knocked Cullum Roberts off his feet. Adam kept on smiling. "You've probably met Karen," he suggested.

Cullum Roberts bowed. He was a courtly man. "Once," he said. "When you and Louis were at the opera in Ramsey."

"I remember," Karen said. She did not. "It's nice to see you again."

"What brings you to New York?" Adam said.

"Director's meeting," Cullum Roberts said. "I have to be here four times a year for those."

"And I have my architects."

"I know. Our deputy mayor keeps busy during your absences."

"If there is ever anything that can't wait I'll fly back, as you know."

"Of course. Nobody's complaining about the hours you keep, Adam."

They stood red-faced in the cold for a few silent minutes. "Nice to have seen you again, Mrs. Starr," Cullum Roberts said, finally.

"Karen and I had a number of things to discuss," Adam said. He could have cut his tongue out. Roberts shrugged.

"Of course," he said. "That's natural enough, Adam. It's good to see a familiar face on a cold day in a strange city. Have a pleasant time. We'll all be glad to see you back."

"Next Wednesday," Adam said.

Roberts waved pleasantly and was gone. Fifth Avenue was crowded. The Christmas shopping season was well under way.

"Is that bad?" Karen said when they were alone.

"No. However, I'm a fool."

"For explaining."

"Unnecessary. Dumb."

"It couldn't be harmful."

"It's not that. I just hate to be stupid. Especially with that bastard." But he did not take her arm again as they walked to the garage.

THEY GAVE each other things for the house that December. His to her was a large, and they thought, beautiful Rosenquist. Hers to him was the antique dining room, eight superb Queen Anne chairs and a magnificent dining table. They were very happy that night. She would be going to her parents' in Long Island for Christmas.

"How will I call you?" he asked.

"You can't. I don't care. You'd be running out to phone booths anyway. Like a school boy, all guilty. I don't like the idea. I'll know everything you feel."

"Will you?"

"Of course."

They did not have to say everything to one another. They did not have to overtalk. It was one of their pleasures.

# 6

Louis had great difficulty sleeping. He began to take Dalmanes. Usually, within half an hour, they put him to sleep for three or four hours. When he awoke, he was always nervous and agitated. He then took a five-milligram Valium and another Dalmane. Eventually, these sent him back to sleep for the rest of the night. But he was often hollow-eyed in the mornings. People did not think he looked well. He did not tell his psychiatrist about the Valium, which he had gotten from Dr. Fry, his medical doctor. The psychiatrist gave him the Dalmane; reluctantly, but it was not a barbiturate: a lesser damage. Eventually, when the combinations were not working as well as they had, he got a Dalmane prescription from Dr. Fry and a Valium prescription from the psychiatrist. But the psychiatrist would only give him two milligrams, twenty-five at a time. He took to having a glass of beer with his second dosage.

He was convinced that he was losing his mind. To prevent this as best he could, he read voluminously in the written reports and the figure charts that were a part of his business. He quoted from them to his colleagues to impress them with the fact that he was on top of things. He marked the fashion magazines and *Women's Wear Daily* to be sure the store had whatever seemed to be in the news. But his buyers noted that he often asked them about the same piece of merchandise a number of times.

He tried very hard to pass time with books and television, but for these entertainments his attention span was too short.

"Try to repeat over and over, 'She is dead and that is final. That part of my life is over. Today begins my new life. Nothing will bring back the old one.'" The psychiatrist told him to do that. Depression due to the loss of a

370

loved one was something the psychiatrist had dealt with. But Louis could not separate in his mind his grief over the loss of a loved one from his fury at: what? And his psychiatrist had no answer for him; only that eventually he could find his own.

The problem seemed to be that he truly felt that the bad things that had happened to him were his own fault. He could not explain to the psychiatrist about his proven inadequacies. He had the strange notion that Adam should go to the psychiatrist and explain these matters. Adam would know how to do it. Adam would detail the inadequacies. In doing so, he might even be able to explain them to him, Louis; not comment on aspects of them, which he had so often done; explain them. Trace them back to their origins. Louis was convinced in his heart that it was Adam he needed to see, not a psychiatrist.

He was shocked to remember one day that he had not done his calisthenics for weeks. It had been years since he had not done his morning exercises. For a few days he returned to them vigorously and also took frequent swims at the club. But soon these things seemed too much trouble. They slipped away from him. The care of his body did not seem very important. Nothing seemed very important.

7

A FEW days before Christmas, Jennifer and Bobby arrived. Nancy thought they were both in especially good form; full of cheer and laughter. The second night at dinner, Jennifer announced that she had got a part in a movie.

"It's all so banal," she said, gaily. "We work in that grubby little theater with one toilet that doesn't have a lock and hope that some producer or director will come. They never do."

"But one did," Bobby offered.

"Martin Rabb, his name is. He does mostly television, but he's producing a movie-movie. And he liked what I was doing."

"What were you doing?" Adam asked. He sat at the head of the table and Jennifer was on his right.

"Marion Froude in *Biography*. You probably never heard of it."

"S. N. Behrman," Adam said, with a smile. "I saw it once in a revival."

"Not with Ina Claire?"

"I would have been about seven when she played it. But I loved whoever did, I remember."

"Of course. The problem is, everybody falls in love with Marion Froude. They forget the actress."

"Not quite," Adam said. "But one does remember Marion Froude, that's true . . . It's a sad play, you know."

"If you play it right," Jennifer said. "Anyway, Martin Rabb, like everyone else, fell in love with that part. But, he did test me for his movie and I got it."

"What kind of part?" Bobby asked. He looked mischievous.

Jennifer looked at him reproachfully. "You know perfectly well," she said, "since I wrote you all about it. I play a hooker who gets murdered in the first ten minutes."

"So we arrive a little early. We can do that for a friend," Nancy said.

"You are too lovely to be killed off in ten minutes," Claude said, quietly.

"Well, but can you *do* anything with those ten minutes?" Nancy asked.

Jennifer was silent for a moment. "Yes," she said, finally. "I can. If I do it well, people will notice me. I'm playing against a character like Tony Perkins in *Psycho* . . . silent, mysterious, threatening. I have all the lines. I have a few minutes of gaiety and then a few of horror. It's a babbling character, at first . . ." She laughed. "My part, obviously."

"Would you like that very much?" Claude asked. "Being in the movies?"

"Oh well, Claude, I'm such an exhibitionist!"

"I was, too, as a model . . ."

"You still make your entrances, Claude," Nancy said, wryly. "You don't come in anywhere by the back door." Claude smiled.

"Do you still play piano on weekends?" Adam asked Bobby while Maitland was serving dessert.

"Oh, no, I gave that up at the beginning of the year."

"Why?" Nancy asked. "I thought you liked it."

Bobby laughed. "Ran out of repertoire," he said.

"No really," Nancy said, having her reasons.

"Hotels are too expensive," Bobby said, knowing her reasons. "I would have lost money."

"I thought you stayed with some friend," Adam said.

"I did . . . but don't." Bobby looked at Nancy, and winked at her. "After a while, it seemed an imposition."

So much for Guy Racquette, Nancy thought, happily. She glanced at Jennifer and thought she looked rather smug. So Bobby had written her, Nancy thought. Well, at least there was that much between them.

After dinner they talked easily and Bobby played for a while. Everyone went to bed early, except Nancy who said she would stay up. She did not feel sleepy and turned on the television, thinking of watching a late movie. But soon, Bobby, in a bathrobe, arrived in the television room and flopped down opposite her. Nancy smiled and turned the sound off.

"How've you been, Nancy?" he asked.

"All right. My work's going well."

"Who's Neal Adams?" he said, with a grin.

She laughed. "Claude's been writing to you. So you know who he is. He's an executive vice-president of the store, he's thirty-seven, he's divorced and he has two small children. He hasn't seen them since he's been here. He plans to go back home after Christmas for a few days. For that purpose. He has sandy hair, he's pleasant and he reads things. Even books. He's lonely."

"Is that why he takes you out?"

"Probably. He hasn't made a pass at me, which I gather is what you're getting at."

"Is that all right with you?"

Nancy hesitated. "I'm not sure," she said. "It's been fine, but since you ask, I'm not sure. I wish you hadn't asked."

He laughed. "Sorry. Will I meet him?"

"I thought the four of us would have dinner during the holidays."

He nodded. "You'll like him," Nancy added. "He's very relaxed. Not like most merchants."

"And Claude's drinking Perrier water."

"I don't know why. But I'm pleased."

"I'll ask her why. And I'm pleased, too. And you're pleased because I've left Guy." He looked amused. "So it's a good start for the holidays. Everybody's delighted with everybody."

"Was it hard? Breaking off?"

Bobby made a face. He was no longer amused. "I had wanted to quit for a long time. If you want to know the truth, I've wanted to quit since we all had that weekend together. But it was hard. He knew it and it was wrecking him. I tried to help and only made it worse. When I finally packed up . . ." Bobby suddenly stopped.

"What?"

"Not wildly pleasant this," he said, dryly. "Taught me a lesson, though. It seems that he kept every letter I ever wrote him. That was quite a few over the years at Harvard. Some of them were . . . affectionate." Bobby took a breath. "Guy told me if I left him he'd send the whole batch to Adam."

"Blackmail."

Bobby nodded.

"What did you do?"

"I talked to him . . . no success. So I beat him up."

"You did *what?*" Nancy was amazed.

"He thought I was going to kill him. I nearly did. I was strangling him when he finally told me where the letters were. If he hadn't told me . . . God knows. By that time, I'd lost my mind temporarily. I got the letters and burned them in front of him with lighter fluid. I almost set the apartment on fire. The last I saw of him, his nose was still bleeding. I was a raving maniac."

"Because of Adam?"

"Because of Adam. I knew it would kill him."

After a moment, Nancy said, "I guess it nearly would. If anything can. Possibly nothing can. Adam and our grandmother. They may be unkillable. The rest of us are all very killable. Have you heard about Louis and Karen?"

"Yes. I was sorry to hear that. Karen was a stunner, and I thought she'd be good for Louis."

"I mean . . . speaking of beating people up . . . what he did?"

Bobby was really astonished. "I don't believe it."

Nancy shrugged. "It's only a rumor. She went to the

hospital. Fell down the stairs, it was said. But it leaked out of the hospital that she didn't look like she'd fallen down the stairs."

"I hope she did. I can live with what I did to Guy. After all, he was about to blackmail me. But Louis would have trouble . . ."

"Is having trouble. He doesn't look well, doesn't act normally. I know Adam worries about him. I think he's not doing well at the store."

Bobby smiled. "Then we'll just have to cheer him up this Christmas. You and Neal and Jennifer and I."

Nancy hesitated, then decided to take a risk. "Does Jennifer . . . mean a lot to you, Bobby?"

He nodded. "Yes," he said, quietly.

"Do you know how she feels?"

"Not really. I know she likes me. But there *was* Guy. When we first met, I mean. She knows he's gone. I wrote her about that. Very lightly. Our correspondence is on the surface. No heavy breathing between the lines. So I wanted her to come for Christmas."

Nancy laughed. "For some heavy breathing?"

He grinned. "Maybe. Do you remember what I told you at the Plaza?"

"What part?"

"That I'd settle down with an appropriate girl some-day?"

Nancy was stung. "Jennifer is not appropriate."

"You bet she is. Unless she gets to be a movie star. *Even* if she gets to be a movie star."

Nancy was suddenly angry. "You don't understand Jennifer," she said. "She's not a well-cut suit you can wear when it matters."

"I didn't mean that . . ."

"She's enormously loving . . ."

"So am I."

"And tender and can be greatly hurt. If that happens . . ."

"No, it won't. Wouldn't . . ."

"I'd be on her side. I'd fight you hard. I love her very much, you know. We are closer than sisters."

He was silent. Nancy was looking at him fiercely.

"I couldn't . . ." He stopped.

"You're stammering."

". . . promise that nothing would ever happen. I could

promise her that anything that did happen would be momentary, quick as the life of a butterfly. And I'd be home."

After a silence, Nancy said, more quietly. "Are you telling me you think you're in love with her?"

He smiled. "That's what I'm telling you."

Nancy's face hardened. She had many conflicting emotions. What had happened between herself and Jennifer was not gone. It would never happen again. She had no desire for that; or for anything like it. But she did not wish to forget it and she did not wish Jennifer to forget it. Or fight it or resent its memory. So it all seemed too pat. Jennifer and her brother. She rose and realized she had let a foot go to sleep. She recognized James Stewart on the television. She would miss his movie. She switched off the set, and looked down at her brother; and saw his beautiful face that she had always adored, but so much stronger now, so much more confident. "How you've changed," she said; paused, "I'm glad for you."

He spoke quickly: "I thought for most of my early life, until just before I went away to Harvard, that I couldn't do anything I wanted to do. That *Adam* wanted me to do. And . . . I had this . . . preference is the best word, maybe. And that was the most hopeless thing of all." After a long pause, Bobby said, still speaking with difficulty, "My mother persuaded me that I could do . . . more than I had suspected."

"Claude did? Bobby, Adam spent his life telling you that!"

"Adam frightened me. Because . . . defending his own image, I guess, he lied to me. He said I was good at things I was bad at. I knew he was lying but he didn't. He was lying to himself and not knowing it. My mother never lied to me. She showed me, eventually, that I *could* do things. Showed me. My father frightened me. My mother saved me . . ."

There was a long silence. Eventually, Nancy rose, walked over and held his head in her hands and then kissed his cheek.

"Some things you can't do," she said, softly. "You can't hurt Jennifer. You can't ruin the sweetness of yourself. That would be selfish, my love. If you ruin those things, you rob me. Because I depend on them. Wherever we are, I depend on them. On us."

"So do I, Nance."

She continued to look down into his eyes. "I'm particularly glad that Claude was able to help you. Somehow she's the one who's always seemed in need. Of something none of us is giving her."

"She probably is that, too."

"But she somehow offered something none of the rest of us could give you. How strange . . ."

He looked down at the floor. "It's so easy to underestimate Claude. She knows things . . . nobody knows. Does things nobody does . . ." He smiled. "It's late."

"Good night, dear."

"Good night."

8

ON THE morning of Christmas Eve, Joe Fox came into Bernie's office and shut the door. His face was gray and his body slumped into the chair opposite Bernie. His eyes were bloodshot. "You still got the bar in here, I guess," he said. Bernie said nothing. He opened the cabinet next to the couch.

"Vodka," Joe said. "Just straight. I already had a couple."

Bernie poured Joe a drink. He took one himself, but he put a couple of ice cubes into it. He knew what was coming, but that did not prevent his hand from shaking. Joe Fox took a belt of his vodka and said, quietly, "It's blown, Bernie. I knew some of it yesterday. The rest this morning. It's all over the market."

"How'd it happen?" Bernie sipped from his vodka and sat down carefully.

"The lawyer the heirs hired smelled something. He did the same kind of detective work you did. When you put yourself on the payroll. You remember that, don't you, Bern?"

"I remember."

"He couldn't reconcile payments supposedly made to stores and promotional efforts given in return. Goods received, in other words. You remember Harvey?"

"The young man?"

"Yeah. The guy who used to pick us up and drop us at the airport. The driver, we all thought. Harvey, my friend, had been living with Sam for five years. Sam Rosengarden was a fag. Now you maybe didn't know that because I never told you, but I knew it. Plenty of people in the business knew it. What I didn't know was that Harvey was bought by Sam. Harvey owned ten percent of that business. He knew everything that happened. Harvey is what is called a hustling fag. So this lawyer faces him down, and like any other fuckin' fag, he cracks and sings. There was a second set of books. Payments made to whom, when, how much. I guess Sam was protecting himself. He had enough on all of us to burn us. And now he has." Joe Fox paused, red-faced and old looking. "From the grave, he hung us." The golden athlete looked through.

"Maybe . . . maybe Adam can do something. Buy off the lawyer."

Joe Fox shook his head. "The U. S. Attorney's office has it, Bernie. Interstate commerce. They got it yesterday. If Adam bought the whole fuckin' business, it wouldn't help now."

"What will happen?"

"The government'll get into the whole industry. Several major stores will be named. Not just us. I don't know who else kept two sets of books. I don't know who else will crack. One's enough."

"Will it . . . will it be in the newspapers?"

"*Women's Wear Daily*, anyway. Probably the *Times*, too. Not so much out of town. The fur business is New York."

"But it definitely will be in *Women's Wear Daily*?"

"Whenever the U. S. Attorney releases it. Like I said, it's on the street. It could break any day. Except tomorrow. They don't publish tomorrow. Enjoy your Christmas, Bernie. Then get a lawyer."

"You're not talking about prison?"

Joe Fox shook his head. "Fines. We'll deny, or plead nolo contendere or whatever and pay fines. And resign. Except you, of course."

Bernie was silent.

Joe Fox looked up and smiled. "It's okay, kid. Payola's been a part of the fur industry since there was a fur industry. In six months we'll all have new jobs. The other buyers and me. I've seen it happen."

"I won't."

"You'll have the old one. Starrs take care of Starrs. What the fuck's your family for, they don't take care of you when you need it?"

"Don't get too drunk down on the floor, Joe," Bernie said quietly. "Adam hangs around furs a lot Christmas Eve."

"I won't. Not this Christmas Eve. I'm goin' home." Joe Fox rose and was unsteady on his feet. "Fun while it lasted, hey, kid?"

"Joe—I can't help you. I'd like to. You helped me when I needed it."

Joe Fox waved his hand. "So we're two kids got caught smokin' in the bathroom. We'll both be okay. It ain't a capital punishment thing. Keep your chin up, Bern. It won't be a great three weeks."

When he started drinking early at home, Becky joined him. "I told you I was with you," she said. "Just let's get through tonight."

"I'll talk to Adam tonight."

"No. Not tonight. Get as drunk as you want tonight. But don't talk to him. Christmas afternoon. Tell him you want to see him Christmas afternoon. Nobody ever has anything to do Christmas afternoon. Tell him then. Make an appointment tonight. But don't spoil tonight for him."

"Okay," he said.

FOR ALL his years on earth, Christmas Eve and other state family occasions had been held at Arnold Starr's house. On the first Christmas after his death, Jenny had moved the locale to Adam and Claude's. He had been curious as to why. "You have the house, the staff. Why change?"

"You are the head of the family now," she had said. "That must be pointed out. Dramatized. My house is a relic."

She had not seemed sad, but rather insistent. So, as they had for nearly five years now, the family gathered at Adam's. Everyone was late because the male Starrs were out delivering personally late presents for customers, as their parents had before them; it is a service great merchants often perform. Drinks were not served until nearly nine. The whole family was present, including Aunt Bessie Goldsmith. Since they already had a guest in Jennifer, and since he had nowhere else to go, Neal Adams was invited. Christmas music came from the radio, but at some point, early on, Claude switched to the phonograph and played the Elisabeth Schwartzkopf Christmas album which Bobby had given them a year ago. Adam felt a mist come to his eyes when he listened to it. Of all singers, Schwartzkopf seemed to be Karen's favorite. She had half a dozen of the great German soprano's records and had made Adam follow the words when she was singing.

The Christmas record, Bobby thought, was the finest record of the familiar carols ever made.

"Nothing is quite as you expect," he said. "When you think you've heard the climax to 'Joy to the World,' there's a second one and better."

So they had listened in silence, and it was as good as he had said.

Now, they played it for the second Christmas, and in the conversational silence, Adam wondered why Bernie had arrived so drunk. He was not staggering yet, but he had a preposterous grin plastered on his face and his conversation made no sense. And Becky was not far behind him. She was in her giggling mood, the one thing about pleasant Becky that could drive him mad. She giggled through Schwartzkopf and whispered to Bernie and irritated everyone. Louis was the opposite. He was somber and withdrawn and scarcely talked at all. Well, that was understandable, Adam thought. Everything, no matter how odd, that Louis did was understandable. So Adam thought. So he told the family. Wait, he would say. Give him time. He needs time. He'll be all right, but not right away; and thus pushed away his guilt as well as it could be pushed away.

"Are you going to read something tonight?" Claude asked Adam. "For Christmas Eve."

He shook his head. " 'Come, bring with a noise,/' " he recited, " 'My merry, merry boys,/ The Christmas log to the firing;/ While my good dame, she/ Bids ye all be free; And Drink to your heart's desiring.' "

"Hear, hear," said Becky, loudly, raising her glass. Claude smiled. They all raised their glasses.

"What was that?" Jennifer asked, curiously.

"Robert Herrick," Adam said. " 'Ceremonies for Christmas.' "

"How do you know it?" Jennifer continued.

"I once published a tiny book with small excerpts from poetry about Christmas. No carols. We sold it in the store. I printed five hundred copies and we sold maybe fifty. I gave the rest away the following year."

" 'At Christmas, I no more desire a rose/ Than wish a snow in May's new-fangled mirth; but like of each thing that in season grows,' " Jennifer recited, seeming proud. "*Love's Labour's Lost.* I have thirty or forty speeches I can deliver, some quite long. I learned them to show what an actress am I. But that's the only one about Christmas, you'll all be glad to know, and I only remember that because we did the play at one of my many schools. Now, on other subjects . . . would you like me to begin?"

Bobby laughing, said, "Please not."

"I also sing and dance," Jennifer offered.

"After dinner maybe," he suggested.

And after dinner, they did sing carols for a while, with Bobby playing for them. Neal Adams had a pleasant baritone and Bobby himself could sing a little. But it was Jennifer, after a while, they listened to. She sang softly, but in a clear, true voice that wound itself around the heart. She sang the second verse of "Silent Night" by herself. No one else knew it. They would not have sung anyway. Adam looked at Claude and she had tears in her eyes. On Bernie's face, they were running down his cheeks. And Louis turned away and left the group around the piano and sat on one of the sofas.

"What else do you know?" Bobby said, when this was done.

"Baez, Mitchell, Collins."

She sang some songs to which he could remember the accompaniment, and this went on for nearly an hour and was a joy to be remembered for many Christmases.

Jenny said, "I adore that girl," to Adam.

He nodded.

"I think you may have company," he said.

"Bobby?"

"What would you think?"

"I would think he'd better get through another year of college before *he* does any thinking."

"And she's on one coast and he's on another most of the year. Bobby could go on to business school, of course."

"Do you want him to?" Jenny asked.

"I don't have strong feelings about it. He'll have learned a few things he'd otherwise have to learn, and some things he'd have to unlearn. But if he wants to, of course . . ."

"There's no question that he'll go into the store?"

Adam hesitated. "It may be hard to believe but it's something we've never really discussed. We've talked around it. But this work at Bloomingdale's . . ."

"He'll go into the store," Jenny said, firmly. "And I don't know that it's necessary that you discuss it with him. You will seem to be pressing."

"Father pressed."

"Your father was a determined man."

"More than I am," Adam said. "If Bobby had something else in his mind, I wouldn't stand in his way."

"I would," his mother said.

Adam laughed. "I know."

His mother smiled. "That's all old ladies have, Adam. Visions of continuity."

"Adam," Bernie said. " 'Scuse me, Mom. Di'nt mean to interrupt."

His mother looked as though she would say something, but decided against it. But her eyes were cool on Bernie's weaving stance. "I'll leave you to hold up your brother," she said to Adam.

"As a matter of curiosity, what is the point of this load you've got on? I'm going to have to get Rivers to drive you home."

"Beck can drive. She quit hours ago, so she could. Thassa point, Adam. Thass what I gotta see you about."

"Well, here I am."

Bernie shook his head ponderously. "Not now," he said. "Christmas Eve. Don' wanna spoil Christmas Eve. Can I come over tomorrow afternoon?"

"Sure."

"Four, five o'clock?"

"Any time you want."

"Five. At five, we can have a legit—legitimate drink. You'll . . . I think you'll want one, too, Adam."

"You're sure you don't want to get this out of your system?"

Bernie shook his head. When he looked at Adam, there

were tears in his eyes. Adam put it down to the drink. He did not doubt that Bernie was in trouble and would have to be helped out of it. Well, Bernie had always been in trouble. So it would happen again. It would happen during all of Bernie's life. That was Bernie.

"An' it has to be alone, Adam."

"Okay. In the study. We'll even shut the door."

Bernie nodded. He took a step forward and unexpectedly hugged his older brother. Then he turned away. In a little while he and Becky left. Adam was glad to see that she was, in fact, in good enough shape to drive. She also did some caretaking, he thought. Before leaving them to go to bed, Jennifer kissed both Adam and Claude.

"It was the loveliest Christmas Eve I can remember," she said.

But then, she, above all the others, had made it that.

OVERNIGHT, A norther swept into Ramsey from the Panhandle, dropping the temperature to below freezing. The skies were gray on Christmas morning, but the sun struggled to break through the layers of clouds and sometimes cast a metallic glint over the land. Around the enormous tree in the living room at Adam's house, the packages were piled high. Everyone had worried that Jennifer would have too few since her family was far away; so she had more than anybody.

"It's embarrassing," she said, in dismay, surrounded by her loot.

"Open a boutique," Bobby suggested. "Sell it all."

But her presents were lovely or useful or both, and she was obviously pleased. The Starrs gave each other and their friends munificent Christmases. They did not think much about it. They had the money, they were generous people. They also got forty percent off at the store. Claude's $12,000 fisher coat from Adam netted out to him at $7,200, but he would have paid the full price because she had the special taste for fisher.

There were many gifts of winter clothing.

"I think we should all get redressed and strut," Jennifer said.

"Strut where?" Adam said.

"Anywhere. Around the grounds."

"Well, let's walk Mother's presents over to her," Claude said. "Instead of waiting until she gets here for dinner."

"I'll call her," Nancy said.

"Tell her we're a touring fashion show so to dress up and break out some early champagne," Bobby said.

Jenny was delighted with the red-faced group which descended on her and indeed gave them champagne. She had had Louis over that morning and even he looked cheerful. And Claude had a glass of the Taittinger; one. Aunt Bessie Goldsmith had to be restrained from having her third. It was a gay morning, and the gaiety persisted through Christmas dinner at Adam's. As was the custom, all the servants shook hands with them and Bobby and Nancy kissed some of them. About four, the guests started dispersing, and Bobby asked his father's permission to use the Rolls.

"Of course," Adam said. "Why?"

"I'm going to take Jennifer for a ride and I think the Rolls would be fun for a change. We may go out to the ranch."

"Is she all right with horses?" Adam asked.

"Haven't you discovered yet that Jennifer is all right with everything?" Bobby said. "She's a blessed one."

Adam smiled. "I suppose," he said.

The young couple left. Claude decided to take a nap and Nancy stayed, happily, to curl up on the sofa with a book. She and Neal Adams had been graced with a private moment during the celebrations.

"We've been seeing a lot of each other," he said, "I don't think it's nearly enough."

Nancy heard herself reply: "I don't either."

She thought with gratitude, "I must be well."

Adam had the greatest luxury of all, he took a long walk, without distraction, without any serious thought and enjoyed it for its own sake.

BOBBY DROVE Jennifer all through the city, the suburbs, even some of the little towns spotted around Ramsey and eventually wound up at the ranch. He parked in front of the remodeled barn and showed her the bunkhouse, the main house where old Ben lived and where his ranch hands were probably gathered with him now, and the stable where some of the horses started neighing because of their presence. Far in the distance, they could see the Black Angus picking at the hay on the ground.

"Someday," Bobby explained, "since it's in the right

direction from town, it'll probably be worth millions for development."

"That's too bad," Jennifer said. She was bundled up in two heavy sweaters and a snow cap over heavy wool slacks against the cold. Her cheeks were pink and her eyes bright. But the wind had died down so it was not too chilly to walk around outdoors. "It's unexpected to think of Starrs owning cattle and horses and land just like the people who settled Texas. It's kind of nice."

"It won't go for a long time. Adam often comes out here to ride and work with the men. He takes out his frustrations here. Or did when my grandfather was alive." Bobby laughed. "In those days, Adam had many frustrations."

"What started you calling them by their first names?"

"Nancy. At age thirteen. She wished to be considered an adult. Or something. So I followed along. In those days, I did a lot of following along."

Jennifer smiled. "And not so much now."

Bobby shook his head. "Not so much. It wasn't so easy being Adam's son. Or daughter. Nancy was angry for a long time. Then that terrible thing happened to her and I got very worried. But she seems better."

"She's not dreaming so much anymore," Jennifer said, thoughtfully. "Those were . . . sometimes horrible. I used to hold her in my arms."

Bobby said nothing. He was pleased there had been tenderness between them; that Jennifer had such tenderness in her. Tenderness was important to him.

"She seems more accepting at the moment." Jennifer plopped down on the ground and gathered her knees up with her arms. "She didn't used to know how lucky she is."

"In what way?"

"Your family. That is a *family*. You can feel the love in that house."

"There's argument, sometimes bitterness . . . all the time."

"That has nothing to do with it. You are all exceptionally close, so you fight. Most families aren't close and don't fight and don't much react at all."

"Is that true of yours?" Bobby asked, quietly.

"Sort of. Daddy drinks, you know. Sometimes he has to go to the hospital. Mother feels very put upon. Says nothing. I find it depressing. Two middle-aged people who haven't really liked each other in years. With nothing but more years of not liking each other ahead. It's not really a family, you see. The Starrs are."

"I suppose. In general, everybody tries to do the right thing. We aren't mean to each other."

Jennifer said, wistfully, "And you have room. For me. For that nice Adams man. There's so much security, there's plenty of room to put up others."

Bobby sat down next to her. "Someday," he began. And stopped. She said nothing and did not even look at him. He touched her on the shoulder. When she turned to face him, he kissed her gently on the lips. In a moment, both of their lips parted and their tongues touched. Then he did put his arm around her, and they slipped down next to each other on the hard ground. They kissed for a long time. At last, he put his hand softly on her breast, but she pulled away her lips and smiled. "I'm overdressed for the occasion," she said.

He smiled also, removing his hand. "And it's a cold climate," he said. "But . . . would you like that to happen —someday?"

She nodded. "Oh, I think so. I'm sure . . ."

After a pause, he said, "I have all the wrong words for what I want to say."

"Maybe it's too early to say it."

"That I love you."

She hesitated. "I guess it's not too early to say that," she said. She suddenly laughed. "Even if you have another year of Harvard to go. And I'm ages older than you."

"Not even two years. Nothing."

"Eventually . . . nothing," she agreed.

"You might want to be a Starr. Part of this extraordinary family," he said.

"I might." She rolled over on her stomach and put her chin in her hands. "If that ever happened . . . would I be hurt often, Bobby?"

He answered immediately, since she had asked the exact question he had not found words to answer in advance. "Not often," he said. "Never for long. And perhaps, not at all."

"Because, you see, I wouldn't have the recourse of payment in kind," she said. "I can take a little hurt . . . I don't expect to live without it . . . but I cannot take trying to give it. That would destroy me, if you understand me."

"Yes," he said.

"I've grown up with repayments. My mother and father are always paying each other back. Ugly games. I have a bad thing about ugliness. I'm not fair to it. I cross the street to avoid it."

"That can be avoided." Bobby paused. "Recently I've learned a good deal about things that are unattractive," he added.

Jennifer smiled. "Well, soon I'll go to make my movie and you'll go back to Harvard."

"Where you can visit me when the movie is finished," he said.

"Perhaps."

"Oh yes. We can't be apart that long."

"We must be apart enough, though."

"God knows we'll be that."

"In a year and a half . . ."

"What?"

"When you're through with college . . ."

"Yes?"

She got to her feet. "Well, now it is getting cold," she said. "We'd better go back."

They talked about small things on the way home. They had said all they could of the larger ones for the time being.

ADAM WAS alone when Bernie arrived promptly at five.

Bernie had once broken his arm by falling out of a parked car. He had opened the door too quickly, lost his balance, stuck out his right arm to brace his fall and snapped a small bone. That happens to boys of five and six, but Bernie had been thirteen. Somehow, it seemed to be within the pattern of his life. He had sneaked smoking before the others, cheerfully broken prep school rules to the point of expulsion, been properly penitent after the expulsions, repeated the sins, drunk too much, gambled too much, spent too much money, handled business with an unbroken record of mild incompetence and never quite grown up. He was a greatly beloved trial to his family.

Nothing in his past prepared Adam for what his youngest brother told him that afternoon. He told his story haltingly. He was close to tears all the time, and his voice frequently choked up on him so that it was a while before he could continue. He sat on the sofa behind a glass coffee table piled with books and magazines, and Adam sat at his desk. By the time he had finished the light had faded, but Adam did not move to turn on a lamp. He was not aware of the fact that his face had not changed expression since Bernie's opening statement: "Adam, I've been taking kickbacks from Sam Rosengarden and other furriers for more than two years. Joe Fox and I both have. It amounts to a lot of thousands of dollars, Adam. And they've found out about it." He explained the procedures they used and every detail he knew himself of the transactions; only Joe Fox knew all the details. He told how he had discovered that Fox was on these various payrolls and what he had done about it. And why. And how, little by little, the worry and guilt that had plagued him at the start had slowly disappeared. Until he had accepted the situation as normal. And the postulate that he and Joe would never be caught. But had intended . . . one day, someday . . . to get out of it. When his finances were secure. Because . . . it was necessary that this be understood totally . . . he had always known, never doubted, that he was breaking the single most cardinal rule Starr's had; had always known that he, Bernie Starr, was corrupting the honor code of the store and of the family. This part of it seemed to break him down completely. For a while he was unable to talk. He simply held his head in his hands, and gulped back the sobs. Adam said nothing. He was too stunned to speak. He had no idea what to say. He was only conscious of his fingers drumming against the desk top.

"Can I . . ." Bernie began. "Can I get a drink?"

And this brought Adam to life. "I'd better get it," he said. "You look sort of beat up and there are servants out there. What do you want?"

"Scotch on the rocks. Please."

Adam left the room and returned in a while with Bernie's drink and one for himself. He no longer sat at his desk. He sat in the black leather armchair and closed his eyes. "I want to be sure of one thing," he said. "You're . . . Joe's . . . positive that this absolutely will be in the papers."

Bernie nodded. "At least *Women's Wear*. Probably the *Times*."

"With names?"

"Yes."

"Well," Adam said, slowly, "if your name is in it, then it certainly will be in the *Times,* too." He paused. "I only know one furrier really well. Marty Weinstein. Have you talked to him?"

Bernie shook his head.

"Are you . . . does Marty do that sort of thing, too?"

"No. Not with me, anyway. Not with Joe and me. Our business with Marty is straight."

Adam went to his desk and thumbed through his address book. He found Weinstein's home number and dialed it. When the voice at the other end answered, he said, "Marty, this is Adam Starr . . . Merry Christmas. Marty, Bernie is in my office. He just told me about his involvement with Sam Rosengarden and others . . . What? . . . No, I knew nothing about it until half an hour ago . . . It's been on the street for weeks? I see. Marty, is there . . . is there any buying off to be done? Is there any device, I don't give a shit what it costs, that I can use? Is there any threat? Any counteraction? Anything?" Adam was then silent for some moments. "I see . . . Maybe this week in the paper? Maybe even tomorrow? I see. So it's too late for anything." Again Adam was silent for some moments. "Yes. I understand. A dumb amateur. Marty, it's always the dumb amateurs, you know that. I could have settled this with a pro in half an hour. Marty, thank you, and I'm sorry. It's a bad call for Christmas night. Thanks again . . . Goodbye."

Adam hung up and returned to his leather chair. He suddenly laughed. "This goddamn lawyer probably cost his clients—old Sam's heirs—a couple of million dollars by blowing the thing to the U. S. Attorney. He had that much coming from the stores. At least. Even if we had to pay the whole fucking tab ourselves." He looked at Bernie earnestly. "I want you to know we would have done that, Bernie. We still would. But it's *too late*."

Bernie did not speak. Adam looked at him for a long time. In the pudgy, tear-stained face, in the swollen eyes, Adam saw many things: He saw the kind of sadness that can nearly paralyze a man and he saw shame and he saw fear. But what he saw, or thought he saw that horrified him the most was hope. Was there even, Adam wondered, more than hope: expectation, really, in Bernie's expression? He had never failed Bernie. Somehow, he felt, it could not happen. Adam Starr could not fail Bernard Starr. It was not possible. It was not in the habit of life, not in the scheme of things. But, sitting in his study silently, Adam could not think what to do. Again, in his present life, for such different reasons, he was without a plan. He said one thing, simply to be saying something: "What about Becky? How much does she know?"

"Everything. From the beginning."

"The beginning," Adam heard himself saying. "Oh, Bernie, the beginning. If only you had come to me then. You don't understand the resources we have. You don't understand your own rights—as a Starr. We could have bought your house and given it to you, or rented it at a dollar a year. We could have provided money over a hundred-year period, for Christ's sake. I put that payback figure on the loan because I thought it would be easy for you. And get you off the hook with Abe. Hell, I would have given you that money. We could have twisted and turned and moved sideways and upside down. That's what we built, Bernie. The ability to do things. Nearly anything. My God, Mother didn't even have to know. Bill King and I could have done that. You never had to get in with sleazy, squalid people like the Joe Foxes and Sam Rosengardens of the world."

"In the industry, people do it," Bernie said.

"People," Adam said, quietly. "Not Starrs. Starrs don't have to. That's what you never understood. The things Starrs don't have to do. Along with the things they can do. Sufficient money . . . sufficient position . . . sufficient authority . . . makes any damn thing possible. Didn't you ever read that, Bernie? Or, for Christ's sake, why didn't I tell you?" Adam stopped short. "Nobody else would have," he said softly. "Not Mother, Father, Louis, even though they all know it. But I could have. And didn't. Because I didn't think you needed to know. There is nothing you could have done, Bernie, that we wouldn't have saved you."

Bernie waited for a while before he spoke. "But now you can't, Adam?"

Adam rose. "Not completely," he said, standing by the desk. "All we can do is minimize. Now, look. I have to get to Mother and Louis and Bill . . . and probably Mindy . . . Before this breaks. I can't let them read about it in the paper."

"I'll tell them, Adam. I don't mind. I've been through the worst. This was the worst."

Adam's eyes filled with tears. He went to his brother,

bent down and kissed the bald spot on the top of his head. "I love you very much," he said. "What we're going to do is cut our losses. We're going to pull out every stop to cut losses. But you don't have to be with us tonight. One of these is enough for you. I'll handle it. If I need you, I'll call you at home."

After a pause, Bernie said: "What about Joe, Adam?"

"Fired," Adam said without hesitation.

"He thought he was doing me a favor."

"Fired. All he did was own you."

"Adam . . . what's going to happen to me? I mean, I never reported any of this money on taxes. I couldn't."

"No, you couldn't. Bernie, this isn't going to be fun. This is going to be lousy for you. And Becky. And all of us. But we're going to cut the losses. Somehow. I promise you, Bernie, there's nothing we won't do. We'll buy somebody or we'll kill somebody, but you won't go to jail."

## 9

THEY GATHERED at Jenny Starr's house at nine o'clock. It was the soonest everybody could get together. There were Louis, Adam, Bill King and Jenny. Adam had wanted Mindy Minsky because of the public relations aspect of the problem, but Mindy's phone had not answered. No one knew why they were gathered except Adam. He had simply explained on the telephone that it was a matter of the highest importance and that it could not wait until the following day. They sat in a semicircle, and Jenny offered them drinks. No one wanted one.

"I'll tell this slowly," Adam said. "Because I don't want to leave out anything and I might. You can interrupt me any time you want, of course."

His voice was calm enough, but he was unsteady within himself. He began with a thorough briefing of Bernie's financial problems. He followed with his offer of the fourteen thousand dollars and the method of payback.

"In this respect, I was a fool," he said. "By not looking into the matter further, by not knowing really the problems Bernie was having, I may have triggered what happened."

"You should get to what happened that you triggered," Louis said, dryly.

Adam nodded. He told the story as Bernie had told it to him. He told of how Bernie himself had discovered that Joe Fox was taking the money and what Bernie had done about it. He came down hard on Fox, pointing out that the practice with him had obviously gone on for years.

"How long with Bernie, Adam?" Bill King asked.

"Over two. Getting on toward three."

"What's involved?" Louis asked. "Moneywise? I mean as far as Bernie's concerned."

"He didn't know when he came to me. He'll have to . . ."

"Check his bank statements?" Louis said, with a cold laugh.

"Something like that. But a lot of thousands is how he put it."

"Of course, none of it was reported on his taxes because that would have involved Rosengarden."

"And the others. There were four furriers paying the kickbacks. Only the one is known to the government right now, but they'll be tearing into the whole industry. No . . . it's all unreported income."

Bill King whistled.

"How many other stores are involved?" King asked.

"At least three. The tops." Adam named them.

"That helps some," King said.

"No it doesn't," Louis said. Adam, looking at him, saw that his eyes were glittering. For the first time in months, Louis was alive. For the first time, something had brought him out of himself; his brother's disaster. What did that say about Louis, Adam wondered. Or anyone. That disaster responds to disaster, he supposed. "The other stores, they've got buyers. At Starr's we've got an owner."

For a long time there was silence. Jenny Starr had not spoken at all. She was rigid in her chair, her eyes fixed on Adam as though hypnotized. Her skin was waxen. She looked like a mummy in a museum.

"And this may break in the morning?" King said.

Adam shrugged. "Or sometime this week. Or next. But it will certainly break."

Louis said, "What is your solution, Adam?"

Adam looked at him silently for a long moment. "I have none," he said, finally.

"Not even a recommendation?"

"Not even that."

"Well, I do," Bill King said. They all looked at him. "There are two things," he said. "Kickbacks and tax evasion. These are legal matters. I'll get Sol Martinson on a plane down here tomorrow. With whomever he wants to bring."

"You think the New York lawyers?" Adam said. "I was thinking we might need to go to Washington."

"We will. Sol will go for us. They have offices in Washington. And people they can call on. The story . . . the actual news story . . . should be a one-day wonder. Then months from now, all the stores'll be paying fines and that'll get two paragraphs. All this is not unheard of, after all."

"The other stores will fire their buyers the day the story appears," Louis said. "What do we do?"

After a pause, Adam said, "Well, obviously, we allow Joe to resign."

"Both men will plead not guilty or nolo contendere," King said. "All the men, in fact. I mean from the other stores. Joe can resign in view of the controversy. Some story like that. Sol can help Mindy with it."

Once again, there was a silence. Adam looked around the circle and he saw, as he had so many times, that no one was going to help him. It was up to him to say what had to be said. "I thought," he said, tentatively, "that we might handle it this way: Joe resigns, and so does Bernie—from his job as divisional merchandise manager of furs. Nothing else is in question. The Men's Department is obviously not involved. The statement would be something like, 'Until the situation with regard to the fur operations is decided by the courts . . .' You know . . . Sol can work on that one, too."

Louis smiled, but did not speak.

"Can that work, Bill?"

King looked dubious, thought and said hesitantly: "Anything can work for a while, I suppose. Then, if it dies down, as I'm sure it will . . . I mean, what the hell, the tax question is one thing; there we're going to have to fight to get away with just a fine and there's no way out of it. There . . . Oh hell, Adam. I don't know."

" 'Bernard Starr fined for tax evasion on kickbacks,' " Louis said, smiling. " 'Gets six months suspended sentence.' Beautiful."

Bill King frowned. "Not necessarily, Louis. Don't be so goddamn down. People can be reached. That's what these law firms are all about. That's why they get what they get in fees. Sometimes these things can be done very quietly. Don't cause a ripple . . ."

"What the goddamn hell are you trying to say, Louis?" Adam shouted. "Fire your own brother? Are you so far gone you haven't got any blood left? Louis the hangman. Is that what you are?"

"Adam," King said, sharply.

"So I'm not my usual self," Adam said, red in the face. "So I don't want to be, either. I happen to love my brother. The purpose of this meeting is to save him, not to hang him."

"You've been holding him up like a coat hanger all his life," Louis said, coldly. "He had to drop sometime."

"Damn you, Louis . . ."

"Please be quiet," Jenny Starr said. She spoke loudly enough to be heard clearly.

"Sorry, Mother," Adam said. Then he looked at his mother carefully. For the second time in his life, he saw tears on her cheeks. Well, of course, he thought. He got up, walked over to her and put his hand on her shoulder. "I really am sorry. I hate to yell. I just want to save that boy as much as you do."

"I don't want to save him," Jenny Starr said, sullenly, her eyes straight ahead of her. No one spoke. "Bernie will be fired in the morning," she continued in the same dead tone. "From the store. As will Joe Fox. Obviously, they will be permitted to resign and I don't care what sort of story the lawyers concoct. They are to be fired from the store in the morning."

After a long time, Adam said, "I don't think I can do that, mother."

Jenny smiled, sadly. "You could fire Emma Goldman and the other old people who built the store because they were not any longer at the efficiency level you like. But

you cannot fire men for dirty stealing. Your brother Bernie
is a . . . dirty . . . thief."

"But, he is my brother. And your son. And he made
the worst mistake of his life. But," he repeated, "we can
cut the losses."

"It is a matter of the honor of the store and of the
family. There is nothing to do about that. It is not a matter of incompetence, laziness, drunkenness or one of those
things. It is a matter of our name itself. Nothing can be
allowed to dirty that name. Nothing! If it were a private
matter that would be another thing. You have made it
clear it cannot be private." She stopped and looked at
Adam directly. "If you cannot fire your brother, then send
him to me and I will fire my son."

Again, there was silence. "How will he live, Jenny?"
Bill King said, finally.

She waved her hand. "Work out something," she said.
"Pay him an allowance. Carry him on the books as a
consultant. But take his name out of the annual report.
He is officially no longer a part of the store."

"Mother—even if we support him—what will he do
with himself?" Adam said. "Bernie has one thing in this
world. The store. One place to go to. The store."

"He cannot have an office with his name on it," Jenny
said. "He can come in from time to time and sit wherever
there is room. Find some room for him." She looked
around at all of them. And then she suddenly screamed,
*"He has betrayed us."* She stopped. Her face was gray.
Without excusing herself, she rose hurriedly and left the
room.

No one spoke for a long time. Then Bill King said,
looking at Adam, "She's right, you know, Adam. There's
no way out. Not really. Your solution won't work. Not
over the long run."

"I know," Adam said, quietly. He sat for a moment,
then got to his feet. "Would anyone like a drink now?"
he said. "I'm going to get Maitland." They all ordered
something. Jenny did not come back for quite a while.
When she did, she looked old and frail. She noticed their
drinks and said to Adam, "Will you ask Maitland to bring
me a cognac, please?" When he had, she took a sip and
turned to Adam. "Do you wish me to attend to this
matter?"

"No," he said. "Of course not. I will tell him your . . . our decision. You'll talk to him in your own time."

She nodded. "You will handle all the questions from the news people?"

"Yes," Adam said.

"Well," King interjected. "Sol can handle a good bit of that."

"Whoever," Jenny said. "Not I."

THE STORY broke within the week in the *Times* as well as in *Women's Wear Daily*. Bernard Starr's name was of course in the headline. The local papers were forced to carry a small stick of type about it, near the obituaries.

"You'll be all right," Adam said to Bernie at Bernie's house the night the story broke. "You can sell anything. You're a born salesman. There's real estate. Insurance. I have connections."

"Okay, Adam," Bernie said.

But he began to drink much more than he had in his life. Up to a point, Becky drank with him. But when he drank in the morning to help himself over the shakes, she did not. For a while, they continued to go out. They were not ostracized by their friends. But sometimes Bernie got very drunk when he was out, and sometimes he got too drunk to go out at all. Adam came over often and talked to him, but it did no good. By early spring, Adam and Becky had placed him in a hospital in Connecticut where he would remain a minimum of ten weeks at fifteen hundred dollars a week.

"That's my tab," Adam said to Becky.

"Thank you, Adam."

"We get him well first. Then we'll remake his life for him."

"Maybe you're a saint, Adam," Becky said.

"No," he said. He put Becky on a plane and drove to Darien.

# PART EIGHT

# 1

TIME, THE ultimate enemy, began now to nibble at Adam. He was running out of devices for postponements as winter became spring and then early summer. The New York work involving the architects and interior designers was done. Workmen would be breaking ground for the new Fort Worth store in July. His visits to New York were becoming something of a nuisance to his planners. Their work now was primarily on location. They were often in Ramsey, meeting with merchandise managers and buyers, working out details. The overall concepts and the basic planning of the store's merchandise departments were finished. In New York, Adam could no longer work his normal day with these men, returning to Darien in the evenings; it was foolishness. He could not bear to be foolish, though obviously he could spend as much time as he wanted in their offices, fiddling with minor changes. The basic reason for his regular trips to New York no longer existed. So he had to invent others. He spent a good deal of time in the market, talking with vendors, hearing their comments and often their complaints about the store, and these manufacturers were flattered that the president of Starr's spent so much time with them; and were also a little baffled. The talks had some value. He smoothed over minor irritations and some major ones, adjusted certain policies at the store and probably generally improved Starr's vendor relationships. He did not have to go to New York every five weeks for this. But he did.

Karen was often silent now. She knew he was having trouble inventing reasons to be in the East and with her. Somewhere down the line, there was a deadline in their life together. They had not quite reached it, perhaps, but it was approaching. This time she said something quite honest; she did not always: "Adam, we're rationalizing."

"Why? Accident of circumstance . . ."

"I don't deny that. But what is essential—and I think we must live with it—is that whatever happened between us, the start of it happened before I married Louis."

He made a face. It was Adam more than she who pushed these things away.

"Not much did happen," he said, and strictly speaking, he was right.

The evening was warm enough for the windows to be open. Insects buzzed against the screens. They were having a before-dinner cocktail and it was his first night with her on this new trip. So she was a little dressed up, as she usually was when he first arrived. Tomorrow, she would be in jeans and a shirt, working outdoors, for it was time for planting and weeding and other spring rituals at which she was new, but which she was enjoying. In a couple of months he would see some of the results of her work and she would have an extra dimension for him. She was inordinately pleased when she did or could do something unexpected which he liked; like pull together, once in a while, a really perfect dinner; like wash and iron his shirts since he could not get them back from the laundry as quickly as he could have in a hotel. She was happy that night. So she was not sure why she took the chance of spoiling it by saying what she now did: "Anyone with a cold, clear eye would call me a calculating bitch, Adam. For example, knowing everything I know about myself and my actions in those days, your mother would call me that. I was not in love with Louis. I told him so. His eyes were open. He was taking his chances. I loved the romance of the famous store in that famous state. But Adam, there was always you."

He said firmly, "You were my enemy. Or at least my adversary. You fought like a tigress for Louis."

"That was all I *could* do then. It was the only relationship I had with you. When I could do something else, my dear, I did it."

After a pause, he said, "Why are you beating at yourself tonight?"

She looked puzzled. "I don't know," she said. "Well, I do know, partly. Something is going to be forced on us, Adam. Some ugly or fine thing is going to happen . . .

well, even if the end result is fine, there will be ugliness. I think I want . . . the worst that can be said about me . . . to be said by me. So that when other people say it, if they ever do, you will have heard it."

He nodded. "I suppose then, that I should do the same for you."

She shook her head. "Not necessarily. I don't live with the guilt the way you do."

"I have less suffering than I had," he said, berating himself for it. "Than I had when you were still in Ramsey. To leave you and go straight home in a car . . ."

"I don't want you to go on," she said, quietly.

"Why?"

"It gets into the question of your lovemaking with Claude. I mean, I know it has to if you're trying to be honest. And that horrifies me. I mean, it *pleased* me to know that this was a serious problem. How vicious that seems . . . But I guess it's normal. I hope so. In the same way . . . I don't wish to hear that . . . that situation has improved. You haven't said it has, you've been careful, but I know it has because I know everything about you and I know that during a month you would want a woman. And you have one. Now you see, it's all right for me to say those things, but it wouldn't be all right for you to say them. Because I am not sure of what I'm saying. And I don't want to be."

He nodded. "Okay." He was uncomfortable and abruptly changed the subject. "I would like to go to the theater. Once in a while."

Her whole face seemed suddenly to glow in a pink spotlight.

"Oh, Adam! Could we really?"

He nodded, and said what had been a good deal on his mind: "You've done wonders with this house, with our life here . . ."

"But it's not enough," she interrupted. "I know. It closes in."

"Sometimes. I love our walks down by the beach. This summer I'm going to buy us a sailboat. And a book on how to sail it. When I was a boy I used to sail a little with boys I visited up here." He smiled. "There isn't much of that in Texas, as you can imagine. So I've forgotten everything I knew. But it would come back."

"Even that . . ."

"Well, that's my point. Even that, even picnics . . . We're civilized people. We need to do some civilized things."

She was eager and dubious. "All these months we've been so careful," she said. "Adam, what would happen if people saw us?"

"I've thought about that. I think, within reason, we can get away with it. A little of it." He smiled. "We were saying, or I was saying, we're civilized people. A marriage just didn't work out, that's all. That doesn't always mean excommunication from you."

It seemed reasonable enough. Deep within him, Adam knew but would not admit that it was not reasonable at all. But he felt he must make a move. He did not have to make a commitment, at least for now, but he did have to act. They were too much by themselves; too limited in where they went, what they did. They would turn inward, eventually. Already he felt restless at times. He was certain she felt the same way. Soon the restlessness would turn to irritations. They would have minor squabbles. They would nurse slight injuries. So much together, they would be forced to talk too much and would inevitably say the wrong thing. He felt they must take some risks; to some extent at least, be a part of the world. Nothing could be allowed to jeopardize the happiness they now had. That much was paramount with Adam. Such a love as he carried destroys judgment. He knew this and allowed it to happen.

So they did begin to go occasionally to the theater, to restaurants in the city, to concerts and museums. Occasionally they spent an afternoon gallery hopping. They did not do this constantly. Twice, perhaps, during one of his trips. But they did do it. To their knowledge, they saw no Texan they knew; that is, they met no one to whom they had to speak, to whom one or the other had to be introduced. They did occasionally run into people one of them knew in New York. "This is my ex-brother-in-law," Karen would say with a smile; or vice versa. They could detect no raised eyebrows.

However, they were seen by people they didn't know; people who knew Adam from photographs in the paper, and perhaps did not know Karen at all; people who certainly didn't know Adam well enough to speak to him and of whose existence he was unaware. But one or two also recognized Karen and mentioned what they had seen to one or two others, not as a scandal but as a mild oddity. By late spring, a small amount of talk had begun in Ramsey. Mostly it drifted off into nothingness, but somebody did mention to Cullum Roberts that he had seen Adam and Karen at a restaurant.

"So have I," Roberts said, goodnaturedly. "They've stayed good friends, I guess. Why not?"

He filed it away, not having any use for it; whatever it was.

THE SECONDARY effect of Adam's invented reasons for continuing his trips to New York was that his very presence began serious talks about the eventual sale of the store. Starr's had always had suitors, but now they were persistent, vague, into discussions that were more serious and more detailed than they had been. Adam continued to be evasive and to tell his suitors that neither he nor the rest of his family was ready yet to sell. But such things as management contracts did come up. Capital for further expansion to other parts of the country was mentioned. The attraction of Starr's was of course its name. Of all store names, it was one of the most marketable in the country. Wherever a Starr's might open, in Chicago, Washington, Atlanta, San Francisco, the event would be major. That point was perhaps not so true, at least in the same way, the way of luxury, opulence and high fashion, of any other store name in the United States. Starr's was magic. The publicity over all the years had done its work.

In addition, the Houston store was now doing exceptionally well. It was keeping pace with the suburban store in Ramsey (this in the face of greater competition) and the sales projections kept being revised upwards. The downtown store remained at a more or less constant level. But by this time, Adam's economy moves were beginning to take effect. Profit was greater. The faces of the people within the organization were changing. They were younger, hungrier, cleverer. The advertising changes resulted in a slow but sharp differential in customer profile. The median age of the Starr's customer was going down. The younger people were beginning to come; beginning to recognize that Starr's more often than not had what they wanted; more often than not at a price they could pay. Still, the store was not really trading down. It was expanding its appeal. It seemed to be losing none of the older, loyalist business it had always had. Jenny Starr was as busy as ever, selling her Bill Blass and her Oscar de la Renta clothes at improbable prices. But in the Sports Shop and in the Younger Set World, where prices varied greatly, traffic was sharply up. Saturdays, in these departments, the downtown store was busy, filled with the secretaries, copy-writers, models and stewardesses who lived closer to downtown than they did to the suburban store. Saturdays had once been like days in a desert.

So, when the major retail chains who wished to buy Starr's or thought they might like to, examined the figures, they saw an upward trend, both as to dollar volume and transaction count. By that spring, Starr's was what is called a "hot" store, not just through its reputation, but through its profits.

Such progress did not disguise the fact, perhaps even emphasized it, that Louis's divisions in ready-to-wear were in a state of absentee management. Week after week, the departments came up for advertising with presenta-tions that had no organization and no unity of thought. Each department was running itself. The momentum of the store was such and the capabilities of the buyers great enough so that no one department was slumping badly. However, they were not producing the kind of gains Neal Adams was producing. Ready-to-wear, the heart and soul of the store, was falling behind its sister departments in growth. And so Adam could no longer postpone his talk with Louis. He had it in his office late one afternoon. He had it at all because Bill King had told him simply: "If you can't straighten that situation out, Adam, the morale of the departments will collapse. It's almost col-lapsed now. The buyers can't get answers, can't get leader-ship, can't get enthusiasm. They're disorganized, don't trust each other and will end up cutting each others' throats with resources. Or quitting. That may be the best group of buyers in the country, Adam. They're why the depart-ments are doing as well as they are. I know them. In mak-ing up the five-year plans for you, I've gone over their departments with every one of them. They're good. And they're disgusted."

"What am I supposed to do, Bill?" Adam had asked. "How do you raise a man from the dead?"

King had said, "Louis can never be a great merchandise manager. We know that. But he can be better than he is now. Because he has been better in the past. Just bring him back to where he was. At least for a few years. We could live with that."

Adam put his brother straight across the desk from him. In that way, the late afternoon sun struck directly at Louis's face. It was the chair in which Adam put men he was about to fire. His major executives, when alone with him, almost invariably sat on the sofa at right angles to the desk; at least in the late afternoon, so the sun would not hit them. Louis twisted his chair so the sun was not directly in his eyes. His face was impassive.

"It seems," Adam began, "that I have to have a talk with you."

Louis nodded. "So what else is new."

"I want to say first that I'm sorry I've had to criticize the advertising presentations so consistently."

"You machine gun them. You destroy people."

"I say the same thing week after week. They're not organized, they have no relationship one to the other. The departments might as well be in different stores."

"I don't happen to agree."

Adam hesitated. Then he said, "Louis, you look at your departments' presentations an hour before the meetings. If they're wrong, it's too late to do anything about it."

"I don't think they're wrong."

"That's not the point. You're not supposed to accept a plan, you're supposed to make it."

Louis shifted in his chair. His expression did not change. "Over the years . . . when I did make the plans . . . I didn't have much more success with you than we do now."

"So you decided the hell with it."

"That's what I decided."

"And," Adam said, "for a moment, at least, you've decided the hell with your job."

Louis suddenly looked startled. "What?"

"Well, that's what you must have said, because that's what's happened."

"Look at the figures," Louis protested.

But Adam shook his head. "They're behind the rest of the store. They look good compared to before, but not in comparison to potential. Don't give me that figure shit, Louis. I know all about figures. So do your buyers.

They're very well aware that their departments can do better than they're doing."

"Then why don't they?"

"Because they're confused. They're confused by you. They say you don't give answers until too late to make plans, that you contradict yourself and that you're too often . . . unavailable. You seem to go for a lot of swims at the club."

"So do Presidents of the United States."

"Maybe they pick their times better than you do. Louis, I want to make this clear—we must have proper leadership in your departments. That is an essential for this store. An essential."

After a long time, Louis smiled. "Or what? You fire another brother?"

"Our mother fired Bernie, Louis. I was trying to find some way to keep him."

Louis nodded. "That wasn't fair," he said. "I admit it. You would have fired him yourself, eventually. Because there was no choice. None. But you did try because you loved Bernie. Love him. You love Bernie, Adam."

Adam said nothing. He also loved his brother Louis. He was absolutely certain of it. In response to Louis's remark, he could not say so. It was too obvious, too blatant.

And then Louis said, to Adam's astonishment, "I'll help you, Adam. You love me, too. I believe that. Somewhere deep inside you is the notion that you love your family. You may wound them and cut them to pieces in the name of the store, but you love them. All right, I give you that. I have the same problem. I love you, too, Adam. It would be easier if I didn't. I would then be free to hate you, as perhaps I also do. But there's no help for it. We are of the same blood. Some families can go about their business, happily hating each other. We can't seem to. Love . . . the love we have for each other . . . Sure . . ."

Louis could not go on for a moment. His voice choked on him and there were tears in his eyes. Adam, his heart breaking, watched him in silence.

". . . fucks us up," Louis finally said.

His face looked older than it ever had to Adam. There were deep lines running from the nose to the mouth, deep furrows in his forehead and a nest of small wrinkles around his eyes. These same eyes, black as his mother's usually, looked somehow pale. All of him was pale. His skin matched his gray suit and Adam was sitting in front of a drab, older man. The sun dramatized the deterioration. It had no sympathy for this diminished person. It even picked out the hairs in the ears of a usually immaculate man who had forgotten to cut them or have his barber cut them. Adam, knowing that he had to speak, could not. It was Louis who finally went on:

"When Dad died, it was a loss and a grief. Remember?" Louis looked at his brother. Adam nodded. "I remember," he said.

"But he was an old man and it was time to go. When Mother dies, she will be an old woman, and it will be a grief but bearable. But now I think I know what it must feel like when someone you love . . . very much . . . dies suddenly. Under the wheels of a truck . . . no preparation . . ."

Adam made himself say, "What is it like, Louis?"

Louis, the old man, groped around for his words: "At first shock . . . numbness . . . it helps for a little. Then such pain. I mean . . . really bad, Adam. Never out of your mind. Emptiness. Endless emptiness. Sometimes breakdowns. Grown-man breakdowns. Five minutes, fifty. You don't know, can't predict. And paralysis. You can't do anything, Adam. It seems . . . like you can barely walk, raise your hand. You wonder whether . . . you're going to survive it. It's so endless. You wake up when the drugs have made you sleep, and sometimes they don't . . . knowing what the day ahead will be like, full of those . . . damn things . . . All day until you can fall asleep again. There is nothing in between. Just breathing and . . . other mechanical actions."

Louis stopped.

"The psychiatrist," Adam said, tentatively.

Louis shook his head. "I go three times a week." He looked up and smiled fleetingly. "I'm not always swimming." The smile disappeared. "He has comments and questions and raises questions about other matters of my life which may be affecting me. Because he has no way of dealing with death. There is no way of dealing with death, Adam. Of the kind I mean."

Adam said, "Karen is not dead, Louis."

"It's the same thing. The same grief. That's why I say I know what death must be like when someone goes under a truck to the person left behind. I mean the one person. Not a group of lesser people. Only the one."

Adam said something for which he never forgave himself: "She could always change her mind."

Louis shook his head. He now spoke briskly. "She wants me to get a Mexican divorce. It's quicker than waiting out a year in Ramsey. I'll go next week and be away a couple of days."

Adam was surprised in a way. She had not mentioned that to him, but she spoke as little as possible of Louis and of her plans for the divorce.

Louis said, "Adam, I will organize things better. I'll meet with all the buyers. I'll try hard."

Adam nodded. "I know you will," he said, helplessly.

That night, he scarcely spoke during dinner. When this was over, he went to his study and tried to read through a pile of *Women's Wear Daily*s. He could not follow what he was reading. An hour or so after eating, he felt ill. He thought he might be sick, but it passed. He felt weak and his hands trembled, and he even felt chilled though it was warm enough. He kept wanting to cry but didn't. He was pale enough so that Claude noticed.

"You've caught something," she said.

"It's nothing. I'll go to bed early. Sleep it off."

He slept fitfully, waking often, but the night finally ended. In the morning, shaving, he thought how much he loathed himself. And also how he would do nothing about it.

2

WITHOUT INTELLECTUALIZING it, which was not her way, Claude Starr had made the major decision of her life by taking the trip to the California health spa. She had decided to keep her life; if necessary to fight for it. At different times over the years, she had wondered whether she even wished to stay with Adam and live up to the responsibilities of being Mrs. Adam Starr. More than once she had contemplated what a divorce would be like, what kind of other life she might have. She had never allowed such thoughts to come to the point of any kind of decision; she had had a few vodkas and lived another day. Now she thought she would have continued this pattern to the end of her days had it not been for the sudden disintegration of their sexual life together and her certainty that he had at last taken a mistress. She knew further that this mistress lived in New York and that the extra days he took on his trips were because of her. And so, at first, she had brooded and drunk more than usual and seen her face begin to puff; and had the matter mentioned to her by her daughter. This mention by Nancy, though brief and not pursued, had a deep effect on her. She realized that she cared very much what Nancy thought about what was happening to her. And Bobby. And Jenny. And the rest of the family and the world; and Adam. She knew her assets. "People who come here," Nancy had once said, "think they have to be fascinating or Adam will be bored. That's heavy. You make them feel they're fascinating just because they're here. You are very loved, Claude." And she had style, served good food, knew flowers. But the most essential thing she had was her looks. Had she been an ordinary woman, she would have been easy to dismiss. It is impossible to dismiss beauty because there is so little of it.

So she stopped drinking because it was destroying her looks. She worried at first that it would be difficult. She found it far less so than she had imagined. She had never been a drinker whose body, once exposed to alcohol, demands more of it. She had drunk to bring on a slight buzz, a certain vagueness that seemed to make it easier for her to get through evenings that promised to be difficult. She found she was better off without it. Alert, she found herself less anxious, not more. When her table was set, she did not wonder whether it was good enough, she took pleasure in how exquisite it was. She gave up her afternoon 'soap operas and visited friends or had them over for tea, and, especially, exercised regularly at their club. Before they entertained, she questioned Adam extensively about each person who was expected, finding out their slots in the city's political machinery and the reasons why they were coming at all; for there had been much of this sort of entertaining since Adam had been elected Mayor. She had rejected participation in it; gone through the motions. Now she was an active partner to him. On evening occasions, when he had to make an appearance somewhere, she usually now went with him. Even during the day, when he opened a new shopping center or dedicated a new building, she often accompanied him. Many photographs of them together appeared in the newspapers; always before he had been alone.

She knew that everything she was doing was surprising to him; and perplexing. But he seemed pleased. Why not? she thought with satisfaction. She was not interfering in the smallest way with his life away from her and was in fact giving the world the ideal portrait of what the Mayor's married life should be. She was helping him to enjoy his affair. Of course she resented that it was taking place (or at least that she was so certain it was). She was bitter that sex between them was inhibited; less so than before, perhaps, but still markedly different. She did have the definite feeling that Adam's mind was elsewhere at times when he was making love to her; that he was mechanical, acting partly from desire and partly from duty; that comparisons might be being made; that the woman's body of his imagination was not hers, and that, no matter what she did, she could not compete with the novelty of a new sexual partner and probably a much younger one at that. Even with this reality in her mind, she by no means simply accepted the sex they had; she did not give up. She initiated matters much more often than she ever had; did not limit her approaches to their bed or to specific times, flaunted her body and used her hands and mouth more than before. She used all the tricks she knew of the strumpet and wished she knew more. She was aware that she took the risk of shocking, even dismaying him, but she took it. She also knew that she faced possible rejection and therefore humiliation; she faced both. And when indeed she was rejected with the "too tireds," "long days," "not tonights," she banished her distress from her mind as best she could and kept her resolve to try again. And she succeeded in keeping alive, at least, the intimacies which had been so important a part of their twenty-five years together.

In all these ways, as she reasoned, she remained in competition. While emotionally she loathed the idea of his affair, intellectually she accepted it as an inevitable part of a married life. She had herself once been the mistress of married men. A few had said they were in love with her; twice, men had wished to break out of the marriages and take her instead; she had ended both liaisons immediately. And so she knew that she might be fighting a losing battle; that Adam might actually leave her for another woman. But not before she had put up the strongest fight she could. And she knew she had weapons. She was liked or loved by every friend he had. She was loved by her daughter and by her son. She was probably loved by Jenny and by his brothers and his sister-in-law. No one Adam cared about, no one whose good opinion he desired, not one of these people in all the world would wish to see Claude Starr hurt. And Adam knew it. In addition, she had the quarter-century of habit going for her; the whole ambience of his adult life had included her. That would be a hard one for him. Adam was no fonder than most men of serious disruptions in his way of life; and like most men, he was pleased by the approval of his peers. In addition—this point always amused her, and she brought it to mind when she was feeling depressed—he was a politician now, and divorces are not beneficial to politicians, especially in a community like Ramsey. So what she had hated was her ally.

But he could lose his head. Men had lost their heads over her; men of intelligence and substance as well as fools. She could do nothing about that. She tried not to think about it.

The possibility of counterattack, of taking a lover, never seriously entered her head. She had no wish to hurt Adam; only to keep him. But there were extra men in Ramsey, divorced, widowed, or, most often, homosexual, so she tried an experiment. When Adam was gone, she had a few small dinners of her own. She had never done this in all the years of their marriage. At first she was nervous about it. She was afraid people would not come. It had not seemed probable to her that anyone ever came to their house because of her. And perhaps they had not. She now found, with enormous gratification, that they would. Her invitations were accepted at exactly the same rate that any of their joint invitations were. She discovered she was a person people would come to be with. She mentioned her pleasure to Nancy, who seemed very surprised.

"You actually thought people would never come here with Adam away?" she said.

"I was afraid so," Claude admitted. Nancy said nothing but kissed her mother on the cheek.

Her little dinners were at least as successful as those she gave with Adam. People seemed to have a pleasant time and were perhaps even a bit looser and more relaxed than they were when Adam was present. He did intimidate some people. Claude found she also enjoyed herself. Once or twice she brought back an ancient afterdinner pastime: charades, totally unthinkable with Adam present, who could not possibly present himself outside of himself. But Claude was good at the game, and Neal Adams, who often came as Nancy's escort, was superb. He was a marvelous, inventive amateur actor and could make people laugh. The new executive vice-president of Starr's made a lot of new friends at Claude's parties; as a result of them, he and Nancy began to be asked places as a couple. Claude viewed this with pleasure. She grew very fond of Neal Adams, understood that his life must often be lonely and began to hope that her daughter might be interested in him; and conversely, that he might be interested in her. She and Nancy did not discuss it.

She had Louis over with Becky one night, and this she found distressing. Louis was withdrawn and remote and looked sad. She felt badly about it because he gave the appearance of trying with all his might not to be so. He would have spurts of talk and would seem alive and interested; and then would seem to run out of energy. When this happened, it was as though he suddenly left them in spirit; not because he wanted to but because he could not help it. In his eyes, at these separated times, there was bewilderment. He himself did not seem to understand what was happening to him. Becky, on the other hand, chattered on as though a few weeks in the hospital would cure Bernie of anything that had ever been wrong with him. She spoke proudly of how well he looked (she visited him every two weeks for a couple of days), of the lectures the doctors gave, the individual psychotherapy he was receiving and the exercise he was taking. She had chosen to ignore the deeper implications of what had befallen him; or perhaps she truly did not understand them. From the things Adam had said, Claude was aware that Bernie's problems were far from over. She knew that tax matters alone could conceivably send him to prison and that the store had the best lawyers it could find working to save him. And they were paying them a fortune with no guarantee whatever of success. Becky did not mention this.

When the guests had left, Nancy and Claude sat up for a while and Claude poured herself a glass of ginger ale. Nancy watched her. After a while, she said, "Claude, why did you stop drinking?"

Claude smiled. "Why did you never ask before, dear?"

"It seemed your private affair."

They were sitting on the two sofas at right angles to each other. Each was dressed in a shirt and slacks. It had been a casual evening which was now drawing close to midnight. They did not often sit up talking. It was not that they avoided it, but Nancy had early classes and enjoyed reading in bed, and Claude often watched late television. And there was nothing urgent to talk about. As Nancy had just said about one particular matter, the things that interested one about the other seemed private matters and this mother and daughter respected each other's privacy.

Claude now said, "I stopped drinking because I wanted to try being a different person than I had been. Also because it was affecting my looks. But mainly, I wanted to see how I would like the world . . ."

"How do you like it?"

Claude hesitated. "Better," she said. She thought for several moments before going on. Nancy, watching her closely, did not interrupt her thoughts. Claude was wondering whether she could trust her daughter. She wished very much in this unexpectedly close time they were now having to talk to Nancy frankly; or if not totally frankly, at least to hint at what she was feeling. But she was not at all sure that Nancy wanted to hear her. It had been different with Bobby, when, sobbing in his room, he had poured out his horror to her and she had had the power to help him. Then he had been in need and come to her. And, during Nancy's own horror, through the long days and nights after the rape, perhaps she had been a comfort. At least Nancy thought that she had once undergone something like her daughter and had survived; not so terrifying, perhaps, not nearly so scarring, but similar; and survived. Lies unchallenged become truth. But she had never involved her children with the difficulties of her life. What they observed was what they knew. This seemed, or had always seemed, proper to Claude. Mothers were to comfort, not to be comforted. Now, sitting on her sofa past midnight, she wondered why this should be so. Where was such a thing written? She was struggling in deep water; for all she knew, she was drowning. And this girl, this woman sitting next to her was her own blood. She, Claude Starr, was a frightened woman. Wasn't it possible to share her fright with her daughter? Even knowing that Nancy could really do nothing to help. Wouldn't the sharing itself be helpful? Wasn't it only fair?

"You see," she began, speaking haltingly, "things . . . aren't the same . . . as they always have been."

Nancy, thinking carefully, said, "How do you mean? Claude . . . Mother . . . don't be afraid."

Encouraged, Claude said, "Your father and I . . . well, we've had a certain kind of marriage, you know . . ."

Momentarily, that much took her to the limits of her courage.

But Nancy was trying hard to help. "I do know. Bobby and I have always known it was 'a certain kind of marriage.' Much better, dear, than many."

Claude nodded. "It may have . . . changed, Nancy. I may have . . . it's possible . . ." She simply could not find the words to finish. For what she needed to say might embitter Nancy toward her father; she knew instinctively that children will always violently disapprove of outside involvements which disrupt what they are used to. It might also embitter Nancy toward her. For mentioning it at all. For not leaving it covered up. She searched her daughter's face for clues. Found none.

Nancy was having her own struggle. She was certain she knew what her mother was trying to say. She did not wish to hear it. She did not know how she would deal with it. But she also could not abandon her mother; and this seemed the only alternative. So at last, when it was clear to her that Claude would not go on, she did what her father would have done. Her voice calm, she said, "You're trying to tell me that Adam is having an affair," she said.

A feeling almost of exultation went through Claude. As this happened, she found words.

"I have no question of that," she said, "I have no proof of it, but I don't need any. It's foolish to say wives always know, because they don't. If Adam were a different person . . . in certain ways . . . maybe I wouldn't. But I do."

"Men have affairs," Nancy began, then switched her approach. "Claude, I wonder how much that would bother me. After all these years. If I were you. I mean, what are you . . . furious, hurt, ashamed, disgusted . . . ?"

Her mother looked at her with clear eyes.

"I'm afraid I might lose him," she said, simply.

Now, suddenly, Nancy was frightened. "That's impossible," she said, automatically.

"Oh, no. Not at all."

Almost desperately, Nancy said, "It must be impossible. I insist it's impossible." She paused. "Claude . . . Adam is one of the most intelligent men in the world. You've forgotten that."

"No. I count on it. But not completely."

"He would have to be mad."

"He might go mad. It's the one thing . . . one of the things . . . men go mad about . . ."

Claude stopped. She realized she had now said nearly all she wanted to say. Nancy could do nothing, of course, except know. But it seemed to her that Nancy's knowing made an enormous difference. And so, it was necessary to make the other thing clear. "So, you see," Claude said, "what I'm doing is fighting."

Nancy then startled her.

"I can end it, Claude. At once."

"How?"

Nancy hesitated. "I would have to have your permission to tell Bobby," she said. "If I had that, we would go to him. We would tell him . . . that he will lose us."

"Would he?" Claude asked.

Nancy said immediately, "Of course." She had spoken so quickly because she was not so certain of what she had just promised. Not so certain of herself, not certain at all of Bobby.

Her mother, sensing this, smiled: "Thank you, dear," she said, "but that's not fair and it wouldn't help. Whatever Adam will do, he will know the risks he runs. In any case, you see . . . well, I have to win, if it comes to that, by myself. That's why . . . so to speak . . . I wanted to try on different clothes."

Nancy rose and sat next to her mother on the sofa. She put her arm around Claude's shoulders and allowed her head to fall on her own. So they sat for a long while until Claude raised her head.

"It's really time to go to bed," she said. "You get up so early."

Nancy nodded.

"I'm very happy that I told you this," Claude said. "I had been feeling . . . awfully alone."

"I'm glad you did, too," Nancy said. She was not at all sure she meant it, but she wished to.

THE OTHER thing Claude did was see Jenny. She had her for dinner and sometimes they went to the movies or watched television. Jenny taught her gin rummy, which she had never played in her life. She enjoyed the game and was good at it. After a while, she won as often as lost. They had casually lunched together hundreds of times over the years in the store. They had scarcely ever spent evenings with each other without Adam. They now said nothing of great importance to each other, but they did not find the hours awkward. Filling them together was pleasant; far easier for Jenny than filling them alone. Possibly, Claude thought, she had another weapon in her mother-in-law; and accepted philosophically and with some humor, the fact that this unworthy thought had at least crossed her mind.

AT HOME, Adam watched his wife in her new clothes. He tried hard not to allow himself to comment on them, even to himself. He did say, once, lightly, "You've become the perfect wife to the Mayor."

"That's what I want to be," she had answered.

This seemed to him gallant. He could not help but admire gallantry. He always had.

LOUIS TOLD the psychiatrist of his talk with Adam and his near breakdown and of his reaction to Bernie's problems. The psychiatrist was silent for a long time. Then the old doctor said: "You have recently beaten your wife and nearly cried in your brother's office. These are types of things you have never done in your life. You are stepping out of character. Out of role. You allowed yourself to be pleased with your brother Bernie's trouble. Because it was worse than anything you'd done . . ."

"Not pleased," Louis protested.

"Not compassionate, either. It's quite normal in distress to be happy about other people's distress. But difficult to admit. You have admitted it. And anger and bitterness. And also that grief about your wife's leaving is only the latest tag on which to blame your illness. Or your difficulties. Not the cause of them. And anger and bitterness turned inward lead to depression."

After a while, Louis asked: "When do . . . anger and bitterness . . . go away?"

The psychiatrist did not answer for a moment. He then said, "When they are released." He shrugged. "And then, sometimes, they keep coming back again and again until . . . Well, we have much work to do, Mr. Starr."

BY THE next time Hayden Calhoun came to Ramsey, four people had announced for his seat in the Senate: two Congressmen, the Governor and a businessman from Corpus Christi. The Senator came to dinner at Adam and Claude's with a number of other people.

"Don't mean nothin' yet," he said to Adam before dinner. "Too soon."

"Of those four, who would win?" Adam asked.

Senator Calhoun laughed. "Ain't one of 'em who can win," he said.

Adam smiled. "Surely the Governor . . ."

"He'd be all right if he just hadn't of been Governor. He read the Book of Mistakes and he made 'em all, politically. You heard anything from Cullum?"

"No."

"Neither have I. Yet. He's bidin' his time. Some of my people tell me he's got the itch somethin' terrible. You done any thinkin'?"

"No," Adam said, truthfully. "We haven't done the busing yet. Though I've worked my ass off on it. We could still have trouble."

"How bad?"

"I don't know. It wouldn't be citywide. It'd be in one or two areas."

"Then you have to be in those one or two areas."

"I have been."

"I mean when school opens."

"I will be."

"What about the newspapers?"

Adam was wry. "I've met with them. I've done everything I think is totally, morally indefensible. I've shut them up."

Calhoun laughed. "Somethin' to be said for a town that's just a little tiny bit Fascist, hey, Adam? At least, now and then when a politician bends, when he needs to soil his white, perfect grace . . ."

Adam laughed. "I'm no knight. I'm no politician."

"The hell you ain't." The old man became serious. "I sure do hope there's not gonna be another Boston down here. I went up to see it and I don't want to see anything like it ever again. That was ugly."

"I'm working on it."

At dinner, sitting at Claude's right, the Senator said, "How do you like the idea of bein' a Senator's wife, Claude?"

Quickly wary, she said, "What are you talking about?"

Senator Calhoun was flustered. "He hasn't mentioned anything to you?"

"Well, it was . . . very casual," she lied.

Relieved, the Senator said, "Maybe it is. He'd be in the very outside post, and he ain't said he wants to try. Maybe it's the poet in me that thinks he just might have a chance."

"Maybe," she said.

Before getting into bed, she said, not at all casually, "I wanted to say if you decide to run for Senate, I think it would be very exciting."

Stunned, he said, "It's too remote." He carefully did not look at her.

"I'm like Hayden. I'm a poet. I don't think it's silly. But, of course, we won't talk about it until you want to. If you ever do."

So time was closing in on Adam. As happens when men would give their souls to stand still, he would have to move.

# 3

AN UNFORTUNATE remark from Karen drew the ropes tighter around him. He was never quite sure why he had done what he did to elicit her remark. It had seemed to him important that the matter of the Senate remain private. He had had no intention of discussing it with Claude or Karen. When Claude had spoken to him, he had been stunned not only that she knew anything about it, but that she had seemed to be pronouncing his own thoughts, repressed though he might try to keep them.

Now, since he was in love with Karen, since he felt he had never loved anyone as he did Karen, since an observer might say that he was obsessed by Karen, he also—after they had held hands, made love, talked of everything, committed themselves to their love—wished to be fair with Karen. Claude knew, so should she. Nonsense, perhaps, but he told her late one night, just before they were going to sleep.

"Hayden Calhoun thinks I might run for his Senate seat," he said.

Lying beside him on her back, she said nothing. She got up and went into the living room. When she returned, she had lit a cigarette. She smoked very little. It always rather surprised him that she smoked at all since she hadn't the habit. He smiled as she sat down on the print chair next to the bed; she did, too.

"All right," she said, "why are you smiling?"

"Because you're smoking."

"Mmm . . . Sometimes, when I need time . . . just a moment or two, I smoke. Hadn't you noticed?"

"I've noticed," he admitted.

She said, "Well, now I've had the time. Do you think you might run?"

"I think it's very unlikely."

"Why?"

He told her his reasons.

"I see . . ." She paused. "Leaving the store aside for a minute. What makes you so sure you couldn't win?"

"Basically, the Jew part of it."

"You are the first Jewish Mayor of Ramsey."

"That's different. In Ramsey, the name—well, not to be pompous, it's a legend. It's above being Jewish."

"Which also may be true of the state."

He shook his head. "Darling, there are still parts of Texas where there are no black men out after sundown."

"And not so many voters, either."

He thought for a moment or two. "I know less personally about anti-Semitism than most Jews, of course. By that, I mean I haven't personally been . . . so demeaned by it. Wherever I've been, even when I was young, I've been a 'show' Jew; like the token nigger. Even so, there are still clubs in town I can't join. And there are clubs I can where I'd be one of maybe three Jews in the place. So I don't join them. Big Jewish communities elect Jews to something, as in New York. There are no big Jewish communities in Texas."

"But the election as Mayor . . ."

"Was something of a fluke. Don't forget, I wasn't just a candidate. I was an issue. Are the people of Ramsey adult and responsible enough to elect their Mayor instead of having him shoved down their throats? I said they were. And there I was, available to show that they thought they were grownups . . ."

She interrupted: "I don't accept all that. Only part of it."

"Why?"

"I watched you work. Adam, I saw you *change minds.* Those people, standing or sitting in front of you, they watched you, listened to you and they switched. You could almost see their minds turning . . . No, not their minds. Their feelings. Their minds turned off . . ."

She stopped, puffed on her cigarette and then put it out.

"If their minds had voted, you might have been . . ."

"That uppity Jew," he suggested.

"Adam, those people loved you. Loved. As a political candidate, you had magic."

Within him, he had the temptation to believe what she was saying. He did not wish to, but he could not help it. For it coincided with a quality that was carved into his soul: that if he wanted anything enough, he could have it. Not that he would be given it: those were feelings appropriate to Bernie, perhaps Louis; that he could earn it; win it. Her words struck home to his conviction. However, he wished not to explore it. With every grain of sense he had, he did not *want* to think he had a chance for the Senate, from which floodlit stage anything, literally anything, could emanate. From every practical standpoint, at this juncture of his life, the whole thing was out of the question. He spoke lightly: "Hearing you, what pleases me is that you love me. And are wildly prejudiced."

She was impatient. "That's not the point."

"Don't dream, Karen. Hayden, out of old affection, is dreaming. I'm not."

She did not reply for a while. Then, she said, "The store part . . . if you won, someone could be hired."

He laughed. "Who could be a disaster."

"Who might not. In any case, the store is simply not as important . . . as the other possibility."

He now became very serious. "Yes, it is," he said. "Don't ever underestimate what that store is to me."

"It has been your life," she agreed.

"Until you."

She smiled. "Maybe including me. Anyway, I won't fight that. It has been your life . . . until, for instance, you ran for Mayor. Which had nothing to do with the store."

After a while, he said, "What are you trying to say, darling? I have a feeling I'm not going to like it."

This time she laughed. "You won't," she agreed.

"Then what?"

To his surprise, she lit another cigarette before speaking. "More time?"

"More time," she agreed, then in a few moments, "Adam, I've always known one thing about you. I both hate it and am in love with it. There is something more important to you than the store . . . than me . . . even perhaps than your children . . . and you would *die* if something hurt them. Walk gladly into any flames to get them out. What I'm talking about is power. Or glory, if they aren't the same thing . . . Your ambition, Adam."

He spoke, he thought, truthfully. "I have everything I want, dear."

She shook her head. "No. Because it's not everything there is."

He spoke sharply. "Karen, the post of junior Senator from Texas is not what might be called exalted. It's not king of the world, you know. And, I should say . . . I think I do a little resent your comments about ambition. There's a nasty connotation to that word."

"I'm sorry," she said, sounding contrite. "I made you sound ruthless."

"So you did."

Karen sat forward and put her elbow on her knee and her chin in her hand. "I didn't mean to," she said. "You feel things very deeply. You can love people. You do. Ruthless people don't love, I guess. But . . ."

"But what?"

She smiled. "Power. Glory. You can't underestimate them in yourself. They're part of the reason I love you. Part of the complications of you. We're very unsimple people, you and I."

Neither of them spoke for a while. They were thinking their own thoughts. At last Karen broke the silence, and he could not forgive what she said.

"If you do decide to run, you know, you should divorce Claude now."

He had been lying on his side propped up on his elbow, sometimes watching her, sometimes gazing off into space. Now he looked at her, first with astonishment and then, quickly, with anger. He said nothing. He got up, slipped on his dressing gown and walked out of the bedroom into the living room. Even this was not enough. He opened the sliding glass doors that led to their tiny terrace and leaned forward with his hands on the railing. It was a dark night. Now and then a sliver of moon escaped shifting clouds, but he could see no stars. A slight, pleasant breeze stirred the branches of the trees. He was left alone there for many minutes, perhaps twenty. Many feelings were clawing at him. Predominant for the moment was anger. He was not aware that he had ever been angry with Karen before. Lovers, under different circumstances they should have fought; they had not. They did not even irritate each other. So anger was unsettling and made him anxious and tense. She was attempting to limit his ability to postpone.

When she did appear, she simply stood in the doorway. She made no effort to come to him.

"I didn't mean you should . . . immediately marry me," she said, softly.

"Didn't you?" He continued to look at the sky. He did not wish to face her.

"Of course not. I know as well as you do the impossibility of that. I know it might be years. That's what I was really saying. There must be a separation . . . decent . . . credible . . . between divorcing Claude and . . . anything that . . . is ever going to happen between us."

"And what is going to happen between us?" he asked.

"I don't know. I've never known."

He did not speak.

"Do you?" she said.

"Of course not," he said, sharply.

"Why are you so angry?"

"Because . . ." He stopped.

"Am I . . . seeming to trap you? Or to try?"

"I should have thought anything concerning a divorce, anything concerning the other part of my life—would come from me."

"I am half of us . . ."

"The half that has nothing to lose." His voice was cruel. He meant it to be. He continued to be so: "When I want to discuss the future . . . any future of ours . . . or its non-existence . . . I will."

"I see," she said in scarcely more than a whisper. "All right. I just thought . . ."

"What?"

"We could talk about anything. That's all . . . I . . ."

This time, he heard the quavering in her voice and turned to face her. She was not crying but she had a hand over her mouth as though wishing to prevent it from uttering any more words. And this he could not stand. He went to her and took her in his arms. But he still had no words of comfort for this girl he loved.

It was the beginning of this trip. Nothing more was said on these matters during the rest of it. In time, the sharpness blurred but did not go away. He did not understand at the time that he was losing control over events and that they were taking charge. So he could not explain his uneasiness, but it was there and did not cease when he got home.

# 4

NANCY WROTE Bobby about the conversation she had had with her mother. She reported it as accurately as she could, and ended:

"It seems hard to believe, but she's really frightened that Adam will leave her. She hasn't a shred of proof that he's even having a casual affair, never mind something serious. But the point is, she *is* terrified and doing everything she knows to fight for him. I told her we would back her. I'm sure I gave her the impression we'd do anything to stop him if there's anything to stop. Will we? Will you? I promised more than I can deliver. Write and tell me what you think . . ."

But Bobby called her one night instead of writing.

"If you can't talk, just listen," he said.

"I can talk. Nobody's around."

"Have you spoken any more to Claude about this?"

"No. I don't think I will. She's said what she has to say. Got it out of her system."

"Well, let me start by saying, I think she's probably right."

"Why?"

Bobby hesitated. "Because she knows him," he said. "Because she knows more about people than any of us."

"I honestly think you're wrong," Nancy said. "I think it's the middle-age horrors. I simply can't imagine Adam going crazy."

"I know Claude better than you do. Better than anybody does."

"That's pretty arrogant."

"I know. I have my reasons. Anyway, you asked will we stop it. The answer is, I will."

"Why you? Why not both of us?"

His voice was chilly. "Because, dear, I can hurt Adam worse than you can. As you know."

Nancy, shocked, was silent.

"You do know what I'm talking about?" he asked.

"Yes," she said. "You couldn't do it to him."

"I could if I have to."

"It may not even exist."

"I'll know that when I see him."

"When will that be?"

"When's his next trip to New York?"

"Well, he goes about once a month. He just got back."

"I'll have to wait then." Bobby sounded disappointed. "I'll find out his next trip and have lunch with him."

Nancy said, "If you hurt him for no reason, I'll never forgive you, Bobby. He's always done his best."

"I hope I won't hurt him at all. But he's not going to destroy our mother. Who gave me life."

Nancy laughed. "Don't sound so special. Me too."

But Bobby did not laugh. "I didn't mean it literally. I can't explain that, Nance, just accept it."

"Okay, okay . . . Just be careful."

"I will."

In a couple of weeks, Bobby called his father and set up a lunch date with him on his next trip, which would be midsummer. Bobby would be at Bloomingdale's for his last season of preparation for the family business. "I just want to talk about presents and futures," he told his father. Pleased, Adam set a Saturday date and they agreed to meet in the Oak Room of the Plaza.

# 5

SHORTLY AFTERWARD, Adam got a call from Cullum Roberts, who also wanted to have lunch. They met at the City Club. The older man was already at the table when Adam arrived. He rose to shake hands. Adam, suspecting what Roberts might want, took the initiative.

"I'm getting too much lip service and not enough action from the councilmen on busing," he said.

"Well, Adam, they got heads to get cut off. They'd like to keep 'em."

"Any riots and we all get chopped up, Cullum."

"Adam, there ain't gonna be no riots. This is a law-abidin' community."

In spite of himself, Adam smiled. "You kill me with that country-boy language."

"It works, Adam, it works. I'm in favor of things that work. Anyway, what is it you want me to do?"

"Break heads. I want you to get those boys you own out in their districts talking to the people. What I've been doing."

"Sayin' what?"

"That it's a dead issue. That there's no point in fighting a dead issue. And—the main thing—that there's no point in keeping their children home."

Roberts frowned. "There're gonna be folks who keep their kids home, Adam. You gotta face that."

"Maybe for a few days. Not more. When the only people who lose are the kids."

Cullum Roberts smiled. "Adam, you're a reasonable man. You have a fault, though. You think people are reasonable. People ain't reasonable. We're gonna have a little hootin' and hollerin' 'round here 'fore all the folks calm down. And that ain't so terrible, Adam. Gets it outa their system."

"You could be talking about blood."

"I could be. I don't think so. Anyway, look—I'll talk to our boys. I won't just talk to them, I'll do like you say: I'll break heads."

They talked of other matters during most of lunch. A dozen or more people came to their table to say hello. A few sat down for a little while. Each man was cordial to the table hoppers. Then when the room was clearing, told jokes idly to each other.

Roberts suddenly said, "What'd you think of old Hayden steppin' down?"

They were now on the minefield they had postponed reaching for nearly an hour and a half. During that time, the club had nearly emptied. Here and there a few men lingered over coffee and there were a couple of stinger drinkers. Near their own table, no one was left. They had privacy.

Adam said truthfully, "I was damn sorry to hear it. He's been a great Senator, good for the state and good for the country."

"You been close to him for many years, of course," Roberts said. "So I guess you know why he's doin' it."

"Wants to come back home, he said. That's all I know."

"Well, I doubt that's all you know, 'cause even I know he had a mild heart attack."

Adam was genuinely surprised.

"How'd you hear that?"

"Washington knows it. I guess it slipped out of the hospital. Things are always slippin' out of hospitals. So, what I mean is, he ain't gonna change his mind."

"No, you're probably right. He's not."

Roberts took a few moments before he continued. "On the other hand, Adam, he's got the most powerful political organization in the state. In the history of the state. For example, it didn't do you no harm when you won that referendum, but especially when you won the election."

"No, it didn't," Adam said, carefully.

"Bodies. And pros. Calhoun's got 'em. And that was just in Ramsey. He covers the state."

"Cullum, why don't you get around to what you're trying to get around to?" Adam said, pleasantly.

"I like to build things up," Roberts said, also pleasantly. "Piece by piece. Like I said before, I like what works. So, when I finish, you'll have the whole picture."

Adam smiled. "So, as you were saying . . ."

"Hayden's gonna want to pick his man," Cullum Roberts said. "He would like to have what you might call continuin' influence."

"Did he tell you that?"

"He didn't have to. I know it. And so do you."

Adam nodded. "I'll go along with that."

Roberts leaned back in his chair. He seemed to squint as though to see Adam better, to catch the smallest flicker of expression on the younger man's face.

"The man who gets Hayden's backin' has a good chance for that job, Adam. It wouldn't be a sure thing, but then Hayden ain't gonna back some halfass who ain't got a chance, right?"

"I wouldn't think so," Adam agreed.

Roberts continued to stare at Adam. "He won't back anybody who's announced so far, Adam."

"Oh, I don't know. He might."

"He won't. He's told some people who talk to me. He's waitin'."

Adam, certain of what Roberts was preparing to say and understanding now what Roberts was preparing to ask, had in mind to be circumspect and evasive. That is what he had in mind before they had ever met for lunch. But now his blood was up and there was excitement in him. The casualness was over. Adam felt the sense of confrontation. After all, this was the man who had betrayed him and who now needed him. In the dialogue which followed, Adam was therefore no longer careful.

"Now, Adam, you know I been givin' the best part of my life to this town. And some of the town's here because I got it here. To do that, I've had to have a lot of friends. Powerful friends. But as powerful as they were, they always turned to me for the word. That's respect, Adam. You and I, for instance, we ain't always agreed on everything, but I'd be surprised if you didn't respect some things I've gotten done in this town."

"I do," Adam said, truthfully.

"Some of those people want me to run for the Senate, Adam. They been talkin' to me since Hayden announced."

Roberts sat back, expressionless but with the same squinting eyes. Adam saw that he now wanted some response.

"Do you want it?"

"Yup."

Adam smiled. "The stage manager wants to be the leading man."

Roberts also smiled, thinly. "I guess you could say that."

"What makes you think you could win? You're pretty local, Cullum."

Roberts looked impatient. "Come off it, Adam. I got friends all over this state. You can't spend your life doin' what I been doin' and not get into the legislature, into Austin, Houston, San Antonio . . ."

"You're talking about the big boys. I'm talking about the people. The people never heard of you."

Roberts dismissed that. "I got a year, a little over. I'll have money. A lot of money."

"So," Adam said, slowly, "what is it you want from me?"

Roberts took a long time to answer. When he did, it was simple enough. "Hayden Calhoun," he said. He quickly corrected himself. "Well, that ain't all. I also want you. You have a following, Adam. A name. You proved that. You can help me a lot."

Adam kept his face expressionless. "You want me to push you with Hayden? You want me to come out for you, even campaign for you?"

"I could be a pretty good Senator, Adam. You've seen me as a persuader. As a doer. You've watched me control people."

Adam now looked away and seemed to examine the Ramsey skyline. It was a long time before he answered and when he did, it was the irresistible attraction of combat which brought forth what he said.

"Funny thing, Cullum." He now looked back at Roberts and smiled. "Some people have come to me with exactly the same proposition."

Roberts looked puzzled. "You mean that you back somebody else?" he asked.

"No. That I run myself."

Roberts seemed so stunned that he appeared unable to speak. His pale face grew even paler. Adam could not help but laugh.

"You look like Muhammad Ali hit you in the stomach," he said. "The world is full of surprises, Cullum. Always expect the unexpected."

Roberts dropped his country boy dialect: "You haven't got a snowball's chance in hell," he said, fiercely.

"Why? Hayden might back me. My name's known. Better than yours."

"You'd be destroyed."

"Tell me why?"

"Because you're a . . ." and Roberts stopped. But it was too late.

"Because I'm a Jew, Cullum? Why, you bastard, you don't even have the guts to say it."

"I wasn't going to say that," Roberts said, weakly. "Not that way. It's not personal. It's just practical."

Adam said, quietly, full of anger: "Well, here's something personal. You double-crossed me, lied to me and lost to me. Because you're a liar and a double-crosser, I wouldn't pull you out of quicksand."

"That was a political decision, not a personal one."

"I don't give a fuck which it was. Now. I'll tell you . . . If I do run, I'll get Hayden's support. And even if I don't win the election, I guarantee I'll sure as hell destroy you. Destroy you."

Adam beckoned to a waiter. They were now the only guests in the club. "However," he said, pleasantly, "I'll also buy you lunch. You see, Cullum, I wouldn't even let you buy my lunch." As Adam signed the check, Roberts said, softly: "You're vulnerable, Adam. You're in the saddle now, but like you said, you are a goddamn Jew. In this town, a blind man can cut down a fuckin' Jew bastard, though it might take him a little time . . . just a little, though not all that much . . ."

On the way to the store, Adam regretted mildly that he had lost his temper. He hadn't realized, it seemed, how bitterly he felt toward Roberts. But he did not consider it serious. Roberts would have done little if anything about the busing anyway. He could think of no way he needed the man for anything else. He could think of no way by which Roberts could hurt him with the city. He was more powerful than Roberts now, and Roberts knew it; from this knowledge had come the old man's violent words at the end. Adam was cheerful as he returned to his desk.

Roberts sat alone for a while in the club. He also could think of no way he could hurt Adam Starr. At that moment. But he also knew that a year, a month, a day, even an hour, can change anything. And he could at least now allow himself the luxury of hating someone; he did not permit himself such a pleasure often, since you never knew whom you were going to need when. This time, he could do it.

# 6

On the birth of his daughter, Adam Starr had been delighted. On the birth of his son, he had been ecstatic, and this had slightly surprised him. He had never consciously known how much he wanted a son. Had Claude produced a second daughter how greatly disappointed he would have been. He had wanted a boy and he had wanted the male line of Starrs to continue through his own genes. He knew these things only after his son was born. He would have sworn that there was no difference in the love he had for each of them, and perhaps there was not. But Bobby was the line from his seed and must continue their name in the generations. Adam wanted it. And now his son, like the latest blooming flower, had turned into the beauty of the garden. The reports Adam had from his colleagues at Bloomingdale's were glowing. Bobby seemed to be showing a good sense of figures, a sharp sense of the importance of profit and above all, at least for Adam, a feeling for fashion and merchandise.

"If you don't want him," Adam's friend at Bloomingdale's had once said, "leave him here. We'll take him gladly." And that remark reinforced Adam's feeling that his son had come into his own.

But the call from Bobby suggesting lunch surprised him. It seemed to suggest his son wanted a serious talk. Bobby had made no such suggestion in his life. Such things had always come from Adam and the results had always been superficial and disappointing. Now it was Bobby, actively seeking his father's counsel. Adam walked to the Plaza Hotel on that hot summer day with a deep feeling of pleasure.

The stately, two-storied Oak Room offers more privacy than most New York restaurants. To Adam, it was one of the city's most familiar rooms. He had lunched, dined and supped after theater there more often than he could possibly remember. The maître d'hôtel and the captains knew him, and he had had a house charge account at the Plaza for so long he didn't even use a credit card as most people did.

On that day, he arrived before Bobby and selected a table for two which had one of the room's splendid old leather wing chairs and a smaller chair at right angles to it. He took the wing chair and ordered a Bloody Mary. He almost never had a drink at lunch, but he was looking forward to this lunch, and what the hell, it was Saturday.

Bobby looked splendid entering the room. He was a tall boy now, though not so tall as his father, he walked erectly, as he had once not done, and his face was as handsome as ever. As he spotted his father and walked smiling toward him, dressed in a white suit and blue-and-white striped tie, Adam was thinking what a great and exciting world it is for twenty-one-year-olds.

"Hello, my boy," he said, standing and receiving and bestowing the ritual kiss.

"Hi, Adam, how are you?"

"Fine."

They both sat down. A captain came over and Bobby ordered iced tea.

"Your suit," Adam said, smiling, "is really white."

Bobby smiled. "This is my lunching-with-distinguished-father-at-the-Plaza suit. Do you like it or is a white suit too flashy for you?"

"For me, yes. Not for you. I don't even know why it is for me. Middle-aged men wear white suits and good-looking seersuckers and all kinds of things and they look fine in them. I can't bring myself to do it."

"Too rakish?"

"I have something in me of those guys who sleep in their suits if they know they're going to have lunch at the Harvard Club," Adam admitted. "So they will appear suitably rumpled."

"Do they still wear button-down shirts and Brooks Brothers suits?"

"Sure. All their lives. So will your own class, I expect, though maybe they don't yet."

"Some of them do off-campus. On the grounds, it's still blue jeans. At Bloomingdale's, of course, anything goes."

"These days. When I first got into retailing, one of the vital rules of any store was dress regulations. Black or dark-gray dresses for the women, suits for the men; appropriately drab suits. God forbid a sport coat or anything like what you've got on. Management was terrified of what salespeople would get themselves up in if they were on their own. Purple leotards, maybe. Middle-aged ladies in purple leotards. I suppose one of the most visible changes in retailing since I've been around has been the elimination of dress regulations. I guess one would speak sharply to a salesgirl who came to work in a bikini. Otherwise, you can't tell the salespeople from the customers."

Bobby half-smiled. "You sound almost as if you regret it."

"Oh, no. I'm not tied to the past. You know me better than that. I've spent a lot of rather . . . painful time freshening faces at our own store."

Bobby looked at Adam with interest. "I know a little about that," he said. "Bits and pieces. I gather there was some blood let."

Adam nodded. "Yes. It hurt some people a great deal to see some of the old faces go. Especially your grandmother. Of course, she had friends among them, which was hard. But also, it signified change. She wasn't—isn't—enthusiastic about change. She distrusts growth and the things you have to do to grow." Adam smiled, ruefully. "Every time we have a computer problem, Mother is secretly delighted. She'd shoot them if they were flesh. She's partially right, you know."

"In what way?"

"Some of the good things about the old retailing have gone as well as the bad ones. Quality, for one. I mean real quality goods."

Bobby disagreed. "We don't sell bad quality at Bloomingdale's," he argued. "We return it. So does Starr's, maybe even more so."

"Well, sure, if it's *bad* quality. No decent store puts up with that. But we'll all settle for respectable quality. As will customers. We sell what is good. We used to sell what was the best."

"Why don't we still?"

"Too few people want to spend the money to buy it. So few people can make it. Therefore, stores don't have it. We carry examples of the superb. We have a store full of the respectable not to say mediocre. Which is what we can sell a lot of, profitably. Profit margins are what matters. Most stores are publicly held, or their owners are. Stockholders don't give a damn whether you have the world's finest vicuña coat. They only care that you're selling enough three-dollar socks. Otherwise, they take their money and give it to somebody whose bottom line looks better."

"I never hear you sounding sad, but you do a little."

Adam shook his head. "Not that. In some ways, it's more fun to run a little store where you know half your customers. What Mother's used to. It's just as much fun and, to my mind anyway, much more challenging to run a bunch of stores which sell good quality by the standards of the day and return a damn good profit. It's certainly more complicated. Well . . . what do you want to eat?"

Adam summoned a hovering captain. Bobby ordered eggs benedict and he a club sandwich. "And I'd like some more iced tea," Bobby said. When the captain had gone, he looked at his father silently for a few moments and said, lightly enough, "I imagine you're wondering why I asked to have lunch with you this trip?"

"A little," Adam admitted. "It's normal enough. We just haven't done it much."

"Not much. Well, of course, I'll be through with college in another year. That's one thing."

"As an undergraduate. There's always business school."

"How do you feel about that?"

Adam thought before replying. "I'm of two minds. I wouldn't be upset if you passed it up and came straight to work. And I wouldn't be upset if you went to it. How do you feel?"

At that point, the food arrived so Bobby did not reply at once.

"I think I might like a glass of white wine, too," he told the captain.

Adam said, "Well, don't do that. I'll join you and we'll split a half bottle. Bar wines are usually insulting. Always order half bottles and leave what you don't want."

Bobby allowed himself a mischievous smile. "Ah, the world of the rich and famous," he said, mildly mocking. "On my salary, I could barely afford the glass."

"Ah, but I'm your father and fathers always buy lunch." Adam ordered a demi-bouteille of the La Doucette Pouilly

Fumé. Bobby started on his eggs benedict. "Adam," he said, calmly, cutting at the English muffin, "did it ever occur to you that I might not go into the store?"

Adam felt a slight chill go through him. But he too was calm in his answer. "Not lately. Years ago, maybe."

Bobby said, mocking himself, "My delicate-plant days, you mean."

Adam ignored this. "You simply didn't seem interested," he said.

Bobby shook his head. "But I was." He looked up at his father. "I was interested in being whatever you wanted me to be, Adam. One of the things you wanted me to be someday was president of that store. But then, you also wanted me to be a good athlete, and I couldn't be that. Still can't. I used to cry sometimes at all the things I couldn't be that you wanted me to be."

Adam attempted to pass this off. "How well you play tennis is really not so important in life," he said. "If I ever made you think it was, I was a fool."

"Tennis is not quite the point," Bobby said. He took another bite of his eggs and sipped his iced tea. "What is the point is that I thought you were the most perfect man in the world, Adam. And that I was the most unlikely son you could possibly have produced." He smiled, coldly. "A disaster, in fact."

Adam felt off balance and remained silent.

"What was worse," Bobby said, his voice steady, "is that I knew how much you loved me. Nancy, too, but I was the son. And I adored you. I was fonder of Mother, she owned my heart, but you were a hero. Hero. And I was failing you every day."

"That's simply not true," Adam said. He regained some of his balance. "Look, Bobby, I'm not going to try to convince you you were wrong for ten, fifteen years, whatever you're talking about. Because that's not what you're getting at. What are you getting at?"

Bobby hesitated. He was considering his order of presentation.

"I could now be at least some of the things you've wanted me to be," he began. "For instance, I think I could be president of Starr's. It now seems feasible."

"Of course it is," Adam said, sharply. "You show me that every day."

Bobby nodded. "Okay. The next thing—I may not consider you a hero, say, in the traditional sense, but I do think of you as larger than life and . . . doing a lot of things I admire."

"But . . ." Adam said.

"Not quite yet," Bobby said. He gave a fleeting smile. "I also love you, Adam."

Adam, taken totally by surprise, did not trust himself to speak for a moment. Then he said, briefly, "And I you."

Bobby had not quite finished his eggs, but he now pushed them away and leaned back in his chair. His face showed no expression Adam could recognize, but the eyes were ice cold.

"I wanted to have lunch today, not about my life, but about yours," he said. "I wanted to tell you that if you ever leave my mother, I will never see you again as long as I live. Neither, I think, will Nancy, but she can tell you that herself. I'll speak only for me. If you write me, I'll not read the letters and I'll hang up on you if you call. If you're ill, I'll ignore it, and if you die, I'll ignore that. You will have no son."

For some time, though he knew he was staring at Bobby, Adam saw only a blur. His heart was beating very fast and he felt such shortness of breath he became frightened. At the moment, he was incapable not only of speech, but of thought. Later on, remembering that moment, he supposed it was unique in the history of his life. He was helpless. Bobby, seeing this, was silent and motionless.

After what seemed like hours, Adam finally spoke: "What . . . possibly . . . makes you think . . . I would leave your mother?"

"Because you're having an affair with someone else," Bobby said, his voice flat.

A measure of relief came to Adam with the words "someone else." Nevertheless, the response he made was automatic and did not even sound convincing to himself.

"That's absolutely not true," he said.

Bobby did not change expression. "It would help if we didn't lie to each other, Adam," he said. "I guess we've probably lied a lot to each other over the years, but now is not the time for it."

"What gives you such an idea?" Adam said, weakly.

Bobby shrugged. "Claude's known for some time."

"What has she known?" Adam said. "There is nothing to know."

"She told Nancy about it. She knows that you have a lady in New York, that she is the reason for all the trips, for the extra days you take, for much of the life you're living right now."

"Bobby . . . We've been married a quarter of a century. At some time during a period like that, a wife suspects her husband of having an affair. And is often wrong."

Bobby's face continued to be expressionless. "Claude isn't wrong, Adam. She knows you. She doesn't even understand how well she knows you. She thinks because she doesn't compete with you intellectually that there is a part of you she can't reach. All right, that may be true. But emotionally there's nothing about you she doesn't know."

"Bobby . . ." Adam began.

Bobby shook his head. "Never mind, Adam. When Nancy told me about this, I wondered myself. I have a great deal of faith in my mother's intuition. I think she's maybe a genius when it comes to human beings and their needs. And what to do about them. But I told Nance I'd only be sure when I talked to you myself. Now I have and I'm sure."

"Why?"

"Your face is gray. You're having to fight to keep your hands from shaking." Bobby smiled and he looked almost sympathetic. "You're a mess, Adam."

Adam sat silently. The captain came back to their table. "Was something wrong with the sandwich, Mr. Starr?" he said. It was nearly untouched. Adam did not seem to hear him. The captain said, "Would you like something else instead, sir?"

Adam roused himself. "What? Oh, no. Nothing. I just wasn't hungry. You can take this away."

"Some coffee, then?"

"All right. Coffee. Yes."

"I'll have coffee now, too," Bobby said. When the captain had gone, he turned back to his father. "I think you want very much to tell me about it," he said. "Maybe it would help if you did."

"There's nothing to tell." Adam was silent again. But Bobby was, of course, right. He wanted to talk to his son. Deeply. And believed from all his training, by every aspect of his nature, that he could not. "I want to speak hypothetically for a moment," he said at last.

"If you like," Bobby said.

"Admitting nothing."

"I understand that."

Adam was speaking very slowly, trying hard to choose his words precisely. "It is possible," he said, "that a man will have an affair. Sometime during twenty-five years. Also, it's possible that a woman will. Or that they'll both have many affairs. You're young and maybe you haven't seen that happen, but I have."

"I grant the point."

"But still, the man and this woman stay together." And then Adam added, to his own surprise: "Usually."

"Unfortunately, you're right," Bobby said. "You would have more experience about that sort of thing than I have."

"Another woman. Or another man . . . is sometimes actually a necessity in people's lives, sometime or other. Sometimes it even helps the marriage."

"I've read that," Bobby said. His tone was derisive. "There are magazines which make a lot of money selling that point. There is also wife-swapping, there are orgies . . ."

"Cut it out," Adam said, sharply. Bobby's mocking gave him the gift of anger. "I'm trying hard. Give me a chance."

"All right," Bobby said.

"I'm simply saying that total fidelity during all those years of a long marriage is . . . well, it's very unusual."

Bobby shook his head and spoke almost sadly. "Adam, you're not understanding anything I've said. I'm not interested in your casual affairs. If Claude had one, I wouldn't be interested in that either. But Adam . . . neither are you."

"Neither am I what?"

"Interested in casual affairs. If you had been, all these years, I would know it. Because everybody would know it. Adam, hasn't it occurred to you you've never done anything casual in your life."

"Of course I have."

"Not really. You don't even play tennis casually. Whatever you do, you do with everything that's in you. You commit yourself. You lose yourself in whatever it is, work, tennis or even a book. You don't know what casual means. My mother knows that, Adam, and so do I."

"So?" Adam said, softly.

"So you're in love with this woman. I won't stand for that."

And now Adam's anger came forward with the force to banish his tentativeness.

"*You* won't stand for it. You're my son and I love you, but you don't run my life. Don't take too many steps, Bobby, you'll fall over the cliff."

"I'm taking that chance."

"What the hell do you know about love anyway? You're twenty-one years old and barely out of your diapers. You don't know love from left field."

"I know something about it," Bobby said, quietly.

Adam scarcely heard him. "You don't know the helplessness of it. The paralysis of will . . . When it happens, there is nothing to be done."

"Then this is where you are now?"

"I didn't say that."

"Of course you did. And Adam, what I'm telling you is I won't allow it."

"Won't *allow* it," Adam said, his voice rising, his face red with fury. "You're a punk twenty-one-year-old kid and you talk like God. Remember who you are, who you're talking to. A man can't help love. Call it a disease if you want, call it anything, it can't be beaten."

"It can be left." Now Bobby's voice was loud. A waiter looked at them curiously. "It can be put out of your life. You can't put disease out of your life, but you can drop love. Or obsession. Or whatever it is. Whatever cruelty it takes—to someone else, to yourself—it can be done. And Adam, you're going to have to do it."

Adam reached out and slapped his son as hard as he could across the face. Bobby's head jerked back and his cheek became red. Tears that Adam could see came to his eyes; whether from pain, surprise or sadness Adam did not know. He could not believe what he had done. He could find no words. But Bobby did not crumble as he would have once. The tears stopped; he brushed them casually away with his sleeve. He did not even seem angry. "Sorry," Adam finally said, looking away. Bobby nodded.

"I love my mother more than anything in the world," he said, calmly. "I think she would be badly hurt if she lost you. Might not recover. To prevent that, I'm willing to do anything."

"I think you already have."

Bobby shook his head slowly. His face was very cold. "No, I haven't, Adam. I can say more."

"What more?"

"I can tell you about myself. I can tell you how I know about love. Would you like to hear that, Adam?"

Adam began to be afraid. "I . . . don't know," he said.

Bobby had no mercy on his father. "I can also tell you about when I was suicidal. Not so long ago, Adam. And what my mother did to keep me from it. I'm sure I would be dead today except for what she did. Do you want to hear about these things?"

Adam now had no courage. Curiously, he felt it in his legs as well as in his stomach and in his heartbeat. He was not sure that, called upon to rise, he could do so. It was as though he were drunk. And he actually did wish to rise. He wanted to run away. He wanted to hear nothing more.

"I don't know," he managed to say. He even played for sympathy. "You know, Bobby, I think I may be in a kind of shock. I don't remember ever feeling this way before."

Bobby was relentless. "If I told you all that I've suggested, you'd be badly hurt, Adam. It would be terrible for me—I've lived in horror of your knowing certain things about me—but it would be worse for you."

"Don't tell me, Bobby," Adam said. And his gray face begged that much from his son.

Bobby then was silent. They were silent together for a long time.

"I've been . . . so proud of the changes in you," Adam said, at last. "At how you've grown up." He smiled a sad smile. "Now I wish you hadn't."

"We can love each other and be proud of each other," Bobby said. "We can still do that, you know. Adam . . . Dad . . . I want that to happen."

After a pause, Adam asked: "What do you want me to say? Now, I mean."

"Nothing," Bobby said. "I know I've hurt you. I know all this has been unexpected and terrible for you. I don't want you to say anything when you're like this. When, God help me, I've made you like this. No, you don't have to say anything now. I'll know what you decide. When Claude does. Maybe you'll even tell me, but even if you don't, I'll know. That's time enough."

Adam nodded. "I'll get a check," he said. When he had signed this, he and Bobby walked out of the Oak Room and into the hot sun. On Central Park South, they stood facing each other.

"I . . ." Bobby began. He did not finish.

Adam did something at which he was awkward. He took a step forward and opened his arms. His son came into them and they stood like this for a time. There was wetness on both their cheeks. Passersby looked at them, but no one stopped. Nothing is surprising in New York.

When they separated. Bobby said, "So long, Adam."

"So long, Bobby," Adam said.

Bobby walked back toward Bloomingdale's. Adam walked aimlessly up Fifth Avenue as far as the Metropolitan Museum. When he arrived there, he walked back. It was late in the afternoon when he finally fetched the car from the garage and started back toward Darien.

He took Karen sailing that afternoon, as they had planned. He did all the other things they had planned during the three days they had left on this trip. She asked him how his lunch with Bobby had gone.

"Very pleasant," he said, briefly.

"Did he have anything particular on his mind?"

"Not really," he said, shortly, anxious to be rid of the subject.

"Of course, there's no doubt that he'll come into the store."

At this, Adam paused. "I don't think so," he said, uncertainly. "But a young man can always change his mind."

She looked at him carefully. "Why do you sound so casual? It would break your heart if he didn't go into the store."

He shrugged helplessly. "Would it? I used to think it would. But it's his life."

She felt that something unexpected had been said at the luncheon. But she did not pursue it. For, although Adam seemed on the surface to be himself, no different, she felt that he was. He seemed more silent than usual. Occasionally, he did not hear at first what she was saying. His mind was wandering. He was distracted. Sometimes, concentrating on one thing or another that was on his mind, he was like this and she had grown accustomed to it. This time he seemed more not to be concentrating on anything; as if his mind were flying off in different directions and he was having a job focusing it. She made no effort to press him. She had resolved to press him on nothing. He was kind, loving, attentive . . . he was Adam Starr, the man she loved. She had no question but that he loved her also.

Things were difficult for him, involving her. She could do nothing about it. He would have to resolve these difficulties. When he wished to come to her with his answers, she would be ready. She sought nothing from him until he was ready to give it. She had made one remark she greatly regretted. She would make no more. She spent the rest of that trip loving him back.

7

ON HIS return and for the rest of that blistering summer, Adam continued to be more subdued than usual. Claude and Nancy noticed it since they lived with him and he was quieter at home than he was in his business affairs. During these, he seemed to his associates Adam Starr as usual. In the pace of his life, he could rise above his personal thoughts and the feeling of sadness he carried with him. It never occurred to him that he could not. For Adam, it was part of the responsibility of being a man not to let private matters interfere with public affairs. It was his nature and his training. He wished his brother Louis could do the same thing. Louis's efforts to improve his operation were obvious, however, and Adam could admire that. He could also admit to himself that were another man holding Louis's job, he would replace him. But Louis was not another man and would not be replaced.

He dealt with the situation involving Bernie in the best way he knew how. Behind closed doors, he discussed Bernie with Bill King.

"The most important thing is taken care of," King said. "Money. We've cleared his mortgage, we rent his house to him for practically nothing and we pay him a damn good consulting fee to do nothing."

"Well, he won't do nothing for that," Adam said. "I'll

see that the Men's Store boys call him in regularly for meetings."

"What's he going to do in these meetings?"

Adam laughed, thinking back to a time long ago. "Well, he might try to bring back spats," he said. "He did once. Oh well. Whatever he has to say, they'll be nice to him. They like him a lot, you know."

"Everybody likes Bernie a lot."

"And maybe he can go into the market with them once in a while. He hasn't a bad eye."

"Well, what's the problem, then?"

"Time, Bill. The hours of the day. We may have given him the money to live on, but we haven't given him a life."

"He could try real estate."

Adam looked thoughtful. "He could, but it's a chancy business. What I've been looking for is something where he'd have guaranteed earnings."

"Like what?"

"Bill . . . the contracting business."

King looked stunned. "Well, I guess he could . . . dig or something."

Adam smiled dryly. " 'Director for New Business.' Our own contractors, Jones and Fenwood. Ted Jones was a poor millionaire once. Because of us he's a very big millionaire."

Bill King was quick enough: "So Ted hits Bernie with the retainer, and the commission. Which he cannot lose, just because of us. The new stores."

Adam mused, "They'll have to bid, of course. But, so . . . they win. Always, unless they get stupid, which Ted won't. And someday . . ."

After a moment, Bill King said: "Adam, you know there'll be twenty or thirty Starr's around this country; and Jones and Fenwood will be doing quite sufficiently, I would say, on just this deal. That is sweet. Ted Jones just might buy a diamond necklace for his wife, with whom I hear he is not getting along so good right now. . . . Adam, I will handle this. Don't speak to anyone. If there is one eyebrow lifted one quarter of an inch, I will attend to the matter."

Adam nodded. There was no necessity for thanks, with Bill King.

So that was how they handled the practical side of

Bernie's life. Meanwhile, the store's lawyers, on one pretext or another, secured innumerable delays in the necessary trial for tax evasion; or at least what had seemed the necessary trial. The lawyers, who worked on many tax cases and knew well many important people in the Internal Revenue Service, hoped they might be able to make an out-of-court settlement for both Bernie and Fox, since the two were inextricably entangled. At worst, they hoped for a suspended sentence and the requisite penalties. Joe Fox, not quite in the way he had envisioned, had done well to allow a Starr to become involved with him.

Bernie himself, when he returned from the hospital, looked better than he had ever looked. The ten weeks had erased the puffiness of the years of hard drinking and the exercise had trimmed him down.

"He's the sexiest man in town," Becky said, gaily, on the night when Claude had them to dinner. "I'm scared. He can walk down the street and practically get raped. He's got groupies now."

She was a very laughing, happy woman that night. And Bernie was funny, too, about his hospital experiences. He emphasized the country club atmosphere, told stories of the vagaries of some of the other patients and of the doctors and attendants, and he made them laugh. But after dinner, while Becky, Claude, Nancy and Jenny chatted of other things, Bernie found himself isolated with his brother and was more serious.

"They say I can never have a drink again," he told Adam.

"Is that so terrible?" Adam asked, lightly.

"It wouldn't be for you. For me . . . hell, Adam, my best friend most of my life has been booze. It cheered me up, gave me courage when I didn't have it and made me talk when I had nothing to say."

Adam, for whom such a reliance was unthinkable, who knew nothing of alcoholism except that it could kill weak people who gave in to it, said, "Then if you have nothing to say, don't talk. Be mysterious. Make people come to you."

Bernie looked at his brother seriously. "You really don't understand, do you, Adam? Well, let me tell you just one thing. I don't think I ever screwed a girl in my whole life without some drinks or without a hangover."

"You're not telling me you can't?"

"No. I can. Thank God. But I don't want to as much. Beck wants it more than I do. Sometimes . . . sometimes, it's really an effort. See, they're the same for me. Sex and alcohol. Mean. They're not separated. It's kind of scary."

"It'll pass," Adam said, with no knowledge of whether it would or not.

"The doctors say it will."

"You know," Adam said, attempting to be helpful, "until you got in this trouble, you always drank, but it didn't seem so bad, Bern. I mean you never missed work or got found in doorways clutching wine bottles."

Bernie was silent for a while. "It was getting to me, Adam. In the last few years, I hit the store with some kind of hangover, big or little, more than I didn't. I nearly got scored twice for drunk driving. I got away with it partly—" Bernie laughed, "entirely because my name was Starr."

"Some night that won't work, Bernie. If you drink now, you'll have to control it. Pace it."

"It's progressive, they say. Maybe I'll never be able to do that. If I can't . . ."

"Try not drinking at all for a long time. See how it goes."

Bernie nodded. "That's what I'm gonna do. But it sure does scare shit out of me."

"What about Alcoholics Anonymous? They seem to have a lot of success."

Bernie screwed up his face as if he had tasted something foul.

"I heard that till it's coming out of my ears at the hospital. I . . . Jesus, this is the snob in me . . . I can't feature me, Bernie Starr, in with fifty-three drunks and me getting up and saying, 'I'm a drunk, too. Just like you guys. I'm the same thing.' Because, goddamn it, I'm not."

Adam understood. All the Starrs, no matter how intelligent, would understand that.

The women came back and the talk became general. Bernie returned to cheerfulness. Quite soon, Bill King had worked out an arrangement for him and he began on-the-job training with a company paid off in millions of dollars' worth of Starr's contracts.

# 8

THE POLICE chief of Ramsey was relatively short, stocky and wore his hair clipped short. His name was Harry McCord, he was fifty-one years old, he was tough and he was able. He was meeting now with Adam in the Mayor's office shortly before the opening of school.

"We'll have some men at every school affected," he told Adam, sitting stiff in his chair. "If there's trouble, we'll have the bodies to stop it quick."

Adam frowned. "If that means the schools'll be crawling with cops, that might start trouble," he suggested. "By itself."

"Adam, there's always a cop or two around schools. Every day. We don't have the problems here New York does, but the schools like to have somebody around just in case. It's not gonna look much different than usual. In most areas, it won't even *be* different. In a few, we'll have squad cars near the grounds. They can be on the scene in minutes if they're needed."

Adam nodded. "What's your sense of the mood, Harry?"

The chief spoke thoughtfully and slowly. "With a little luck, we won't have any serious trouble, Adam. Now, people don't like this. I'll be frank. Neither do I. I got two kids of my own that're gonna be bused seven miles. I wish they weren't. They wish they weren't. But they are and that's that. My people have talked and listened around town pretty good. They've found nothin' we can't sit on quick."

"Demonstrations?"

McCord shrugged. "Maybe some banners. Placards. Some people hangin' around. In a couple of places, especially. That's okay, they got that right. But we don't see any real

445

pullin' and haulin', like buses gettin' turned over. We don't expect that."

"You mentioned a couple of problem areas."

"One really. South Ramsey. It's always been white. The elementary school, that's been nearly lily white. When nearly a hundred black kids from six to eleven years old move in there that's gonna make one hell of a difference. And people are more emotional about younger kids than they are about older ones. With the older ones, we might get problems later on with the kids themselves. With the little ones, we might get problems with the parents Tuesday."

Adam thought for a moment.

"That's the Hayes school."

"Robert E. Hayes. One of the oldest schools in the city."

"How many buses will be arriving out there carrying the black kids?"

McCord looked surprised. "Two. Three. I dunno. They'll be comin' from the west and the east mostly. Which, of course, is where some of the white kids will be goin'."

"Can you find out for me which one of the buses for Hayes is likely to be the most crowded?"

"I suppose so. Why?"

Adam said, "I'm going to ride in it."

The police chief's mouth fell open. "You what?" he said.

"You heard me, Harry. Ride in it. Arrive at Hayes with the kids."

"Adam—what the hell good's that gonna do?"

"Maybe not any. But I'll have been on television the night before. I'll have been saying what great people Ramseyites are. If I get off the bus with those kids, I'll at least be the symbol, doing it right. If there's any trouble, it'll have to be with me."

McCord looked worried. "I don't like that, Adam."

"Why not?"

McCord paused for some time before he spoke. "The people who hate this haven't got anybody to hate. No physical body. Just some court that ain't even in this town. Washington. New Orleans. They can't hate you for it because you didn't have nothin' to do with it. But if you get off that bus, Adam, they sure as hell can."

"That's okay, Harry," Adam said, slowly. "They can hate me. I'm a big boy. Whatever they want to yell, let 'm yell at me. If they want to throw something, let'm throw it at me. Not at the kids."

McCord stared at him. "You talked this over with the rest of the Council, Adam?"

Adam smiled. "No. I don't always do that. I wish every one of those men would ride a bus, but I know they won't."

"Because they'd think it would be suicidal. They'd think —and Adam, they'd be right—that people would say they was in favor of this busin'. Not just enforcin' the law. Pushin' it. Which is what they'll say about you."

"I know. I can ride that out."

McCord did not speak for a while. "We'll have to have a few more people at Hayes than I was expectin'," he said.

"Why?"

"Because it's a crazy world. And you're a flesh-and-blood politician. You're not gonna announce this in advance?"

"Nope. Just arrive. And Harry, I don't want to see fifty of your goon squad. I don't want to see *any* of your goon squad."

"You won't see 'em, Adam. But they're gonna be there. A few in plain clothes on the grounds. The cars not far away. I take my orders from you, Adam. You're the Mayor. But I'm the Chief of Police and I got my responsibilities."

"Just so long as I don't see them, Harry. And nobody else does, either."

For Adam's television talk, he had five minutes at the end of each of the local newscasts on the Monday night before the busing would start. He did not call reporters in for the occasion. It was not a press conference. He did not wish a press conference because he did not wish questions. Instead, he spoke quietly and calmly of education, the need young people have for it and the joy they take from it, and the necessity that it be given equally to all children. It was no longer possible, as it had never been desirable, to have black schools and white schools. From the next day forward, there would be in Ramsey only schools, and good ones.

"We all wish there were a better way to do it than by busing children out of one area and into another," Adam said. "The problem is, no one's been able to think of such a better way. So this is the way we're going to do it. And, since it is our tradition in Ramsey to be successful, we're going to be successful at this. We're going to be the model for the whole country. As we have before at difficult times and over difficult issues. What we are doing tomorrow is nothing new. It is the completion of a process that began years ago. Let me tell you a little about that."

And Adam traced in factual terms the progress of integration of hotels, restaurants, stores, housing developments and so on; the great Ramsey success facade, as he knew, but no more a facade than in other cities, he was certain. And the process had been effective enough to inspire many stories in the national news media about the success of integration in Ramsey, Texas.

"Many businesses, bringing many jobs, moved into Ramsey just because we were sane and sensible people," Adam said. True; no riots. "And we found, once it was done, that it hadn't been hard at all. That it not only didn't spoil our lives here, it improved them."

Adam looked directly into the camera and allowed himself a moment's silence.

"Tomorrow morning," he said, "we face another challenge. Tomorrow night, I'm certain, we will all be very proud about how we met it. Good night, my friends."

Since the speech was taped, he could watch it later at home with Claude and Nancy. He studied himself carefully. It seemed to him that he came through pretty much as he had hoped. He was serious without being ominous, unblinking, not fumbling with his words, and contacting his audience as well as he knew how. He was also, as he had meant to be, positive. He made it seem that disturbances would be unthinkable. In his projection he did not allow such a possibility. For that reason he had carefully made no mention of the deployment of the police.

"What do you think?" he asked his daughter and his wife, who had watched as intently as he.

"Very good," Claude said. "You're always good on television, but I've never seen you better."

"Will it work?" Nancy wondered. "All the speeches in the world—I mean, the whole thing's such a red flag. My God, I'm a long way from being a redneck and I don't know whether I believe in it or not myself."

"Well, we don't have an alternative to it," Adam said. "Not now, anyway. As to whether it'll work, we'll see in the next few days."

"I can't help but wonder . . ." Claude began, sounding worried.

Adam, understanding, said, "Wonder what, dear?"

"What good it's going to be for you to be there? And how dangerous that is?"

"Well, not dangerous at all. There'll be plenty of protection, though not obvious. At least I hope not."

After a pause, she said, "Do you want me to go with you? Because I will."

He was deeply touched. He was about to say no, but did not immediately. He was remembering how good and kind and easy Claude had always been with small children; their own and any others who had entered their lives for even a few hours. He was thinking, too, of his own awkwardness in similar situations. He was uncertain around children. He did not bounce them on his knee joyfully, as his father had. He found conversation with them difficult until, at least, they had reached their teens. He had been born an adult. Claude had always had touch with the very young. She could talk to them. She could even listen to them; she was truly interested in them. In the perplexities of how the adults would react to an unpopular change in their condition, Adam had given little thought to the children. As he now began to do so, Claude put what he was thinking into words.

"They'll be so terrified," she said. "Going into a whole new world. So unknown. So scary."

"There might be," he said, tentatively, "some unpleasantness at the school. I think it will be minor. But it may happen."

She looked at him intently. "I can take that," she said. "You ought to know me well enough. I can take anything you can take."

He made his decision. And he made it, he suddenly realized, because he was nervous and felt he needed her. Need. Adam had not been much conscious of needing people during his life. It now seemed to him that he needed his wife. Though it was difficult for him to admit it, he did.

"I think I'd like very much for you to come with me," he said. "I think you would make things much easier."

"Then we both have to get up early." Claude sounded gay.

Nancy said nothing.

Early September had not finished summer in Ramsey, and at six o'clock, when they climbed into the Rolls Royce, the day was already blistering hot.

"We'll leave the car at the bus depot," he said. "When it's all over, we'll take the bus back to the depot."

The depot looked like a bus graveyard. Somehow, looking at the black-and-yellow vehicles lined up side by side in a wasteland the size of a football field covered with gravel, Adam was reminded of pictures he had seen of battered World War I fighter planes preparing to go out at dawn. The buses, too, for the most part were old and bruised. The Board of Education replaced one only when it could not go a mile farther. Otherwise, it was repaired again and again in the huge hangar-like shed which adjoined the parking lot. Adam parked the Rolls at the outskirts of the field. The thought fleetingly crossed his mind that he might have no hubcaps when he returned to it. It was that kind of neighborhood. Near the warehouse, a short, red-faced man was meeting with his drivers. They were all in light-gray shirts and dark-gray trousers and they wore badges identifying them as school bus drivers. They did not wear caps. As Adam and Claude approached, they began to hear what the red-faced man was saying:

"Is there any son of a bitch here who ain't sure of his route?" he was questioning, loudly. The men, young, old and in between, were silent. "Because all we need is for one of you fuckers to get lost so the kids don't get to no school at all."

"Murph, it's all written out. Been mapped twenty times. We all been through it. We'll get there." This was a young man wearing glasses. He sounded weary before his day had begun.

"You better." The red-faced man paused, as though pondering something. "You know what to do if somethin' happens, right?"

"What happens?" another young man said.

"I dunno what happens, meathead. Somebody throws rocks or eggs or bombs or whatever." There was some tight laughter. "You keep on drivin'. You don't stop. The routes'll be clogged with cops. Any serious trouble, they'll be there. Don't argue, don't yell back, don't do nothin'. Just drive. Okay?"

That was the end of the meeting. The drivers started off toward their buses. It was a quarter to seven. The Ramsey schools opened at eight-thirty. The drivers would be covering greater distances than they ever had before. The children would be on time or they would be left behind. In the old days a driver would often wait a minute or two for a known, tardy child. But now the children were unknown. Some of the drivers had had little friendships, back-and-forth kidding relationships with some of their small riders. In many cases these were now ended by the new routes. The drivers had their difficulties, like the parents and the children.

Adam introduced himself to the dispatcher.

"Oh yeah, Mr. Mayor, they tole me you was comin'. You're takin' number fifty-seven, I think."

"Is that it?"

"Yeah, there it is. I'll walk you over."

Adam introduced Claude and the dispatcher took them to their bus and presented their driver, a pock-marked young man named Evans.

"Make yourselves comfortable," he said, cheerfully. "As comfortable as you can in this broke-down old rattletrap. Don't you have no influence down there at City Hall? Couldn't we even have a new bus for the Mayor and his wife?"

"I guess not," Adam said, smiling.

"We're goin' west so it'll be twenty minutes or so before we pick up our first passengers."

Since there was no air conditioning, all the windows were open, but the air remained stifling inside. When they started to move, the bus rattled like a dying soldier. They sat up front in one of the dirty-yellow cane seats and Claude took his hand. But their palms were soon sweating and she released it.

Later, he wondered what he would have done without her during their ride. He could do the things he had expected to do; she did the rest and the rest was more important. As the children got on board at the various stopping points, Adam let them take seats and went to each one of them. "My name's Adam Starr," he said. "I'm the Mayor of Ramsey. I wanted to travel with you this morning." The children, with the exception of a few Spanish-Americans, were all black and nearly all young. He guessed that none of them was more than nine or ten. That had been the plan; let the older youngsters finish at the schools where they now were. Integrate with the younger ones. And these small children looked up at him with dumb amazement as though they could not believe what they were hearing. Indeed, it seemed that they did not understand what they were hearing. Perhaps, he thought, they don't even know what a Mayor is. Some of them wore afros, wild or modified, and some had their hair screwed into braided plaits all over the head culminating in twin pigtails. All the girls, without exception, wore dresses; home sewn, some washed to bleached-out rags, but dresses. And the boys in their pants and white shirts were scrubbed cleaner than they perhaps had ever been in their lives. Sunday best. At each stop the mothers, and a few fathers, were on hand to see their children off, and they too were dressed up: the kind of clothes most of them would wear to baptisms, funerals and revival meetings. All the faces were solemn, parents and children. Behind these faces at the bus stops were the drab and broken houses where these families lived and fought to survive. Again, war images came to Adam's mind, and he imagined these scrubbed youngsters as refugees from the havoc of a bombing, going places where their parents could not follow them; taking this first step to escape all their parents had ever known, the depth of America.

"What's your name?" Adam asked each child. Some gave a first name, Willie, Reggie, Ray, Emma, Sue, whatever, no last names; and others did not answer, a few staring silently at him, most looking away. They did not at first do much talking even to each other. But as Claude moved through the bus, dressed in an old pair of slacks and a blue cotton shirt, something about the radiance of the smile she wore seemed to bring response from them. She sat on the edge of seats and could talk at once to as many as four of the children. He could not hear what she was saying but now and then she laughed at whatever it was. After a while, a couple of the kids grinned, then more, then there were six or eight of them standing around near where she was, lurching as the bus lurched, unable to take their eyes from this creature unlike any they had ever seen. When they began talking to her, she answered smilingly until they were also talking to each other. She made forays into other areas of the bus and wandered back and forth until he could hear, not only a steady buzz of conversation but occasional peals of laughter, raised voices, arguments and friendly insults. He would have liked to be a part of it, but he knew he would spoil it. At every stop, he went through his ritual, but now the serious faces were entering a noisy, natural children's world and the solemnity broke quickly. By the time they reached the Hayes school, their bus was much like any other carrying any children to any school.

In all, perhaps two hundred adults stood on the grass in front of the school. As far as Adam could see from the moving bus, two-thirds of them seemed to be women. Some carried white cardboard placards with black lettering:

BUSING IS A COMMIE PLOT
BUSING IS UNCONSTITUTIONAL
KEEP OUR CHILDREN WHERE THEY BELONG

And a few like

NIGGERS GO HOME.

The men, he supposed, were mostly at work, but as he had long since learned, women were far more ferocious than men anyway, at least the ones who had nothing to do but live with their frustrations. Of the men, a few, he was aware, were plainclothesmen. He couldn't believe they would be needed; this was scarcely a mob. He felt less tense.

The school's principal stood, by prearrangement, on the steps of the massive pile of bricks that was the Hayes school. He would wait for the children there. Most of the men and women of his faculty were behind him. Adam got off the bus first and walked over and shook hands with the principal. He was a youngish man, not more than forty, and he looked pale.

"Everything okay?" Adam asked.

"Some of the white kids are missing. Quite a few. But the buses aren't all here yet."

From Adam's bus, the children came toward the steps. Two of them walked hand in hand with Claude. She continued to smile. From the other arriving buses, the young people trooped out and walked slowly toward the old school. The principal and the faculty members had also forced smiles and slowly the faculty began to disperse, leading the children to wherever they were supposed to go inside the building. None of them carried books on this first day of the new year. Soon they were all inside.

"It begins," Adam said to no one in particular.

"That's all," the principal said. "Just begins. Now the work starts."

Adam turned to Claude. "You go on back to the bus and wait for me," he said.

"What are you going to do?"

He nodded in the direction of the people standing back of them on the grass.

"I'd better talk to them," he said.

She nodded and walked slowly away from him. Adam strode forward into the sea of sullen faces. From standing in the blazing sun, many of them were sweating. He was himself. He went directly into the mass of bodies, his hand outstretched. "I'm Adam Starr," he said. "I wanted to shake hands with you this morning." His confidence and especially his celebrity took precedence over any other emotion for most of them. They shook hands with him. In another situation, he might have been asked for his autograph. Many even smiled. "Great day for our city," he said, and other such things. But there were a few people who turned away as he approached them. He did not pursue them. And then suddenly, something struck him on the top of his head. It was not heavy enough to stun him, but he staggered momentarily before he could wheel around. A thin, middle-aged woman stood before him, her arms already grasped by two men so that she could not move them. Her face was contorted in fury; white, wild-eyed, crazy. On the ground in front of her was the placard with which she had struck him. It was the one which read NIGGERS GO HOME. He stared at her in wonder. There were quickly two men at his side and he knew they were police. "It's all right," he told them, quietly. He looked steadily at this woman and said, "Why did you do that?"

"Jew bastard," she screamed. The men gripped her arms tighter as she strained against them.

"What good did it do?" Adam asked, quietly.

"Christkiller," she said, but this time she was quieter. Adam studied her. As much as anything, he felt curiosity. He had never in his life been face to face with the crazed.

"Did it help you?" he asked. "Do you feel better?"

The men had her arms but not her head. She leaned forward and spat in his face. The saliva trickled down his cheek.

"You better let us take her," one of the plainclothesmen said.

"Where?" Adam said.

"It's assault," the cop answered.

Adam shook his head. Slowly, he took his handkerchief from his hip pocket and wiped his face.

"I am so sorry for you," he said. He looked around at the people nearest her. "Do any of you know her?"

A stout woman stepped forward. "I know her," she said. "She's a neighbor." She looked at Adam coldly. Noting this, Adam looked closely among the faces in front of him. At least half, he thought, were foreign and hostile. It might take madness to strike him, but not to hate him. He came back to the stout woman: "Can you get her home?"

"After you've gone. She gets funny sometimes. You just go and she'll be all right, I reckon." The men still held her.

"Sorry this happened, Mr. Starr." This came from one of the other men in the group. "Warn't nobody plannin' for nothin' like this." He was clearly sincere.

Adam said, "It doesn't spoil anything." He raised his voice and tried to make them all hear him. "It's okay," he cried out. "It doesn't spoil a thing. We've done it. We've done what the law says. We've done it together." And he clasped his hands and raised them above his head like a fighter who has just won a championship. "We're good people, all of us," thinking, "Well, the bad ones are impotent. I made them impotent."

And so, as he walked away from them, he did feel something of what a champion must feel. He had trained, as it were, for this moment for months and he had won. He took Claude's hand and helped her aboard the bus to return to the bus depot.

"I was terrified," she said.

"Just a crackpot. Like the ones you sometimes see on the streets screeching out their poison." He looked at her and smiled. "You were amazing with those kids," he said. "What on earth were you talking about?"

She laughed. "I don't know. But I love children. I hate to see them afraid." She paused. "When all they need is an arm around them. Whatever I said . . . about how they were having a big adventure, how exciting it was going to be . . . I was putting my arm around them. I don't know what I was doing . . ."

Adam said nothing. He patted her hand as they started the clanking, hot, dusty ride back to the depot. For the rest of his life the faces of hatred often came into his vision and reminded him that reason has little to do with life.

On that day, in isolated areas of the city such as the one Adam had visited, only about sixty percent of the white children attended school. These were the poorer areas, where tensions were great at all times and merely exacerbated by the first day's busing. That, too, had been expected. "As a boycott, it's half-assed," Adam said to his wife and daughter. "If twenty percent had showed up, we'd be in bad trouble."

By the end of the second week, all the children of the public schools of Ramsey, Texas, were in their classes. No in-school incidents of importance were reported. The Associated Press and *Time* magazine interviewed Adam on the processes by which such success had come about. He told the reporters of the preparatory work that had gone on in all the communities of the city. He said the entire City Council had participated. The Councilmen were grateful for his lie. The stories praised them all. Senator Calhoun called him.

"Very good," he said.

"Well, it worked."

"The national stories were things of beauty. They could be a joy forever."

Understanding him, Adam said, "I'm still pretty negative about that, you know."

"You still got time. And, Adam, let's get one thing straight. I'm not twistin' your arm. It's your move all the way."

"I know."

What had happened was, of course, his greatest triumph as Mayor: a high point in all his life. But he saw Claude, who had helped him through it, saw Nancy and knew that she and Bobby had talked, and remembered so vividly his lunch with his son that the thought of it sometimes woke him in the middle of the night. The essential feeling within him was not the exultation he might have had but the deepest kind of sadness; close to despair.

# 9

CULLUM ROBERTS and Louis Starr did not move in the same circles. Roberts was nearly fifteen years older than Louis, for one thing, and had his own friends. Also, he did not need Louis Starr. They did, however, know each other. In cities like Ramsey, the people who take any interest at all in civic work are bound to know each other. Roberts and Louis knew each other that way.

A number of coincidences brought about what happened one night between them. The first was that Roberts had heard some of the talk about Adam and Karen having been seen together in New York, and had idly recalled having seen them himself. He had given the matter no thought. The second coincidence was that they were both invited to an enormous barbecue on the grounds of the palatial home of R. E. (Bob) Meadows, an oilman. Still a third was that Louis decided to go. He had been going to very few parties. He did not think he was capable of making much of a contribution to festive evenings, and he felt that the other guests looked at him and said to themselves, "He couldn't keep his woman." That this was his own feeling and not that of other people he understood intellectually. He knew other people didn't care much. Yet he persisted in projecting his personal disgrace into the minds of the people he saw. He decided to go to the Meadows' party because he had never seen the grounds, on which he had heard millions had been spent just on the sculpture garden, and because the party was to be so large he would be able to leave it at any time without being missed. The final coincidence was that out of the more than one hundred tables scattered throughout the enormous rolling lawn of Meadows' estate, Louis and Roberts ended up at the same one. They sat down, having procured their dinners from one of the five buffet tables, and found they were separated only by Roberts' wife, a pleasant, gray lady, rather stout, whose name was Isabel.

"Well, Louis, I'm glad to see you," Roberts said, cordially. "I wonder if you know Isabel, my better half?"

"We've met before," Louis said, shaking hands with her.

"Many times," Isabel Roberts said. "I used to watch you announce the store's fashion shows. I love fashion shows. You don't do that so much any more, do you, Louis?"

"Not so much. They take a lot of preparation and time, you know. And Pete Shaw does a good job."

"Oh I think he's just wonderful," Isabel Roberts said. "So amusing. I mean, fashion isn't all that serious, is it? And some of the new looks . . . you have to laugh."

Louis, picturing Isabel Roberts in some of the new looks, agreed that fashion should not be ponderous.

The woman on Louis's left said something to him, and he was engaged in talking with her for a while. Two orchestras were working, taking turns. One of them played waltzes, two-steps and foxtrots, the other was a rock band. Both of them played loudly so that conversation at the tables was limited. One spoke to those immediately around one. The others at the table could not hear. A great wooden platform for dancing had been set up, and there were many dancers. Louis did automatically what he had done all his life. He danced with his partner on the left and he danced with Isabel Roberts. It was his training to dance with all the ladies at his table.

Though the days were still scorching hot in September, there was relief in the evenings, and this night a pleasant breeze rustled through the trees and cooled the dancers. The grounds were lit expertly and expensively, but it was one of those Texas nights when the stars and the moon might have been sufficient by themselves.

As he and Isabel Roberts were returning to their table, Louis said idly, "Later on, I want to take a walk through the grounds and have a look at some of the sculpture."

They sat down. Roberts, who had overheard this last remark, asked, "You never have been out here before, Louis?"

"Never."

"Bob took a few of us around himself a few years back. It wasn't all done, then, but you could see what it was gonna be. I doubt there's a place like this in the whole United States of America."

"Well," Louis said, "he has all the big names. And a lot of them. Somebody told me he has eleven Henry Moores, something like seven Hepworths, two or three David Smiths . . ."

Roberts smiled. "Whoever he may be. I can't say I'm much for modern art. Oh, I don't light into it like some folks do. You know people actually get mad at it?"

"I know. I've seen it," Louis said.

"Speaking of that," Isabel Roberts said, "how are things going with the Museum? Acquisitions. You were all mixed up with that, weren't you, Louis?"

Disconcerted, Louis said, "Well, I don't really know too much about what's been going on lately."

"How come you didn't keep up with it?" Cullum Roberts asked. "Seems like it would be right up your alley."

"Well, you know my former wife was really into that more than I was. When she left town, I drifted away . . ." He trailed off. He was beginning to sweat on this cool night. "Couldn't hold his woman . . ." Texans held their women.

It was at this point that Cullum Roberts had his notion. He did not know what he was talking about and was aware of this. He could not know whether what he would say would damage Adam Starr or not. He simply hoped it might. He said, smiling and shaking his head, "You know, I've always had the greatest admiration for you Starrs. You're not like any other family I ever knew."

"How's that?" Louis asked.

"Well, I don't mean just that you built a great business, which you did. You just have an attitude that most folks don't have. And I admire it. I suppose you'd call it sophistication, and a country boy like me can sure admire that."

Louis smiled, but was nervous. "Sorry, Cullum, you've got me. I don't have any idea what you're talking about."

"Well, I mean about a divorce in the family. You take most people, a divorce, that's the end. Whoever leaves, by God he or she has *left*. Gone, out of sight. You know what I mean, Louis: bitterness all up and down the family. Now every time I see Adam and Karen together in New York, I think how different you Starrs are. You and she maybe got a divorce but that don't mean she got banished, right?"

After a moment, Louis said, his voice steady, "No."

"And they seem to enjoy each other, have fun together, like any old friends. Other people seein' 'em say the same thing. What I mean is, if Isabel left me, ain't nobody in my family'd ever talk to her again. Or vice versa." Roberts paused. He could see no change in the expression on Louis's face. Obviously, then, what he had said had neither upset, nor surprised Louis. It didn't much matter to Cullum Roberts. It had only been a shot in the dark. Some day, some way, he would cut Adam Starr. He scarcely listened to what Louis was mechanically saying: "Adam and Karen were always good friends. Nobody in the family hates Karen. We had problems, but she didn't have problems with the whole family. Adam keeps me up to date on what she's doing. I'm . . . naturally interested."

"That's what I mean," Cullum Roberts said. "Sophistication. I think the thing about your family, Louis, and what a great family it is, from your parents on down to Adam's children, is that it's so sane. Sanest family I ever knew. That's something in this crazy age."

Louis managed what he supposed was a smile. "I guess it is," he said.

When he could, he excused himself and began to walk around the grounds. He did not feel like going home. He thought he would look at the sculpture and the terraced gardens and let the moon and stars shine down upon him and the breeze play through his hair. Once in a while, someone spoke to him, and he nodded and smiled appropriately. What Roberts had told him did not strike him like some sudden hammer blow. Rather, it trickled into his brain as something to be considered when it was better formulated, had a more solid consistency. Later, he told himself he had never had a doubt from the moment Cullum Roberts had spoken. That was really not true. He did have doubts. It seemed quite possible that Adam might have had dinner with Karen and that people would have seen them together. There was actually no reason why he shouldn't have done so. Or gone to the theater with her.

But, of course, if there were no reason why Adam should not have done such things, then Adam would have told him that he had done them. That was the point Louis could not escape.

And then, as he wandered the grounds, drove home, sat up late in the apartment, had a drink or two and tried to cope with the hours, he did become convinced in spite of himself that his wife had left him for his brother. He was not convinced because of evidence; he had never sensed an attraction between them when they had been together and what Roberts had told him was not conclusive. He was convinced because it seemed to be inevitable. Karen had always wanted an Adam and had settled for a Louis. That much he knew. The other thing he sensed, not quite sure how to intellectualize it, was that the pattern of his having been crushed down by his older brother all his life had not ever had an appropriate completion. Adam had not destroyed him. He had sliced pieces from him and never rent him open. It seemed to Louis late that night, that must be the inevitable completion of the pattern.

He was a careful man. On the following day, he went to see the store's security officer, an ex-FBI agent, and told him that a friend had asked his help in finding a reputable detective agency in New York. It was, he said, a matter of prospective divorce and delicate. The security man gave him the name of an agency run by a man with whom he had once worked. Louis took it and early the next morning called the detective from his home and explained the circumstances. The detective, whose name was March, asked some questions. Among other things, Louis told him was that he did not need or want anyone bursting into bedrooms with flashbulbs. Such dramatics would not be necessary. March seemed happy to hear that. Louis promised to let him know when his brother would next arrive in New York.

# 10

KAREN DID not usually meet Adam at the airport, but on this trip in late September, she did. She waited, well away from the arriving passengers early on that Sunday evening, until she could be certain Adam was alone. She was aware that he might have picked up an acquaintance on the airplane, in which case her trip would have been fruitless. But as she watched him walk briskly to the baggage terminal, she saw that no one was with him and that he spoke with no one. She went up behind him and tapped him on the shoulder.

"Hi," she said. "Want to have some fun tonight?"

He turned and smiled and took her in his arms.

"What are you doing here?" he asked, releasing her.

"Well, I should say I couldn't wait to see you. But the truth is, I felt like meeting you."

"I'm glad you did. The flight was boring and I felt like being met."

He collected his luggage while she got the car, and came around and picked him up outside.

"St. Regis?" he asked.

"Of course."

They drove downtown, and she waited for him in the car while he checked in and deposited one of his bags in his suite. He had developed an unvarying routine on these trips. During the days in New York, he stopped in at the hotel at some point and collected any mail and messages. And then at night, from Darien, he telephoned in case anyone had been trying to reach him. There were always a couple of calls from people who knew where he stayed and wanted to have lunch with him. He returned them and made his dates. Once or twice, during all the months, some member of the family had called him at the hotel, or Bill King or some other member of the store's executive organization. At no time had he ever been unreachable. Only the hotel's chambermaid knew that he never slept in his bed. He always left her the usual tip. On this night, when he had gone through his usual routine, he walked outside into the cool air.

"The King Cole Room's practically empty," he said. "Want to have dinner in town?"

"Sure. I haven't got anything much prepared and the thought of Chuck's Steakhouse somehow doesn't thrill me."

He found out from the doorman where the nearest garage was and drove over with her while she parked the car. Then they walked back to the hotel and took a table in the King Cole Room. The room was indeed three-quarters empty, though a few people did stroll in while they were having their cocktail. One of those was a square-built, cropped-haired man in his forties. By himself, he took a table a good bit away from them. They noticed him come in as they did others, but paid no attention. The fact of being with Karen had, for the moment, at least, blunted most of Adam's sadness. He felt the same lift, the same delight he always felt when he saw her after absences. Over and above his love for her, he took great aesthetic satisfaction in her. He loved watching her changing expressions, the sly amusement that sometimes came into her eyes and the delight that spread all over her face when she laughed.

"This was my father's favorite bar when he was working in New York," she told him. She pointed up at the huge Maxwell Parrish mural over the bar. "He especially loved that. He thought it was the faggiest picture he'd ever seen."

Adam examined the painting of Old King Cole and his courtiers and his fool. They did indeed have a smirking, mincing look. "I see what he meant," he said. "I want a drink and I'm hungry. What would you like?"

They had roast beef and a fine bottle of wine. With their coffee they had cognac. He had not planned to get into anything serious between them tonight, anyway. His vague plan was to talk with her toward the end of his trip; but it was vague. They would talk, he supposed, when the moment came when they had to.

The man with the crewcut left when they did.

That night in Darien was like all the other first nights when he returned to her. They sat up late in what was now a comfortable living room and talked and often touched and were happy. He told her about his success with the commencement of busing in the city, but he told this story sketchily, leaving out Claude's part in it. He felt guilty doing this, but he also felt it would be part of what they would talk about later in the trip. Later in the trip. All that was important, all that mattered would come later in the trip. For her part, she had now become thoroughly involved in her art gallery.

"I'm there at nine o'clock every morning when I'm in the city, which is most days when you're not here, and I don't leave until six. I see painters and printmakers and critics and magazine publishers for lunch. I've become an expense-account-lunch girl. Needless to say, the lunches with the painters and the critics are on me. Painters and critics never pay for anything. It's the only thing they have in common."

"How are you getting on with your partner?"

"Very well," she said with enthusiasm. "She's an extremely good businesswoman. She does all the books, the finances, the taxes, all that sort of thing. And she works with me on product."

He smiled. "Product. You've become a marketing executive."

"Paintings, when you're in business, are product. Just like soap. Only I'd much rather sell them than soap." She was working into an excitement he had never seen in her before. "The thing is, Adam, I have a flair for it."

"Of course, you have. You have a flair for everything."

She was impatient. "No, I don't mean that. I mean I have a good sense for spotting work that will sell. I used to think my taste was too special. It isn't. I'm not talking about second-rate stuff. I can find work that is very good —not just promising, very good now."

He said seriously, "The great buyers have that. It's a born thing in the best of them. Can't be taught. They're born liking the things other people will like. You can teach a buyer to be very professional and successful but you can't teach her to be great."

She smiled. "Then I must be great."

"The gallery's doing that well?" he questioned, becoming impressed and also pleased and—relieved? he asked himself, that she had a serious project.

"Yes. So well, we're going to expand. Our graphics section is too small. We have the potential for three times the volume we're doing now, just in graphics. But we haven't room."

"Will that mean changing location?"

"I don't know yet. There's a bookstore next to us and there are rumors that it's going to move. If we can get that space, we'll stay where we are. I like Madison Avenue in the mid-seventies."

"Pretty expensive, I should think."

"We can afford it." She paused and looked rueful. "At least we can if my projections come true. If they don't . . ." She burst out laughing. "Daddy, dear Daddy, bail money, please."

"How do you find these young painters?" He was genuinely curious.

"Contacts. That's what all those lunches are about. And I go to a lot of parties. Everywhere from Park Avenue to Soho lofts. Well, Soho is getting to be the Park Avenue of loft real estate now. I go into a lot worse neighborhoods than that."

"And you see a lot of bad work."

"No. My contacts steer me away from really rotten stuff. Oh well, sometimes I have to spend two hours talking with some poor painter whose work is hopeless. That's embarrassing and sad and I lie a lot. But most of what I see has possibilities for us, at least someday."

"And you're busy and excited and I've hardly ever seen your eyes so bright," he reflected, aloud.

She was silent a few minutes and then said, "You did that for me, Adam."

Surprised, he said, "I? How do you mean?"

"You taught me the fun of work. I had thought . . ." She stopped, embarrassed.

"What?" he said, interested.

"I thought it was something other people did. Only because they had to. Hating it."

"Well, that's true of most people. Sadly."

"But not of you. I used to watch you work and see how much pleasure you took from it for its own sake. And it seemed to me that I had at least the same possibility. In the gallery." She paused. "As it turned out, I did. And of course I have you when you come."

"Yes," he said, quietly. He rose from the sofa and walked idly around the room. The curtains were all up, the paintings were hung (the Rosenquist he had given her looked very strong, he thought) and all the furniture there would ever be was in place. The second bedroom, which was their study-television room, was complete except that there was room for many more books and records: to be added in time, they had expected. The Queen Anne chairs and the fine old dining table she had found at an antique shop in Southbury were unexpected in this house, but he had grown very fond of them. He had not had the time to do all the selecting with her, but these things which she had bought seemed very much a part of him. And occasionally he had gone with her to make final decisions. Doing a house together, he was thinking, is a powerful and loving experience. They had shared it. Perhaps it was not much of a house by the standards both of them were used to, but they had been very happy in it. His sadness returned enough to make him blink against it.

"What *are* you doing?" she asked, jokingly. "You look like a real estate agent."

"Just thinking what a nice place this is." He came over and sat on the sofa next to her and took her in his arms with her head resting on his shoulder. "And how happy I am when I'm in it with you."

She said nothing, but remained in his arms for some time. There was plenty of light in the room by which the man outside could take his pictures without flashbulbs.

That night, their lovemaking was especially sweet to him. He could not get enough of her and when at last they were both exhausted, they fell asleep in each other's arms; and made a pretty picture with the coming of daylight.

Waking in the morning, he found that she was still asleep in his arms. Unusual. From the very beginning of their Darien experience, she had made it a point to be up first and have the coffee made so he could have a fast cup even before he dressed. He liked a cup of coffee before he did anything else in the mornings. In Ramsey, Rivers brought it up to him in the mornings. In Darien, Karen gave it to him in the kitchen. On this morning he disengaged himself carefully, threw on his robe and made the coffee himself. Looking outside, he saw that the day was gray and misty. The leaves on the trees were yellowing now and there were many scattered over their front lawn. Soon it would be leaf-raking time. Adam enjoyed that sort of mindless physical work now and then: weeding, raking, mowing the lawn. He had enjoyed very much the changes of season in the East; in Texas they are less pronounced, less affecting. And he loved the beach by the Sound, jogging or walking on it, or simply lying on it, taking the sun and reading. And he had enormously enjoyed their little sailboat. His old knowledge of sailing had come back easily, and the pleasure he took in sailing it through a good breeze and choppy waters with Karen crewing for him was sensual. Well, it was not too cold yet. They had a sail or two left. A picnic or two. Some long walks in the autumn weather. Some lovemaking, some tender words, some unexpected, sudden touches. But they would buy no more for their house in Darien. The sadness in him seemed almost like a physical attack.

"What on earth time did we get to sleep?" she said,

standing in the kitchen door, her hair tousled, her eyes still heavy.

"Pretty late," he said, smiling, forcing himself into cheerfulness. "Was it worth it?"

"Mm . . ." she said. "What lechers we are."

"Still," he said. And went off shortly to work.

On that trip they did all the things they normally did. They went to the theater a couple of times, went to a concert, went for long walks, sailed over the weekend, read books, listened to records, made love, ate her dinners, drank his wine and talked without ever saying what had to be said. The difference for Adam was that the waves of sadness sometimes choked him silent without warning. His mind could not always follow what she was saying and sometimes even lost track of the play they were watching. He fought to keep from seeming distracted and winced when Karen said at dinner one night, "Adam, your mind's on another planet. Come back to me."

Adam smiled and brushed off the comment, but through the rest of that evening it was Karen who was silent; and Karen who attacked him so fiercely in bed that night he could barely manage to stay with her.

Their last Sunday was glorious. The sun shone brilliantly all day and they took out the boat not even wearing sweaters. They brought a couple of bottles of white wine with them and some sandwiches and made a day of it on the water. When they returned to the house and showered and changed, they were starving and drove down to the steakhouse for dinner. But, after having proclaimed their starvation, neither of them could eat much. Nor did they talk much. It was the first difficult dinner they had ever had together.

When they were back at the house, Karen curled herself up on the sofa and he sank into the armchair across from her.

"Well, darling," she said, kindly. "I'm afraid the time has come."

He nodded. "Yes," he said, softly. "Time . . . that's what I've run out of."

"Well, then, Adam . . . one thing: I think it's good you didn't say anything till now. I knew it was coming, of course, but I could pretend it wasn't for a week. It's been a lovely week. One of the loveliest weeks we've ever had. So thank you, dear."

As he told her what he had to say, his eyes were quite misty and his throat caught many times. He was often very close to tears. But he could not, it seemed, just stop talking and cry. Perhaps it would have helped him. And Karen. But he could not do it.

He began by telling her simply enough that he was not going to divorce Claude. He told her of the changes she had made in herself and of the busing experience she had shared with him. "I'm not in love with Claude today as I am with you," he said. "You know that."

She made her first comment. "Men have divorced their wives to marry other women whom they loved."

"I know they have," he said, sadly. "And I thought I would. I really thought that for a time. But, Karen, she is a physical part of me."

"What you mean," she said, rather sharply, "is that she couldn't do without you."

He shook his head. "If I just thought that, I might leave her. But that's not it. I couldn't do without her. We are just not separate people, each to do as he wishes. We're one thing. Joined. Locked together. Too much is involved."

She waited and then said, "I'm having a hard time with that, Adam."

So he told her about his lunch with Bobby and he reported it all as accurately as he could. "Some things he said, I don't even know what he meant but I understood enough. He had talked with Nancy, he told me. They . . . are together."

Karen thought she understood what Adam had not of Bobby's threats; but she also realized it did not much matter. She had always known she had no chance against Adam's children. Her only hope had been their acceptance of whatever he did. She had not hoped for their blessing, only for their acceptance, and not even of their acceptance of his marriage to her. She had been quite willing to postpone that indefinitely, or, quite possibly, forever. She had told herself a thousand times that she would take Adam on any terms. But she could neither take him nor have him on these fierce terms delivered by a twenty-one-year-old boy whom she now hated, or assumed she did. She began to say something and found that she was quite incapable of speech. She could not sort out what was happening in her mind: grief, despair, anger, they were all going through her, and she did not know what to do with them and so was silent.

Adam said, dully: "I've said to myself, it doesn't mean we have to end what we have. But you see, Karen, I really haven't had a reason to come to New York this often for months. I've invented them. I've run out of inventions. I would be in New York four times a year, ordinarily. With some quick, two-day trips sometimes."

She shook her head. "It wouldn't work anyway . . . Not without hope. I always had to have that."

She got up and walked around the room, looking aimlessly about her, unseeing. "This house," she said, distractedly, "what will I do with this house?"

He had thought of that. "Our good landlord will take it back, I'm sure," he said. "He can rent it again like a shot. Up here, a rental place like this is a jewel."

She smiled half-heartedly. "Or I could rent it myself, furnished. And make a profit. As you can see I've become very business-oriented."

"I can see that," he said, gently.

"All these things we bought," she said, wonderingly. "What fun it was. Everything we did was so damn much fun. Every day we spent together seemed proof . . . absolute proof . . . of what I had always thought. From the very beginning."

His voice continued to be soft and kind. "What had you always thought, Karen?"

Now she looked at him and her eyes were bright with tears. "That we were born to be together. More than . . . anybody . . . ever was. More than my mother and father, and they've been happy enough, more than any friends I've ever had, more than . . ." She paused. "Ugh," she said, softly. "It's all so banal. I thought we belonged together forever. It's a word I didn't understand until I knew you, Adam. Forever. Nothing was forever. But we were. I was so sure of it. And I acted horribly to Louis because of that. I was a bitch because of that. I was everything people would have called me, if they had known. All because I was so sure of us."

He spoke uncertainly. "If it helps any, I agree with that. I've never known what it was to be so happy. If the world were kinder . . ."

"Well, it isn't," she said, bitterly.

"No. Nor even fair. We aren't the only ones. People are

always finding out things at the wrong time. When nothing can be done."

She looked at him intently. "Adam, I have one last question. Is it true, then, that nothing can be done . . . *ever?* I mean two years from now, five years . . . ?"

He spread his hands helplessly. "I don't know. When the kids are married and have their own children . . . If Claude falls in love with someone else. If . . . God help me . . ." He did not finish. Karen did.

"If . . . she dies . . . You see how low I've sunk. I can say anything. Well, she won't and I'm terribly ashamed I said that. I'm going to make myself a very stiff drink, Adam. Would you like one?"

"Yes, I would," he said.

She made them scotches, something she almost never drank. She also put on the record player the fourth symphony of Mahler. "This is supposed to be his most cheerful symphony," she said. "I must say I never found it exactly hilarious. But we can listen and not talk for a while, because I can't think of anything to say."

They went to bed very late that night, after playing one record after another. For the first time since he had known her, she was a little tight. He had no idea what to do about making love to her; had no idea whether she wanted it, none as to whether he even could. She solved the problem. "I'd like for you to just hold me," she said. "If I should cry, just let me. Say nothing and go on holding me."

So he did. She did not cry. At some point during the night, she touched him and turned her face up to him, and they did make love. The experience was gentle and tender.

"I didn't know whether we could," she said softly when it was over.

"Neither did I."

"I'm glad it happened. It would have been too unfair if we couldn't have." Sometime during the night he woke up, disturbed by something. He found then that she was crying. He did not touch her for fear of making it worse.

In the morning, his last day, she said, briskly, "Today, I'll go to the gallery and work all day. Tonight, it would be nice if you took me to the theater or even the movies and to supper. Then you can stay the night at the St. Regis and I'll go to the apartment. I don't want to come back here tonight. I don't want us to be alone very much.

I'll work out everything about the house. I won't call or write and I may go somewhere for a little while. I have some friends in London. I might visit them."

"I'll pack, then," he said, hopeless.

At the end of that evening, they walked back to her apartment from Sardi's, which happened that night to be full of theater people, a few of whom Adam knew. So their supper was not difficult. When they reached her apartment building, she said, "Don't come up, Adam. It's . . . it's as far as we can go."

"All right," Adam said.

"Kiss me on the cheek and walk away and for God's sake, don't say goodbye."

Among the countless airplane trips he had taken in his life, none was ever like the one he took on the following day back to Ramsey. A four-year-old cried nearly all the way. Adam had the deep conviction suddenly that small children should not be permitted in first class. The elimination of children should be one of the things one paid for. All the people on the plane seemed like creatures from another planet, and he had the feeling they were all watching him, all conscious of the turmoil within him. Sometimes people with terrible hangovers feel like that, walking the streets. The mixture of emotions within him was too complicated for him to understand. He was aware what his grief would be like over the weeks and months, perhaps even the years; or at least his regrets. But there was also the feeling of which he was aware and which he received with difficulty, yet also with gratitude. It was relief. Adam Starr, who had spent most of his life trying to do his honorable and considerable best, could now at least cease to loathe himself. But for Karen, there was not even relief to help her, and her pain, not greatly dulled by time, struck her like a blow any time at all that she saw a very tall man walking down some street with a long stride and his jacket flying in the wind.

# 11

MARCH, THE detective, called Louis at home on the morning after Adam's return.

"Good morning," he said. "I hope I didn't wake you."

"No, no. Not at all."

"I have the oral report of the man who covered this case for us. He and I just finished."

"And?"

Mr. March seemed to hesitate. "Of course, I don't know whether this is good news or bad news for you. If it's bad news I'm sorry."

"Thank you. What did your man report to you?"

"The situation turned out to be pretty much as you expected. At least the important part of it. Your former wife and your brother have been together for the full eight days."

"When you say 'have been together' you mean, of course, they've been sleeping together?"

"Oh yes. The documentation is complete on that. As a matter of fact, considering your restrictions on our activities, that particular documentation is more detailed than I expected."

"How do you mean?"

"Apparently we have some pictures taken from outside a window."

Louis interrupted quickly: "Your man wasn't seen? No one suspects . . ."

"He was never seen. Neither of the parties involved has any idea they were followed. I guarantee that."

Louis felt great relief. "That's very important," he said.

"It'll take a couple of days to put together the report in written form. The pictures will have to be developed and enlarged. I glanced at the negatives. They aren't great photography, but they'll do the job for you. They'll give you all the evidence you need of adultery. They'll stand up in any court, and of course my man is available for depositions and even testimony if that should be necessary."

Louis said, "That won't be necessary."

"Is there any special way you want this report delivered? I mean do you want it personally delivered? Not sent through the mails?"

"No. Send it to my house. That's sufficient. I open my own mail here. No one will see it."

"Now as to the bill . . ."

"Oh yes, that's important. I want the bill, absolutely complete and final, sent with the report. I want to receive them both simultaneously. You will be paid by return mail."

March laughed. "Your credit's good, Mr. Starr. Even up here, we know about Starr's. We don't figure a Starr to be slow pay."

"Thank you," Louis said.

For the next two days, Louis did not seem to feel anything at all. He had his plan in mind, but he did not even give this much thought. There would be time enough for that when he had studied the detective's report. Instead, he went through the routine of his days exactly as he normally did. He had scheduled a series of meetings with his buyers and he held these. By this time of year they were planning what they would be selling at Christmas, and he carefully reviewed the ideas presented to him and the samples they had managed to secure from the manufacturers. Then he and Neal Adams had a review meeting with Adam, and his brother seemed satisfied with the projections. He did say, quite gently, to Louis, "I'm concerned, of course, that you'll be covered on these goods in all the stores. Branch-store coverage is not yet your greatest strength, as we've discussed."

"I've been over that at great length with the buyers," Louis said. "It's possible we could be overstocked on some items, but we won't be caught short."

Adam nodded. "Good," he said.

Neal Adams, who had not been asked, thoughtfully volunteered that he had had the same kind of meetings. He was uncomfortable when criticism, actual or implied, came to Louis in his presence. In this meeting and in several encounters in hallways with Adam, Louis was examining his own attitude toward his brother. He could detect no feeling of hatred or betrayal. The only essential difference he could note was that he was no longer afraid of Adam. He had nothing to fear from Adam ever again. That brought him relief.

At the end of each day, he went for his swim at the club. He was now doing thirty laps without pause and was in the best physical condition he had ever been in, he supposed. He followed the exhausting swim with a long sauna and a shower. He also kept his Friday therapy appointment.

"You seem less tense than you have been," the psychiatrist told him toward the end of the session. "Are you taking the Valium as prescribed?"

"Yes," Louis said.

"The prescribed dose? No more?"

"Yes. No." Louis was amused. The doctor studied him.

"Mr. Starr," he said, "I am wondering if there is something you have to tell me that you have not," he said.

"Not that I'm aware of," Louis said. He had not consciously lied to his psychiatrist before. But then he no longer considered this man very important. He did not consider anyone very important.

The psychiatrist did not let go. "The reason I ask is that you seem dazed to me."

"Dazed?"

"You have been in here for months, consumed with repressed anger, depression and occasional suicidal impulses. You've been intense and collaborative and got as deep within yourself as you knew how. Today, you are mechanical."

"I'm now swimming thirty laps," Louis said, mischievously. "I'm in the pink of health."

The psychiatrist permitted himself the smallest smile. "That would not seem to answer all the questions," he said. He became serious. "Today, as I push buttons or pull strings, so you react. Mindlessly. You are floating. Ectoplasm. Something has happened."

Louis looked perplexed. "What could it be, I wonder?" Sly.

The doctor looked at him with kindness. "I hope I'll know soon, Louis." He had never before used Louis's first name.

Louis remembered this last exchange through the next

few days, and it made him happy. To be mindless: what relief. To be emotionless: how marvelous a feeling. To be out of control: how free it felt.

And with this sense of absence of responsibility he examined March's report when it arrived on Saturday morning. As it happened, it was his Saturday off. He would not be going to the store. He studied the report most of the morning. It had been done in the form of a diary, beginning at Adam's arrival at the airport and being met by Karen, and concluding when he left the St. Regis alone to catch his plane. The detective assigned to the case had even followed Adam to the airport to make sure that he had not been seen off. The days in between were fully documented as to the comings and goings of his brother and his former wife. The detailing included their theater evenings, the concerts, the restaurants in town, the sailing, the walks on the beach and the time of night the lights were turned out. All that was missing was the conversations that had taken place between them behind their door in the Darien house. Especially interesting to Louis, in the prose part of the report, were the details of any physical touches the detective had observed between them, from the embrace at the airport to the hand holding on their walks.

Louis saved the photographs for last. With a telephoto lens and fast film, an experienced photographer can be out of sight and yet present quite an intimate picture of the movements of two people who have no idea they are being watched. The pictures taken through an open window of them asleep in the morning in each other's arms were almost artistic, Louis thought.

He pored over all this for hours. He had expected from the moment Cullum Roberts had made his remark exactly the situation he now saw documented before him. So there were no surprises. He was faintly amused that his clever brother should have been distracted sufficiently not to notice that someone had been following him for more than a week.

At some point, he realized he was hungry. He had eaten no breakfast, and it was now one in the afternoon. He had his project for the afternoon, but there was time enough for it. First he went to a restaurant nearby and had a solitary luncheon with a half bottle of wine. Then he drove back to his apartment. In the kitchen he fumbled around the bottom drawer of one of the cabinets. It was full of old wrenches, hammers, nails, picture hangers and other kinds of household tools, but eventually he found the pistol. He took it out and looked at it curiously. It was the pistol he had taken from his mother the night of his father's death. Five years before. He had stuck it in this drawer, and apart from the time Karen had discovered it and wondered what they were doing with it, he had not thought of it since. Until now. It was an old weapon, but obviously it worked. His mother had for whatever mysterious reasons of her own fired six shots into the air with it that night. It was an ugly thing, cold to the touch. And it was empty. That was his project for the afternoon. It would have to be checked to be sure it was in working order and it would have to be reloaded. There were fifty, maybe a hundred gun stores in Ramsey, but he went to none of them. Instead, he drove out to Branchville, a suburban town not far from Adam's ranch, where he knew there was such a store because he had passed it. And where he would be unlikely to be seen going inside. This was only prudent. He did not actually care whether anyone saw him going inside a gun store or not.

Branchville had a diner, a broken-down post office, a tiny liquor store, a laundry, a couple of beer bars and the gun store. It hadn't much else, but the gun store probably did all right because there were many ranches nearby, and hunters abounded in season. It didn't have to do very well. It was tiny and the rent must be absurd.

The man who waited on him, obviously the owner, was quite elderly. He was tiny, wrinkled and his sandy hair was scant. He was dressed in an old blue work shirt and khaki work pants, and his eyes twinkled behind his spectacles as he examined the gun.

"Good Gawd awmighty," he said, "this is one ancient son of a bitch. They ain't made one like this in twenty-five, thirty years. Where'd you get it?"

"Belonged to my father," Louis said, easily. "I came across it the other day and thought it might be fun to shoot at a few tin cans. This is if the damn thing'll still work."

"Well, we'll see," said the old man. "You know this might be forty years old and that's the truth. So, for one thing, it needs cleanin' up. But . . ." He was inspecting the gun with great care. "I don't see no reason why it wouldn't fire." He grinned at Louis and startled him because his front teeth were missing. "Now that don't mean you're gonna hit nothin' much with it, lessen you stand 'bout three feet away. I don't know how straight this little fella'll shoot, but I reckon not very."

"Well, how about cleaning it up and selling me some bullets?"

"Shore," the old man said. "We can even fire a couple of rounds out back, make sure it goes off. Forty years old, my Gawd!"

It seemed to take forever for the pistol to be cleaned, for the owner to show Louis the workings of it and then for them to fire a couple of shots into the air over the blackland prairie that was in back of the store.

"So you're all set," the old man said. "Jess' don't depend on it for nothin' more than tin cans."

Louis smiled. "I won't," he said. He bought several boxes of cartridges. He didn't know why. He really didn't care about track covering. For what he planned to do, it didn't matter what tracks he left.

As a lark, more than anything else, he did drive out to the ranch and walked lazily to the shooting range, where, as children, they all had fired at the bull's-eye.

Later, it had been used primarily at the store's Western parties at which, carefully supervised, the New York slickers could take a Texas shot at a target. The skeet shooting, on the other hand, had been a common family recreation in the days when the ranch had been used more than it was now. Even his mother and father had tried their luck with the shotguns. And he, Louis Starr, had been very good at it; usually the best in the family, though as Nancy grew older she got pretty fair herself and could give him a run for his money. Adam was erratic and Bobby was hopeless, but the family had had some pleasant afternoons on this ranch. A moment of sadness passed through him as memories of happy days came to him. There had been some once. But they seemed far away. His sadness did not last. He loaded up his pistol and from various distances, tried his hand at hitting the target. He didn't hit it much, but he also didn't care. He was simply familiarizing himself with the pistol, as a child does with a new toy. In half an hour or forty-five minutes, he was manipulating it with ease, and from five yards away was hitting the bull's-eye consistently. He would not need five yards.

When he got home, he put the pistol, unloaded, and the

boxes of cartridges back in the drawer where he had found it. It was late afternoon and he had an evening to kill. The reason he had an evening to kill was that he knew Adam and Claude were going to a benefit ball that Saturday night. He had been invited himself and had turned it down. He was rather sorry now that he wasn't going. He would rather have enjoyed that night the bustle of people all dressed up, many of them in the clothes his family store had sold them. It occurred to him that he could still go if he wanted to. All he had to do was show up at the door and purchase a ticket. They would find somewhere to seat him. There was always a way to seat a Starr.

And so Louis did spend the evening in black tie in the big Sheraton ballroom. He danced with many of the women he knew (some of whom he had known most of his life) and laughed and joked and there were people who remarked that he seemed more cheerful than he had in ages. He might be mad (he was now quite certain he was) but he was certainly enjoying his madness. At home, he took his sleeping pill and did not wake up once during the night.

Sunday morning, he called Adam and asked whether he might come over and see him late that afternoon.

"Sure," Adam said. "Anything important?"

"Not really. I've been doing some thinking, which may be along the same lines as some of yours, and I'd like to chat." Louis laughed. "It's one of those 'study' conversations." Adam's study had a hallowed significance within the family.

They settled on six o'clock.

Louis dressed carefully. He wore slacks and a sport shirt with a dark blue blazer. He had showered and shaved and combed his hair immaculately. As he got into his car and drove off, he felt more light-headed than ever. On the seat next to him was the envelope containing the report from Mr. March. The first part of his plan was to present Adam with that.

At the house, Adam, Nancy and Claude were sitting around the living room, reading the Sunday paper or magazines. They were all in casual shirts and pants, and they were quietly relaxed. Louis was sorry Claude and Nancy had to be there, but there was no way out. He could scarcely suggest that they leave the house for an hour. Claude suggested a drink, and Louis said he would take a glass of white wine. So that was what they all had, while they talked of nothing much. But he did not feel awkward in this small talk.

"Well," Adam said, at last, "should we go back into the study?"

"Sure," Louis said.

"Business," Nancy said, making a face. "Business even on Sundays."

Claude smiled. "If he weren't talking with Louis, he'd be dictating. This is normally dictating hour."

"I'll do that later," Adam said. "A week away and the paper piles up."

And what a week away, Louis thought. He almost smiled.

Adam took his usual seat at his desk, and Louis sat in the black leather armchair which had the reading light. He looked at his brother curiously, and found himself admiring the familiar strong nose and jaw, the supremely intelligent eyes, the short, graying hair that must need so little attention.

"So what's up?" His brother's voice penetrated into his brain. And the intelligent eyes were kind.

Louis put his hand on the brown envelope in his lap, and suddenly, without the slightest warning, his hands began to shake. The hand that was on the envelope shook so violently, he could not grasp it. In a matter of seconds, his whole body was shaking and his teeth were chattering. He opened his mouth to say something, but nothing would come out. He sat helplessly while Adam watched him; at first just curiously.

"Cat got your tongue?" he said, lightly. He did not see the extent of his brother's distress. A wave of nausea now struck Louis, and he hurriedly rose, clutching his envelope with both hands as though he were saving a baby from a fire and unsteadily made his way to the bathroom in back of the study. There, for several minutes, he first threw up and then dry-retched. When this had passed, he was drenched with sweat. It was pouring down his face and he could feel it trickling all over his body. When he emerged from the bathroom, Adam was waiting for him, frowning with concern.

"What on earth is it, Louis?" he said.

"Suddenly . . . felt sick . . . to my stomach," Louis managed.

"You're green," Adam said. He reached for the envelope. "Here, give me that and lie down on the couch for a minute."

But Louis snatched back the envelope. With one last, desperate gesture, he reached in the pocket and felt the coldness of the pistol. With horror, he snapped his hand out of his pocket as though he had burned it. As no other thing in all his life had been necessary, it was now necessary for him to get out of that house.

"Something I ate," he managed. "Must be."

"I'll call the doctor," Adam suggested, but Louis shook his head.

". . . go home and lie down. It'll pass."

"Well, you certainly can't drive," Adam said. "I'll drive you and Nancy can follow in her car and bring me home."

And Louis was indeed not sure he could drive. He nodded, helplessly. And so Adam drove to his home the brother who had planned to kill him.

"If you aren't feeling better after a while, call Fry," Adam said, obviously worried.

"All right."

"I'll check you later, so answer the phone. It'll be me."

Louis nodded, dumb. Unsteadily, he walked away from the two cars and back into his apartment. In despair, he sank down on his sofa and closed his eyes. The envelope lay on the floor beside the sofa. He continued to shake periodically for some time, but the nausea slowly left him. The horrors in his mind which made him twist and turn on the couch were not only about the fact that he had failed again, but that his failure had been so undignified, embarrassing, absurd. He had not even been able to salvage dignity from his defeat.

It was well after dark when Adam did call. Louis told him he was feeling much better. His voice sounded steady enough. His brother had no reason not to believe him. They were not on the phone long.

And so, as the night wore on, Louis Starr was reduced to writing letters. He sat at his desk and wrote letters to Adam. They were bitter, sometimes brutal, more often measured and controlled. Some were very sad. He must have written all or parts of ten or twelve letters that night. None of them was any good. None of them said what he wished to say. His whole *life*? This was because there was, really, nothing to say. No comment he, Louis, could make.

Nothing he could add to the brown envelope with the report and the pictures in it. In addition, his handwriting was shaky and crabbed. Toward midnight, he tore them all up. Instead of tossing them into the wastebasket, he took them outside to the garage in a plastic bag and buried them in the middle of a garbage can with the other plastic bags, the beer bottles and the orange peels.

A little after one o'clock in the morning, he transferred the contents of the envelope from March into a plain large manila envelope of his own. He took one of his business cards, and after a great deal of thought, wrote on it, "I suppose you couldn't help it. God forgive you both." He did not sign it. He paper-clipped this to the material, sealed the envelope, addressed it to Adam at the house, marked it personal and also Fourth Class Mail. Since he had done so, he only put thirteen cents in postage on it. Perhaps it was too little and Adam would have to pay the difference.

He then walked out into the darkness, got into his car and drove to the mailbox in the shopping center near him. He imagined it would be three days or so before the envelope arrived. Time enough to have done with the formalities. He drove back to the apartment and mixed himself a drink. He drank it slowly, not to give himself courage, for he had that. And he had relief; which in time passed into a profound and lovely calm which gave him deep pleasure. He supposed other people knew often such joy, but he had not and so he savored it and grasped it close to him.

When he had finished his drink, he washed out the glass, returned to the library and sat down in the chrome and leather Breuer chair of which he had always been so fond. The pistol was on the glass table in front of him. He picked it up, and in less than one minute, Louis Starr had done what he had set out to do. For the first time in his short life, he had made a complete success of something; and something few people have ever been able to manage. He had died when he wanted to.

# 12

SINCE HIS maid discovered the body early the next morning, matters moved very quickly, and the services and burial were held Tuesday afternoon. Under the circumstances, these functions were limited to members of the family. He was buried next to his father. This time, not even Bernie cried. This was not because of stoicism so much as the fact that they were all numb and unbelieving. Rabbi Moskowitz again officiated, but his graveside prayers were much briefer than they had been for Louis's father. The Ramsey newspapers that day carried moderate space on the death. There was no way to avoid printing the police verdict of suicide, even in New York. Karen was somewhere in Europe. Jenny made no effort to communicate with her. That was that.

The family had supper at Adam and Claude's. No one had much to say. It occurred to Adam that not a single person asked the question aloud: "Why did he do it?" Perhaps it was because there were too many rather than too few answers to such a question. After supper, Jenny said to Claude, "I wonder if I could go home and get a few things and spend the night here?"

"I'd like you to," Claude said, meaning it. "It will help us, too."

So Jenny drove home and packed an overnight bag and returned. After a while, the long silence became oppressive to her, and she decided to go for a walk. "I feel like some air and being by myself," she explained. "I'll just wander around the grounds."

Outside, the air was cool and pleasant and the skies were clear. Almost immediately the breeze began to clear her head of the confusions and puzzlements which had been skittering through her brain since she had got the news. Strangely enough, it was not the suicide as such which was the focal point of her thinking. There had never been a suicide in her own family or in the history, so far as she knew it, of the Schatzkis-Starr-Goldsmiths, but she was not feeling at this moment a sense of disgrace to family honor or anything of the sort. And it was too early for her to feel the kind of grief for her second son she might one day feel.

What was in her mind was the pistol. She had not seen it since she had fired it off the night of Arnold's burial, and she had had no idea what had become of it. And no interest. But she could visualize it perfectly. She knew exactly what it looked like and how it felt in the hand. It was extraordinary that, bought forty years before for the purpose of killing a Starr, now it had. This astonishing coincidence brought to consideration what a pistol meant. Well, it meant many things, but among them, it was a symbol of military rank. Officers wore pistols. Starrs were officers, never enlisted men, and had worn invisible pistols all their lives. Now, this visible one made her think of war and that war, indeed, was what they had waged, these Starrs, all through the years. The early wars of starting the business, and scraping and borrowing to keep it going until it could gain a foothold; the war, genteel though it had been kept, between her husband and herself ever since the Sunday night in the kitchen when he had explained a hotel bill to her and she had lost her hope of Heaven forever; the wars between Arnold and Adam, between Adam and his brothers and between Adam and herself. She thought of the casualties: all the elderly men and women Adam had eased out to improve productivity; expendable troops; Bernie, now Louis. Someday soon, herself.

So, then, she thought, sitting now on a lounge chair by the swimming pool, life was war. And what on the surface seemed so sane and plausible was underneath absurd, outrageous and murderous. Even for the Starrs, sanest of families.

Wars were, of course, fought to attain victory. So far as Jenny understood what victory was, the Starrs had attained it. They had their stores. They had won success. The world judged the Starrs as victors. Not as saints. Jenny supposed that saints had victories, but she did not understand saints.

She could only understand what the world around her had taught her.

She felt very tired tonight. She lay back in the lounge chair and thought of Bobby who might marry Jennifer and Nancy who might marry Neal Adams; upcoming officers, training to take command. Of bigger armies, too. Adam had not yet talked to her seriously about it, but she knew that he felt the store must be sold and become a national enterprise. Well, why not? she reflected. If the casualties were bloody, why should not the victory be extraordinary and not limited to local engagements. The management contracts would be secure. Adam and Bill King would see to that. Bobby and Neal Adams would have to prove themselves, but so had she and Arnold. She would not, she realized that night, any longer stand in the way of the sale of Starr's. It must go on occupying territory, using all the methods of modern warfare. And if they were not her methods, then she, too, was expendable. And old. And tired.

After a while, she walked slowly back. Bernie and Becky had left. She said good night to the others and went to bed. She was glad, somehow, that she was not alone in her big house.

They all retired early. As Bobby left for his room, Adam followed him to the door. He said, with difficulty, "What we discussed in New York . . . has been disposed of."

Bobby said nothing. He leaned over and kissed his father on the cheek.

Two mornings later, Adam, Claude and Jenny sat at the breakfast table, lingering over coffee. Nancy had already left for class. The mail was piled at Adam's right as it was every morning. Normally he opened it in the study, but the plain manila envelope was much larger than anything else and he picked it up idly. It was taped at the closure so it took him a little time to open it. Neither woman was watching him as he began to look at the contents. It was not until the low moaning began to escape from his throat that they looked at him. He seemed to be fumbling through papers and photographs, scarcely glancing at them. Some of them dropped to the floor. His face was clown white. The moaning continued.

"Adam, what . . . ?" Claude began.

And then suddenly, Adam dropped all the papers on the

floor and from his mouth came the most terrible scream either woman had ever heard. It came twice. He rose and left them, going straight to his study, leaving the papers and the photographs strewn on the floor.

Claude bent down and gathered them together. Almost the first thing she saw was Louis's card. She read a few lines of the text and then glanced at a few of the photographs. She looked at Jenny. Her face was calm but her hands were tight on the chair's arms.

"It was Karen," Claude said, dully.

She shoved the material across the table toward her mother-in-law.

"What . . ." Jenny began.

"I have known for more than a year that he was having an affair. I didn't know who. It was Karen." She indicated the report. "This is from Louis . . . he had found out."

Jenny's face turned to stone. "I don't wish to see this," she said.

Claude said, slowly, "So we know . . . why he . . . finally . . . took his life." She stopped, puzzled.

And then she remembered the Sunday evening when Louis had left them shaken and sick. "I suppose," she said, her voice sounding matter of fact, "he meant to kill Adam, too. My God."

For some minutes the two women sat like statues.

"What will you do?" Jenny asked. Her voice sounded faint and terrified.

Claude rose from the table and went into the study. Adam sat in the leather chair, his head in his hands. The low moaning was still coming out of him. Silently, she took the scissors from his desk and the wastebasket from under it, and brought them both back to the breakfast table. She placed the basket at her feet and began cutting up the report. It was too bulky to cut as a whole, so she took it in sections. She cut the sections into minute pieces, crushed them and threw them into the wastebasket.

As she was doing so, she said to Jenny, "There are four people in the world besides the detective who know about this. Adam, you, me and Karen. I can do nothing about Karen. But I would think she will say nothing. Would you agree?"

Jenny said, "I would agree."

Claude finished the cutting up and crushed the tatters

with her foot into the basket. She rang for Rivers. "Rivers, take this out and empty it into the garbage," she said.

"Yes, Madam," he said, taking the basket from the floor.

Claude looked at Jenny. "As to what I'll do, I won't know until I've talked to Adam," she said. "I'll do that now."

"Is now the time?"

Claude shrugged. "It is for me."

"Do you want me to stay?"

"Yes. I do."

Claude went into the study and shut the door. Since Adam was in the reading chair, she sat at his desk, reversing their positions of a quarter-century.

"I have one question," she said. There was, at this moment, no sympathy or kindness within her. "You'll have to stop your moaning, or whatever you are doing, long enough to answer."

He raised his head, and then she was shocked. He looked sixty years old.

"Does this end it?" she said.

With great effort, he said, his voice cracking, "It was already ended. I finished it . . . on that trip."

"Why?"

"Because of you and Bobby and Nancy. I chose."

"I see. Thank you."

She left him alone, shutting the door behind her. She looked at Jenny, still white-faced and gripping hard the arms of her chair.

"Mother," she said. "I'm going to stay and get us through it. Will you help?"

Jenny nodded. "Yes," she said. After a pause, she added, "Claude . . . we can do this together."

Claude looked at her and was silent a moment. "I suppose," she said. "We . . . must . . . enough strength, after all." She paused. "Today, I would like to buy some clothes and go to the movies. Would you go with me?"

"Of course."

"We'll have lunch at the store." She hesitated and then a wan smile came to her face. "You see, I think we may as well start now."

"Should he . . . be alone?"

"He'll be all right today. He needs to do his . . . retching privately. I'll get him to his office in the morning . . ." She paused. "He has work to do."

Claude walked slowly over to her mother-in-law and touched the old lady's smooth cheek with her fingers. "There is a position in the store to be filled," she said.

*Osborne Hill Road*
*Sandy Hook, Connecticut*
*1977*